New York Times and *USA Today* bestselling author Emily March lives in Texas with her husband and their beloved boxer, Doc, who tolerates a revolving doggie door of rescue foster dogs sharing his kingdom until they find their forever home... raduate of Texas A&M University, Emily is an avid ...n ot Aggie sports, and her recipe for jalapeño relish has made her a tailgating legend. You can find out more about Emily March and her books – including bonus content and sneak peeks – at www.emilymarch.com and follow her on Twitter @emilymarchbooks or facebook.com/emilymarchbooks.

Praise for Emily March:

'V th passion, romance, and revealing moments that will t ch your heart, [Emily March] takes readers on an un-h ried journey where past mistakes are redeemed and a more l utiful future is forged – one miracle at a time' *USA Today*

...ly March's stories are heart-wrenching and soul-isfying. For a wonderful read, don't miss a visit to Eternity ngs' Lisa Kleypas, *New York Times* bestselling author

...ters you adore, a world you want to visit, and stories iat tug your heartstrings. Bravo, Emily March. I love ternity Springs' Christina Dodd, *New York Times* bestselling author

'Readers will be breathless as Eternity Springs works its romantic magic once again' *Pu Review)*

By Emily March

Emily March

DREAMWEAVER TRAIL

headline
ETERNAL

Copyright © 2014 by Geralyn Dawson Williams
Excerpt from *Teardrop Lane* copyright © 2014
by Geralyn Dawson Williams

The right of Geralyn Dawson Williams to be identified as the Author
of the Work has been asserted by her in accordance with the
Copyright, Designs and Patents Act 1988.

Published by arrangement with Ballantine Books,
an imprint of Random House,
a division of Random House LLC.

First published in Great Britain in 2014
by HEADLINE ETERNAL
An imprint of HEADLINE PUBLISHING GROUP

1

Cataloguing in Publication Data is available from the British Library

ISBN 978 1 4722 0205 5

Offset in Sabon by Avon DataSet Ltd, Bidford-on-Avon, Warwickshire

Printed and bound by CPI Group (UK) Ltd, Croydon, CR0 4YY

Headline's policy is to use papers that are natural, renewable and recyclable
products and made from wood grown in sustainable forests. The logging
and manufacturing processes are expected to conform to the environmental
regulations of the country of origin.

HEADLINE PUBLISHING GROUP
An Hachette UK Company
338 Euston Road
London NW1 3BH

www.headlineeternal.com
www.headline.co.uk
www.hachette.co.uk

Family is my heart.
For John and Kim.
I wish you much happiness in your marriage.

And to Nicole Burnham, Mary Dickerson,
Christina Dodd, and Susan Sizemore.
Friends like you are the real magic
of Eternity Springs.

ONE

Valentine's Day
Eternity Springs, Colorado

"I've never seen so many hot men in one room at the same time," Gabriella Romano muttered over her champagne glass. Wasn't it just her luck that they were all either married or related to her?

Earlier today, her brother Lucca had married the love of his life, Hope Montgomery, and now their wedding reception was in full swing at the new event center at Angel's Rest Healing Center and Spa. Gabi was thrilled for her brother and his wife and the new family they'd formed. Hope's daughter, Holly, was a sweetheart, and with a new baby due to arrive this summer, Lucca's world was as bright as sunshine atop snowy Murphy Mountain.

Gabi just wished that Lucca's happiness didn't make her so aware of her own world's gray skies.

A wave of melancholy rolled over her as the music switched to something slow and romantic, and guests paired off with their spouses and significant others. Gabi watched her brother Zach give his wife, Savannah, a twirl. She sighed when sexy Jack Davenport nibbled at his Cat's ear and again when Cam Murphy stroked a finger down the path of his Sarah's spine as they swayed with the music. When Richard Steele let his hand slide south of her mother's hip, Gabi turned away and gazed out at the snow-covered grounds of Angel's Rest standing silvered in moonlight. *I'm a wallflower.* "Maybe I should draw a big *W* on my forehead."

"W for what?" her brother Max asked, his green eyes dancing with amusement as he moved to stand beside her. "Whiner?"

She shot him a glare. "I don't whine."

He arched a cynical brow but wisely remained silent. Gabi's scowl deepened for a long moment before she relented. "Do I whine?"

"Not usually. Lately . . ." He shrugged. "You're obviously unhappy, Gabriella."

"Not unhappy, Massimo," she said defensively. "I'm . . . drifting."

Since leaving the sheriff's department last fall, she'd helped with her mother's project—turning a dilapidated old house into Aspenglow Place Bed and Breakfast. The B&B had opened for guests two weeks ago, and Maggie Romano had the running of her new business well in hand. "I need a job."

"So you've definitely decided not to work with Mom at Aspenglow?"

"I'm not cut out to be an innkeeper."

Max grabbed two flutes of champagne from a passing waiter and handed one to his sister. "Lucca says you've been out of sorts since you resigned from the sheriff's department. Why don't you go back?"

"No," she swiftly replied.

Max sipped his champagne and studied her. "You know, honey, there's a reason most departments require an officer to see a counselor after a shooting. I know Zach said his department would pay—"

"No." Gabi cut him off. "I'm not against further counseling, and I promised him I'd see someone if I thought I needed it."

"But—"

"That's not the problem, Max. I have no regrets about killing Francine Vaughan." The memory of that moment flashed through her mind, and she repressed a reflexive shudder before continuing, "Killing her saved Zach's life, and that's the best thing I've ever done. But I don't want to carry a weapon anymore. It's as simple as that."

"I hate to see you give law enforcement up for good, honey. I remember how you stood up to Dad when he disagreed with your decision to become a cop. You fought hard for what you wanted. You always do. You know, there are jobs in the field that don't require you to carry a weapon."

That much was true. "Eternity Springs isn't London. Our police carry guns."

"Maybe it's time you come back to Denver."

"Maybe," she said, the word rife with doubt.

Max's expression clouded. "Look, honey, if you're worried about Sobilek, you can give me the green light to have that talk I've been dying to have with the scum-sucking bastard. He won't bother you. I can promise you that."

She couldn't help but smile. Most of the time, big brothers acting like big brothers cramped her style, but she always recognized that it demonstrated their love. "No, Max. Frank Sobilek has nothing to do with this. Maybe I did leave Denver because of him, but I stayed in Eternity Springs because of me. Besides, if I wanted to be in Denver, I wouldn't let him stand in my way. I won't give him that power. My broken heart has mended, and it's stronger than ever before."

That's what she told herself, anyway. She wasn't certain she'd pass a lie detector test.

She heard the sound of Nic Callahan's laughter drifting across the room. Smiling wistfully, she observed, "I don't think Denver is where I need to be at this point in my life. I don't really want to leave Eternity Springs. I love it here. I love the people here."

"Don't you miss your friends back in Denver?"

"Friends come and go," she said lightly, burying the twinge of pain.

"That doesn't sound like you," Max observed. When she didn't respond, he added, "Speaking of friends, what's the news about Cheryl these days? I guess she's still jetting off to Hollywood to be interior designer to the stars?"

At the mention of Cheryl Oliver, Gabi's heart twisted. "Yes, she's still living in Aspen and traveling to California quite a bit."

"Now there's someone who never had any career doubts. Every time she came over to play with you, she'd haul in that huge bag full of furniture and accessories for your Barbie Dream House. I'm not at all surprised that she's working for the rich and famous."

"I don't think Hollywood has been a good influence on her," Gabi replied with the understatement of the day. "She does get to travel a lot, though. I got a postcard from her last week from France."

"Maybe you should hire on as her assistant."

"I don't think so." Gabi would rather work for a rattlesnake. Once upon a time, she and Cheryl had been inseparable, best friends who'd played Barbies, experimented with makeup, and crooned along to the Backstreet Boys together. Cheryl had been the sister Gabi had always wanted.

Those days were over. Their friendship was over, killed by Cheryl's selfishness and stupidity and by Gabi's inability to forgive such a personal betrayal.

Her gaze drifted back to the couples on the dance

floor, and she changed the subject. "You're not with anyone these days, Max. Don't you ever get lonely?"

"Sometimes," Max said, a shadow crossing his face. Just why the shadow, Gabi didn't know. Of all her brothers, he was the least open about details of his private life. "Not enough to brave the Denver dating scene, though."

"At least Denver has a dating scene."

Max gave her a brotherly thump on the nose. "If you're lonely here, go somewhere else. You can always move back to Eternity Springs."

Perhaps Max was right. Perhaps it was time for a change of scenery. Gabi had never been one to sit back and wait for life to happen. She believed in being proactive. When she wanted something, she went after it.

"I want passion."

Max winced. "Too much information, little sis."

"Not that kind of passion. Well, okay, maybe that kind of passion, but not only that kind of passion. I want more than a relationship, and more than a job. I want a life that I'm passionate about."

"That's a good goal. Though it's a little weird to be thinking about it at our brother's wedding."

"This is the perfect time to be thinking about it," Gabi protested. "Look at Lucca and Hope. Don't they inspire you? They've both gone through so much emotional pain and heartache, but they fought their way through it and triumphed. Now they glow. They're euphoric. They show us what life should be."

"For a tough broad, you are such a starry-eyed girl."

"Bite me, brother. Look—Lucca and Hope, Zach and Savannah, and shoot, even Mom and Richard are all actively living their lives. Somewhere along the way, I quit living mine. I've been simply marking time. That needs to stop. I need to find my passion."

"If you want it, you'll find it, Gabriella. Of that, I have no doubt. You're as hardheaded as they come."

"You say the nicest things to me, Max," she drawled.

"I'm about to do something nice for you."

"Oh, yeah? What?"

"Hold on." He set down his champagne glass on a nearby table, then moved to intercept a waiter. A moment later, he returned with two dessert plates filled with pieces of the Romano family Italian cream cake that had quickly reached legendary status in Eternity Springs.

He handed one plate toward her. Gabi eyed it wistfully. "Mom said we're only supposed to have one piece."

"I thought you wanted to live a little."

"By ignoring Mom's rules? That's a death wish."

Max took a big bite of cake, then tauntingly licked the tines of his fork. "Live dangerously, little sis."

Laughing, she did so. After finishing her cake, she accepted the groom's invitation to dance and managed to hold her melancholy at bay for the rest of the celebration. But later, as yet another Valentine's Day drew to a lonely close, she crawled into bed with a paperback that couldn't hold her interest because her thoughts kept drifting back to the wedding reception and her big revelation.

It was time to live. Time to search for her passion. How? Where? What could she do to get the ball rolling?

Maybe she should begin with baby steps—get out of town, do something fun and spur-of-the-moment. Unfortunately, the sad state of her bank account limited her options. What she needed was another gig like the one she'd had last fall for the Thurstons, the über-wealthy owners of a vacation house outside of Eternity Springs who had taken her along on their Mediterranean vacation to babysit their beloved dog. A girl could do a lot of thinking while walking a dog along a beautiful beach.

One sleepless hour and then two ticked by, and the thought wouldn't leave her alone. When she finally fell asleep, she dreamed she was in line for an adventure ride at an amusement park.

First thing the following morning, she looked up the phone number for the Thurstons and made the call. The Thurstons didn't need her, but they had friends who had friends who were desperate for a caretaker for their four-month-old puppy.

By the end of the week, Gabi was boarding a plane in Gunnison. Thirty-six hours of bumpy flights, boring layovers, and a harrowing boat ride later, she arrived at her home away from home, a small, sparsely populated Caribbean island named Bella Vita Isle.

After meeting her employers, the Fontanas, and her charge, a Newfoundland puppy with a solid black coat and a playful disposition named Bismarck, she explored the house where she'd be staying for the next four months and had to pinch herself to be sure this wasn't just a fantasy. Oceanfront view? A swimming pool? An electric massage chair in her bedroom?

Paradise wasn't lost. She'd found it on Bella Vita Isle.

Flynn Seagraves glanced up from the legal document he was reading and smiled when Matthew Wharton stepped into his office. The silver-haired barrister had abandoned his usual Brooks Brothers look for island wear. "That's some shirt you're wearing, my friend."

"Margaret bought it at the market in town yesterday. She said I should wear more red, orange, and yellow, but I think it's a bit bright for me."

"Not at all," Flynn replied. Then he pulled a pair of sunglasses from his desk drawer and put them on.

"Very funny," Matthew said as he took a seat across from Flynn. "She asked me to tell you that if you want your morning swim, you should do it now. She doesn't want to try to cook tomorrow since we'll be heading back to Miami early, so she's decided you need a full breakfast today. Can't have you wasting away, you know."

"Not a chance of that. Have you seen all the meals she's put into my freezer?"

"She thinks you need to gain back those ten pounds you've lost." Matthew frowned and patted his bulging stomach. "And she wishes I could give them to you. She doesn't cook like that for me anymore. I've been put on notice that carbs are not in my future."

Flynn returned the sunglasses to his drawer, grinning at his friend's glum tone. "Why don't you leave her here when you go? I'll take good care of her."

"In your dreams, boss." The lawyer buffed his nails on his shoulder. "She wouldn't leave me for you. If you were short and pudgy with a receding hairline, I might worry, but she's not impressed by rich pretty boys."

"Just my luck," Flynn said as he flipped to the last page of the document. "Women like Margaret are few and far between." He'd learned that lesson from bitter experience.

"Do you have any questions?" Wharton asked, nodding toward the papers, his tone shifting to business. Serious business.

"No. It's straightforward and clear."

"And final. And unnecessary."

Matthew appeared ready to ramp up his arguments yet again, despite the fact that they'd already been over this a dozen times before. Flynn headed him off by picking up a pen and signing the top sheet of a stack of paper. "It's what I need to do."

Matthew set his teeth but didn't comment further as Flynn worked his way through the rest of the documents Wharton had prepared. When they were all done, Flynn returned them to a file folder and handed it over to his attorney. "I need a new start, Matthew. I know it's symbolic, but symbolism matters."

"So do patents. You are walking away from so much."

"I *walked*," Flynn corrected, gesturing toward the file folder. "Past tense. It's official now, right?"

"I have to file the paperwork, but yes."

Conflicting emotions swirled through Flynn. He was both happy and sad, relieved and disturbed and regretful. Of course, that seemed to be his default these days. "Flynn Brogan," he said, testing his new name aloud. "My mother's father would be proud that I've taken his name. He told me one time that one of his biggest regrets was that since he'd fathered only girls, the name would die out."

"From what you've told me about the old Irishman, he'd kick your daddy's ass for his actions these past few months. But back to those patents . . ."

"No longer my property. It's okay, Matthew. This is the way I wanted it. Don't worry so much."

"After the past three years, it's a habit." His attorney and friend shook his head. "You do know that selling your company and changing your name won't keep the vultures away. They'll track you down."

"I expect they will, but now that I'm living on the island, it won't be easy for them. Plus, I'm determined to be boring. They'll lose interest, and pretty soon I'll be old news."

"I swear, the worship of celebrity in this world is a disease."

"Look on the bright side," Flynn advised. "If not for my celebrity status, you wouldn't have an open invitation to visit my island paradise anytime you'd like. Now, I'd better hit the pool so I have a big enough appetite to do Margaret's efforts justice. Want to join me?"

"Are you kidding?" Matthew looked appalled. "If I exercised, I might lose my pudginess, and my bride might take a second look at you."

"Damn. You saw through me." Flynn pushed away from his desk and stood. "How long do I have?"

"Forty-five minutes, I'd say. Maybe an hour. She's still whipping up her famous breakfast casserole, and it has to bake. She's also making homemade biscuits to go with it, fruit salad, freshly squeezed orange juice, and who knows what else."

"In that case I'll swim an extra couple of laps."

Flynn took the stairs two at a time to reach the master suite, sparing only a glance for the spectacular ocean view out the west-facing window. Despite all of the banter with his attorney and friend, today's actions weighed upon him. He'd worked hard to build Seagraves-Laraby, and he was proud of what he'd accomplished. Cutting those ties hadn't been easy. A man didn't turn his back on his very identity without acquiring a bruise or two.

He changed into his swim trunks, looking forward to the distraction of a good hard swim and a hearty breakfast. He exited the suite by way of the iron spiral staircase that led down from his bedroom verandah. A dozen varieties of tropical flowers perfumed the air, and thick green grass provided a soft path for his bare feet as he crossed the lawn toward the pool. There he discovered a couple of trespassers—two large lizards swimming in the water along with leaves and flower petals that had blown in during last night's storm. He retrieved the skimmer pole from the storage shed and set about cleaning his pool.

His thoughts returned to the stack of documents and contracts he'd handed to his attorney this morning, and with his focus on paperwork, he didn't immediately notice the noise. However, the movement caught his attention.

A fluffy black dog dashed through the evergreen hedge at the far side of the yard just as Flynn scooped a lizard into his net. The small dog—no, a large puppy—spied him and altered his course, heading directly toward Flynn, yapping all the way. Flynn started to grin at the puppy when another figure fought through the hedge. He instantly went on guard.

The woman was beautiful. Supermodel tall, tanned, and nicely curved, she wore a yellow bikini top, jean shorts, and flip-flops adorned with sunflowers. She had her dark hair in a ponytail pulled through the back of a Colorado Rockies baseball cap. She did not have a camera in her hands or hanging around her neck, but experience had taught him that didn't mean a damned thing.

"Bismarck! Get back here," the woman called as she plucked leaves from her ponytail. "You can't just . . . Oh." Her gaze meeting Flynn's, she flashed an apologetic smile. "I'm so sorry. Bismarck and I are still establishing who the alpha is in our little pack."

The dog dashed up to Flynn, then plopped down at his feet. The woman scowled down at the puppy, who studiously ignored her. "It's only been two days. It's bound to get better." Then she extended a hand toward Flynn. "I'm Gabriella Romano—Gabi. I'll be pet-sitting next door for the next few months while the Fontanas are on an extended vacation." Her lips twisted as she added, "Bismarck wasn't invited to tag along. I can't imagine why."

His neighbors were named Fontana, although he had yet to meet them. Maybe she wasn't a paparazzo after all. Maybe.

"I'm Flynn." He shook her hand, then spoke his new name publicly for the first time. "Flynn Brogan."

It sounded good, he decided. Not weird at all. An underlying tension about his decision to change his name dissipated. He had done the right thing.

"Nice to meet you, Flynn. Do you service next door, too?"

He blinked. "Excuse me?"

She closed her eyes and her cheeks stained pink. "Oh, jeez. That didn't come out the way I intended. Pool service. Are you the pool guy for next door, too? The Fontanas didn't leave me a number for the pool service they use, and I need help. There is something growing in the water, which totally stinks because I wanted to swim this morning. Once I got a good look at the pool . . ." She frowned and shook her head, sending her ponytail swinging. "It's nasty. I've never owned a pool, so I'm not sure what it needs."

She thinks I'm the pool boy. If Flynn had been 100 percent certain that this wasn't a setup, he'd enjoy this exchange a lot more. "I'm afraid I don't clean the Fontanas' pool."

"Oh. Well, I'll figure it out. I'm resourceful." Then she stared down at the dog and sighed. "Except when it comes to a certain Newfoundland puppy, I guess."

"He's a Newfie? I think of Newfs as cold weather dogs."

"Yes. Well." Her lips twisted in a rueful smile. "Don't get me started. He sheds everywhere. He jumps on everything. He barks constantly and chases and nips at everything that moves. He's as stubborn as my brother Max, and believe me, that's saying a lot."

"Love your job, do you?"

"I sound awful, don't I? I do love animals, dogs in particular, and he's a sweet little guy, honestly—for about five minutes every hour. We're in an adjustment period. He's a puppy being a puppy. I'm sure it will get better."

She reached beneath the lounge chair for the dog, but before she could grab hold of him, he scooted out the other side. With that, he was off the way he'd come. She darted after him. "Bismarck!"

Flynn should have set down the pool skimmer and attempted to help, but two things prevented it. First, while he tended to think otherwise, the dogsitter thing could be a ploy. Second, and of more immediate concern, he couldn't drag his gaze away from the lovely sight of a scantily dressed, long-legged beauty racing across his lawn.

The dog darted back through the hedge, and before she dashed after him, Gabriella Romano paused and waved. "Nice to meet you, Flynn. I'll be seeing you around."

Flynn watched her disappear into the hedge, her voice bellowing out, "Bismarck!" He set down the pool skimmer and prepared to dive into his pool, a hint of a smile playing on his lips.

Gabriella Romano. Dogsitter or snoop?

It served his best interests to find out. He imagined he could discover everything he needed to know in five minutes on the Internet followed up by a couple of phone calls. But where was the challenge in that? Flynn was a sucker for puzzles, and one had just blasted through his hedge.

As he executed a sleek racing dive into the deep end of the pool, Flynn decided that putting the pieces together just might be the most fun he'd had in months.

TWO

Once Bismarck collapsed into sleep on his bed, Gabi spent time on the Internet, continuing her reading on the Newfoundland breed of dogs and developing a plan for how to best care for the puppy. She had already ordered half a dozen books on dog training, two on dog grooming, and a variety of chews, toys, and treats—all on the Fontanas' dime—and they should be arriving any day now. However after this morning's adventure, she decided she needed more immediate help, so she placed a call to Eternity Springs seeking advice from her favorite veterinarian, Nic Callahan.

After the two women exchanged greetings, Gabi explained the reason behind her call. "I've never tried to train a puppy, especially not a high-strung, purebred one. I'm afraid I'm in over my head."

"Nonsense," Nic responded. "You'll do fine. I'm not so sure about his owners. What were they thinking? You don't get a puppy, then leave it alone for months."

Gabi had a list of unflattering comments she could make about her employers' behavior where Bismarck was concerned, but she refrained from voicing them. After all, they'd given her the opportunity to spend four months living in paradise. She owed them some loyalty. "I want them to come home to a well-behaved dog. Except for housebreaking, he's had no training whatsoever. I'm not entirely sure where to start. I've ordered books." She listed the titles, then added, "Do you have any more to suggest? Any other guidance?"

Nic thought a moment, then gave Gabi the address of a website to read. "It's full of excellent information. Between it and your books, you should have everything you need. My best piece of advice is to be consistent. That, and to be sure to keep Bismarck clipped. He's not suited for the Caribbean heat, poor thing."

"Will do."

They discussed the puppy for a few more minutes, and Nic insisted that Gabi feel free to contact her anytime with questions. Then she changed the subject. "So, tell me about Bella Vita Isle. Is it paradise? Are all the beaches filled with Latin gods wearing tiny little bathing suits?"

"I haven't seen all the beaches yet, and I don't think he's Latin, but the guy who cleans the pool next door is worthy of a fantasy or twelve," Gabi replied, her thoughts wandering back to Flynn Brogan.

"Oh, yeah? Dish."

Gabi explained about Bismarck's dash for freedom and the studly surprise she'd found on the opposite side of the hedge, adding, "The man is ripped. Flat belly, shoulders a mile wide, biceps you can't miss. He's gorgeous, too, with a long, angular face and sun-streaked, beach-boy hair that he wears just a little long."

"Really, now?" Nic said, drawling the words. "What color eyes?"

"I don't know. I wasn't close enough to see them, and besides, I had a horrible time pulling my gaze away from his six-pack."

Nic laughed at the picture Gabi painted, then teased, "Who knows? Maybe you just met the love of your life.

Lucca met Hope because of a dog. Maybe it's a Romano thing."

"I'm not looking for the love of my life on Bella Vita Isle. Though I wouldn't be opposed to a summer romance." She paused, recalling how Flynn Brogan had looked during that last peek she'd taken of him through the hedge as he worked the long pole with a skimmer net attached. A grin flirted at her lips as she added, "Actually, I might relax my position against one-night stands if Mr. Six-Pack Cabana Boy is part of the equation. He appeared to be quite the expert using his . . . pole."

Nic snorted, then said, "Wait one minute. It's February. There's three feet of new snow on the ground, and the thermometer hasn't topped fifteen in a week. Is this your way of bragging about the weather in the islands?"

"If I were bragging, I'd tell you that it's eighty-seven degrees and sunny here."

"I hate you."

"Then my work here is done."

"Of course, you do have an untrained, high-maintenance puppy to watch over. I suspect that getting my twins into snow gear might be an easier proposition."

The two women spoke a few more minutes, and Nic offered one last bit of guidance about the dog before ending the call. "Bismarck will be much easier to manage if you give him plenty of exercise. Walk him all over that island and you'll both be happier. Let him play in the surf, too. Newfies are water dogs, excellent swimmers. Wear him out, and he won't wear you out."

"Thanks, Nic. I'll take your advice to heart."

Gabi did just that. She changed into sneakers, and when the puppy awoke and started wandering, she grabbed a leash and the grocery list she'd made that morning, and they headed out.

Bella Vita Isle was shaped like a boomerang, ten miles

long and six miles across at its widest point. Her employers' estate, Palmetto House, occupied five acres at the southern end of the island. The island's only town, Corazón, sat at the inner bend of the boomerang, protected by a ridge that showed the island's volcanic origins, approximately seven miles from Palmetto House. For transportation, Gabi had the use of a bicycle, a scooter, a four-wheel-drive utility vehicle, and a BMW convertible.

At the key rack, Gabi didn't hesitate. To Bismarck, she said, "I've never driven a Beemer before. Let's grocery shop in style, shall we?"

She put the top down on the car, buckled Bismarck into the doggie seat belt harness, slipped on her shades, and headed into town.

Too bad Bella Vita didn't have a road that wound along a hillside, she thought as she zipped the powerful car along the winding road. She could wear a silk neck scarf and pink lipstick like Grace Kelly in *To Catch a Thief*. Except she wasn't blond, pink was not a good color for her, and her picnic companion was a Newfoundland puppy rather than Cary Grant. Bismarck was cute, but she didn't want him grabbing her scarf to pull her into a searing kiss.

Now, the pool boy was another matter entirely.

She allowed herself a moment to fantasize, then shook off the image, downshifted, and punched the gas. Knowing her luck, she'd have an Isadora Duncan moment, and the scarf would get caught in the rear wheel and snap her neck.

Upon arriving in Corazón, she found a parking place on Bay Street in front of the bank, and a short distance away from the open-air market that served as the island's primary retail sales area. This was only her second visit to town since arriving on the island a week ago, and even though the setting and style of the little town were totally different from Eternity Springs, the similarities were striking.

Like in Eternity Springs, the tourist trade contributed to Corazón's economy. It wasn't a port of call for cruise ships, but the harbor saw the arrival of a steady stream of private sailing vessels. A coral reef just offshore attracted divers, and the deep blue water off the eastern bank teemed with fish that lured sports fishermen from better-known destinations.

Yet the town had only one inn, two restaurants, and a permanent population of under a thousand. The majority of the residents had lived in Corazón all their lives, and they made their living doing a hodgepodge of jobs—as did many of the residents of Eternity Springs. Moneyed people built oceanfront estates just like they built mountain mansions back home, providing jobs and a nice boost to the island economy.

Gabi decided she was going to love it here on Bella Vita Isle. It was the perfect escape. "And I don't have to think too hard about the future when my present is something out of an old movie."

She released Bismarck from his harness and fastened his leash to his collar, then the pair headed for the market.

It was a gaudy assembly of colors, scents, and sounds that catered to both the tourist trade and the needs of local residents. Stalls offered fresh fruits and vegetables, baked goods, and local delicacies for sale, along with straw hats and baskets, carved wood, jewelry, beach towels, and a variety of other items. The energy in the air put some pep in Gabi's step and a smile on her face. Even Bismarck seemed happy, sniffing his way from stall to stall and basking in the attention paid to him by the vendors and customers alike. Nic was right—activity seemed to agree with him.

On Gabi's previous market visit, she'd breezed from stall to stall picking up necessities. She hadn't taken time to explore. Today, though, she had all afternoon . . . and a puppy to wear out. She wandered, buying a gorgeous straw basket to carry her purchases, choosing fruits, a shell bracelet, pastries that made her mouth water, and a lemon-yellow cotton scarf. Grinning, she wrapped it around her neck, gave her hair a Sophia Loren toss, and turned around.

And bumped into Flynn Brogan.

"Oh," she said as his hands came up to steady her. She looked up into his eyes, and it struck her that she really was looking up at him. Since she was tall herself—five nine and a half—that didn't always happen. And the eyes that she looked up into were . . . wow. How best to describe them? Stunning? Piercing? Intense?

She had blue eyes, but his were *blue*. Not just one shade of blue, either, but a swirl of shades that reminded her of the stretch of ocean between Bella Vita Isle and Nassau where the turquoise waters fell into a deep, fathomless blue.

"Where's your camera?"

It took a couple of beats for his question to filter through her lost-in-a-blue-eyed-hottie haze. Her camera? Good idea. The girls at home would appreciate photos of the pool guy. She grinned at the idea, then asked, "What? Do you think I'm a paparazzo come to stalk the rich and famous on Bella Vita Isle?"

Those gorgeous eyes narrowed. "Are you?"

She laughed. "Yeah. Me and Bismarck. We like to sneak up on unsuspecting celebrities."

The expression on his face changed, and she'd have palm-slapped her head had her arms not been full. "Oh, wait. You work for a celebrity, don't you?" she babbled. "The Fontanas told me that a country music star built Tradewinds for his parents. So I guess you actually work for a celebrity's parents. That's close enough, and I shouldn't tease. No, I'm just a dogsitter."

Judging by the stiffness in his stance, she thought, the jury was still out, so she added, "I'm afraid I'd be a total failure as a paparazzo. I wouldn't recognize most celebrities even if they bumped into my shopping cart at the grocery store. I don't pay attention to that whole nonsense."

"Photographers use some sneaky ways to gain access to private property around here," he said. "Do you know the Wayfarer estate at the other end of the island? The paparazzi have been a problem there ever since—" He paused, glanced around, then lowered his voice and murmured a Hollywood power couple's name. "They vacationed there last fall. Rumor is that they might be coming back."

Now it was Gabi's turn to shrug. "Frankly, I'm not impressed by celebrity. Singers and sports studs and movie stars are just people as far as I'm concerned. True heroes are cops and firefighters and other first responders who go to work and put their lives on the line each day, and the teachers and doctors and clergymen who make a significant difference in the lives of others."

Flynn relaxed, and the suspicion melted from those spectacular eyes. She almost got sucked back into a hormone haze before he grounded her by asking, "Have an opinion about that, do you?"

"I do," she said. "Maybe it's because two of my brothers have been minor celebrities. They both played NBA basketball, and one of them now coaches in the collegiate ranks. They're good guys, don't get me wrong, but my brother who is a sheriff is more deserving of attention and adulation. So you don't have to worry about me stalking Tradewinds unless Bismarck has gone on the lam again."

His mouth lifted in a slow grin. "I like your style, Gabi Romano."

"Thank you." She returned the smile until his gaze

dropped to the fruit-filled basket she held tucked against her breast.

His eyes gleamed. "So, you and Bismarck are out doing some shopping, are you? Nice melons you have there."

Gabi followed the path of his stare to the pair of admittedly large mangoes nestled against a bunch of bananas. *Very funny, Captain Obvious.* "They're mangoes. Mangoes aren't melons."

His lips stretched in a slow, wicked smile full of straight white teeth that brought out the laugh lines at the corners of those mesmerizing eyes. "My bad."

Behind the shield of her sunglasses' dark lenses, she rolled her eyes before giving him a lingering once-over. Her stomach tightened in response.

He was incredibly sexy, with a light stubble on his strong chin and jaw. His broad shoulders and wide chest filled out a Manchester United T-shirt that hung loose over his flat belly. He wore navy board shorts and worn leather sandals that looked like they might blow a strap at any time. Gabi smothered a sigh. That grin. Those eyes. *Yes, I'll bet you're bad. And to my shame, I'd love to discover just how bad you can be.*

"What makes a melon a melon and not just any old fruit, anyway?" he asked as he hunkered down and scratched Bismarck behind his ears.

As the puppy preened, Gabi considered the question. "Well, melons grow on vines."

"Grapes grow on vines. They're not melons. Blackberries aren't melons."

"True. I guess I don't know what makes a melon a melon, and frankly, I don't care."

That didn't appear to matter to the man one bit, because he continued, "Fruits are the matured ovaries of plants. Technically, tomatoes are fruit. So are almonds. Chestnuts, on the other hand, are seeds."

"Who are you, Barney Botanist?"

He stood. "I'm Flynn Brogan. We met this morning. Remember?"

"Very funny. If you know about plant ovaries, you should know what makes a melon a melon."

"I know. I'm rather embarrassed about that gap in my education," he confessed, and managed to sound sincere and look just a little sheepish while doing so.

The fact that someone this good-looking could be anything less than smooth appealed to Gabi. So did the evidence that the hunk apparently had a little bit of nerd thrown in. Pretty boys were nice to look at, but brains attracted her most of all. Just because he made his living as a pool boy on a tropical island didn't mean he didn't have smarts.

"All right, professor. Fruit me this one." She reached beneath the bananas and pulled out a wrinkled yellow fruit. "Is it a fruit? Vegetable? Seed? Melon? What is this? The woman at the fruit stand didn't speak English, and I don't know enough Spanish to comprehend what she said. I thought it looked interesting, so I decided to give it a try, but I'm not sure what to do with it."

Those Caribbean-blue eyes lit with interest. "So, you're culinarily adventurous? What's the most exotic food you've ever eaten?"

"Hmm . . ." Gabi folded her arms, tapped her finger against her lips, and considered a moment before saying, "Dorm cafeteria food."

He laughed, then gestured toward the section of the market where meats were offered for sale. "Have you ever tried iguana?"

"Depends on your definition of 'tried.' I did date a lizard for a while."

"Bitter, hmm?" he asked, his lips twitching.

"Turned rancid very fast."

"It hasn't turned you off adventurous dining, has it?"

Gabi's spirit was dancing. She hadn't flirted like this in a long time, and she was enjoying herself. That said, she didn't want to give the wrong impression. She shrugged and said, "Not turned off. Cautious, I'd say."

"There's nothing wrong with cautious." Flynn reached out and plucked the fruit from her hand. "This is a good place to start. You really don't know what this is?"

"No."

His gaze remained locked on hers, his lips lifted in a grin, as he tossed the fruit up like a juggler's ball and caught it once, twice, three times. Just as Bismarck leapt to his feet apparently ready to chase, Brogan fired out a stream of Spanish she couldn't translate and pitched the fruit to a woodworking vendor two stalls away. The man laughed as he caught it and replied in a fast stream of Spanish. He set the fruit on a table, picked up a cleaver, and whacked it in two.

Flynn showed her that wicked grin again, and Gabi recognized that she hadn't experienced this little hum of attraction in a very long time. Not since Frank, the lying, cheating, pond-scum bastard.

A woman in another stall joined the conversation, and Flynn went over to her booth and accepted the white plastic spoon she offered. He picked up the sliced fruit and sauntered back toward Gabi and the dog.

"No," he said in a stern, firm tone to Bismarck.

To Gabi's surprise, Bismarck sat. Brogan displayed the inside of the fruit. Gabi pursed her lips. It was yellow and slimy and seedy—not at all appealing. "Kind of makes me think about the first person who ate an egg," she observed. "Why would you try it?"

"Hunger," he replied.

The sound of the word on his tongue caused Gabi to shiver a little. He dipped the spoon into the slime, then held it up for her to taste. "Now, Gabriella, let me teach you about passion—"

Passion!

"—fruit."

Oh. Passion fruit. "This is passion fruit? I know passion fruit. Though I've only had it in juices. You eat the slime?"

"Yes. But I suggest you don't bite the seeds. They're bitter. Let it all play on your tongue, then slide down your throat."

"They look like tadpole eggs to me."

"You've eaten tadpole eggs?"

"Ick. No." Gabi closed her mouth around the spoon and tried the pulp. Flavor exploded on her tongue. Sweet, with a hint of bitter, fresh, tropical, and citrusy. A bigger flavor than what she was accustomed to from juice. She savored, then swallowed. "Yum. Okay, that was really good."

"Glad you like it." He offered her the second half. "Passion fruit is a favorite of mine."

"In that case, why don't you enjoy the second piece? I think I'll go back to the fruit stand and buy some more."

"Thank you. I will. And you should definitely buy more. A person can never have enough passion . . ." He winked at her. ". . . fruit. Now, I'd better finish my errands. I'll see you around, Gabriella. Maybe we can get together sometime and try some of the other delicacies Bella Vita Isle has to offer."

He sauntered off whistling, and Gabi watched him go with a curious smile on her face. Well, now. Wasn't that an interesting exchange, and wasn't he an interesting combination of smooth-talking swagger and nerdy uncertainty?

She had come to the island to thaw out and do some soul-searching. Since the population of Bella Vita Isle wasn't much bigger than that of Eternity Springs, she hadn't counted on meeting anyone. Maybe . . .

"Hold your horses," she muttered. "You don't know

anything about the man." He could be married with six kids for all she knew. He could be another lying, cheating weasel.

Or he could be a nice guy who would be fun to spend some time with while she was here on the island. She didn't know enough from two casual encounters to make the call.

She looked down at Bismarck, who was sniffing happily at a tuft of grass, and said, "We need to remember that we're on island time. Don't rush. Don't worry. Be happy." She paused and added with a touch of exasperation, "And don't eat that beetle!"

She strolled off through the market in the opposite direction of Flynn Brogan to continue shopping, slowly, without concern, and with a light heart—the island way.

Gabi added a straw hat and a beautiful sarong in shades of orange and yellow to her purchases, and when she turned a corner to visit the next row of vendor booths, an explosion of color stopped her in her tracks.

A wide wooden beam stretched between two poles some six feet apart. Dozens of glass ornaments hung from the beam, positioned so that they caught the rays of the afternoon sun. Spheres and starfish and seahorses sparkled like jewels, drawing Gabi as though they were magnets. The colors simply took her breath away—fiery reds and icy blues and every shade in between. Gabi had always been a sucker for color, and these colors seemed to reach right inside her and grab hold of her heart.

A young man with multiple piercings and wild Rastafarian braids stood beside the display. "Hello, beautiful lady. You need a dreamweaver for your kitchen window, do you not?"

"A dreamweaver?" Gabi asked, unfamiliar with the term.

He removed a yellow starfish from the beam and handed it to her. "These are no ordinary suncatchers that simply color sunshine and make a pretty sight in your window. Our creations capture the sunlight on our beautiful island and weave it into dreams of your days spent on Bella Vita Isle. Where are you from, beautiful lady? Is it winter where you live? You must buy a dreamweaver and take our warm sunshine home with you so that on dark, dreary days you can look at it and see your dreams."

"They're lovely. How much . . ." She stopped as she caught sight of a sculpture on a shelf, a mermaid in shades of blue that reminded her of Flynn Brogan's Caribbean-colored eyes. "Oh, wow. That's gorgeous."

"Isn't it? It's a new piece from Cicero."

"It looks like it belongs in a gallery."

"Most of his pieces are destined for galleries, but this one didn't match his vision, so it is offered here."

"It's beautiful. The colors are fantastic."

"You must buy it." He named a price that had her eyes bulging.

"I'm afraid that's way beyond my budget. I do love it, though. The color is just fabulous."

"If you like the blues, you should consider this." He pointed out a six-inch seahorse-shaped dreamweaver that hung at the far end of the display. "The colors are very similar. Blue like your eyes. Shall I wrap it up for you?"

"Not my eyes," she murmured. Flynn Brogan's eyes. She wanted the ornament, badly, but she'd already overspent her budget at the market today. "How much?"

He named a price, and Gabi decided to make her first stab at bargaining. She offered him half of what he'd asked. "Ah, beautiful lady. You pierce my heart with such an offer. I spent a substantial amount of time on that piece. It is no beginner glassblower's work. Why, look at—"

"You made this?" she asked, intrigued.

"I did. I am Cicero's apprentice, Mitch."

"So you have a studio here on the island?"

"We do." He folded his arms and studied her. "I see interest in your lovely eyes. Would you like to watch Cicero at work?"

"He wouldn't mind? I would totally love that."

"Cicero welcomes the occasional visitor, and he especially likes to display his talents to lovely women. Invitations are at my discretion, so yes, you are welcome to visit our studio." He gave her directions to the workshop, then added, "Come next Wednesday at noon. Now, about the seahorse dreamweaver. How much did you say you're willing to pay?"

Gabi laughed and surrendered, opening her wallet and removing the full amount. Mitch wrapped the seahorse in tissue paper, and Gabi tucked it carefully into her basket.

Ordinarily she'd make purchases like this one to give as a gift, not to keep for herself, but she'd had a visceral response to the seahorse. It was hers. Her suncatcher. Her dreamweaver. A symbol of . . . what? Adventure? A new beginning? A spring fling?

The possibilities put a spring in her step, and she gave the yellow scarf another jaunty toss. A spring fling with a pool boy?

Her brothers would have a cow.

THREE

The following day Flynn delivered the Whartons to Lynden Pindling International Airport on the island of New Providence in time to catch the four o'clock shuttle to Miami. Outside the terminal, he wrapped his arms around Margaret and hugged her tight. "Are you absolutely certain I can't convince you to leave that cranky old curmudgeon and run away with me?"

"You are a temptation, darling, but my heart belongs to Matthew."

"I'm crushed."

"You'll get over it." Matthew gave Flynn an elbow to the ribs. "Now, let go of my woman and go find your own."

Flynn's mouth twisted in a rueful smile. "See, I'd rather steal yours. Last time out, my own woman proved to be a disaster. I don't trust my judgment anymore."

"Now, Flynn." Margaret reached up and touched his cheek. "Don't be that way. You have excellent instincts. Listen to them. You're starting a new chapter in your life. I have faith that it's going to be filled with good things."

He wanted to believe that was true, but recent events made him wary. "I don't know, Margaret."

"Well, I do. You have so much to give, Flynn—your

brilliant mind, your generous heart. Don't let the vultures and the naysayers and the closed-minded idiots win. Matthew always says you're an inventor, but I know better. You're a dreamer. Don't give up on your dreams. Chase them. Let them grow and change and fit the man you are today. Don't quit creating new dreams."

Flynn recalled those words later that day as he guided his forty-two-foot Formula speedboat out of the harbor for the cruise back to Bella Vita Isle. Funny that Margaret had called him a dreamer. When he was growing up, his mother had said the same thing. *You're like me, Flynn. Just another dreamer.*

His mother had been a mystery writer who sold her first book to a New York publisher when he was in sixth grade. She used to walk around the house in a daze plotting murder and mayhem. She'd died from heart disease six months before the crap hit the fan with Lisa. He'd miss her until the day he died.

"Just another dreamer," he murmured as he gave the throttle a little bump. He used to spend days on end turning over ideas and tinkering with machines out in his father's workshop. He'd loved losing himself in what-ifs and if-I-tried-thats. When had he quit spending time in dreams? Not in high school. He'd had a great shop teacher who had turned him on to industrial technology. Certainly not as an engineering student in college. That's where he'd conceived the design that became his very first patent.

It wasn't that he'd quit dreaming, he realized. He'd quit devoting time to it. After he and Will Laraby established Seagraves-Laraby Technical Solutions shortly after college, he'd gradually taken over CEO responsibilities and left development up to Will. He hadn't realized how much he'd missed designing until he'd played with an idea he'd had for the steering system of his new sailboat.

Thinking about the boat he'd commissioned made Flynn smile. He'd been trying to come up with a name for it. Maybe he'd call it *Dreamer*. A man could do a lot of thinking while sailing. He tested the name, much like he had done with his own new name. "*Dreamer. The Dreamer.*"

Yeah. He liked the sound of that.

With the decision made, he reconsidered his current destination. Instead of returning directly to Bella Vita Isle, maybe he should pay a visit to his boatbuilder in Hope Town and check out the latest on the boat's construction. He could have dinner at the Salvadoran restaurant his builder had introduced him to and overnight on the Formula. Or he could get a hotel room if the spirit moved. He wouldn't mind being around people tonight— not the people of Hope Town, anyway. They didn't read the *National Enquirer* or *Star.* At least, not that they let on, anyway.

Happy with the plan, and having reached open sea, he turned the speedboat into the wind and opened up the engines. The salty sea breeze sent his shaggy brown hair whipping around his face, so he grabbed the Georgia Tech ball cap from around the throttle and put it on backward.

He flew across the water. Speed suited him today, he recognized. The rush of the wind, the thrum of the powerful engines, and the sometimes violent lift and crash of the hull against the swells fed his mood. More symbolism, he decided. Here he was hurtling balls-out toward his new life.

Or fleeing from the old.

The nasty little thought crept into his head and wouldn't go away. Was that all this adventure in paradise was? Had he been lying to himself? Had the move to Bella Vita Isle, the sale of his company, and changing his name been nothing more than a grown man's attempt to run away and hide?

The questions slithered through his brain like eels, and Flynn's enjoyment in the speed of his journey slipped away. He pulled steadily back on the throttle until the speedboat slowed and the engines idled. Then he switched off the engines and allowed the Formula to drift.

The boat drifted. Flynn drifted. Nothing new here. Hadn't he been drifting for the past three years? Drifting wasn't all that different from running. Why did the thought of running bother him so much?

Because innocent people don't run. Guilty people run.

Flynn filled his lungs with briny air and lifted his face toward the cloudless sky. Despite being surrounded by brilliant shades of blue—azure and turquoise and sapphire—he now felt black and stormy. He exhaled harshly.

Memories rocked him like ocean swells. *Flynn Seagraves, you are under arrest. Mr. Seagraves, how do you plead? Hey, Flynn, why did you do it?*

For God's sake, son, how could you?

As always when he thought about his father and the events that had caused the break between them, anger and frustration and bone-deep hurt swirled through him like a whirlpool.

He hated these feelings. Hated the way they pulled him under to a cold, dark place. A time or two they'd come close to drowning him.

Will the defendant please rise . . .

Drumming his fingers against the wheel, he absently gazed at a gull as it dive-bombed the sea in its quest for food. *Don't give up on your dreams. Let them grow and change.*

Margaret's advice was fine, but it didn't address the nightmares. How could a man turn his mind toward new dreams when the old, ugly ones consumed his mind?

So get rid of the nightmares. Throw them overboard. Send the old crap to the bottom of the sea and get on with your new life.

"Channeling Dr. Phil now, dumbass?" he muttered. Still, it was a good plan. Easier said than done, though.

Of course, he knew what he needed to do in order to rid himself of some of the nightmares. Symbolism be damned—he needed to take action. He needed to take one particular action. But did he have the guts to do it? Could he bring himself to make that call?

He lifted the ball cap off his head and finger-combed his hair before replacing the hat. Guess the answer to that question depended on just how serious he was about this new start he was making. Honestly, he could change his name, address, hair color, eye color, and dental records—hell, he could go all in and have a sex-change operation—but unless he confronted this particular demon, how could he truly move forward?

The Formula rocked on a swell and shook Flynn from his funk. He muttered, "Screw this."

Nightmares . . . dreams . . . action or inaction. He couldn't do a damn thing about any of it while adrift in the Caribbean Sea.

He started the engine, engaged the throttle, and continued on his course toward the Abaco Islands. He traveled fast and the miles flew by, and soon he spied the red-and-white striped Elbow Reef Lighthouse on the horizon. Taking care to avoid the reef that lay just off the eastern shore, he guided the Formula into the harbor and moored at the marina.

Twenty minutes later, he arrived at the boatyard. A bell rang as he opened the office door and stepped inside. His designer, Marcus Yarrow, glanced up from his computer with a scowl on his face that melted away when he identified his visitor. "What did you do? Transport by way of the starship *Enterprise*? I only sent the email fifteen minutes ago."

"I haven't checked email in hours. I had to make a Nassau run, and since I was out, I decided to stop by. What's up?"

"You have great timing," the builder said. "We're ready to wrap her up, so if you have any adjustments or additions, now's the time to say. Want to take a look at her?"

"Absolutely," Flynn replied. "You're ahead of schedule."

"She's been a pleasure to work on. That design change you suggested in the rudder assembly was brilliant. You might want to consider a patent for that idea."

Flynn smiled. It had been the only design idea he'd had since Lisa died. "Thanks. My lawyer has the paperwork in process."

They spent the next forty minutes going over the thirty-two-foot sailing cruiser from stem to stern. Delighted with the workmanship, Flynn couldn't wait to get her out into open water. "We'll have her ready to deliver by the end of next week," Yarrow said.

"Excellent." They discussed delivery arrangements for a few more minutes, then Flynn shook the boatbuilder's hand, said his goodbyes, and took half a dozen steps toward the Jeep he'd rented at the marina before his steps slowed, buried thoughts and memories reasserting themselves.

Guilty people run. Stop running.

You're a dreamer. Don't give up on your dreams. Move forward.

Take the first step. Someone has to do it. Just do it. Don't put it off. You're Flynn Brogan, a new man with a new life. Maybe . . .

Emotion flickered to life inside him. Not the pain, not

the anger, not the sorrow to which he'd become accustomed. For the first time in a very long time, Flynn dared to hope.

Maybe his father would listen this time.

He turned around. "Marcus?" he called. "I almost forgot. I need to make a private phone call. Could I use one of your offices?"

"Sure thing."

The boatbuilder showed him to an empty room, then shut the door behind him as he left. Flynn took his cell phone from his pocket, wiped sweaty palms on the fabric of his khaki cargo shorts, then thumbed the number.

A gruff voice answered, "Hello?"

Flynn swallowed hard, then said, "Hello, Dad."

A long moment of silence dragged out. "Flynn?"

"Yes, Dad. It's me. I'm calling to—"

Click. Flynn closed his eyes and spoke to the empty office. "Forgive you."

He sat at the desk for a long moment trying to fight back the wave of ugly emotions. He shouldn't be surprised. He hadn't expected anything different, had he? Army Colonel Nolan Seagraves had court-martialed and convicted him and levied a sentence of banishment for life. In the beginning, Flynn had believed that his refusal to consider Flynn's side of the story lay rooted in mourning for his wife; maybe that had been part of it. Grief hadn't affected his intractability, however. Once Nolan Seagraves took a position, he stood firm.

Well, now Flynn didn't have to wonder or second-guess himself. He'd taken action. He'd made that one final effort to mend a fence, so now he could in good conscience wash his hands of all of it. Finally.

So why did it make him feel like hell?

Because he still remembered playing catch with his dad in the backyard and the fishing trips wherever in the world they were living at the time. Because he would never forget the pride on his father's face when he gave the valedictorian's speech at his college graduation. Because his father was the only family Flynn had left.

Now, unfortunately, he couldn't forget the disgust on Nolan Seagraves's face the last time Flynn had seen him.

"Well, same right back at you, old man," he said aloud. He was done with it. From here on out, he'd consider himself to be a one-man family. Better to be alone than have a blind, stubborn, unforgiving asshole dragging him down.

Brooding, he decided not to overnight on the boat. He'd get a room, and after dinner he'd camp out in the bar and watch some basketball. He wasn't in the mood to be alone.

He drove to the five-star resort at the northern tip of the island and strolled inside. He and Lisa had vacationed here on four separate occasions, the last time only ten days before he discovered her infidelity, when he'd still thought a romantic weekend getaway might be the medicine his ailing marriage needed. The staff was courteous, the accommodations excellent, the bartender generous with his pours. Lisa had claimed the spa services were some of the best she'd ever had. Flynn had never tried them. Good thing in hindsight, he thought, giving a bitter snort. She might have given the massage therapist poisoned oil to use on him.

He left his rented Jeep with the valet and strolled toward the front door, then hesitated. Maybe this wasn't such a good idea after all. The staff was so good that they might remember him. They might recognize him. Would he be able to be Flynn Brogan here?

"Guess there's no time like the present to find out," he murmured, and pushed open the revolving door.

The lobby was unusually crowded, and he heard a

steady hum of conversation coming from the restaurant off the lobby. He hesitated, questioning whether or not he wanted to be around a crowd that was bigger than he'd anticipated, but before he could make up his mind, a woman and her entourage exited the grill. He heard a feminine voice gasp, "Flynn!"

Oh, hell. Wendy. Why . . . oh, the damned spa.

Half a dozen faces turned his way. Cameras came up, clicked and flashed. His former sister-in-law started toward him, and Flynn didn't move. Despite the fact that a freight train full of ugliness was bearing down upon him, he had to stand his ground. *No more running. I'm done.*

He hardened his jaw, and the Academy Award–winning dramatic actress didn't disappoint. Wendy Stafford drew back her hand and let loose a hard, stinging slap. "You vile, evil bastard," she declared loudly, her famous green eyes flashing. "To see you walking free . . ."

Flynn considered it a victory that he'd managed to keep his head from turning, because the woman packed a punch. He chose not to speak to her—experience had taught him the futility of that—so instead he simply waited for the end of act one, hoping she'd decide to skip acts two and three.

The onset of her tears proved his hopes were in vain.

One of her people moved in and put his arms around her. "Ms. Stafford, perhaps you should sit down."

Flynn didn't move a muscle, nor did he break eye contact with his former sister-in-law.

"Take me out of here," Wendy said. "I cannot bear to be in his presence one minute longer."

Flynn waited to turn away until she'd swept from the hotel lobby. He decided to make his way to the poolside bar. He wouldn't stay here tonight, but neither would he run. Not now.

He'd taken two steps toward the side door when a lanky, bearded boy stuck a recorder in his face. "Flynn Seagraves. Bart Feyen with the *Hollywood Clarion.* How did you feel when you heard the verdict?"

On Wednesday of her third week on the island, Gabi woke before dawn. Today she planned to visit the glass studio, and she was as excited as a child on Christmas Eve. She had a lot to do before she left the house, however. First on her list was a run on the beach with Bismarck. When she went to the studio, she would put him in his dog crate, which was better described as a dog mansion. He obviously liked the crate, so he'd be just fine, but she'd feel better about leaving him behind if he'd been thoroughly exercised first.

She rolled out of bed and pulled on her running gear. When she carried her sneakers out of the closet, Bismarck leapt to his feet and ran around her legs in circles of delight. They exited the house just as the eastern horizon went aglow in shades of pink and gold.

Gabi liked to run. Though basketball had been her primary sport, she'd run cross-country in high school, and after basketball season her final year in college, she'd begun training to run a marathon. Her friend Cheryl had talked her into signing up for the race, but unfortunately, Gabi hadn't followed through. She'd always regretted that she'd allowed a romance with a computer engineer to distract her from her goal.

It hadn't been the last time she'd let a man derail her aspirations, either. She'd let Frank talk her out of going for her detective shield.

"Idiot," she murmured as she led Bismarck along the path to the beach. Well, she was over being the submissive girlfriend. Never again. It shouldn't be a hard habit to break. After all, she'd never been submissive to her brothers.

Maybe she'd take another shot at a marathon. Nothing was stopping her. She could train while she was here on the island, and then she'd be ready to step up her game once she went home. "I could enroll in one of the mountain marathon training programs, Bismarck."

The dog ignored her, but Gabi pretended otherwise. "Yes, I know. I've always thought mountain marathon runners had a screw loose, but I shouldn't judge. Cheryl said doing it gave her time to clear her mind and put things into perspective."

Cheryl. There she was again, popping back into Gabi's memories. Her best friend since the second grade, Cheryl had always been a constant, a welcome female presence in Gabi's male-dominated world. The product of a broken home racked by alcoholism and sadness, Cheryl had been welcomed into the Romano family bosom.

"And look how she returned the favor," Gabi muttered, her spirit sinking at the memories. The hurt, the unbelievable betrayal . . . Gabi didn't think she'd ever get over it. Or forgive it. No matter how many apology letters, postcards, and emails the witch sent.

Shoving the old ugliness aside, she declared, "Running a mountain marathon is the worst idea I've ever had."

At this comment, Bismarck grunted, then veered off the path to sniff at a clump of grass. "No, all this running off at the mouth doesn't mean I added a snort of vodka to my orange juice. Though I should probably stop imagining that you're talking back to me. You're good company, Bismarck, despite the fact that you shed like a bear, eat bugs, and lick your privates."

Because she'd had one of those months when menstrual cramps laid her low for a couple of days, she hadn't left the estate since her visit to the market. She was overdue for a visit with two-legged creatures. Gabi liked people, and she thrived on social interaction. She needed to make some friends here on the island. Maybe Mitch and this Cicero person would be the first ones. "Of course, there's always the pool boy. He did say, 'See you around.'"

Bismarck spied a bird perched on driftwood on the beach and let out a yap.

"Don't worry. I won't ignore you. I won't quit talking to you. I just think it's best if you quit talking back to me."

She led Bismarck across the sand to the water's edge, where she did her stretches, then headed off. *Just another day in paradise,* she thought as she ran on the packed sand, the happy dog at her heels. As was her habit when she ran, Gabi allowed her thoughts to wander freely. Today for some weird, disturbing reason, they wandered to a time she'd have preferred to remain unvisited.

Gabi was strolling down Cottonwood Street a block and a half away from Savannah's soap shop when her radio squawked and Zach's tight, tense voice repeated the call sign requesting immediate backup. "Heavenscents. Savannah is in trouble." He added a description of what *she was wearing, then added, "Hurry, I'm going in."*

She was running even as she spoke into her radio. "Zach, wait! I'm two minutes away."

She knew he wouldn't wait: Savannah was his love. Gabi summoned a burst of speed and cut ten seconds off the trip. She entered the back door with her gun drawn.

Immediately she heard sounds of a struggle. Upstairs, they're upstairs. Instinct told her to hurry. Training required she be methodical and cautious. She did both, confirming that the kitchen was empty and pausing just long enough to peek into the dining room as Savannah's nephew, TJ, called from the front of the shop. "Savannah? The credit card machine has quit working. Savannah?"

In that instant, the situation went to hell. Savannah

screamed. A gunshot sounded. Gabi rushed for the stairs as she heard Zach's strangled voice shout his nickname for the woman he loved: "Peach!"

Halfway up the stairs, she caught sight of Celeste Blessing—only it wasn't her friend. That woman wasn't Celeste. Seconds passed like hours as she processed what her senses were taking in. Panic in her brother's voice as he cried his lover's name. Stealth in the woman's movements.

A gun in her hand.

Gabi lifted her own gun, a shout forming on her tongue, as the stranger's finger moved on her gun's trigger.

From below, Gabi fired. Her aim was off. Instead of hitting the target's center mass, her shot sailed high, striking the head. A chunk of skull flew. The woman dropped.

On a beach in the Bahamas a year and a half later, Gabi's steady stride faltered, and she almost tripped over her own feet.

"What the heck?" she muttered. Why in the world had she gone back to that sorry time and place?

Gabi had been too slow on the draw, and Francine had gotten off a shot, hitting Zach. He'd barely clung to life, and only by the grace of God had her brother been saved. Gabi had nightmares about that horrific scene and terrifying moments to this day.

"So quit thinking about it in the daytime, idiot," she murmured. Then she picked up her pace, trying to outrun the sick feeling in her stomach that thoughts about that day inevitably produced. "Think about something else. Something bright and beautiful."

Movement farther up the beach caught her attention, and upon identifying the figure entering the surf, she murmured, "Well, well, well. Just what the doctor ordered."

Flynn Brogan was definitely bright and beautiful.

Today he wore a formfitting racing suit that left nothing to the imagination. She wasn't surprised to discover that he was a swimmer. A guy didn't get shoulders like that without physical exertion.

She watched as he dove into a wave and surfaced swimming freestyle. He proved to be just the distraction she needed, and she continued her run with her attention diverted from the past and directed toward the swimmer. He was out early, and she didn't see a vehicle of any kind. He must live on this end of the island.

"Of course he does," she murmured as she observed his long, strong strokes through the water. He'd told her as much that first day, hadn't he? He'd said he took care of things around Tradewinds. He wasn't a pool service guy. He must be the estate's caretaker. A live-in caretaker at that.

The notion made sense. Tradewinds was twice the size of her employers' estate. She imagined that keeping it up could be a full-time job. The Fontanas used a concierge service on the island to arrange for housekeeping, yard work, and, Gabi had discovered, pool maintenance. People were in and out of the house all the time.

But according to Veronica Fontana, the owners of Tradewinds were the parents of the famous country music star Sam Wilcox, and they took their privacy seriously. Gabi had seen an older couple who she assumed were the Wilcoxes walking hand in hand on the beach her first night on Bella Vita Isle. If they valued solitude so much, it made sense that they would limit access to their estate to as few people as possible. Hence, a live-in caretaker. "See, I would have been a great detective," she remarked to Bismarck.

She wondered how Flynn Brogan had come to make a career out of serving as caretaker for the wealthy. Probably just fell into it like she had, and then one rich contact led to another. It was all about networking, really.

Although she shouldn't ignore the possibility that it might not be his only job. Maybe he had a passion that being a caretaker allowed him to indulge.

At that, her imagination took flight. Perhaps he got the job because he had connections in the country music industry. Perhaps he was a songwriter. She could imagine someone with a name like Flynn Brogan creating a moody, soulful ballad. And those Irish eyes . . .

Or maybe he was a writer who lived in a garage apartment where he crafted murder mysteries or suspense thrillers on an old manual typewriter. Maybe he needed a research assistant. After her years as a police officer, she had plenty of stories she could share.

Or what if he was an undercover private investigator working for the Wilcoxes in the islands trying to track down any offshore bank accounts that Sam's accountant had opened to hide his ill-gotten embezzlement proceeds?

The fanciful line of thinking made her laugh aloud, and she decided she'd run the dog far enough for now. They both could use a cooldown. "Then I need to stop thinking about Flynn Brogan," she said.

The dog's ears perked up. "What do you think, Bismarck?" she asked. "Is there more to Flynn Brogan than meets the eye? Not that being eye candy isn't enough."

Bismarck looked up at her expectantly. She reached into her pocket and pulled out one of the treats she had at the ready.

As they walked back toward Palmetto House, her thoughts shifted away from Flynn and toward an idea that had been bouncing around the back of her brain since she arrived on the island. Lots of people made their living by providing a service to others. That's what she was doing now, wasn't it? Frankly, this gig was hard to beat as short-term work. But as much as she liked the lap of luxury, she wouldn't want to sprawl in it permanently. She had family she loved and whom she wanted to be part of her everyday life.

So maybe the answer for her was to take this business model and plop it down into the middle of Eternity Springs. In the past few years, dozens of vacation homes had been built in the mountains around her little town, and Cam Murphy's recent decision to sell acreage and right-of-way for a road on his Murphy Mountain land promised more to come. Gabi suspected that a person could make a decent living providing concierge services to vacation homeowners. Maybe building a business—her own business—in Eternity Springs would solve her dilemma about what to do with her life.

The idea held merit, and it was something she should explore. She could start by talking to the concierge service here about their business.

Who knows, maybe one of those vacation home owners in Colorado is a fabulous single guy who has been yearning for an excuse to move to the mountains. I can be an excuse. The Marlboro Man—minus the nicotine—wouldn't be something to turn down.

"I'm pathetic," she muttered. If she kept up this sort of thinking, she'd have to surrender her strong-and-kick-ass-woman card. She didn't need a man to make her life fulfilling. Hadn't she been perfectly happy as a single lady while working for the sheriff's department? The problem wasn't the lack of a man in her life. It was the lack of too many things. If she had even one of the big things—a great job, a great love, a great passion—she doubted she'd feel the absence of the others quite so keenly.

"So, get to work, Romano." After her visit to the glass shop this morning, she would pay a call on the concierge service and invite the owner out to lunch. She'd seemed like a lovely lady when she'd returned Gabi's call about scheduling a repair for the mangled sprinkler heads inside the dog run that Bismarck had used as chew toys.

Making that decision gave Gabi a little extra spring in her step, so she kicked up into a run once again. She'd almost completed the run and was nearing the beach access to Palmetto House when she spied Flynn Brogan emerging from the sea. Eye candy galore.

Well, it was only neighborly to stop and say hello, wasn't it?

FOUR

Flynn reached for the beach towel he'd left lying in the sand and dried first his face, then his torso. Spying Gabi Romano's approach, he paused mid-wipe. Exercise looked good on the woman.

She wore a black sports bra and little running shorts that showcased those amazing legs of hers. Her skin glistened with a fine sheen of sweat, and her full breasts bounced just enough in that constricting bra to be interesting. But it was her open, friendly smile that attracted him the most. She didn't look at him like he was a killer.

Of course, she thought he was a cabana boy, and he'd done nothing to dissuade her of the notion. He felt a little guilty about that. After all, one of his big takeaways from his whole marriage debacle was the destructive power that lies had in every sort of relationship, and he'd made it a personal tenet to avoid even white lies from then on. He really should correct the misunderstanding.

"Hello," she called. "How's the water?"

"Salty." Flynn grinned at the dog, who plopped down at her feet. "Looks like someone is done with his run."

"That's the plan. He'll be spending time in his crate this morning—I can't leave him in the dog run, since the last time I left him there, he got into mischief."

"In his dog run?"

"He ate three sprinkler heads."

"Puppies will be puppies." Flynn hunkered down and scratched Bismarck behind his ears.

"I share some responsibility. I should have left him with more than one chew bone, but I had no idea he'd go through it so fast. I'm glad he stopped with sprinkler heads. A friend of mine has a Boston terrier that will eat anything and everything. He's a true devil dog. But Bismarck really is a sweetheart."

The sweetheart under discussion suddenly hopped to his feet and took off running, catching Gabi by surprise and tugging the leash right out of her hand. "Bismarck!" she called.

The dog darted right into the water.

"Oh, for crying out loud," Gabi muttered as splashing commenced. "What is he doing? Bismarck, heel!"

Flynn grinned. "Looks like he'd rather swim."

"Yeah, well, he should reconsider. You know what happened to the *Bismarck*. The British sank it."

"Know your naval history, do you, Ms. Romano?"

"I grew up with brothers. We played Battleship." She sighed and added, "He is too cute, isn't he? Look at how he's nipping at the sea foam."

Flynn gave her a measuring look. "So, you're enjoying your dogsitting job?"

"I am." She cocked her head and added, "Speaking of jobs . . . it's early for you to be on this beach. Do you live at Tradewinds?"

Warily he answered, "Yes."

"You're the caretaker?"

Flynn hesitated. *Now's your chance.* "Would you believe that I own it?"

She flashed an easy grin. "Sam Wilcox's parents own it."

The words "not anymore" hung on his tongue. Technically, he wasn't really lying to her, and he had made an attempt to be honest. Was it his fault that she chose not to believe him?

Lame, Brogan. Yet he enjoyed this regular-guy anonymity more than he would have guessed, so he let it go for now. "I do take care of the place."

"I'm curious about how you got started. Would you mind answering a few questions for me about it? I have an idea for something I might like to try when I go home."

"Where is home?" he asked, curious and just a little wary. He still didn't completely trust her—another justification for allowing her to continue believing he was a pool boy.

"Colorado. Sleepy little mountain town in the middle of nowhere that you've probably never heard of."

"Try me."

"Eternity Springs. So, about your job . . . ?"

She was right. He hadn't heard of it. Flynn didn't want to answer questions about his "job," but neither did he want to lose that friendly smile. "What do you want to know?"

"I'm afraid I have an appointment, and I don't have time to go into it all now. Maybe later?"

Out of nowhere, he found himself saying, "Come to dinner. I'll cook for you."

The smile warmed, and so did Flynn. "I'd like that, unless . . . you won't serve lizard or fried ants, will you?"

"No reptiles or insects on our first date."

She hesitated a moment, the tilt of her head indicating that she was pondering a question. "So, this is a date? Then let's be clear . . . you're not married or in a relationship?"

Surprised at her candor, he replied, "I was married. Not anymore. I'm not in a relationship. Are you?"

"Nope. Never married. Have some baggage, but right now I'm free as air."

Good. That was really good. "In that case, seven o'clock."

"Sounds great. Now, I'd better see about getting the canine Bismarck into dry dock so that I can make my appointment on time." She toed off one running shoe, then the other before wading into the surf to retrieve her charge. Bismarck didn't make it easy for her, however, and by the time she waded out of the surf, she was almost as wet as the dog. And laughing about it.

Flynn found her reaction refreshing. Lisa would have gone into a high snit, then complained that she'd contracted some dreadful disease from the seawater. Of course, Lisa had hated dogs.

As Gabi Romano exited the beach, Flynn's thoughts continued in the direction he'd shied away from for a very long time: his wife.

He'd met Lisa Stafford while in graduate school at the University of Michigan. She'd had the fair-skinned, blond-haired beauty that displayed her Scandinavian ancestry, but her mind had been the main attraction. A medical student, she'd been smart as a whip, and when they first started dating, they'd spent hours in coffee shops and bars talking and debating subjects that most people didn't consider or care about. Flynn would never forget the look on his roommate's face when he told him he'd spent three hours with a girl talking about number theory and Fermat's Last Theorem.

They'd moved in together the week her sister had received her first Academy Award nomination. Lisa's health problems started a couple of months after that. It hadn't been any one serious ailment, but a series of minor illnesses one after the other that added up to her missing a ton of classes. Flynn had never felt so helpless, especially when she'd made the decision to withdraw from medical school.

They'd married the weekend after he'd graduated

with his master's. Wendy had been Lisa's maid of honor at the destination wedding she'd hosted on Maui. It had been Flynn's first encounter with paparazzi, the first time his photo had ended up in *People* magazine.

What he wouldn't give if only it had been the last.

Flynn sighed. They'd been happy those first few years. Lisa had helped him build the business, and when those first patents paid off big-time, she'd been as important a part of the team as he and Will.

He'd never really been able to pinpoint just when their relationship began to head south. Maybe it was all those trips to the West Coast to see the doctors her sister recommended. Maybe it was when Seagraves-Laraby broke ground on the new facility and he began spending so much time at the site. He knew her constant excuses to delay the start of the family they'd always planned had begun to wear on him long before he'd discovered her affair.

Sadness weighted Flynn's heart as he turned toward home, but for the first time in a very long time, anger was absent.

Maybe his plan to move forward was working. How had Gabi put it? Free as air? Could he claim to be free as air?

Polluted air, maybe. He still had some baggage bringing him down. "But not as much as I had a week ago."

And he had a date tonight with a beautiful, friendly woman who didn't appear to have an agenda. Well, except for learning about his "job." He'd better decide just how he wanted to handle that. So far he hadn't actually told her a lie. He would like to keep it that way, but he'd also like to go on being Mr. Nobody in her eyes. She wouldn't spot Mr. Nobody in the tabloids. Neither would she want something other than company. It had been so long since anyone had simply wanted his company.

He'd figure something out. In the meantime, he'd better make a run to the market. He had a meal to plan, something exotic.

Flynn liked to eat exotic foods, but he'd never cooked an exotic meal in his life. Luckily, he knew just whom to go to for help. Upon reaching the house, he went straight to the phone and dialed a number from memory. At his home in Florida, Matthew Wharton said, "Hello?"

"Matthew, I need your wife."

"So what else is new?"

Gabi drove the scooter into town for her appointment at the glass factory, wearing khaki capris, a sapphire-blue short-sleeved cotton camp shirt, sandals, and her scarf. She'd driven a Harley one time, but never something this small. She might just have to get her one of these to drive around Eternity Springs.

Because she was still a little early for her appointment, she parked the scooter near the market, where she purchased a glass of freshly squeezed mango and passion fruit juice—a new favorite of hers. Sipping her juice, she strolled the two blocks to the glass studio's location with a spring in her step. What a great start to her day! She'd enjoyed a lovely run, and then her sister-in-law Savannah had called to whine that her outdoor thermometer had registered twelve below zero just about the same time Gabi had been frolicking in the surf with a puppy. With the visit to the glass studio this morning and her first real date in just about forever on the docket for tonight—with a blue-eyed, bona-fide hottie, no less—it didn't get much better. She'd said as much to Savannah, who had then teased, "So, you'll be playing with fire this morning and again tonight?"

"Not on a first date, no," she'd replied. "Not playing. Flirting."

"Flirting with fire," she murmured now, smiling, as

she approached the studio's front door. That sounded like the title of a romance novel. One she'd like to read.

The building housing the studio was fashioned out of corrugated metal that had begun to rust in places. She stepped up to the glass front door and read the gold-painted logo: CICERO. As a rule, Gabi considered the whole going-by-one-name thing to be pretentious, but she did understand the need for businesses of all kinds to create a brand. Marketing 101. Gabi opened the door and stepped into a small retail shop. A teenage girl showed her a friendly smile. "Can I help you?"

"My name is Gabi Romano. Mitch invited me to visit."

The girl's smile widened. "Yes, he mentioned we might have a visitor. Welcome, Gabi. My name is Shannon, and you've come at a great time. They're just getting started on a commission, a sculpture. Come on into the studio and you can watch."

Shannon opened the door, and a blast of heat rolled over them. Gabi followed her into the studio.

Her life changed in that instant.

As classic rock pounded through speakers set high on the walls, Mitch handed over a long metal rod with a red-hot blob of molten glass on the end to a seated figure who wore his midnight black hair long and tied back at the neck. Gabi quietly shifted her position for a better angle on the proceedings and got her first good look at the broad-shouldered man. She drew in a quick breath.

Not just a man, the fanciful part of her suggested. He could be a fallen angel.

His face was long, his features chiseled like the granite cliffs at home. She couldn't see his eyes; they never lifted from his work. He had a long, thin nose that showed signs of having been broken, dark eyebrows, and lashes thick and long enough to make any woman envious.

Full lips wrapped around a tube, and as the molten blob began to expand, she realized he'd blown air into the glass. Gabi watched the scene with awe. *He's a fallen angel molding fire.*

His big hands never stopped moving. He picked up something with his right hand—a pad of some sort. Surely that wasn't a stack of wet newspaper? He held the pad against the glowing molten substance slowly turning from a blob into a shape. Steam or maybe smoke rose from the pad as his left hand kept the metal rod constantly spinning. He dropped the pad onto a table and reached behind him. Gabi jumped when he hit a lever and a blue flame erupted from a torch.

He held the torch to the glass for a moment, then picked up a large pair of metal tongs. Now the form stretched, elongated. His movements constant and fluid and sure, he used one tool, then another. At one point he transferred the glass from one rod to another.

The form slowly took shape in shades of red. It was a woman wearing flowing robes. Following some sort of unspoken signal between the artist and Mitch, it went into the fiery oven to heat, then came back out to be worked some more. They repeated this dance time and again.

How long it lasted, Gabi didn't know—two hours, two days. Time seemed suspended. Without uttering a word and with Mitch's perfectly choreographed assistance, the artist danced a ballet, conducted a symphony. The man made magic.

Inside Gabi, a flame of desire began to burn.

Not, to her complete surprise, for the man. For the art. She wanted to do that. She wanted to create something like that.

When he used a tweezer-like tool to pull the glass along the figure's back and she realized he'd created wings, she sucked in a breath. Wings made her think of angels, which made her think of her friend Celeste Blessing and the awesome changes she'd brought to Eternity Springs. With the opening of Angel's Rest, the town had been reborn.

Angels. New starts.

New passions.

Gabi's mind began to spin.

She thought about the booth Mitch manned in the market and the trinkets he sold. Dreamweavers. She pictured the seahorse she'd bought. Hadn't it appealed to her in part for exactly the reasons Mitch had given? Because she knew she'd look at it and remember her visit to Bella Vita Isle?

Souvenirs. The shops in Eternity Springs did a brisk business with souvenirs in the summer. Tourist towns all over Colorado did. Throw in the ski resorts and you had a year-round clientele.

And locally made items sold best of all. Savannah's success with her Heavenscents soaps had proved that. Why couldn't Gabi learn to blow glass and make souvenirs to sell in Colorado?

Maybe because you don't know the first thing about it? Or because it probably takes years and tons of practice to learn? You've never even attempted to make anything. How do you know you'll like it?

She knew. It was a bone-deep knowledge that she recognized as surely as she had known that she never wanted to pick up a gun again. She wanted to learn to do this. Badly.

Gabi held her breath as Mitch donned a pair of thick gloves and held the figure while the artist—Cicero, she assumed—tapped the piece gently until it separated from the rod. Then Mitch carried it to another metal box set against the wall and set it carefully inside. He shut the door, set a dial, then turned around and smiled at Gabi. "Beautiful lady, welcome!"

"Thank you."

The artist rose gracefully to his feet, picked up a bottle of water, and, locking his gaze with hers, drank half the bottle down. Gabi wanted to fidget. Instead, she summoned her inner calm and waited, sensing that these next few moments had the power to change her life.

Mitch wiped his sweat-dampened brow with a dingy yellow towel, then said, "Cicero, this is the lady I told you about. Ms. Gabriella Romano."

Cicero lowered the bottle. "Gabriella," he repeated, his tone serious, his countenance unsmiling.

Oh, holy cow. His voice was sexy, too.

"Watching you work was amazing."

He took another long pull on his water. "You're a tourist?"

"I'm dogsitting for the owners of Palmetto House. I'll be here four months."

"You want to learn. It shows in your eyes."

"I do want to learn. I want it very much."

He studied her for a long minute. Gabi held her breath. She told herself that it didn't matter what he said. She could find another place to learn when she went home. Maybe not in Eternity Springs, but somewhere. Surely.

"Help her make a flared bowl," he said to Mitch, then turned and left the room.

Gabi broke out into a wide smile and did a fist pump. Mitch waved a hand. "I knew he'd agree. You're beautiful. Cicero seldom says no to beautiful ladies."

"Oh, would you stop with the ridiculous flattery and show me what to do?"

Mitch placed a hand against his heart and made a thumping motion. "You wound me. I speak but the truth."

"Can it, Romeo. So, what is the pole called?"

He laughed. "It's a blowpipe."

"But he didn't blow through it. He blew through a tube."

"Patience, bug. Let me get set up and then I'll take you through it step by step."

"Bug?" She'd gone from beautiful lady to an insect?

As he walked around the studio preparing his tools and supplies, he explained, "That's what Cicero called me when I first started working as his gaffer."

"Gaffer?"

"His apprentice."

"How long have you been his apprentice?"

"Three years."

"Oh. It takes that long to learn to blow glass?"

"It takes a lifetime to become an artist. You have to live glass. It must be your entire world. It must be your passion."

Passion, Gabi thought. *There's that word again.*

Mitch asked, "Ready to get started?"

"Definitely."

"All right, then. We start with color. Color is achieved by using different metal oxides. What colors would you like to use in your bowl?"

Gabi immediately thought of Flynn Brogan's eyes and the beautiful blue of the dreamweaver she'd purchased. "Do you remember the seahorse I bought? I'd like that blue, please."

"Cobalt. What else? Pick a couple more."

"I'd like it to look like the sea off the beach at Palmetto House."

From a shelf against the wall, Mitch chose three plastic jars filled with what looked like small rocks. He poured a sample of each color into three separate dishes lined up on a metal table. "Achieving the color you're going for in glass is tricky. You can use the exact same method and the exact same supplies, and get a different result from one time to the next. That's all part of the fun. The colors coming out of the annealing oven will be different from when they went into it."

"So how do you get the color you want?"

"Practice and prayer." He shot her a grin. "Now, all is ready. I want you to pick up the blowpipe. You're going to always hold it here." He pointed to two positions. "That's important. Otherwise, you risk a burn."

"Okay."

"Now, the furnace is the heart of any studio, Gabi. Glass is made by melting natural raw materials inside a ceramic pot called a crucible that rests inside the furnace. The glass is clear. It's a clean canvas for the artists at this point."

"How hot is the furnace?" Gabi asked.

"Around two thousand degrees. It's kept on all the time, seven days a week. So, are you ready?"

"I am."

"Then extend the pipe into the furnace. We're going to let it heat for a minute so that the glass will stick to it."

"This is so cool," Gabi said.

"Actually, it's two thousand degrees."

"You know what I mean."

The young man grinned, then said, "Now you're going to get a gather of glass. Look into the crucible. Find the reflection of the molten glass. See it?"

"I do."

"Dip the pipe into the glass. Turn it, and dip. There you go," he added as she did as he instructed. "Again."

Once she had a blob of glass—a gather—he said, "Good. Now, remove it from the furnace, and we're going to carry it over to the table and apply color."

He instructed her to dip the glass into the first dish of color crystals, turn, dip into the second, turn, dip into the third. "Excellent. Now, into the reheating furnace to melt in the colors."

Gabi extended the pipe into the smaller furnace he

indicated. After a moment, he said, "Now you're going to marver in one spot."

"Marver?"

"Twist in the colors. That's the marver table." He pointed to what looked like a stainless-steel table. "Roll it. Flatten it out a bit. Keep turning the blowpipe. The glass is the consistency of honey, so if you don't keep it moving, you'll have a mess."

Gabi followed his instructions, her gaze never lifting from the orange glow at the end of the pipe.

Mitch continued. "Now it's time to put in the starter bubble. Let me take the pipe, and you go sit on the bench. Grab a bottle of water on your way. Need to stay hydrated in here."

She took a seat where Cicero had sat earlier and wiped her sweaty palms on her capris. It was blazing hot in the studio, and the water tasted delicious.

For the next fifteen minutes, he took her step by step through the process. She blew the initial air bubble, shaped it with wet newspaper, added air through the blow hose, and added more glass. He showed her how to apply the punty—another rod, only without a blowhole—and open up the lip of the bowl. Gabi was fascinated, challenged, and, when Cicero reentered the studio, distracted. If cobalt made the color of Flynn Brogan's eyes, she wondered what metal oxide would create that dark chocolate brown of the artist's.

"Hello? Are you with me?" Mitch asked.

Gabi winced, embarrassed, and redirected her attention to the project, but not before she spied the smirk on Cicero's lips.

"This is the fun part," Mitch told her, handing her the tongs. He put his hand over hers and showed her how to widen the lip and shape it. Once it was done, he said, "Now, we flare it. We're going to turn it upside down and let centrifugal force do its thing by spinning it faster and faster and faster."

"We are? It won't drop off?"

"Nope."

"I don't know, Mitch. I don't think—"

He handed her the punty saying, "Spin and flip. Quick."

She was nervous and excited but did as instructed, twirling the punty until she saw the glass flare out into waves.

"There you go. Perfect."

Not perfect. Her waves were totally lopsided. Nevertheless, a heady sense of utter delight rushed through her.

Mitch carefully tapped the punty with a knife and detached the bowl. He heated the bottom with the torch, smoothed away the punty mark, then carried Gabi's bowl to the annealer. "All completed pieces are put in here. It's kept at about 950 degrees during the day."

"Isn't it done? Why do you have to bake it?"

Cicero stepped forward. "You can't leave hot glass out at room temperature, because extreme temperature changes will cause it to explode or, at a minimum, crack. We'll put all our smaller finished pieces inside, then at the end of the day, the annealer is set to automatically and systematically cycle down to room temperature. This typically takes eight to twelve hours for standard bowls and vases."

"The figure you made this morning is different?"

"Yes. The sculpture we made earlier is dense, and it will take days to bring it to room temperature. That's why it's in a separate annealer."

Now that Cicero had joined the conversation, Gabi took advantage of it and peppered him with questions. Because every answer he gave invariably led to at least three more questions, the exchange went on for some time. Totally engaged in the impromptu lesson, she didn't notice that Mitch had left the studio. She was a sponge, and she wanted to absorb everything.

Cicero used his work to demonstrate the points he made about color and design. He gave her different items to hold as he talked about weight and balance. When he took her hand and placed his index finger atop hers to trace the cool, emerald-green ridges and valleys of a sculpted piece he'd named "Time," she grew hypersensitive. The rough velvet sound of his voice mesmerized her. The sensation of his skin against hers gave her the shivers.

But it was the work itself that seduced her.

Deep down in the very marrow of her soul, she yearned. *I want to learn,* she thought. *I want to learn to do this.* Never one to shy away from being bold, Gabi turned and faced Cicero. "Will you teach me?"

Intensely he studied her, and Gabi held her breath. Even though her pulse pounded and the ten-year-old inside her wanted to jump up and down and clap her hands and beg "Pretty please," she wouldn't be devastated if he refused. Because while those interminable seconds ticked by, she realized something else. This man wasn't the only person in the world who could teach her. One way or another, she would find a way to learn to blow glass. After a long moment, he shook his head regretfully. "You feel it, don't you?"

"Feel what?"

"The passion. For the work."

Passion. Yes. That was the right word. This was what she'd been searching for. Finally!

Nodding, she affirmed. "I do."

"You're certain."

"I am."

Cicero sighed and slowly shook his head. "Such a pity."

Gabi's stomach sank. Shoot. Even though she was certain she could find another place to learn, she really didn't want to wait the four months until her stay on Bella Vita Isle was over.

"I have a rule," Cicero continued, his voice a low, sensual rumble as he gave her a slow once-over. He reached out and brushed his thumb across her lower lip, then repeated his sigh. "I don't hit on students. Such a sacrifice I make."

The sensual note in his voice evaporated as he added matter-of-factly, "Be here at nine a.m. tomorrow, Legs. Wear long sleeves and closed-toe shoes and bring a sack lunch for three and a big jug of water. Now go. I have work to do, and I don't need you in my way."

Student. He'd said "student." "I'm in."

"You. My way. Leave. Now."

The seducer had disappeared, leaving an autocratic dictator in his place. As a law enforcement officer, Gabi had plenty of practice taking orders from her superiors, so she drew from experience: she turned on her heel and beat feet.

Outside of the studio, she abruptly halted. Excitement welled up inside her like an ocean swell. She'd found it. She knew in her heart of hearts that she'd finally found the road she'd been seeking. Perhaps she'd discover that she had no talent for blowing glass. Maybe she'd decide that the craft wasn't the one for her after all. There was even a chance she'd show up tomorrow at the studio and decide it had all been a big mistake and she needed to keep searching.

Except she knew it wasn't true.

She threw out her arms, lifted her face to the sun-filled sky, and smiled up at the heavens. Gabriella Romano had found her passion.

FIVE

Flynn spent the afternoon severing one of the few remaining ties with his old life. He worked at his computer making a final pass at the email received at his personal address before he deleted the account. He'd put off the task until now because he'd known he'd find land mines awaiting him in his inbox, and until today he hadn't had the energy to deal with them. Guess the thought of having a dinner date with a beautiful woman was just the shot of caffeine he'd needed.

Sure enough, in addition to dozens of emails requiring his response, he'd found an excoriating message from Lisa's best friend and a long, vicious diatribe from Lisa's sister. He'd expected hateful words, but to know that other human beings wanted to stab his balls with an ice pick, pull his teeth without anesthetic, and cut off his fingers and toes one at a time was disturbing. Nevertheless, he read them through to the end. Self-flagellation or penance or a combination of the two, perhaps, but he did it anyway. Doing so felt like flinging that last shovel of dirt onto the grave of his previous life.

Reviewing the eighty-seven attack emails from his former friend and business partner, Will Laraby, took his thoughts in an unexpected direction. Rather than focus on the vitriol and grief Will expressed, Flynn thought about the man himself.

He had met Will in September of their freshman year in the hallway of the science building as they both waited for their physics professor to arrive for office hours. Within five minutes they'd formed a bond of brotherhood that had lasted fifteen years. If he were being honest with himself, losing Will had left a bigger hole in his life than losing Lisa.

Will had a brilliant mind, but everyday life tended to defeat him. He often forgot to eat. He seldom remembered to pay his bills. He habitually left his possessions trailing behind him like bread crumbs. But it wasn't those absentminded tendencies that Flynn was reminded of when reading the emotion-filled, nonsensical emails today. The emails reminded Flynn of just how clueless the man was when it came to dealing with people.

It was that cluelessness, that innocence, that had made him susceptible to Lisa's machinations. Flynn had been too wrapped up in his own pain and grief to see it until today. Will wasn't blameless in this tragedy. Far from it. But neither was he the villain Flynn had perceived him to be for these last three years.

Flynn pushed the delete key on the last of Will's emails, putting a period to that part of his life. A heavy weight lifted from his heart.

He shut the lid on his laptop, shoved back from the desk, and turned his attention to a more pleasant topic. It was time to get started on dinner. Thinking about Gabi Romano, he smiled. She didn't know it, of course, but the evening with her would mark a fresh start, a new beginning, to the rest of his life.

Flynn seldom went to the bother of cooking for himself, but he did know how to do it. With Margaret's assistance, he had planned a menu that he felt comfortable preparing that qualified as exotic without containing any lizards or insects, just as he'd promised.

He hadn't said a word about snails.

When he left his house to pick up his date shortly before seven, he had a table set for two, perfectly positioned to watch the sunset, and a jazzy Latin guitar instrumental playing softly on the sound system. Flynn kept only one vehicle on Bella Vita Isle, a Jeep, so he climbed into it and prepared to make the short drive to the estate next door.

To his surprise and consternation, he realized he was nervous. He hadn't been on a date in over twelve years if you didn't count those few weeks of sport screwing after his marriage ended, and Flynn didn't. He tried not to think about that period. He'd been in an ugly, self-destructive state, and it had left him feeling dirty, despite the fact that all the women he'd been with had been on the prowl themselves. Then after Lisa died, the weirdos had come out of the woodwork, and some of the propositions he'd received had been downright frightening.

He didn't think he had to worry about that sort of nonsense with Gabi Romano. She seemed genuine, open, honest, and normal. "Normal" was his highest compliment these days. She certainly wasn't after his money, since for all she knew, he didn't have any. Best of all, she wasn't a permanent resident of Bella Vita Isle. He could dip his toes back into the dating pool without needing to worry about drowning in the deep end.

"So, nothing to be nervous about," he reassured himself as he turned into the drive at Palmetto House. Dating hadn't changed that much in twelve years, had it? But for all he knew it had, given how the world had changed in the past decade. If the two of them enjoyed themselves, would she expect to sleep with him? How would he react to that? As much as he'd like sex, he didn't want to experience that sucky one-night-stand feeling again.

Although, he argued with himself, if it happened naturally at the end of a nice date, that should feel different from picking up a skank in a bar, right?

Was that justification talking there, or did he really believe it?

He had no more time to ponder the question or his own nervousness because she answered his knock with a bright smile and a harried look in her eyes. "I'm so sorry. I'm running just a little bit behind. My mother called with some family news, and I'm afraid I lost track of time. I still need to see to Bismarck."

"Why don't you bring him?" Flynn suggested. "I haven't had a puppy to play with in a long time."

"Are you sure?"

"Yes. I've been thinking about getting a dog. It will do me good to spend time with one before I make my decision."

The wattage of her smile doubled. "I'll get his go bag."

"A go bag? You have a go bag for a dog?"

"It's not a go bag in same sense as a bug-out bag, of course," she said, casting a look over her shoulder as she hurried away.

So the lady's vocabulary included bug-out bags? Interesting, Flynn thought. But then, she did say she lived in the mountains in the middle of nowhere. Probably good to have a pack of basic survival items handy.

Two minutes later she returned with Bismarck on a leash and a tote bag on her shoulder. Flynn took a moment to enjoy the picture she presented. Gabi wore a batik dress like the ones sold in the stalls at the island market. It flowed around her in shades of green and tied over one shoulder, leaving the other bare. She had lovely shoulders, tanned and toned and utterly feminine. And she walked with a swing of her hips that made Flynn want to lick his lips and growl.

Instead, he turned his attention to the dog, squatting down and scratching him behind his ears. "Hey, Bismarck. Were you a good boy today?"

"He was," Gabi replied in a proud-mother tone. "When I came home from the glass studio he was snoozing happily in his crate. I opened the door, but he didn't leave it for another twenty minutes. That made me feel so much better about crating him when I go somewhere without him."

Flynn rose and opened the Jeep's passenger door for Gabi and Bismarck, his gaze locking on her legs as her skirt rode up on her thighs as she took her seat. He whistled beneath his breath as he walked around the back of the Jeep to the driver's seat, his nervousness gone and his spirits high.

"So, what did you do today after your run?" he asked.

"I had an absolutely awesome day." Her expression turned a bit dreamy as she added, "I visited the glass studio and totally fell in love."

Well, that's a helluva thing to hear at the beginning of a date. Blandly he observed, "Cicero has a way of doing that to women."

"I meant I fell in love with the art," she said with a laugh. "Though I'm not surprised at the comment about Cicero. He strikes me as a player."

"Not just a player. A whole ball team of players. Not a basketball team, either. A football team."

"So you know him well?"

"Yeah. We're both regulars in a weekly poker game at a bar in town. We've become pretty good friends over the past few months."

Gabi gave him a measured look. "So does that mean that you're a football-team-sized player, too?"

Flynn's mouth twisted. "Hardly. You're my first date since I split with my wife."

"Oh? How long ago was that?"

He hesitated, deciding how best to present the facts. He could fudge the truth, but since he was already guilty of allowing her to believe he was a pool boy, he couldn't in good conscience do that. "I filed three years ago, but my wife died before the paperwork was finalized. So technically I'm a widower."

"Oh. Well." Curiosity lit her eyes, and he waited for the inevitable question: *How did she die?* Except Gabi Romano surprised him. "My condolences. No matter what happened between you two, that couldn't have been easy."

You don't have any idea. "Thank you."

He relaxed when she returned the conversation to glass. "What Cicero does with glass is amazing. He's agreed to teach me."

Teach you what? Flynn drawled, "I'll just bet he did."

Gabi frowned at him. "I know what you're thinking. It's not like that. Well, it could have been like that, but apparently he has a personal standard not to mix business and . . . that." She lifted her chin and added, "Besides, I'll have you know that I have personal standards, too. Just because he might have been willing to mix doesn't mean that I would be."

"No offense intended, Gabriella. It's just that I know Cicero very well, and he never misses a chance to make a pass at a beautiful woman. Now enough about him. Talk to me about the lessons. Is this something you've always wanted to do?"

"No, but as crazy as this sounds, I think it's something that I'll want to do always."

She launched into a description of her time at the studio with an enthusiasm he envied. It reminded him of how design work used to make him feel, and soon he was caught up in her enthusiasm, asking questions about her wishes, hopes, and dreams.

As he pulled the Jeep to a stop in front of his house, she said, "I'm sure it would take years and years of training to even begin to reach the point where I could be considered an artist. However, I think I could make the process work for me in the meantime. That's where you come in."

"Me?"

"I'm curious about your job."

Well, damn. Flynn delayed his response by exiting the car. He really didn't want to kick off the next portion of their date by admitting that he'd failed to correct her mistake about his identity. He opened her door and attempted to distract her by saying, "I'm very boring, Gabi. I'm happy to answer your questions, but why don't I pour you a glass of wine and give you a tour of the house first?"

Interest lit her eyes. "Ooh, I love to peek into the lives of the rich and famous. I have friends at home who are seriously wealthy, and they have this great house in a valley up above town. It has the most amazing pool designed by another friend of mine."

"You have a lot of friends."

A shadow crossed her face. "I haven't always. I was the girl who was happy to have her one BFF and a small group of special friends, but something happened to change that. Now I'm making a concerted effort to expand my social circle."

From his experience, large social circles weren't always a good thing, but he wasn't going to tell her that. As he opened the front door he observed, "Sounds like there's a story there."

"I need a couple of glasses of wine to share it," she replied, stepping into Tradewinds.

Flynn took his time showing her the house. He had

done very little redecorating since buying the property, so it was easy for him to speak truthfully about the Wilcoxes' decorating. He showed her the living areas first, then the guest rooms upstairs. He deliberately skipped the master bedroom because it showed signs of occupancy that he didn't want to explain—unless he had a reason for showing the room later.

She oohed and ahhed over the bathrooms and marveled over the views from each window. She liked the reading nook in the library better than the theater room and was surprised when he mentioned the game room, which was part of the pool house wing.

"They have a theater room and a game room?" she asked, giving Bismarck's lead a tug to bring him back to heel.

"The game room is an arcade. I have to admit it's pretty awesome. I can waste hours in there if I let myself."

She shook her head and clicked her tongue. "Boys and their toys."

Next he led her into the kitchen, and he spied special interest in her expression. "Are you a cook?"

"Yes." She shot him a quick grin. "A horrible one. At least, that's what my brothers tell me. I'll admit that except for a few weeks last year after I quit my job, I've never put much effort into culinary learning. My mother is a fabulous cook, and she tried to teach me when I was growing up, but I was never interested. I regret that now. How about you? Are you a good cook?"

"Considering that I'm fixing dinner for you, we both should hope so."

"Should I be worried?" she teased.

"No. I don't cook often, but when I do, I think I'm decent at it. Some old friends of mine are foodies. Margaret, the wife, has given me plenty of tips through the years."

Gabi pulled a swivel peeler from a pottery jar filled with kitchen tools and studied it. "What are we having tonight?"

Flynn spoke casually but watched her closely as he replied, "Snail salad."

Her eyes rounded with horror and she dropped the peeler. Flynn laughed. "Since you've been on the island at least a week, I'll bet you've already tried it. Conch salad?"

Her lips rounded in a circle. "Oh. I've seen it for sale, but I haven't tried it. Conch is a snail?"

"Yes."

"Oh."

He smiled at her uncertain expression. "What did you think it was?"

"I don't know. I didn't think about it. Just like I don't think about oysters or shrimp. Shoot, I'm a city girl. I like to think that chicken and hamburger starts out as little plastic-wrapped packages in the refrigerator case at the grocery store."

Flynn shook his head. "Gabi, Gabi, Gabi. And to think I worried tonight's meal wouldn't meet the exotic standard."

Warily she asked, "What else are you serving?"

He was tempted to tease her, but instead offered the truth. "We'll have grilled triggerfish that I caught today, rice, and *plátanos maduros* as a side dish. So, too risky for you, city girl?"

"Not at all," she fired back. After a moment's hesitation, she asked, "What is *plátanos maduros*?"

He laughed. "Patience, grasshopper. Trust me."

She wrinkled her nose. "When it comes to men and trust, I am extra careful."

"Sounds like there's a story there, too."

"It's the same story, actually," she replied, her mouth twisting in a rueful smile.

"Then I'd better pour the wine. I have a nice chardonnay that should pair very well with our meal. Is that all right?"

"Sounds lovely."

While Flynn busied himself with the wine, Gabi wandered through the kitchen, inspecting the appliances. "My mother would go bonkers over this kitchen. She recently remodeled an old Victorian house and opened it as a bed-and-breakfast. She spent weeks and weeks on her kitchen design. She chose this brand of appliances, but she only has the basics due to the size limitations of the room."

"So your mother is an innkeeper? How does she like it?"

"She's happy as a clam. She says she always wanted to have a career, but my dad didn't want her to work, even after the kids were all grown. When he died three years ago, she moved to Eternity Springs to be closer to me and one of my brothers. We all thought she was crazy when she said she wanted to open a B&B, but she just loves it." Showing him a crooked grin, she added, "Of course, it doesn't hurt that she's got something going with her handyman."

"A jolly widow, then."

"Oh, yeah. Although she told me in our phone call that the handyman is contemplating a move. He wants to be closer to his grandchildren, which is the same reason my mother won't consider leaving Eternity Springs."

"Will her heart be broken if he goes?"

Gabi pursed her lips thoughtfully. "I don't think so. He's a nice man and he's been good for her, but I don't think she's head over heels in love with him."

Flynn handed her a glass filled with a crisp, buttery wine. "Tell me about the rest of your family. I think you mentioned you have brothers?"

"Four of them, bless my heart."

Flynn could hear the obvious love for her relatives as she gave him a rundown of their identities and occupations. He followed college basketball, so when she mentioned that two of her brothers were coaches, he placed them right away. They talked a little hoops, and then she asked him about his family. Flynn carefully considered his words. "I'm an only child. My mother passed away a few years ago, and my dad lives on the West Coast."

"I'm so sorry you lost your mom. I know I'd be devastated."

"It was a difficult time."

"Do you see your dad often? The West Coast is a long way from Bella Vita Isle."

"I don't see him as often as I would like," he said truthfully. Then he picked up the wine bottle and changed the subject. "Shall we continue our tour? I thought we'd eat out by the pool. You can let Bismarck off his leash to go exploring."

"That sounds perfect."

Flynn did his best to make it exactly that. He led her and Bismarck out of a side door and along the walk to the covered breezeway where he'd set a table for two. It was one of his favorite places on the estate, with a view of the pool and gardens on one side and a view of the ocean on the other. "Oh, wow. How gorgeous," she exclaimed. "I didn't notice this spot the other day when I followed Bismarck over here. This faces west, right? Bet you see fabulous sunsets!"

"They can be pretty awesome." He flipped the switch on the rice cooker and set the bottle of wine into the outdoor kitchen fridge next to the filleted and seasoned fish. He'd prepped everything ahead of time, so the only thing left to do was to wait for the rice to cook and grill the fish. "It's still a little early to start the fish. Do you have any throw toys in that go bag of yours?"

"I do."

"If we run this pup a bit, he might crash while we have dinner."

"Excellent idea." Gabi fished inside the bag and pulled out a tennis ball.

"Mind if I play?"

"Be my guest." She handed him the ball.

While Flynn threw the ball for Bismarck to chase, Gabi strolled through the garden. She looked just beautiful, he thought. And what pleasant company she was proving to be. No demands, no unreasonable requests. He'd almost forgotten that spending time with a woman could be like this. It hadn't been good with Lisa for a very long time before the split.

He realized he had what was probably a goofy grin on his face.

But Flynn was happy. For the first time in a very long time, he felt good. About life. About the future. About the possibilities in his future. He felt as if he'd truly turned a corner and left the misery of his past behind him.

And best of all, the ideas had begun to float through his brain again. His creativity had been mostly MIA since he learned about the affair. He'd mourned the loss of that vital part of himself almost as much as he'd mourned the death of his marriage.

He threw the neon-yellow ball one more time, and Bismarck bounded after it, brought it halfway back to Flynn, then plopped down on the green grass. "I think he's done," Gabi said, a note of humor in her voice.

"I think you're right." Flynn snapped his fingers, but the dog didn't so much as perk his ears.

Gabi braced her hands on her hips and laughed. "Give it up, Brogan. I know him. He's done. He probably won't move for an hour."

Perfect. "All right, then. I'll get the fish on the grill."

Flynn crossed to the outdoor kitchen, washed his hands,

and fired up the grill. "You cook with gas," Gabi observed.

"Tonight I am. Is that a problem?"

"Not at all. Now, if you were having dinner with my brothers instead of me, there would be a discussion."

"Ah, I see. So you have some barbecue purists in the family? Charcoal men?"

"Charcoal hardheads. Honestly, I recognize the importance of good barbecue. I'm a sports fan, and I know that barbecue can make or break a tailgate. I'm the one who gave them all the Barbecue-Meister control that they rave about for Christmas, but—"

"You gave your brothers a Barbecue-Meister?" Flynn interrupted, inordinately pleased. It was his personal invention, the first technology of its kind that controlled temperature in wood-burning or charcoal cookers. Totally separate from Seagraves-Laraby, the Barbecue-Meister patent and his shares in the business that had grown from it was the only thing he'd had Matthew hold on to in the divestiture.

"You know it? Do you use one, too?"

"I do. Cooking low and slow is what makes barbecue great. The Barbecue-Meister affords the cook predictability and consistency with his meats without having to constantly monitor his cooker."

"Which is why my brothers think it's the greatest invention since the DVR."

Flynn couldn't help but preen. He was also curious because, after all, he knew his way around grills. As he removed the platter of fillets from the fridge, he asked, "How do your brothers usually grill their fish?"

"They don't. They pan-fry the trout they catch, but that's about it. When it comes to grilling, they are all about being carnivores. So, what can I do to help?"

"Have a seat and enjoy your wine and the sunset. Dinner will be ready in just a few minutes."

Her warm, friendly smile made Flynn plenty warm himself.

While he tended to the final dinner preparations, Gabi stood staring out at the ocean, sipping her wine. Nature was providing quite a show tonight, with the sky a fiery riot of oranges, reds, and golds. "I can't believe I'm here. It's probably ten degrees at home right now." She glanced over her shoulder and asked, "How did you come to be here, Flynn?"

He didn't want to lie to her. While he could say, *After my murder trial, I needed somewhere to hide,* he didn't want to spoil her appetite, so he offered a different truth. "I needed a change. My personal life wasn't all that great, and I wanted some time to sort through the possibilities. I had a chance to come to Bella Vita Isle, and it seemed like a good place to do some thinking. I've discovered that I can figure out a lot about myself while I have a fishing rod in my hand."

"Really?" Gabi replied, giving Flynn her complete attention. "That's why I came to Bella Vita, too. So your caretaker gig isn't a permanent position?"

Again he carefully chose his words. "I don't intend to make the island my permanent home."

Flynn checked the fish and judged it was time to turn it. He squirted a little fresh lemon juice on it and over the steam and sizzle asked, "So tell me why you needed a change. Something to do with your BFF?"

"Maybe a little bit, but that's not the main reason I've been floundering. My whole world changed when I killed someone."

Flynn dropped his grill spatula, and Gabi winced. "Guess I should have chosen my words a little better. Don't worry. Don't let it spoil your appetite. You didn't invite a murderer to dinner."

This is bizarre, Flynn thought as he bent to pick up the tool.

Gabi continued, "The synopsis is that I used to be a cop, a deputy sheriff, and I shot someone in the line of duty. I worked for my brother Zach, who is the sheriff in Eternity Springs. There was an incident, and I was seconds late reacting. A woman shot Zach before I took her out. He almost died. The event was . . . life-changing for me."

Flynn heard the hitch in her voice and regret filled him. *I understand. Believe me, Gabriella, I do understand.* "I'm sorry," he told her as he brought individual bowls of conch salad to the table. "I didn't mean to bring up something upsetting, especially right before dinner."

"That's okay. Don't worry about it. Nothing spoils my appetite." She took a sip of her wine, then added, "I've actually found it does me good to talk about it."

He waited for her to say more, but as he removed the *plátanos maduros* from the warming drawer and plated them along with rice and the triggerfish fillet, she appeared content to watch. "Wow, if it tastes as good as it looks . . . even the snails look appetizing."

"It's actually just one snail," he explained. "A big one. With tomato, bell pepper, onion, and lime. A few seasonings. Now, go ahead and take a bite."

She picked up her salad fork, then hesitated. "Life is all about new experiences, right?"

"Absolutely."

"I should forge ahead."

"Definitely."

"It probably tastes just like chicken."

Grinning, Flynn shook his head. "Only one chicken at this table."

Gabi sucked in a bracing breath, then speared the salad with her fork and took a bite. Flynn watched her over the top of his glass, a grin hovering on his lips, as she cautiously tested the taste. Her eyes went round and wide, then she closed her eyes and savored. She took a second bite, and her little moan of pleasure sent his blood flowing south. After she swallowed, she looked at him and observed, "That is sinful."

"Caribbean Viagra."

That startled a laugh from her. "Excuse me?"

Flynn shrugged and dug into his own meal. "Locals believe conch is an aphrodisiac."

She held his gaze for a long moment. "It's only our first date, Mr. Brogan. Getting a little ahead of yourself, don't you think?"

The look he returned was all innocence. "I'm a Boy Scout. We're always prepared."

Gabi laughed, then tried first her fish and then the plantains. "This is all simply fabulous, Flynn. You could open a restaurant."

"Hardly," he said with a laugh. "Unless it's a sandwich shop. I pretty much live on those."

"The single person's staple," Gabi agreed. "What's your favorite?"

The conversation continued with get-to-know-you type of talk. They discussed music they liked and books they read. Gabi liked fantasy and paranormal romance along with the thrillers he gravitated toward. They agreed not to discuss politics, and they spent a good amount of time talking about sports. When they'd finished their meal, he suggested a stroll on the beach, which Gabi agreed to enthusiastically. "I need to walk. I ate too much. Dinner truly was fantastic, Flynn. I admit I'm a little jealous. Do you cook for the Wilcoxes when they're here?"

"No, I've never cooked for the Wilcoxes," he replied, rising from his chair. As he topped off their wineglasses, he made a quick attempt to change the direction of the conversation as he escorted her out onto the beach. "So, earlier you said you're a city girl. You've mentioned that you used to live in Denver. Is that where you grew up?"

"Yes. I grew up there, went to college in Connecticut, then returned to Denver after I graduated. When I decided to move to Eternity Springs, I admit I was a little worried about small-town living, but I love it. Eternity Springs is truly a wonderful place to live."

"What makes it special?"

She considered the question a moment before saying, "A friend of mine has a bit of a mystical air, and she claims that the area has a healing energy. I know it sounds hokey, but after living there awhile and learning people's stories, I tend to think there might be something to it. People arrive in town with broken hearts, and before you know it, they're falling in love and getting married and having babies."

They fell silent for a few moments watching the last of the scarlet colors of sunset bleed into the sea. The shadows deepened and a sense of intimacy surrounded them, prompting Flynn to take the conversation to a more personal level. "Was a broken heart what brought you to your little town?"

She sipped her wine and considered a moment before saying, "No, or at least I didn't think so at the time." She told him about going to Eternity Springs to work with her long-lost brother. "In hindsight, I can admit that I did have a broken heart when I moved there. I'd recently discovered that my fiancé had slept with my best friend."

Whoa. She and I have so much in common, it's almost frightening. Flynn shook his head. "People can be such scum."

"So I've learned. Funny, I haven't spoken about this to anyone. Must be the wine."

Flynn sensed a crack in one of his defensive walls as the need to share a bit of himself welled up inside him. Before he had time to reconsider, he said, "Could be you can talk to me because you and I are kindred spirits. The good thing is that you discovered the truth about him before you married the idiot, Gabi. I wasn't so lucky."

Softly illuminated by the silvered light of the rising moon, Gabi turned toward him. "Really? Your wife cheated on you?"

"Yep."

She touched his arm. "I'm so sorry. That totally sucks."

"Yep. He was my best friend, too."

"You're kidding. That's not exactly the most wonderful thing to have in common with someone, is it? That's why you filed for divorce?"

He hesitated. Just how much did he want to share? His defenses were cracked, not destroyed. "I filed the day after I found out about the affair. The man was my business partner, too, so that complicated matters."

Following a moment of silence, Gabi said, "So you and I really do have a lot in common, don't we? I take it your career goal wasn't to be a caretaker for the rich and famous?"

"No more than yours was to be a dogsitter for deep-pocketed idiots who chose to raise a cold-weather breed in the tropics."

"Poor Bismarck," she said with a sigh. "He'd be in doggie heaven if he lived in Eternity Springs. Our cold winters are perfect for him. So where are you from, Flynn? What did you do before becoming caretaker at Tradewinds?"

He'd anticipated the questions, so he had his reply at the ready. "I'm from the South. After college I went into engineering and design."

"You're an engineer? Jeez, now I'm embarrassed. Why did you let me think you were the pool boy at Tradewinds?"

"I am the pool boy at Tradewinds," he responded. But before he could expound and claim ownership of the estate, Bismarck interrupted the conversation by leaping to his feet and darting toward the beach, barking.

"I wonder what that's all about. Think someone is walking on the beach?" Gabi asked as she rose to follow the dog.

"No. We're private here. May be a critter of some sort."

Instead of wildlife, it appeared that Bismarck had been spooked by the moonlight shining on the gently rolling surface of the sea. To distract him, Flynn picked up a sun-bleached stick of driftwood and threw it in the dog's general direction, calling, "Fetch, Bismarck."

With a series of yips, the dog dashed toward the stick and brought it back to Flynn. He pitched it again, this time throwing it back toward the house. "He's picked up that game fast. The dog is smart."

"He's loving and loyal, too. This world would be a better place if people like Frank and . . . what was your wife's name?"

"Lisa."

"If people like Frank and Lisa learned some lessons from dogs."

Flynn stifled a comment about butt sniffing, and when Bismarck became distracted by some unseen scent beneath the breezeway, he turned his attention back to the sea. It really was a fine night. "We're doing this all wrong, Gabriella."

"What do you mean?"

"I'm standing on a moonlit Caribbean beach with a gloriously beautiful woman." He slipped his arm around her waist and gently pulled her toward him. "Why waste time dwelling on old, ugly memories? I say we make a new one."

Flynn lowered his mouth to hers.

SIX

Gabi's heart raced as Flynn slipped his hand around her waist and deliberately drew her toward him, his intention clear. She wanted to giggle. Two come-ons from two different hotties in the same day? Score! Then his mouth touched hers, just a whisper, a tease, drawing the moment out, and Gabi forgot all about Cicero.

Flynn took his time, nibbling at her lips as if testing their softness, tracing them with his tongue. "Gabriella," he murmured, drawing out her name just like the kiss. The sound of it made her shudder, and she opened her mouth to respond. He took advantage of the moment and deepened the kiss.

Gabi's head reeled as sensation battered her. His probing, playing tongue. The firm, hot press of muscles against her. The taste of wine and the scent of salt and sea and man.

Her knees literally went weak, and she twined her arms around his neck and held on as heat washed through her and need flared within. When finally he lifted his head, sucked in a deep breath, and eased away, the sudden sense of loss caught her by surprise.

"Well, then," he said. "That was . . ."

"The conch salad?"

"No, Gabi. That was you, all you." He reached up

and trailed the pad of his thumb across her swollen lower lip. "About that first-date caution you mentioned a time or two . . . are you firm in that decision?"

Is he asking me to sleep with him? She thought so, but she wasn't sure. It had been a long time since she'd been in a position like this: hot guy, surf lapping at the beach, full moon.

Shoot, she'd never been in a position like this. She'd better take it slow.

Darn it.

"Yes, I'm afraid I am."

He sighed, shook his head, then leaned back down and gave her one brief, hard kiss. "All right, then. I've enjoyed tonight very much, and I'm not ready to see it come to an end. Since you have this first-date no-sex policy, I see only one solution available to us. Follow me, Gabi."

He started back toward the house, leaving her behind in the sand. "Well," she muttered, a little bit peeved.

She started after him, torn between wanting to tell him off for leaving so rudely and wanting to preen because he'd obviously felt the need to put some distance between them. Flynn returned to the breezeway where they'd eaten their dinner, but instead of turning back toward the house, he stopped and waited for her to catch up. "Are you a game player, Ms. Romano?"

Now she really was annoyed. "I'm not a tease, Mr. Brogan."

"Not that kind of game player." He led her toward a door on the wing of the house that stretched alongside the pool. As he stepped inside, he said, "Not those kinds of games." He flipped on a light switch. "These."

Gabi's chin dropped, and her pique faded as a smile spread across her face. A game room. No, more than a game room. "The arcade!"

"What's your pleasure, my dear? Pinball? Shuffle-board? Pool? Hoops? Car racing? Video games?"

"This is awesome," she said, walking into the room and turning around in a slow circle. "My brothers would be so jealous."

"So, you want to play?"

"Absolutely!"

"Pick your poison, Romano. One word of warning: I play to win."

Grinning, she surveyed the room. Among the video games, she spied the game Call of Duty, something she'd mastered after playing Zach daily during the winter downtime at the sheriff's office. Since the shooting, the game had lost its appeal, so she kept on moving. She loved pinball, but she'd played basketball all of her life.

"I don't know. I haven't played any arcade games in a very long time. What are the rules for that game over there?" The picture of innocence, she gestured toward the basketball game.

Flynn studied her with a long look. "You think I'm stupid?"

"Excuse me?"

"Two of your brothers played professional basketball. You're a long drink of water, yourself. I know a ringer when I see one. I'll bet you played basketball in college, didn't you? At Connecticut?"

She stifled a smile and shrugged.

"Scholarship?"

She nodded. "Full ride."

"Not just any college, but a basketball college."

"So what are you saying, Brogan? Chicken to play me?"

His slow grin warmed her all the way to her toes. "How about you put some money where your mouth is? Two bucks a point?"

"Make it five."

He flipped the switch on the game, and as the lights flashed and bells rang, he tossed her the little basketball. "I knew you were going to be fun. Maybe next time we'll play for different stakes."

"Is five dollars a point too much for you?"

"Oh, I'm thinking of something more interesting than money." He waited until right before she released the ball to add, "Have you ever played strip basketball, Gabriella?"

The ball hit the rim with an ugly clang and bounced out.

Flynn Brogan laughed maniacally.

The next few weeks flew by as the term "island time" took on a different meaning for Gabi than what she had anticipated. There simply weren't enough hours in the day to fit everything in. But by the end of her second week in the studio, she had settled into somewhat of a routine. Flynn Brogan became a vital part of it when, on the morning following their first date, they again crossed paths during their morning runs and he offered to watch Bismarck while she was at the studio. So far the arrangement had worked out well for them both. Flynn enjoyed having Bismarck around, and Gabi was able to concentrate on her work without having to worry about her four-legged charge.

At the end of her workday she'd return to Palmetto House, shower, and clean up—blowing glass was hot, sweaty work—then stroll over to Tradewinds to collect the dog. More often than not, she and Flynn ended up spending the evening together, though not the night as of yet.

For all his talk about strip basketball and the like, Flynn wasn't pressuring her for sex. The man could and did kiss her senseless at every opportunity, but they had fallen into a pattern of taking it right up to the point of no return, then returning. On their fourth official date, they'd talked about it, and doing so gave Gabi insight into the man.

He'd said, "After going a little crazy following my split with Lisa, I concluded that for me, casual sex isn't worth the emotional hangover. I feel like crap afterward. I know that it's old-fashioned for this day and age, but I'd rather wait until it means something more to both of us than just getting off."

Gabi respected that point of view, and while it made her like him all the more, it also gave her pause. The better she got to know Flynn Brogan, the more she liked him. He was kind, witty, wicked smart, and upon occasion just quirky enough to be endearing. All that made him dangerous.

She could fall for him. It wouldn't be difficult at all to tumble into emotions stronger than what was safe for a summer fling.

That reality had her second-guessing the request she planned to make to Cicero today. Flynn had invited her and Bismarck to go along with him when he accepted delivery on a new sailboat for Tradewinds and took the *Dreamer* on its maiden sail. She'd accepted with the caveat that Cicero had to okay her being away for up to three days, since Flynn wanted to make it a leisurely trip and show her some of his favorite Caribbean destinations.

She honestly didn't know how the glass artist would react. Her position at the studio hovered somewhere between slave and student. Some days she did nothing more than sweep the floor and watch. Other days she filled the role of gaffer for Mitch. Her favorite days were those where he turned her loose to experiment and learn from her own mistakes. She'd made a lot of mistakes.

But she'd also enjoyed some victories. When she'd removed the angel figurine she'd made from the annealing oven on Monday and seen that it had turned out exactly like the way she'd wanted, she'd actually burst into tears.

She knew that today Cicero planned to work on a commissioned piece, which meant it would be a broomstick day for her. She didn't really mind. Watching him work was both a lesson and an inspiration. However, considering the schedule, she expected he would have his artist attitude on until after his day's work was finished, so she'd probably put off asking her question until the end of the day.

As was her habit, she began pulling her hair up into a ponytail as she entered the studio. Her hands were still in the air when she caught sight of Cicero and stopped abruptly. The man stood stiff as a board, staring down at his phone. He was as white as a sheet. Gabi slowly lowered her hands. Something was wrong.

She made a quick survey of the room and was relieved to see Mitch standing in front of the wall where Cicero pinned his sketching. Her relief was short-lived, however, when she spied the look on the teen's face.

Something was very, very wrong.

She stepped farther into the room and approached her teacher. "Cicero?"

He acted as if he didn't hear her. For the first time ever, she used his given name. "Hunter? What happened?"

He lifted his head and met her gaze. The anguish in his eyes broke her heart. "I need to go home. Today."

"Why? What's the matter?"

He opened his mouth, then shut it. He closed his eyes and shook his head.

Gabi didn't press him, but instead followed her instincts and enfolded him in a hug. At first he stood stiff and resisting, but after a moment he melted into her, his arms going around her and holding on tight.

Whatever the reason for him needing to go home, it definitely wasn't good.

Then Cicero's moment of dependency ended and he stepped away from her. He began to pace, prowling the studio, rubbing the back of his neck. "I have to go to Oregon. Gabriella, book me a flight. I want to get there as fast as humanly possible. Mitch, I need you to look at the schedule and start contacting people. I don't know how long this will put us back. At least two weeks, but likely longer."

"What about the chandelier?" Mitch asked. "It needs to ship in sixteen days."

Cicero grimaced, and Gabi turned her head to look at the pieces of what was to become the centerpiece of the lobby in a new hotel in Sydney. Although most of the design had been completed, six pieces still needed to be done. Cicero said, "You finish it. Include a note with it saying I've been called away from the studio on a family emergency. Offer them a twenty percent discount, plus another five percent if they can accurately determine which pieces you contributed."

Mitch's eyes went round and wide. "Really?"

"They won't be able to tell," Cicero said. "You're ready, Mitch. Now, make your calls, people."

While Gabi and Mitch got to work, Cicero climbed the stairs to the loft where he kept his easel and the art supplies he used to make his sketches. He shut the door behind him.

Within minutes, Gabi had narrowed down his flight choices to two possibilities. Taking the phone away from her ear, she spoke to Mitch. "Are there any helicopters available for rent on the island?"

"No, you have to call for one out of Nassau."

Shoot. That would double the time it took to get to the airport. "That stinks. Connections would be so much better if he could wait."

Even as the idea occurred, she was dialing the number. Three rings later, Flynn answered. "Hello, beautiful."

In concise sentences, she explained the problem, then asked, "I thought about the Wilcoxes' speedboat. Any chance we could—"

"I'll get it gassed up. If we leave in the next forty minutes, we should be able to get him there in time. Come with him, Gabi. After we drop him off, we'll go on to Abaco and pick up the *Dreamer*."

"Oh. Well." She glanced at Mitch. "I'd love to go with you to Abaco, but I don't think I can leave the studio now. With Cicero gone, Mitch will need my help more than ever."

Hearing her, Mitch shook his head. "Go, Gabi. Don't take it personally, but you don't know enough yet to provide the help I'll need. I have a friend in Key West who apprenticed with Cicero when I started here. He'll come help. He's been wanting to visit."

Knowing her own limitations, Gabi was relieved. "Are you sure?"

"I'm sure."

"All right," she told Flynn. "I'll come with you. Do we meet you at Tradewinds?"

"No. The gas dock at the marina."

"Do I need to bring anything special for Bismarck?"

"No, I have everything ready for him."

"Okay, then. We'll be there as soon as we can."

She disconnected the call, then climbed the stairs and knocked on Cicero's door. "Sorry to disturb you, but time is tight." Speaking through the door, she explained the problem and her solution.

"Good. That's good." He opened the door and she

looked up into swollen, red eyes. "I need to go home and grab my passport, but I'll be there. Thank you, Legs."

Legs. He hadn't called her that since he'd accepted her as his student. "Glad to help."

She hurried home, packed a bag, then drove the scooter to the marina. Upon arriving, she spied the Formula floating beside the gas dock, Cicero handing a credit card to the marina employee who'd pumped the gas, and Flynn buckling Bismarck into a doggie life vest. She parked the scooter, grabbed her bag, and went to join them.

The trip to Nassau proved to be both exhilarating and tense. Flying across the water at an average speed of over eighty miles per hour thrilled her. Watching Cicero stand stiff and silent while facing into the wind broke her heart. What in the world had happened? she wondered.

As they entered the harbor, Cicero phoned the car he'd arranged to transport him from the marina to the airport. Then he turned to Flynn and spoke his first words since leaving Bella Vita Isle. "Thank you, Flynn," he said, extending his hand for a handshake. "I am in your debt."

Flynn shook Cicero's hand, then clapped him on the back. "No, you're not. You're my friend. If you decide you want to talk, you have my number."

Cicero nodded, then turned to Gabi. "Thanks for your help, Legs."

"You're welcome. Good luck. I'll be thinking about you."

He gave her a crooked smile that didn't reach his eyes. "Of course you will." He leaned down and kissed her, then vaulted from the boat onto the pier and walked hurriedly away.

"Just because we're friends doesn't mean he gets

to . . . Does he do that often?" Flynn asked, annoyance in his tone.

"Kiss me? Not really."

"Not really?"

She ignored Flynn's question as she watched Cicero climb into a waiting car that then sped away. "I wonder what happened. Something with his family, I'd guess. What do you know about them, Flynn? He never talks about his family."

Flynn didn't respond, and she glanced around to see a shadow pass over his expression. For the first time she realized that except for one mention of his parents, he never spoke about his family, either. How had she missed that? Family was such a big part of her life, she couldn't believe she'd overlooked it.

"I think he has a sister," Flynn finally said, his tone brusque. Then he changed the subject. "I thought we'd grab some lunch here, then head out. Is that okay with you?"

"That sounds like a great idea," she said, turning her attention to brighter thoughts. "I love the speedboat, but I'm really excited about sailing. This will be my first time aboard a sailboat."

"You're going to love it."

While Flynn tied the lines, she clipped Bismarck's leash onto his collar and climbed out of the boat.

Flynn led them away from the pier to a street teeming with people and a fair selection of available food choices. She chose conch salad—she'd grown to love the snail— while he made a beeline for a pizza place. They sat at picnic tables along the wharf and ate while watching the seabirds dive for the bread crumbs dropped by squealing, laughing tourist children. Gabi licked her fork, then said, "This is delicious. Maybe not as good as your conch salad, but still wonderful."

"Bet it's not as good as my pizza. That's the biggest drawback to living on Bella Vita. I can't get pizza."

"You have stacks of pizza boxes in your freezer."

"Frozen pizza is a poor substitute for this," he said, offering her a bite.

Flavor exploded on her tongue—tomato, garlic, and pepperoni. "It is good," she agreed. "Not as good as my mother's."

"Your mom makes pizza?"

She nodded. "It's one of her specialties. She put a pizza oven in her kitchen at Aspenglow."

"Really?" he said, his gorgeous blue eyes lighting with interest. "I never thought of that. That really would make Tradewinds paradise."

"Think you could talk the Wilcoxes into adding one to their kitchen?"

He shifted his gaze away from hers. "That wouldn't be an issue. I'll have to look into having that done. Say, there's an ice-cream shop just around the corner. How about I score us a couple of cones to take with us?"

"Lime sherbet for me, please. While you're doing that, I'll walk Bismarck."

"Sounds like a plan."

Half an hour later, they were once again on the open sea. Flynn opened up the engines and the boat roared, flying across the water, and when he switched on the most excellent sound system and classic rock pounded through the air, Gabi felt more alive and carefree than she had in ages.

And she wanted to yank back the throttle, throw Flynn Brogan down on the cushioned bench seat, and have her way with him.

Judging by the looks she caught him throwing her way, she thought he might have the same idea. However, neither of them acted on the urge, and the cruise continued. Gabi made an effort to distract herself by trying to decide what she'd be doing right now if she'd stayed at home. Shoveling snow? Scraping ice off her car window? Spending ten minutes piling on clothes so she could walk outside just to check her mail?

"This is heaven, Flynn. Pure heaven."

He shot her a grin. "It is pretty wonderful, but hold off with the heaven comparisons until you take a ride on the *Dreamer*. I'll be curious to see which mode of water transport you like best."

It seemed like no time at all before Flynn pointed out an island on the horizon. "In just a minute you'll see Elbow Reef Lighthouse. That's Hope Town. We're going around to the other side of the island. The builder has the *Dreamer* moored in the cove where his shop is located."

"So, tell me about this boat. How big is it?"

"Forty-six feet," he replied, his voice eager. "It's a single mast with in-mast furling, a twin-wheel cockpit, and all the amenities of home. It's a cruiser, but built fast enough to race if the spirit moves. The builder promises that it will slice through a shimmering tide on cruise control and cradle us like babies when we're anchored in a safe harbor drinking a martini."

"I've never seen you drink a martini."

"Actually, I asked Marcus to stock us up with champagne for our maiden voyage."

"I like the way you think," Gabi said, folding her arms and studying him. He seemed awfully excited for a man who was picking up someone else's boat. "I'm surprised the Wilcoxes aren't taking the *Dreamer* on its maiden voyage."

"I intend to explain all of that to you later," he said.

"All of what?"

Rather than respond, he pulled back on the throttle

and turned the boat toward shore. Moments later, they entered a cove, and Gabi spied a large building with a sign on the top that read YARROW BOATS.

Floating some twenty yards from shore was the boat. The hull was white with a blue stripe the same color as Flynn's eyes. "She's pretty."

"She's beautiful. Almost as beautiful as you."

He guided the Formula toward a dock. Having learned from watching him with the lines earlier, Gabi played first mate and assisted in securing the boat. While Flynn grabbed their bags, Gabi gathered up Bismarck and climbed out of the Formula.

Flynn introduced her to Marcus Yarrow, and they made small talk for a few minutes until Flynn asked her to excuse them while they completed the last bit of paperwork involving the sale. "Take your time," she responded. "Bismarck and I will go for a walk on the beach."

The two men disappeared into the boatyard's office, and Gabi made her way to the white sand beach nearby. She had just let Bismarck off his leash to run around when a buzz in her pocket indicated an incoming call on her cell.

She recognized her brother Zach's number. "Hello, Sheriff."

"Hello, little sister. Have I caught you in the middle of scooping up dog poo?"

"Hardly. I just finished a ninety-mile-an-hour cruise on a Formula speedboat, and I'm getting ready to take a sail on a forty-five-foot yacht."

He laughed, his disbelief obvious. "I was right, wasn't I? You are on potty patrol."

"You think whatever makes you happy, brother. You could even pretend that I'm not contemplating taking a dip in the lagoon in order to cool off."

A moment's silence came across the connection. "You're being serious, aren't you? Dammit, Gabriella, that's just mean."

"I love you, Zach. So, was there a special reason for this call, or did you simply miss my sweet voice?"

"Sweet as a lemon, love. However, I do have a reason for calling. Savannah found out the sex of the baby today."

Gabi halted mid-step. "She did? What did she do, bribe the obstetrician? I thought Hope and Lucca decided to wait until the baby is born to learn what they are having."

"They are. We're not."

We're not? "Zach, are you saying . . . ?"

"We're pregnant, Gabi. We're having a girl. She's due in August. She'll be two months younger than Lucca's little one."

Gabi squealed. "Oh, Zach. I'm so thrilled for you. Have you told Mom? What did she say?"

"We haven't told anyone yet. We're having a family gathering tonight, and we'll announce it then. I wanted you to know first."

Gabi's heart warmed, and tears stung her eyes. "Thank you, Zach. That makes me feel special."

"You are special, Gabi. If not for you, I wouldn't be alive to enjoy all this happiness. You are a blessing to me, to my new little family, and to our entire family."

That caused her tears to swell and overflow and trail down her cheeks. She asked how Savannah was feeling, then caught up on other family members. Zach had just asked her about her days on the island when Flynn and Marcus Yarrow exited the office. "I have a lot to share, Zach, but I don't have time right now. I don't want to miss my boat."

"So who are you going boating with? Some wealthy Greek tycoon?"

"The pool boy next door."

"Oh, yeah. Savannah mentioned something about a pool boy. If he's taking you out on his yacht . . . that's some pool boy."

She could have said something about the Wilcoxes, but she didn't. Lately she'd begun to suspect that there was more to this engineer than he'd let on. "Yes. Yes, he is."

They said their goodbyes, and Gabi wiped the remnants of tears from her cheeks before turning to meet the men. Flynn took one look at her expression and frowned. "What's wrong?"

"Nothing. Nothing at all. My brother called with happy news. Our family is expecting another baby." She smiled brightly and said, "So, is it time for us to set sail?"

His relief obvious, he gestured toward the small aluminum boat floating at the end of the dock. "Our tender awaits."

Gabi couldn't help but grin at his obvious excitement, and as they boarded the boat and Marcus and Flynn did one final inspection, she realized why. This wasn't simply a sailboat. This really was a yacht. No wonder Flynn was so excited. Who wouldn't be thrilled at the idea of sailing the Caribbean aboard a brand-new yacht?

The boat had two staterooms, two bathrooms—heads, Flynn corrected her—a gourmet kitchen, and a swim dock. The lines both above deck and below were sleek and elegant, the amenities luxurious. As the shipbuilder took his leave and Flynn hoisted the anchor, Gabi felt her own excitement rise. "Darn it, I should have brought my neck scarf."

"Excuse me?"

"I'm channeling my inner Grace Kelly."

"Because I'm such a prince of a guy?"

"No. You're much sexier than Prince Rainier."

"Well, now. That's not a bad way to begin our cruise." He hit the switch and the engine fired. "And we're off like a herd of turtles."

"Okay, my father used that expression. You need to stop. This is too romantic a scene for my dad to be anywhere near it."

"The romance of the sea is the real deal." Flynn flashed her a sexy grin and added, "And you're right. We don't need family or baggage along. It's just you and me along for the ride this afternoon."

"And Bismarck."

"Of course." Smiling widely, Flynn navigated the sailboat out of the cove and into open sea. There he paused a moment before asking, "Ready for the ride of your life, Gabriella?"

Oh, yeah. And it has nothing to do with sailing. "Absolutely."

Flynn unfurled the jib, raised the main, and cut the engine. The boat wallowed for a moment, but then the sails filled, the rigging groaned, and power transferred from propeller to wind. Like a butterfly released from its cocoon, the puttering powerboat transformed into a sailboat.

Flynn let out a shout, and Gabi's mouth went dry. He'd done it for her when he was piloting the speedboat, but now . . . "Holy Moses," she murmured.

Windblown hair, bright smile, sparkling eyes, tanned and taut skin stretched over muscles that flexed and relaxed as he worked the wheel—yum. As if that package wasn't enough, over the course of the past few weeks she'd come to know the man beneath the breathtaking good looks. She liked him. She genuinely liked him. They clicked.

She'd never in her whole life made the first pass at a man, but that might have to change today. She couldn't ever recall wanting a man quite so badly before. When he gave her a safety lesson, she had trouble paying attention. She wanted to bite at his earlobe and let her hands wander across the broad, tanned expanse of his shoulders.

The trip was glorious. Gabi sat with Bismarck stretched across her lap, dividing her gaze between the sea and the man at the wheel. For the first hour he paid her little mind as he learned the boat. In the second hour he offered her the wheel.

"I want to try, but what if I do it wrong?"

"I'll be right beside you."

"Okay, except . . . let me put Bismarck below first. That way I can concentrate without worrying about what he's up to."

A few minutes later, she took the wheel. Flynn stood next to her and spoke about sailing.

"Some believe that sailing is an art. To me, it's a song, a rhythm that lives deep inside of me, one that the ocean brings alive."

He put his hands on her hips and moved her to notes she did not hear. "The tempo is always changing. Sometimes I have no trouble picking up the new beat and matching my steps to it. Other times I'm awkward and clumsy and no matter how hard I try, I can't manage the dance. Then the music changes again and I find my rhythm once more."

With that, his fingers on her hips tightened, and he spun her around. He reached behind her, flipped a switch, then backed her against the wheel.

"It's sanctuary. A music that shelters me from storms and allows my heart to dance free and fresh and filled with passion. I feel the power of the wind and the water and I know that I am small and should be frightened, but I'm not. I'm strong in my weakness. I can conquer Nature herself."

Then he kissed her. Hard and fast and furious, and Gabi went up like dry brush.

He'd kissed her before, but this was different. She couldn't remember a man ever kissing her like this. Her body tightened and her heart raced as she matched his every move.

Raw hunger, need, and all the pent-up emotion that had been dormant for so long came to life, and Gabi was shocked by the intensity. She told herself it was because it had been so long. Told herself that it was because he was hot and hard and needy, and she was, too. Told herself that she wanted to just escape into the bliss of being this close to someone again.

She moved in, her arms encircling him, her fingers diving into his hair. His body slammed into hers, and he slanted his mouth across hers, licking, invading, possessing. Deep in her core, the exquisite throbbing increased, and Gabi moaned against his lips. Flynn's response was quick, almost vicious in his delight. Whispering against her lips, he said in almost a warning, "I want you."

"I . . ." She tried to say the same, but simply kissed him back. God, she was turned on. Instead of replying, she grabbed at his shirt with impatient hands, desperate to press her bare skin against his. His mouth left hers to trail a path of hot, wet kisses across her neck. "Gabi . . ."

The way he said her name . . .

He tugged off her shirt and his gaze fell upon her tiny bikini top. He breathed a curse. "Tell me no, Gabriella. Tell me no right now, or we're going to finish this."

A shred of sensibility pushed through the erotic fog. "Wh-what about the boat? Will we drift?"

"Autopilot."

"Hallelujah." She tugged the string bow between her breasts and her top spilled open.

"Gabriella." He said it like a prayer as he filled his

hands with her breasts, kneading her, flicking his thumbs across her sensitive nipples, sending arrows of pleasure to her very core. Having his hands on her breasts, his fingers tugging . . . her head lolled back and she arched to the touch, her eyes closed against the sunlit sky. Feeling his hands rove and explore, Gabi experienced the warm rush of anticipation. Then, finally, his lips closed over the top of her breast, and she sizzled.

At some point he picked her up and carried her to the cushioned sun deck at the back of the boat. He laid her down and stripped her naked. His hands skimmed over her and she writhed with need.

But Gabi Romano gave as good as she got, so she tore at his shorts and ripped at his shirt until he was as naked as she. Finally! She pushed him back onto his back and straddled him, then looked her fill. He was gorgeous. Toned and sculpted, he lay against the white cushion with those brilliant blue eyes glittering like sunshine on the surface of the sea as they scorched a hot path across her skin.

"You take my breath away," he told her, breathing hard, stroking his big hand down the center of her torso.

"My thoughts exactly," she replied, her own breath panting as a wild, reckless energy pulsed inside her. Wanton, she thought, remembering a term from the books she loved.

She touched the hard, heavy heat of him, and Flynn sucked a breath past his teeth. "There's storage at your eleven o'clock. Little door, see it?"

"Yes."

"Condoms."

Oh, right. "Bless you."

"Hurry," he urged, thrusting up against her hands.

The instinctive movement thrilled Gabi, and she rushed to help him take care of business. "Yes."

Their coupling was fast, furious, and bordering on violent. She took and he demanded. They met as equals, as partners, and somewhere deep inside herself Gabi recognized the difference within her when she was with him.

Her strength didn't threaten Flynn Brogan's masculinity. He reveled in it. Shared in it. Respected it. Respected her.

The pace quickened as they moved together, their bodies sensing what was to come. Flynn's arms locked around her as he called out her name in a shuddering shout. From deep in her soul came a matching cry of sheer triumph. As the climax burst over her, Gabi Romano tumbled a little bit into love.

SEVEN

"I need water," Flynn said, lying naked amid the destroyed linens of his bed, where they'd spent a good portion of the hours since he'd anchored in a protective lagoon of an uninhabited island.

Lying beside him, Gabi lifted her head. "There's a bottle on the nightstand."

"Getting it would involve moving. I don't think I can. I'm not certain I'll ever be able to move again."

Gabi levered up to a seated position. She slapped his butt and said, "Well, I have tons of energy, but I'm hungry. I'm going to go finish the rest of my supper that you interrupted." Then she teasingly added, "Do you need me to bring you some conch salad?"

"In an IV," he murmured into his pillow. She laughed as she made her way to the galley, and Flynn grinned and reached for the water. Only spectacular sex could make a man feel this drained. The sex he'd had during his season of self-destruction had never come close to this. Sex with Gabriella Romano was different. Gabi was different.

Once he'd chugged three-quarters of the bottle, he plopped back down on his pillow and dozed off. When he awoke, he sensed he hadn't slept long—twenty minutes at the most. A perfect postcoital catnap that recharged his batteries and left him humming with energy.

He rolled out of bed, took a quick shower, pulled on dry swim trunks, and went looking for his lady. The galley was empty. In the guest stateroom he found Bismarck snoring in the crate he'd set up for him. Flynn went up on deck and found Gabi seated cross-legged toward the bow. She wore her bikini top and running shorts, and her beauty rivaled that of the setting sun, which was especially glorious tonight, a western sky filled with crimson, orange, and gold. The pensive expression on her face brought a frown to his.

"Hey there," he said.

She gave him an easy smile. "Hey."

"Are you okay?"

"I'm fine." She patted the seat beside her in unspoken invitation. "I'm pretty darn wonderful, actually. I've been sitting here thinking that I'm starring in my own classic movie."

He laughed. "I've always wanted to go boating with Sophia Loren or Gina Lollobrigida."

Gabi shook her head. "Nope, this is my fantasy, so I'm Grace Kelly. All my life I wanted to be blond and fair-skinned."

He gave her look that told her he thought she was crazy. "I don't understand women. You have beautiful skin and gorgeous hair." He lifted his hand and let a strand of midnight silk glide between his fingers, remembering how it had tossed around while they made love. The memory caused him to stir, and the reaction surprised him a little. She made him feel eighteen again.

"It's all about the fairy tale, don't you see? I'm the penniless ingenue who chased a dog and met a prince masquerading as a pool boy, and he's taken me out on his yacht to an isolated private island and made earthshaking love to me. It's the perfect plot."

"I like the earthshaking part of that, though you do seem to be stuck on princes."

"I'm doing classic film. If I were doing paranormal romance novels, then you'd be a merman who brought me here to seduce me into joining you in an underwater world."

"A tail? You'd give me a tail? Why don't I get to be a vampire or a werewolf?"

"Fangs don't do it for me, and besides, you already have a mighty fine tail." She leaned back on her elbows and stared up at the darkening sky. "Thank you for today, Flynn. And when you talk to them next, thank the Wilcoxes, too. For a day that started out totally crappy, it has become a day I will always remember."

The Wilcoxes again. *Okay, enough of this crap. Tell her now.* When this trip began, he had intended to come clean about the Wilcox illusion before inviting Gabi into his bed, but events had spun out of control. This wasn't an honorable way to treat the woman he was sleeping with, so he would end it right now.

Except he hadn't yet decided just exactly how much of the truth he owed her. Should he simply say that he'd bought Tradewinds from the Wilcoxes and leave it at that? Or should he go all in? *Guess what, Gabi? You're dating an infamous accused murderer. One who the world believes pulled the wool over a jury's eyes.*

"It's not all about the fantasy, either," she continued before he worked up the courage to speak. "I think that if Celeste Blessing were sitting here with us, she'd award me my Angel's Rest blazon."

He blinked, distracted. "All right. You've totally lost me now."

Gabi gave him a crooked smile. "Sorry, I'm waxing philosophical. Shall I stop?"

"No. I'm intrigued." He was also glad for the respite from making his confession.

"My friend Celeste owns Angel's Rest Healing Center and Spa. She's sort of . . . I don't know how to describe her. She has the most uncanny intuition of anyone I've ever met. She's a lovely woman. Everyone credits her with literally saving the town when it hovered on the edge of bankruptcy. She opened Angel's Rest and made it a success, and now Eternity Springs is thriving."

"So what's this about a blazon? That's not a word you hear very often."

"I know. I had to look it up. It's a pendant. Anyway, Celeste hired another friend, an artist, to design a pendant that Celeste named the official Angel's Rest blazon. It's a beautiful interpretation of angel wings, and Celeste gives it to people who have—and I quote—'embraced healing's grace.' I've been really jealous of my friends who earned their wings. Right now I feel I can make a good case for scoring an Angel's Rest pendant for myself. I've turned a corner both personally and professionally."

Flynn studied her and guessed. "I'm the first guy you've slept with since your breakup?"

Gabi nodded.

"Are you going to get a medal for that?"

"It's not about that!" she exclaimed with a laugh. After a moment's hesitation, she added, "Well, I guess in a way it is."

He smirked. "I'm glad I didn't know that ahead of time. I'd have been stressed about my performance."

"You have to think to be stressed. Not much thinking going on our first time. That was all primitive animal instinct."

"True. Which is why I'm having a bit of trouble with the idea of earning angel's wings as a result. Though, I guess if you got them, I could bill myself as a sort of spiritual advisor. Instead of a faith healer, I could say I'm a sex healer."

"Very funny," she scolded. "And I hate to burst your bubble, Dr. Feel-Good, but my earning my wings has nothing to do with you. It wasn't the sex that healed me.

I'd already healed, which is why I was ready to have sex. You're just the beneficiary."

"That role works for me." Then he took her hand and abandoned his teasing to speak seriously. "Good for you, Gabriella. I wish I could say I was angel-wing qualified, but I still have some work to do. I'm trying, but it's hard."

He realized then that telling her half of the story wouldn't do. She needed to know the whole ugly thing, and he needed to tell her. Dare he do it? No telling how she would react.

Well, if she bailed on him, better to know it now before he got in any deeper, right? Because he sensed he could go deep with Gabriella Romano. Fast.

I'll do it. I'll lay out the entire story. It was the best thing for them both, the fair thing to do for her. The right thing. Because unless the past twelve years had totally screwed his perception where females were concerned, Gabi Romano showed every sign of jumping into the deep end right along with him.

"I have some pretty ugly wounds, Gabi," he said, attempting to tie the previous conversation to the one he wanted to have.

Rather than ask him about those wounds, as he expected, she said, "It's very hard to heal, Flynn. I haven't been able to manage it until now. You've helped me do it. You've been the right guy at the right time, and I'm glad I waited until now. Who knows, maybe I'll help you in return."

He brought her hand up and pressed a kiss to her palm. "You have helped me. No matter where we go from here, I want you to know that. I feel like you've become . . . well, a friend. That's a big deal for me, considering. I value it—I value you—very much."

"Thank you." She leaned over and kissed him lightly. "That's a lovely thing for you to say. Friendship is totally important to me. I think maybe my friendship with you has helped advance my healing, too. Something has changed within me, healed within me, these past few weeks, and it's allowed me to stop looking backward and move forward. Ever since I learned that my fiancé and friend were sleeping together, I've been so angry. More angry than hurt, even. Outside of my family, they were the two people in the world who were supposed to love me most. How could they have done that to me? It totally ticked me off. I hardened my heart and wrapped it in a shield of indignation."

"That's understandable."

"Understandable, but unhealthy. I gave them and their actions power over me. Well, today I took my power back. While you were asleep, I took advantage of your offer to use the computer, and I checked my email. I read the dozens of emails that Cheryl has sent me over the past year, and then I answered her back. I told her that I accepted her apology and I forgave her."

"Wow. You're not kidding about the whole healing thing, are you?"

"Nope. I admit that it earned a solid three on my list of the top ten hardest things to do, but I managed it. She begged for forgiveness over and over and over again. I looked inside my heart and I found it."

"Good for you."

"Yes, good for me."

She looked so pleased for herself that it made him smile.

"Forgiveness is a powerful thing. I'm afraid you're a better person than I am. I made a stab at that recently myself," he said, thinking about his father. "I couldn't pull it off. Frankly, I don't know that I'll ever be able to pull it off."

When he saw the curiosity in Gabi's expression, he wished he'd bitten his tongue rather than open up even that much. But instead of pressing him, she simply said, "You'll have to make a visit to Eternity Springs sometime."

"You're saying your time in the tropics isn't what did the trick?"

"No. Not at all. I think this trip is the best thing I could have done." She grinned at him and added, "Present company definitely included. But I also think that my time in Eternity Springs helped me build a foundation of strength for forgiveness to balance on. I think it took getting away from home to recognize it."

"I can't imagine you being anything but strong." He could picture her in a Wonder Woman outfit easily.

"You should have seen me after the shooting. I managed to fool the people around me, but inside, I was Jell-O. Every morning when I strapped on my gun belt, I felt a little sick. It took me forever to admit to myself that I couldn't be a cop anymore. I'd fought so hard to win the battle to get there to begin with. It killed me to face the fact that I needed to walk away."

"Why a battle? Did you face sexual discrimination along the way?"

"I faced my father. He did not want me to go into law enforcement at all. We had a major fight about it. It was my biggest act of rebellion, one he held against me until the day he died." Her lips twisted ruefully. "It could be argued that he was right. Maybe Dad knew me better than I knew myself."

"Did you always want to be a cop?"

"No. My career goals changed when Cheryl and her mother found themselves in a horrible domestic violence situation and a policewoman literally saved their lives. It made a huge impression on me. I wanted to make a difference like that, too. And I did make a difference. I saved my brother's life, and now he's married and expecting a baby, a little girl. Because of my actions. My training. Because I did my job. I've known that in my head, but until today, I've never managed to take it into my heart. I regret having taken a life. I don't regret the reason I did it."

"Good for you." He stroked his thumb across her knuckles. "So, does this revelation of yours mean that you're ready to consider returning to law enforcement?"

"Nope. Call it karma or destiny or the hand of God, but I believe I was meant to be in Eternity Springs that day to save my brother. I also know that now it's time for me to do something else. So much of my life as a law enforcement officer revolved around destructive elements. Now I'm all about creation."

She looked at him then, her eyes glittering with purpose and excitement. "It may take me a while to make it happen, but eventually I'm going to make my living working with glass. I'll learn from Cicero and Mitch or somebody else if need be, but that's what I want to do. It's what I'm going to do. I have a path to follow now, one that excites me, and I'm free to travel it without looking over my shoulder. I dropped my baggage and kicked it to the side of the road."

"Good for you. I have to tell you, Gabriella, I find strength exceedingly sexy in a woman."

"Oh, yeah?"

"Yeah."

"Good. Because I've a mind to continue my classic movie fantasy." She gazed toward the beach, then back to him. "Have you ever seen *From Here to Eternity*?"

He knew she was referring to the iconic beach kiss scene, and he was tempted. Oh, so tempted. "No, but there was this one episode of *The Simpsons* where Homer and Marge get frisky on the sand. . . ."

Gabi laughed and rose gracefully to her feet. "With a visual like that, how can I resist? Race you, Brogan."

Still, he hesitated. "Maybe it should wait. I need to tell you something. I don't feel right—"

"Let me guess," she interrupted. "You own this boat and you own Tradewinds."

His brows winged up. "You know?"

"I tell you, I would have made an excellent detective. You can explain it all later, Flynn. I'm feeling too good to scold you for failing to correct my pool boy assumption. Come and get me, pool prince."

She stripped off her shorts, then made a shallow dive into the water as Flynn climbed to his feet. He watched until she surfaced and began taking long, sure strokes toward shore. "You're a weasel, Brogan," she called back.

But since he'd already delayed this long, why not let them both have this fantasy? He could make a good argument that today was about her, not about him. He could tell her the truth tomorrow when they returned to Bella Vita.

His conscience assuaged, Flynn tucked a few foil packets into the pocket of his swimsuit and dove in after her.

Half an hour later, having rolled in the sand with such wild abandon that they both had sand in places where sand shouldn't be, Flynn lay on his back, his eyes closed, the surf lapping at his feet, with Gabi draped bonelessly on top of him. As he stroked his hand slowly up and down her back, he couldn't recall the last time he'd been this happy. This at peace.

He allowed his mind to wander. He liked Gabi Romano. A lot. Her talk about healing made him realize that during the time he'd spent with her, he'd definitely done some healing, too. Maybe the Eternity Springs effect had rubbed off on him. Whatever the reason, being with Gabi made him optimistic about the future again.

He smiled without opening his eyes. Maybe he was fooling himself, but he also believed that the Gabi he'd come to know would listen to his side of the story and give him the benefit of the doubt. If that happened, then . . . well, who knew? Maybe he could earn a pair of those Eternity Springs angel's wings for his own.

Except she was a short-timer on Bella Vita. Right now, anyway. She'd said she wanted to be home in June when her brother's baby was due, but that didn't mean she had to be gone for good, did it? Sure, the Fontanas would return to Palmetto House and displace her, but that didn't mean she had to leave the island. She could rent a place near the glass studio. She could move into Tradewinds.

Whoa, there, Brogan. Getting a little ahead of yourself, aren't you?

He was. He definitely was. But honestly, he didn't really care.

For the past two years, life had been dark and ugly and empty of anything good. He'd come to Bella Vita seeking light, and while he'd made some progress on his own, it had taken Gabi bursting through his hedge and into his world for him to believe in possibilities again.

He pressed a kiss against her hair and said, "I'm so glad that Bismarck wandered over to Tradewinds that day."

"I am, too." Gabi lifted her head and smiled at him. "I never knew it could be like this. Nobody ever kissed me the way you do. . . ."

He recognized the *From Here to Eternity* quote, but before he came up with an appropriate response, she added, ". . . Homer."

He flipped her over on her back, and as he settled himself between her legs, he replied, "Wait until you see what I have in mind to do next, Marge. It'll turn your hair blue."

The *Dreamer* weighed anchor at seven the following morning. Flynn charted a course that would take them through some good fishing grounds and to another small, private island—one that Flynn was currently negotiating to purchase. It was a beautiful spit of land of volcanic origins whose primary appeal was an isolated beach at the base of a picturesque waterfall. Flynn intended to build a small, rustic home there that would be his new getaway. Now that the paparazzi had found him on Abaco, it was only a matter of time until they tracked him to Bella Vita Isle. In the meantime, it would be a great place to have a lunchtime picnic. He and Gabi could snorkel in the lagoon and give Bismarck a little land time to do his business ashore, though he'd adapted to his role as a boat dog just fine. He'd picked up without mishap the habit of using the pee carpet Flynn had provided for him.

After lunch, they would turn toward home, taking a leisurely route that would deliver them to Bella Vita around dinner time. While they sailed, he'd tell her about Lisa. That way if he'd figured her wrong and she turned out to be like his dad and everyone else, they wouldn't be in forced proximity for long.

Happy with his plan, Flynn motored out of the cove where they'd moored overnight, then with the help of his enthusiastic crew member set the sails. Gabi cheered the flapping sound they made as they filled with wind, and Flynn flipped the brim of his hat backward as he stood at the helm. The boat heeled and the *Dreamer* cut across the surface of the sea with that magical near silence that lifted his spirits every time.

It was a great morning, with high, puffy white clouds floating across a cerulean sky. Upon reaching the good fishing waters, he rigged a couple of game rods, and they trolled a pair of lines. They had little luck at first, but the payoff came when a wahoo struck Gabi's line. Watching her wrestle her first wahoo into the boat was the most fun he'd had since . . . well, since last night. It made him look forward even more to showing her his island. Fresh wahoo was one of the best-tasting fish in the sea. "We'll build a fire and grill this fellow," he told her. "Conch salad pales beside fresh wahoo."

Four and a half hours after leaving their overnight mooring, as they sailed around the windward side of the island, he said, "Watch off to starboard now."

He kept a close eye on her expression, and his anticipation was rewarded. "Oh, my," she said, wonder filling her expression. "It's like Fantasy Island. I've never seen anything so gorgeous."

Without taking his gaze off of her, he said, "Me neither."

Flynn set the anchor in twenty feet of water, and they used the inflatable tender to transfer to shore. Gabi helped Flynn gather wood and played fetch with Bismarck while he built a fire and cooked the fish. Lunch proved to be as delicious as he'd promised. Afterward they attempted to snorkel in the cove, but Bismarck kept disturbing them. After the third time he'd swum thirty yards out to meet them, Flynn planted his feet on the sandy bottom in about five feet of water and asked, "Shall I swim to the boat and get his leash? We could tie him to a tree."

Laughing, Gabi dislodged the snorkel from her mouth and turned the swimming dog toward shore. "That's okay. I'm ready to go ashore myself. Something keeps nibbling at my toes and it's freaking me out. I'm worried that next time it'll be a shark who wants more than a nibble."

He gave her a smile full of teeth. "You read my mind."

She shook her finger at him. "Back off, Jaws. As lovely as last night was, I've showered three times since then, and I still have sand in tender places. I love romance as much as the next girl, but you have two perfectly comfortable beds aboard the *Dreamer*. I don't see what's wrong with making use of them."

"Well, if that's the way you really feel, I guess I'll abandon my fantasy about beneath-the-waterfall sex."

She twisted her head around toward the natural phenomenon in question. "Oh. Well. Hmm . . . Maybe I was a bit hasty."

Flynn gave her a wicked wink. "I'll race you."

They played in the water like children until their play turned to something more adult. Afterward, they lay drying in the sun on the beach towels they'd brought from the *Dreamer*. "This trip is just one piece of paradise after another. I have to wonder, why is it that people like the Fontanas have these stupendous homes and toys like the *Dreamer,* and not only do they not use them, they hire people like me to take care of them? It's crazy."

Rolling onto his side, he rested his head in his hand and said, "I think it's different for everybody. From what I understand, the Fontanas are trust-fund wealthy. They've never known another lifestyle. When Sam Wilcox originally built Tradewinds, his parents were younger. They loved coming to Bella Vita Isle, and they regularly spent half the month here. Once Mr. Wilcox started having health issues, they didn't want to be too far away from his doctors."

"That's understandable," she relied. "So you bought the estate from him?"

Flynn took a deep breath, then said, "Yes."

"Are you a prince?"

"Definitely not. I'm still an engineer. I, um, invented a gadget that's been a commercial success."

"Oh, yeah? What gadget?"

Telling her risked giving the game away prematurely, though only a slight risk, he thought. Only a few of the articles written about him had mentioned the Barbecue-Meister connection, and she hadn't mentioned the trial when she talked about buying ones for her brothers. Besides, Gabi didn't strike him as someone who watched Trial TV.

He licked his lips. "I patented the Barbecue-Meister."

She sat up. "No. You did not."

"I did."

"Really? And you didn't say anything about it that night?" Scowling, she added, "You dog."

"It was our first date. I wanted you to like me for me, not for my patent."

She wrinkled her nose. "Well, I guess I can understand that. I've seen how women are with my brothers. So, are you a celebrity at home shows?"

Dryly he said, "My booth almost outdraws the kiddie fish tank."

"Wow, I'm impressed," she teased. Then she rolled to her feet, saying, "Enough of this lazing around, barbecue boy. Let's weigh anchor and do some more fishing."

"'Boy'? Listen, sweet cheeks, I think that after this trip I've earned the term 'man,' don't you?"

Since she was already walking toward the tender, he couldn't see her face, but he could hear the smile in her voice as she said, "'Barbecue man' doesn't have the same ring to it. How about 'barbecue big boy'? Or would you prefer 'big barbecue boy'?"

"You've got a mouth on you, woman."

Now she looked over her shoulder. "Play your cards right and I'll use it on you . . . big boy."

Lust got Flynn's tongue, and before he could manage a comeback, she paused where beach met water to gather up their towels. Her arms full of primary-colored stripes, she stood staring at the waterfall for a long minute before turning to him with a smile so brilliant that it took his breath away once more.

"This has been a trip I will never forget. Thank you so much for this, Flynn."

"You are very welcome. It's been an unforgettable trip for me, too, Gabriella. I will never forget it . . . or you."

Back on the water and with the trolling lines out, he continued Gabi's sailing lessons. "I can't believe I've gone my whole life without experiencing the joy of sailing," Gabi said as she took a turn at the helm. "Where did you learn to do it, Flynn?"

"Mobile Bay, when I was a kid." he replied. "My dad loved to fish, and I grew up on the water. When I was ten, I pestered my parents to send me to summer sailing camp, and that's all it took. I went back every summer after that."

"So you're an Alabama boy? I thought I heard the South in your voice. So, I guess the big question is, Auburn or Alabama?"

"Auburn," he replied, knowing she referred to his collegiate loyalties. "I chose on the basis of mascot when I was eight years old. Tigers were way cooler than elephants to an eight-year-old."

"Where does the war eagle enter into it?"

Flynn explained about the difference between Auburn University's mascot, the tiger, and its battle cry, "War Eagle!" and then conversation expanded to other Southeast Conference schools. Considering that she'd played collegiate basketball and that two of her brothers were coaches, he wasn't surprised that she displayed a thorough knowledge of sports. However, he enjoyed her enthusiasm. Lisa hadn't liked sports one bit.

"So did you attend Auburn?" Gabi asked.

He smiled and sang, "I'm a ramblin' wreck from Georgia Tech and a hell of an engineer."

The last note hung in the air as Flynn drew in a breath to sing the next line. But before another sound issued from his throat, a terrific force hit his head.

Flynn Brogan's world went black.

EIGHT

Bright red blood burst on Flynn's forehead, and he crumpled to the deck. For seven wasted seconds, Gabi didn't process the sound that she'd heard or the sight that met her eyes. Had she been on the beat in Denver or even walking the streets of Eternity Springs, she would have put it together faster.

One didn't expect a gunshot to occur in the middle of the freaking Caribbean Sea.

Yes, a gunshot. Flynn had been shot. The truth hit her like a wave of cold seawater, and she started toward him. "Flynn!"

But even as she took that first step, a hand clamped around her ankle, halting her progress flat. Momentum carried her forward, and she lost her balance and hit the deck hard. Pain radiated from her right knee as she fell upon a cleat, but it helped to jolt her into focus. *We're under attack.*

And teetering on defeat.

Fear for Flynn and for herself threatened to overwhelm her, but then Gabi's training kicked in and she began to think. *Flynn is down, bloody. No help there. You're it, Romano.*

The hand released her as a figure scrambled over the railing onto the deck. Gabi crawled forward, away from him and toward the ladder. She had to get below, get to the gun Flynn had showed her during his safety lesson yesterday.

Behind her, a short, burly man found his feet and lunged for her, shouting in Spanish. Gabi was slippery with coconut-scented sunscreen, and she evaded his first grab. In the periphery of her vision she spied movement. Not Flynn. Another man. Two men. *Hurry. Hurry. Hurry.* Three more steps. The ladder leading below remained two enormous steps away.

"*Cabrona.*" A hand clawed, managed to grab the waistband of her shorts. Gabi screeched and fought against the pull, but he was strong. His grip held.

Until a snarling Bismarck launched himself at the man.

Gabi heard the man scream and other men's shouts and then Bismarck's pained yelp. Instinct made her want to whirl and see to the dog, see to Flynn, but training and experience kept her pointed to the ladder.

The attackers' guttural shouts followed her. Then she was down the ladder, reaching for the door. *Move. Move. Move.* Adrenaline humming, she slammed it shut, got her hand on the lock and started to turn it, and—

A hard shove on the opposite side of the door dislodged the lock before she could get it fastened. A frustrated scream emerged from her throat as she pushed back.

She couldn't budge him. He was stronger. He had a better angle. *Plan B, Romano.*

She leapt away from the door and landed on the lower deck with both feet, ready to run. Knowing the floor plan gave her an edge, and she used it to full advantage, gaining a few steps on her pursuer as she flew through the galley, praying it would be enough.

She burst into the master stateroom and, knowing that seconds counted, slammed the door but didn't take time to attempt to lock it. She lunged across the bed and put her hand on the compartment pull as the assailant entered the stateroom.

The drawer opened. She reached inside. Her hand went unerringly to the grip of the Smith & Wesson .32 revolver.

"*Puta!*" he yelled, and he was on her, swinging that big, meaty fist at her head.

Pain exploded in her cheek and nose, and her eyes automatically watered. But Gabi's focus never wavered. She yanked the gun free of the compartment, pointed, and pulled the trigger.

The explosion roared. Blood spattered. Her attacker collapsed on top of her, but Gabi couldn't relax. The gun was trapped between them, and at least two more men were right behind this bastard.

She tried to shift him enough to yank her arm free, but a voice speaking English stopped her cold. "Move and I'll blow your head off."

Tall and dressed in camo print in shades of blue, he had long black hair and evil black eyes. He stood in the doorway with a Desert Eagle .50 caliber pointed at her head. Gabi didn't have a chance.

He called out three or four sentences in Spanish, and then a second huge bear of a man wearing a black T-shirt, jeans, and a scraggly beard followed camo guy into the stateroom. He also pointed a gun at Gabi and approached the bed. Camo guy said, "I want to see your hands. Left hand first. Leave the gun behind. Any sudden move and we shoot."

Her thoughts racing, she debated her options, but failed to find a way to avoid following his instructions. She pulled her left hand out from between her body and the dead one, then hesitated. If only Flynn had loaded the gun with different ammunition. Hollow-points might be suited to a boat, since they wouldn't go through the hull, but they did her no good now. With hollow-points, she couldn't shoot through the dead man and take one of these guys out.

She showed them her empty right hand. Bearded guy reached between her and the dead man and confiscated the gun. Camo guy said something, and the bearded man sighed heavily and handed the weapon over. Then he grabbed the dead man by the arms and dragged him off Gabi and onto the floor. Camo guy's hard gaze never left Gabi, and the look he gave her sent shivers up her spine. He snapped out another sentence and the only word she made out was "diez." Ten. *Ten what? If I get out of this alive, I swear I'm going to learn another language or twelve.*

Then the big man shot Gabi a leer and she figured she'd translated it just fine. Fear rippled through her and she sent up a quick prayer for strength. She would survive this. She would use her brains and other God-given gifts and she would be ready to act when the opportunity presented itself. She would save herself, save Flynn and Bismarck, too.

The big man said something to camo guy as he slipped his hands under the dead man's arms and hauled him up the ladder. Before he disappeared from view, he pursed his lips and blew Gabi a kiss.

She couldn't hide her shudder, and camo guy showed her a slow, evil smile. "You are covered in the blood of my *compadre*. I do not like that. Take off your clothes."

"Who are you?" she asked. "Why are you doing this?"

"You have big tits. I like big tits."

Oh, God, please help me.

"Now, *puta*."

Yes, now. Seconds count. Flynn needs help. The sooner you get him within striking distance, the better. He can't rape you from across the room, and when he gets close . . . you have weapons, Gabi. You're smart. You're strong. *Pick your moment and you can crush his balls or break his neck.*

"Bastard," she said, and as her hands went to the hem of her T-shirt and lifted it over her head, she rolled up onto her knees—making the movement appear natural, but putting herself into a much better attack position.

"No, that is one thing I am not. I am the eldest son of Vicente Moreno Villarreal."

Eldest son of Lucifer is more like it, Gabi thought.

"The top," he demanded.

Gabi wore a halter-style swimsuit top, and as she reached up to the neckline, her thoughts flashed to Eternity Springs and the other time she'd taken a life. That day Savannah had faced rape and sought to delay the attack by drawing out the disrobing part. But Savannah had been in the middle of a town full of people who potentially could help. *I'm in the middle of an ocean surrounded by sharks. I don't have time to attempt to seduce this son of a bitch.*

"No," she said flatly, lifting her chin and squaring her shoulders. "You want to see me naked, then you're gonna have strip me yourself. I'm not going to cooperate with rape."

He laughed, and the sound brought the hairs on the back of her neck to attention. "I do enjoy a woman with fight. It makes it all the more enjoyable when I hurt her."

"Come and take me, big boy. I'll be—" For a split second, movement behind camo guy distracted Gabi. Her heart all but stopped, but she recovered fast enough not to give the game away. "—the death of you."

At that, as the villain stepped toward Gabi, Flynn moved forward swiftly and silently. As his left hand grabbed the attacker by his long dark hair and pulled his head back, exposing his throat, the long, curved fillet knife in his right hand sliced deep. A fountain of blood spurted, splashing Gabi in the face. Recoiling instinctively, she cried out.

"It's okay, Gabi," Flynn said, his voice weak. He was pale, his face streaked with his own blood, the gash that ran up his forehead into his hair still bleeding freely. "It's over. They're dead. You're safe. I killed them."

Thank God.

But before she could say more, he emitted a sound she couldn't quite identify—a laugh? A sob? A cry?—then added, "I'm a killer. They had it right all along."

Then Flynn Brogan wove on his feet and collapsed to the floor.

Pounding pain in Flynn's head greeted him as he floated up to consciousness, and he wanted nothing more than to sink into blackness again. But the sound of heart-wrenching sobs tugged him back. He opened his eyes and recognized the galley. He lay just outside his stateroom door on the floor with a pillow tucked beneath his head. The sound came from above deck. It was Gabi, crying from the depths of her soul. Then he heard the sound of the engine. The boat was under way.

The events of the day came roaring back. He lifted his head as he started to sit up, and the waves of pain and nausea that resulted almost made him pass out again. It took him a few minutes, but he made it to his feet. He lifted his hand to his aching head and touched a gauze bandage, then wobbled his way toward the ladder.

Climbing almost killed him, but the sound of her tears pulled him forward. She stood at the helm, but her gaze was on the sea. He opened his dry mouth and croaked, "Gabi?"

She looked up at him, then wiped her tears away with her knuckles. "You're awake. Good."

"Did they hurt you?"

She hesitated a moment. "No. Physically, no." She

crossed the cockpit to the passage and supported him as he took the last two steps onto the deck. She urged him toward the nearest seat, saying, "Come sit down before you fall, Flynn. You may be the luckiest man on earth right now, but you still lost a lot of blood. A bullet hit your forehead and skimmed over the top of your head, leaving a ditch in your scalp from front to back. I've radioed for help, and the U.S. Coast Guard responded to my mayday. They're on their way, but I don't know when they'll get here."

Flynn's thoughts processed slowly. She never stopped looking at the sea. He wanted to reach for her, to take her into his arms, but it was as if the Gulf of Mexico stretched between them. "Was there more than one boat of pirates?"

"Pirates? Oh, I thought they were drug dealers. This is the Caribbean, not Somalia."

"Are there more, Gabi?"

"No. Not that I've seen." She had a catch to her voice as she added, "We seem to be alone on the ocean."

He hadn't taught her how to plot a course yet. Why was the motor running? "Then why are we under way?"

She didn't say anything. She didn't look at him. Tears began to stream down her cheeks. Then it hit him. "Where's Bismarck?"

Her voice sounded strangled. "I don't know. I haven't seen him since I went for your gun. He's ..." She stopped and cleared her throat. "He's not on the boat, Flynn. I've searched everywhere."

Flynn closed his eyes, feeling sick.

"I tried to go back the way we came, but I'm not sure that my direction is right. I'm afraid to go too far because help is coming for you, and they have to find us. He could be out there, swimming. He tried to protect me and I heard him yelp. They could have kicked him off the boat."

"You're right. Newfies are strong, excellent swimmers." Flynn rose and manipulated the boat's electronics to display the *Dreamer*'s course. He made a few adjustments to their current heading, then pulled a pair of binoculars from a cockpit storage compartment. "Use these."

While she scanned the water, Flynn radioed the authorities, updating their position and condition. He watched the water, too, though his fuzzy vision reduced his ability to see much. Twice Gabi thought she saw something, but both were false alarms. Flynn knew they needed more help, so after thinking through the possibilities—not an easy task considering his raging headache—he placed a call to Matthew Wharton and cut the attorney's greeting short. "I have a situation here. I need you to organize a private search-and-rescue mission in the water at the coordinates I'll provide. We are looking for a dog, a Newfoundland puppy, black coat, twenty to twenty-five pounds. He went overboard . . . hold on. Gabi? Can you estimate the time between Bismarck's yelp and when the big guy hauled the body above deck? Five minutes?"

"It seemed like forever, but no more than that."

Flynn continued to Matthew, "I set a boat adrift approximately five minutes after the dog went overboard. A seventeen-footer running an Evinrude outboard, painted blue. Hard as hell to see against the water if you're not looking. We weren't looking. This is high priority, Matthew. Unlimited resources are at your disposal. I want so many people out here that they are tripping over each other, and I want them here fast."

"You know I'll do whatever you ask, Flynn," Matthew said. "But . . . all this for a dog?"

Flynn's gaze returned to Gabi, noting the fresh tears on her cheek. His heart weighed a ton. "He's a great dog. Now, get on it, Matthew. Speed is vital. I'll give you the rest of the story after you set the rescue in motion."

"Yes, sir."

The moment Flynn took the phone away from his ear, Gabi said, "Thank you, Flynn."

"We will find him, Gabi."

It wasn't beyond the realm of possibility, he thought. Newfoundlands might not be suited to the tropics, but they were damned good swimmers. Bismarck was strong and he was smart, and while they'd need good luck to spot him in the sea, it wouldn't be impossible for him to make his way to one of the dozens of small islands in the area.

That is, if the damned pirates hadn't wounded him before they sent him overboard. Gabi would have heard a shot, but if they'd used a knife . . . Shying away from that possibility, he added, "We'll have a lot of people looking for him."

"That's good."

She lifted the binoculars and returned her attention to the sea. They searched in silence from then on until he heard the sound of a motor approaching. He should get the gun, just in case, he thought. As he started below, her voice stopped him. "Where are you going?"

"To get the gun."

"I have it."

She didn't look prepared to give it up, either. Well, she had been a cop. "If you'll give me the glasses, I want to see if I can identify the boat headed our way."

She did as he asked, then returned her gaze to the water. He identified the patrol boat and breathed a sigh of relief. "It's the Coast Guard."

He started to hand Gabi back the binoculars, but stopped when he heard the *whop whop whop* of a helicopter. "Good. I knew Matthew would get the job done."

The Royal Bahamas police arrived on the heels of the Coast Guard, and after that, Flynn had little opportunity to speak with Gabi. The police interviewed them separately, Gabi above and Flynn below deck in the guest room. As a medic cleaned and dressed his head wound, Flynn was asked to explain what had happened aboard the *Dreamer,* and he could no longer avoid the memory of the afternoon's events. The sick feeling made him want to curl up in a corner.

He had taken a life. Two lives. They'd been two sorry-ass scumbags who didn't deserve to live, for sure, but that didn't negate the fact that he was responsible for their deaths. They likely had family somewhere who would mourn them. Mothers. Wives. Children. That knowledge weighed on his heart.

The memory of the sounds, the resistance and then the give of human flesh beneath his blade, and the sticky warmth and coppery scent of blood flowing across his own skin would haunt him until the day he died.

Emotion clogged Flynn's throat, and he felt pressure at the back of his eyes. He'd be damned if he'd cry. He fought off the urge by lashing out at the cops. "I check the crime reports regularly. I haven't seen a single mention of pirates in this part of the Caribbean. So this was the third attack by pirates in the last ten days and nobody has bothered to let the public know? Why the hell wasn't a warning issued?"

The policeman rattled off a bunch of excuses that didn't placate Flynn one bit. He was working up to a good rant when one of the Coast Guard guys exited the master stateroom and gave Flynn a measuring look. "Do you know who you killed in there?"

Flynn shrugged. "He told Gabi his name. It didn't stick with me."

"Villarreal. Tomás Villarreal. He was Vicente's son."

"And Vicente is who?"

"One of the most powerful politicians in Mexico. He's

been living in the Bahamas, and he's had a few brushes with the law. Didn't know he'd taken up piracy."

"Seems to be a lot of ignorance going around," Flynn grumbled.

The Coastie didn't like that. He snapped back, "You should be glad we know who he is, Seagraves. Otherwise we might look at this as something other than an attack and peg you for a serial killer after what you did to your wife."

Flynn stiffened. His passport still listed Seagraves as his name because his replacement had yet to arrive. He felt the rage swell inside him. He was so damned tired of this. Forget the results of a court of law—he'd been judged guilty in a court of public opinion, and in this day and age, that was an ugly sentence.

He turned to the policeman. "Do you have any more questions for me?"

"A few." The policeman continued his interrogation, and Flynn buried his bitterness and kept his answers quick and succinct. The sooner this was over, the better. His head was killing him.

They'd just wrapped up the interview when news was received that one of his search helicopters had spotted a body floating in the ocean. "What sort of body?" he asked. "Canine or two legs?"

He'd be damned if he'd call the son of a bitch he'd thrown overboard human.

"From your description, he's our missing perpetrator," one of the policemen said.

"Good. Now, if y'all are done with me, I'd like to take a shower. Any idea how soon we'll be free to continue our search for our dog?"

After some consultation, the policemen declared they'd need to take possession of the *Dreamer* and sail her to Nassau in order to process all the evidence. Flynn sighed.

He should have expected that. By now, Marcus Yarrow would have returned the Formula to the Tradewinds slip. "In that case, Ms. Romano and I will need a lift to Bella Vita Isle."

The arrangements they made gave Flynn time to take a badly needed shower. In addition to the head wound, he had bruises and scrapes from his struggle with the ass he'd sent overboard. The hot water felt like heaven, because inside Flynn was so cold. Clean and dressed, he looked at himself in the mirror and grimaced. Gabi was right. He was one lucky, hardheaded son of a bitch. The bullet had struck his forehead an inch below his hairline. His face looked gaunt, his eyes haunted. He'd had that same bleakness in his expression the day he'd been arrested for Lisa's murder.

"Screw it," he said to his reflection. He'd go home to Tradewinds and oversee the search for Bismarck. Once the Newfie had been found, Flynn would indulge in a good old three-day drunken binge, then pick up the pieces of his life again. He'd been down this road before. He knew how to do it.

He climbed the ladder and stepped onto the deck. Gabi sat alone at the back of the boat, her arms wrapped around her knees, her face turned away from him. She, too, had showered and changed clothes. Good. She'd been covered in blood, and he knew she would have hated it even worse than he did. "Gabi?"

Her dark hair swung like a velvet curtain as she looked his way. Flynn sucked in a breath. The bright, vivacious, happy woman had disappeared. It was as if all the light that had been shining from within her had died.

No wonder. Bismarck was gone, likely for good. She'd been attacked and almost raped. And she'd been forced to kill again. What an effing cluster. He felt terrible that he'd brought her into this situation. It was just like Lisa all over again. He wasn't responsible for the horrible things that had happened, but he felt like crap for having failed to prevent them.

Oh, Gabriella. I'm so sorry.

Gabi wanted her mother.

When she arrived back at Palmetto House, she would place the call to the Fontanas and then immediately call her mother. She'd seriously considered making the calls from the satellite phone on the *Dreamer,* but she needed privacy for both. The sooner she was off this Coast Guard boat, the better.

She asked the nearest sailor, "How much longer?"

"About ten minutes."

"Thanks."

Her gaze drifted toward the aft of the boat where Flynn stood alone, staring out at the sea. Except for saying her name that one time, they hadn't spoken directly since the Coast Guard pulled along next to the *Dreamer.* He walked away after seeing her face and she didn't bother to call him back. She needed a little time and space to deal with what had happened today before she could offer support to anyone else.

Still, she couldn't walk off this boat without thanking him for calling out the troops to look for Bismarck. By the time they'd left the search area, the place had been crawling with helicopters and boats. That, together with a couple of swimming-dog stories one of the Coasties had shared with her, gave her a glimmer of hope that Bismarck would be found.

Though the realist in her knew better. Bismarck had attacked that man. She suspected he had struck back. She put the chances of the dog having entered the water uninjured at less than 10 percent.

Taking a deep breath, she wiped her sweaty palms on her thighs, then stood and walked to the back of the boat.

It was as if Flynn had an invisible force field around him keeping everyone away. Standing awkwardly just outside of his space, she said, "Flynn, I want to thank you for what you're doing to find Bismarck."

He didn't look at her, and long seconds ticked by before he replied. "It was the least I could do."

Following another awkward pause, she asked, "How is your head?"

"I'll live." At that point, finally, he looked at her. "I'm so sorry that you were forced to defend yourself, Gabriella. The last thing I ever wanted was for you to pick up a gun again."

Hearing that, she couldn't hold back the tears that swelled and overflowed. The events of the day had awakened her demons and her fears, and at the moment she was barely holding herself together. She wanted Flynn to hold her and tell her everything would be okay, but he looked so forbidding, so unapproachable. Didn't he need a hug as badly as she?

She cleared her throat and took a single step forward, hoping to breach his walls. "I'm not the only one who took a life today. I know you must be wrestling with demons of your own."

He didn't move. Didn't look at her. Didn't speak. His whole body language told her to stay away.

Despair and disappointment made her want to whimper, but she swallowed back the sound. Well, okay. This was his first time taking a life. He was understandably shaken. She'd been there. She knew what the aftermath felt like. It took some time to wrap your brain around what happened, and he was probably in shock. She was the experienced one in this instance. She should give him a little time to deal with it and not burden him with her neediness.

You're a strong woman, Gabriella Romano. Be strong.

Find it inside yourself. Give him some time. He'll give you your hugs later.

Yes. She'd be strong . . . even if it killed her. She cleared her throat. "I'm going to call the Fontanas when I get home. If you hear anything at all from the searchers, you'll let me know?"

"Of course."

Before she moved away, Gabi did reach out and lightly touch his arm. Then she returned to her spot near the bow of the boat and focused on the picturesque waterfront of Bella Vita Isle's little town, Corazón. Soon she noticed the crowd congregated at the marina. That was unusual, and she wondered what was going on. She hoped there hadn't been a drowning.

Unless . . . could this be good news? Could one of the helicopters have done a water rescue? Could Bismarck be waiting for her at the marina?

It was a wild hope, but it rose within her like champagne bubbles. She grasped hold of the railing and stared hard at the shore, hoping, praying. Wishing one of those Eternity Springs miracles might have followed her to Bella Vita Isle.

As the Coast Guard boat pulled nearer to the marina, the crowd did seem to surge, but she did not see any sign of Bismarck. Her stomach sank. Stupid of her to have gotten her hopes up. Surely if they'd found him, someone would have radioed and reported the news to the man who was paying for the search.

That quickly, she no longer cared about the crowd congregating on the wharf. She wanted to be home with the Fontana phone call behind her and wallowing in her mother's long-distance comforting. So mired was she in her own misery as the Coast Guard docked their boat that at first she didn't realize that cameras were turned her way. Lots of cameras.

Then she heard Flynn spit a vicious epithet. *What the . . . ?*

"There he is," one of the photographers called.

Cameras began clicking. Voices shouted. "Hey, Seagraves! Are you a serial killer?"

"Flynn! So you switched from a syringe to a knife?"

"Flynn Seagraves! Do you have a statement to make to the families of the men you killed today?"

"Like the one you made to Wendy Stafford after you murdered her sister?"

Gabi froze. Murdered her sister? Wendy Stafford's sister? Her jaw gaped. Flynn Seagraves? *The* Flynn Seagraves?

Shocked, she whipped around. He stood staring at her from ten feet away, an unreadable expression on his face.

Horror filled her tone as the question burst from her mouth. "You're Flynn Seagraves?"

His beautiful blue eyes blazed with emotion for the briefest of seconds before going flat and glacier cold, and he gave her a barracuda smile. "Surprise."

With that, his head held high and his spine straight as a board, he stepped off the boat and was swallowed by the mayhem.

Gabi stood watching him go, frozen in shock. She hadn't recognized him. She should have recognized him. Everybody who stood in the checkout lane at a grocery store should have recognized him! His picture had been on the front of every tabloid in the racks.

They'd called him the GQ Killer.

He'd worn his hair short instead of long and dressed in Brooks Brothers suits rather than swim trunks and tees, but those eyes were the same.

She'd dated the GQ Killer!

She'd made love with the GQ Killer!

"Un-freaking-believable." It was simply too much,

that final straw that broke the slim hold she'd had on her control. Damn him! He'd lied to her from the start! Let her believe he was Flynn Brogan, cabana boy. Then, when she'd figured out he was more than an impoverished servant, he'd trotted out Flynn Brogan, barbecue king. But he'd never gotten around to mentioning that he was also Flynn Seagraves, tabloid cover star, aka the GQ Killer. He'd lied to her and slept with her and sailed her into pirate-infested seas in which she'd killed a man intent on rape and lost the dog she was supposed to protect. She'd lost Bismarck.

Pain and anger and fear and devastation swirled within her like an F5 tornado. She wanted to throw back her head and scream long and loud. Instead, after giving the Coasties a tight but sincere thank-you, she marched off the boat and onto the wharf. The paparazzi had followed Flynn, so she had a clear path to where she'd left the car what seemed like a lifetime ago. Once inside, she held the wheel in a shaking, white-knuckled grip all the way to Palmetto House.

There she went straight to the phone. She needed to get this call behind her ASAP and then she could fall apart.

She looked up the emergency numbers and placed the call. As expected, it was ugly. Mrs. Fontana wailed at the news, then screamed at her, and finally demanded she leave Palmetto House.

"Of course I will," Gabi replied. "I just . . . all hope is not lost, ma'am. A local has organized a search, and there's a chance—"

"Nonsense," her employer snapped, venom in her tone. "If those thieves didn't kill him, the sharks surely have by now. I should sue you for neglect. I will have you arrested if you're still in my home this time tomorrow."

Gabi's hand trembled as she disconnected the call following another five minutes of verbal abuse. She didn't blame the woman. She deserved every word. She'd failed Bismarck. Sighing raggedly, she started to thumb her mother's number when the doorbell sounded.

"What now?" she murmured. She didn't want to talk to anyone but her mother. The bell rang again, and she started toward the door. *Unless they're bringing Bismarck home . . .*

"Please, please, please, please," she murmured, reaching for the knob. She released the latch, swung the door open, and received yet another shock.

"Surprise!" Maggie Romano said, her blue eyes shining, her smile wide. She wore a blue travel dress and flats, and the sassy cut of her auburn hair was new since Gabi had last seen her. Gabi looked down at her diminutive mother. "Mom! What . . . ?"

"Celeste had a pair of airline tickets that were about to expire."

"Hello, Gabi dear," Celeste Blessing said from behind Gabi's mother. "We thought you might welcome some company."

Gabi threw herself into her mother's arms and burst into tears.

NINE

Gabi cried so hard that she got the hiccups. She only vaguely noticed that Celeste took charge, ushering them inside and into the living room, where Gabi collapsed onto the sofa, laid her head in her mother's lap, and sobbed. Maggie Romano stroked her hand up and down Gabi's arm and back, crooning, "Hush now, baby. It's okay. Everything is going to be all right."

"No, it's not," she wailed.

Celeste spied a box of tissues and brought it to Gabi as, in fits and starts and sobs and interrupted by hiccups, she poured out the story. So distraught was she that she barely heard her mother's responses until Maggie went stiff and burst out, "Pirates?"

"I shot him, Mama. He fell on top of me and his blood spilled onto me and he died. I killed him. I killed again and I was a dogsitter, not even a sheriff's deputy!"

"Oh, baby." Now Maggie's voice had a tremble and fear to it that Gabi could hear even through her tears, and Maggie wrapped her daughter in a tight hug. "Oh, honey. Thank God you're okay."

"I'm okay, but Bismarck isn't." She told them the dog part of the story and finished with, "I don't think they'll find him."

"Now, Gabi," Celeste said. "You mustn't lose faith.

Take a lesson from your new sister-in-law. Hope never stopped believing that she'd see her Holly again, and she had her happy ending. You need to believe that you can have yours."

Had that assurance come from anyone other than Celeste, she would have dismissed it, but Celeste had an uncanny way of being right.

Maggie patted Gabi's leg. "We'll take you home tomorrow to your family and friends and give Eternity Springs a chance to work its magic all over again."

Gabi rested her head on her mother's shoulder, thought about sharing the GQ Killer part of the tale, but now that she'd poured out the rest of it, she didn't have the energy. "I wish we could go today."

Celeste stood and brushed her hands together. "Gabriella, why don't you go take a long, relaxing bath? Your mother and I will fix us supper, and maybe after dinner you can show us around this island. I'd hate to leave without seeing the glass studio you talked about in your emails."

Thinking about working with glass gave Gabi the first glimmer of warmth she'd felt since Flynn had collapsed to the deck of the *Dreamer*. "That sounds lovely, Celeste. You always have the best ideas."

"I do, don't I? I also give excellent advice. Aristotle said that hope is a waking dream. Never stop dreaming, Gabriella. Only then will you see where life is meant to lead."

Flynn swam until he could swim no more. Fatigue gripped at his muscles, and instead of using the side to hoist himself out of the pool, the way he usually did, tonight he climbed the steps. He was physically, mentally, and emotionally exhausted, which was not a bad thing. He figured now he might actually get some sleep.

He grabbed a towel and dragged it across his torso,

then whisked it across his back. Only when he turned to toss it onto a chair did he spy the dark figure seated on one of the bar stools at the outdoor kitchen. Immediately he tensed. *What the hell?*

"Who are you?" he demanded.

"I'm a friend of Gabi's, Mr. Brogan. My name is Celeste Blessing. I came through the hedge that separates your estate from Palmetto House, and I'm sorry to intrude on your privacy, but I wanted to thank you for saving our beloved Gabriella."

Glad I didn't swim bare-assed naked tonight. Apparently Eternity Springs women didn't think anything about trespassing through hedges. "How did you get here so fast?"

"We made an impromptu trip to surprise Gabi, and arrived this afternoon. Her mother is with me."

Good, Flynn thought.

"We plan to take Gabi home tomorrow."

His teeth clenched against a protest, and he told himself that Gabi's leaving was good, too. It was over. No sense dragging it out. His visitor slipped off the bar stool and stepped forward out of the shadows. An older, attractive woman, she reminded him of the actress who'd played M in the recent Bond flicks. He tried to place her in the list of hometown friends Gabi had told him about. "You're the lady who runs the spa."

"Yes. Angel's Rest Healing Center and Spa. It's a lovely place, Mr. Brogan. Peaceful and serene. Eternity Springs is a very special town. The valley where it sits has a special energy that heals and soothes the soul. You should pay us a visit sometime."

He laughed. "Somehow I don't expect I'd be welcome. Not by Gabi, and certainly not by all her brothers."

She chastised him with a look. "You saved her life. The Romano family will have conflicting emotions where you are concerned, true. However, they are fair people. They will recognize that you are not the villain here."

"It doesn't matter. Gabi and I are done, and I don't see myself visiting Colorado anytime soon, so I probably won't run into any Romanos on the street."

"You might be surprised," Celeste replied.

Her amused smile annoyed him, so his voice had a bite to it when he said, "If you'll excuse me now, Ms. Blessing, I need to go in and get dressed. I'm cold."

She shocked the hell out of him when she walked over to him and wrapped her arms around him. Her hug warmed him from the inside out, and damned if he didn't feel tears press at the back of his eyes. "You are a good man, Flynn. You are being tested, but your heart is true. They will not destroy you."

His arms came up and hovered. He wanted to return her hug, to hold on for dear life, but she was a stranger. This was weird. He swallowed a lump the size of a tennis ball in his throat and closed his eyes. "Look, lady— Ms. Blessing. I appreciate the thought, but you don't know me."

Her arms around him tightened for a gloriously warm moment, then she released him and stepped back. "Sure I do. You are Flynn Brogan, inventor. You've been blessed with a brilliant mind. You will find comfort in using it. And listen to your heart to know when it's time to come to Eternity Springs to heal."

He ignored the urge to protest when she turned and walked away, leaving him alone. Alone in darkness.

He spent the next few weeks searching the islands for Bismarck. He used the Formula, since the *Dreamer* was better suited to be called the *Nightmare* now, and he stayed gone from Bella Vita Isle days at a time, sleeping in the cutty cabin and catching his meals on a hook.

He tried not to think about Gabi. He tried not to think

about much of anything. During the daytime when he trekked across uninhabited islands calling Bismarck's name or knocked on doors on the populated islands with a picture he'd taken of Gabi and the Newfie, he managed to keep his mind on the goal. It was only during those long, lonely nights aboard his boat or in his bedroom at Tradewinds that the memories haunted him and the night terrors returned.

On Tuesday of the fourth week after the attack, he awoke from a nightmare drenched in sweat, his heart pounding. He knew he was done with sleep for that night.

He unlocked the door and exited the cabin, thinking he'd dive in and swim off the sweat and stress. That's when he heard it, a sound that could only be one thing: barking. Bismarck barking.

"Bismarck!" he shouted, standing on the seat as he scanned the shore. "Bismarck? Boy, where are you? Bismarck!"

Arf. Arf. Arf. Arf.

Flynn didn't hesitate. He tossed boots, his phone, and a flashlight into his dry bag, then dove in. He reached the moonlit beach in minutes. "Bismarck?"

Arf. Arf. Arf.

Flynn's lips lifted in a wide grin. He recognized that bark. Bismarck had survived! "Here, boy! C'mere, Bismarck. Hey, boy, where are you?"

The barking grew louder and a little bit frenzied and came from somewhere inside the trees. Flynn switched on the flashlight and followed the sound, continuing to call the dog's name. Since Bismarck was as black as midnight, he wouldn't be easy to spot beneath the canopy of leaves.

As it turned out, neither was the man who struck him on the side of the head with a huge, meaty fist. Once again, Flynn's world went black.

* * *

When consciousness returned, sunshine warmed his body. His head ached. He recognized the faint scent of chloroform at his nostrils. What the hell?

Then it all came back. Bismarck.

Flynn tried to sit up, but he couldn't. Something restrained his arms and, he soon realized, his legs. He opened his eyes and saw nothing but blue sky. He was staked spread-eagled on the beach.

"Well, now. Good morning, Mr. Brogan."

He turned his head toward the sound. He saw a dark-haired man, probably in his mid-sixties, sitting in a folding chair. Bismarck was nowhere in sight.

"What is this?" Flynn croaked.

The man's smile telegraphed pure evil. "I'd say it's the beginning of the worst day of your life."

Another one? Flynn almost laughed.

The man rose from the chair and moved to stand over Flynn. Sunlight glinted off the blade of the knife he pulled from a sheath at his belt. "My name is Vicente Villarreal. I have come to avenge my son."

When the sun set the following night, Flynn lay on the beach a broken man. With the frayed end of a three-quarter-inch dock line hanging around his neck, Bismarck lay beside him.

TEN

Eternity Springs, Colorado

Summer sunshine shone down on Gabi as she pedaled her bike up Cemetery Hill. It was a beautiful morning in June with a clear blue sky above, wildflowers blooming along the roadside, and birdsong whistling from the trees. Nevertheless, halfway to the top of the hill, she lost heart in her bike ride, so when she reached the turn-off into the cemetery, she took it. Upon reaching the graveyard, she leaned her bicycle against a tree near the headstones of the Eternity Springs founders and took a seat on a concrete bench beneath the shade of a spreading oak.

So much for thinking exercise might lift her from her funk. Gabi had been in a moody funk ever since returning from Bella Vita six weeks ago. She hardly slept for the nightmares. She barely went an hour without thinking about Bismarck.

She spent a shameful amount of time on the Internet surfing for information about Flynn Seagraves, aka Flynn Brogan, aka the GQ Killer.

Most of America believed that he had drugged his wife, then stuffed her unconscious body into a freezer in their basement.

The acquittal had shocked the nation almost as much as the O. J. Simpson verdict had. The televised GQ Killer trial had been every bit as dramatic as that one, what with Flynn's devastated former best friend's public accusations and his former sister-in-law's change of allegiance. After standing beside Flynn for months, halfway through the trial Wendy Stafford had abruptly changed her mind about his innocence. She'd refused to explain why.

The tabloids had had a field day. What secret had poor Wendy uncovered? Daily television ratings doubled. Everyone had assumed a guilty verdict would be forthcoming. But Flynn's criminal attorneys had presented a brilliant defense, poking holes in the circumstantial case. Then they'd all but given the pundits apoplexy when they put Flynn on the stand.

Gabi had pored over photos from the trial. Seeing Flynn in a classically cut suit and conservative tie that perfectly complemented his eyes made it obvious why the moniker "GQ Killer" had stuck. He'd looked serious but confident.

According to published reports, he wasn't shaken by the prosecutor's cross-examination or even his former sister-in-law's outburst when she stood up and shouted, "Liar!"

The summary she'd read of the rest of the trial spoke of a motion for mistrial, and a gleeful prosecutor when the motion was denied. But Flynn remained calm, cool, and collected, and when he finally left the stand, pundits agreed that had it not been for Wendy Stafford's outburst, he might actually have gotten away with murder.

But then, after six and a half days of jury deliberation, that's exactly what happened—at least, according to almost every newspaper in the country.

Gabi thought otherwise. She believed in Flynn. He hadn't killed his wife. He might be a liar, but he wasn't a murderer. Anyone who knew him should know that. Maybe someday she'd have the chance to tell him so, too.

She still felt horrible about her reaction upon learning who he was. For just a second there, a stricken expression had flashed across his face before he'd gone cold. Hard and cold.

"Just one more thing to feel like crap about," she muttered.

Lifting her face toward the warmth of the summer sunshine, she closed her eyes and sighed. When tears built behind her eyes, she didn't even try to stop them from falling. If the past six weeks had taught her anything, it was the futility of attempting to hold back her tears.

When her cell phone rang, she almost didn't answer. But then she checked the number and saw that it was most likely the call she'd been waiting for. She thumbed the green button, then said, "Is it baby time, Lucca?"

"Hope's contractions are five minutes apart. We're heading for the clinic now."

For the first time in what seemed like forever, her spirits rose. "Would you like me to call the others?"

"No, thanks. I've already called Mom, and Hope is sending out a text to everyone else. Holly is due back from day camp at two. Can you—"

"I'll pick her up and bring her to the clinic. Don't worry. Is the plan still to have her join you in the delivery room?"

"If everything is going okay, and if she still wants to do it, yes. Our plan is to just have her there for the actual birth. I'll come get her."

"Excellent. That way we'll all know when the newest little Romano is about to enter the world."

"Great. Thanks, sis."

"You're very welcome, brother. Now go have a baby."

She accomplished the ride down the hill with much more enthusiasm than she'd had for the journey up it. When she got home, she had time for a shower and to pack a basket with sandwiches, fruit, and snacks. The medical clinic in Eternity Springs was equipped to handle emergencies and had a state-of-the-art birthing suite, but it didn't have a cafeteria. It never hurt to have munchies in the waiting room, especially when people were nervous. Considering that this was the first of a new generation of Romanos, Gabi anticipated there being plenty of nerves to go around.

She and about a dozen other people were waiting at the school when the bus arrived from the summer camp sponsored by the charitable foundation Jack and Cat Davenport had established in the name of their late daughter, Lauren. This week was local kids' week, and when the bus door opened, children swarmed out like ants. Holly emerged in the middle of the pack, looking around for Hope or Lucca.

Her gaze breezed right over Gabi, then abruptly stopped and returned. Hope sparked to life in her eyes. "Aunt Gabi? Are you here for me?"

"That I am."

The eleven-year-old clasped her hands in front of her. "Is it baby time?" she asked.

"That it is. Lucca and your mom are at the clinic."

"Hurray!" Hope threw out her arms in joy.

"Do you want to go by the house and change clothes, or would you rather go straight to the clinic?"

"To the clinic, please."

"Hurray!" Gabi cried, throwing her arms out in imitation of the girl. "I'm so excited, too, Holly."

They both giggled like schoolgirls all the way to Gabi's car. Once she was seated with her seatbelt fastened, Holly peppered Gabi with questions. "How long has Mom been in labor?"

"Honestly, I'm not certain. Lucca called me"—she glanced at the dashboard clock—"about an hour and twenty minutes ago. Hope's contractions were five minutes apart, and they were headed for the clinic."

Holly nodded knowingly. "She probably was having contractions this morning when she made my lunch for camp. I thought she was distracted. She promised that they'd call the camp if I needed to leave early."

"I'm sure if events had started speeding up, that's what they would have done." Gabi gave the girl a sidelong glance. "So, are you excited about seeing the baby born?"

Holly's little cupid's bow of a mouth pursed. "I'm a little scared. Part of me wants to watch really, really bad. Another part of me doesn't want to see all that stuff. I know what to expect. Mom and I watched a video on YouTube."

"An educational video?"

"No. The real thing."

"Someone put a video up of their baby's birth?"

"There's a whole bunch of them."

"Good heavens." Call her old-fashioned, but Gabi thought that as a rule, the world today suffered from TMI—too much information.

They arrived at the clinic a few minutes later, and Gabi could tell by the parking lot that word of the pending delivery had spread. She saw her brother Zach's Range Rover, Celeste's Honda Gold Wing motorcycle, Sage Rafferty's and Cat Davenport's SUVs, Sarah Murphy's truck, Ali Timberlake's BMW convertible, and three bicycles, two of which were pink and equipped with baskets, bells, streamers on the handlebars, and training wheels—which meant the Callahans were here, too. She observed, "Looks like the party has already started."

"Party?" Holly's eyes went round. "Mama didn't say anything about a party. Do I need a gift?"

"No, honey," Gabi said with a smile. Kidnapped by her babysitter as a five-year-old and reunited with her parents only last Christmas, Holly's adjustment to her new circumstances had gone relatively well. However, insecurity reared its head upon occasion; the little girl needed desperately to belong. Lucky for them all that Eternity Springs was the perfect place for that. "I said that as a figure of speech because our family and many of our friends are here to wait for your brother or sister's birth."

"Oh. Okay." She paused a moment, then asked, "Think Mrs. Murphy will bring any cookies?"

Now Gabi laughed—her first genuine laugh in weeks. "I sure hope so. We need to keep up our strength during the waiting."

They walked into the clinic hand in hand and followed the noise to the maternity waiting room. Celeste saw them first. "Holly's here."

"Excellent," Sarah Murphy said. "Now Hope will feel free to speed matters up."

"What's the latest?" Gabi asked. Then, taking a good look around the room, she added, "And where's my mother and Zach? Are they in with Hope and Lucca?"

"No," Celeste said. "They're with Sage and Rose. They're taking X-rays of your mother's foot."

Rose Anderson was Sage Rafferty's sister and a part-time physician at the clinic. "X-rays!" Gabi exclaimed. "What happened?"

Savannah spoke up. "She was pumping gas into her car when Lucca called her to say they were headed here, and she got all excited and tripped over the gas hose. Landed hard on her foot. She was complaining about it, so Rose looked at it and said she needed X-rays. Your mom refused to leave the waiting room until Sage checked on Hope and Lucca. She said we're still a ways away."

"My mom is doing okay?" Holly asked.

"Your mom is doing fine," Savannah responded. "She said if you want to pop in and say hi when you got here, she'd like that."

Holly glanced up at Gabi. "Should I go in?"

"Up to you, sweet pea. But I'd go in a heartbeat if I had the chance."

"Okay." She drew a deep breath. "I'll go. Where do I go?"

"I'll show you." Gabi led her around a corner to the birthing suite. Holly knocked on the door, and a moment later, Lucca opened it. "Holly Bear! Just the lady I was hoping to see. Guess what? It's finally . . ."

"Baby time!" Holly giggled, the phrase having become a game for the growing family.

Lucca opened the door wider for her to enter. Seeing Gabi, he included her in his grin. "Want to come in and say hi?"

"I'd love to."

She found Hope up out of bed, wearing a fluffy yellow bathrobe over her hospital gown as she hugged her daughter. "Wow, you look great for a woman in the throes of labor," Gabi observed.

"I'm doing great now that Holly's here," Hope responded, leaning over and kissing the top of her daughter's head. She looked at her husband, saying, "Lucca, I could use some fresh crushed ice. Could you show Holly where it is, please?"

He frowned and checked his watch. "You're due for another contraction in a minute and a half. I don't know—"

"Gabi will help me through it, won't you, Gabi?"

"Sure. I've got it covered."

"But—"

"Don't worry, Lucca. Remember, I delivered a baby in a cab one time."

"That doesn't give me any sense of security, Gabriella."

"Hurry and go, Lucca, so you can get back," Hope said. When the door closed behind him and Holly, she let out a loud, exasperated sigh. "Your brother is driving me crazy!"

Oh, dear. Maybe I should have stayed in the waiting room.

"He's supposed to be the labor coach, but giving birth isn't a basketball game. There are no free throws or slam dunks. He's treating this like an NCAA tournament game!"

"The Sweet Sixteen or Final Four?"

"Gabi!"

"I'm sorry. I'm sorry. I couldn't resist." Giggles were bubbling up inside her, and they felt so damned good that she had a hard time swallowing them back. "What can I do to help?"

"Tell him not to be so . . . tactical! If he gets his clipboard out one more time, somebody is gonna get hurt."

"Clipboard! Why does he have a clipboard?"

"I don't know. He makes notes. He checks items off a list. He's Captain Clipboard! Why can't he hold my hand and say 'There, there, dear'?"

"Have you had any pain meds, Hope?"

"No. I've been trying to go natural."

"Well, it's a personal decision, but maybe you should consider that epidural. Think of Holly. It'd be easier on her."

The door opened, and Lucca and Holly stepped inside. Both carried white Styrofoam cups filled with shaved ice. Both gazed toward Hope anxiously.

Gabi made her move. She kissed Hope's cheek and said, "Good luck, little mama. Love you." Then she turned toward the door and her brother and said "Good luck, big daddy." As she leaned over to kiss him, she whispered in his ear, "Hold her hand, dumbass." She repossessed the clipboard and continued into the hall, swinging the door closed behind her. Just before it shut, she heard Lucca say, "There, there, sweetheart."

"My work here is done." Gabi strutted down the hall toward the waiting room, Lucca's clipboard tucked beneath her arm. She couldn't wait to see what he'd written, but after she snooped, she'd put the notes someplace safe for the baby book.

She felt better in that moment than she had in the past six weeks. Then she sauntered into the waiting room . . . and spied her mother in a wheelchair, plus totally weird looks on the faces turned her way. "What is it? Mom, are you okay?"

"I'm afraid not. I broke my foot. I'm going to need surgery and screws."

"Oh, Mom. No. I'm so sorry!"

"Me too. I won't be able to help Hope with the children like I'd planned. I know she'll be fine. Lucca will be there. It's just that . . . I wanted to help."

Gabi took a seat beside her mother, then gave her a hug. "You know, this might work out better for you. You'll get full-time baby holding; you won't get shafted into doing laundry."

Maggie Romano patted her daughter's knee. "I'm glad to see you thinking so positively. It's nice to see you smile again, honey."

"And she hasn't even heard the exciting bit of news yet," Celeste piped up. "Zach, why don't you tell her?"

Gabi glanced up at her brother. Why was he and everyone—except Celeste—looking at her so strangely? "Tell me what?"

"Right before I learned that Mom had been hurt, I got a phone call from an attorney in Miami. He had a message for you."

For her? She didn't know any attorneys in Miami.

Then she figured it out. This had something to do with Bella Vita Isle. "Are the Fontanas suing me?"

"The dog has been found. He's okay."

Gabi took an inadvertent step toward Zach. "Bismarck? Flynn found Bismarck?"

"Somebody found him, the attorney didn't say who. The lawyer said he's skinny and has a few scratches and scars on him, but he's been living on an island not far from Bella Vita."

A weight as heavy as a chunk of Murphy Mountain granite lifted from her shoulders. Bismarck was alive! He'd survived! "Thank God. The Fontanas must be so thrilled."

"Apparently, not so much. The attorney said they didn't want him back."

"What?"

"The guy wasn't very complimentary about them. Anyway, the dog has a good home to go to, a home where he'd be cherished and, according to the lawyer, of significant help to the new owner, but knowing Bismarck's circumstances, he wanted to offer him to you, first."

"Oh." Gabi was taken aback. For one thing, she was disgusted with the Fontanas. The way they'd gone on and on about how much they cherished their puppy and how her irresponsibility had destroyed their happiness . . . they'd kicked her when she'd already been down. It must have all been a bunch of bunk if they didn't want poor Bismarck back now. "The Fontanas made me feel like dirt. Those jerks."

"Absolutely. So what do you want to do about the dog?"

That, she realized, was the reason for the strange looks she'd been receiving. What? Did they think she couldn't take good care of a dog? Gabi wasn't one to let things slide, so she confronted them. "Why are you all giving me those strange looks?"

Nic, Sarah, Sage, Cat, and Ali shared a glance. Zach, Savannah, and her mother shared their own. "What is it?" Gabi demanded. Then she knew. "It's Flynn, isn't it? The lawyer told you something about Flynn? You think I'm going to freak out if you tell me?"

"Something like that, yes," Savannah said.

Gabi scoffed, though inwardly she admitted they had good reason to be wary of her reaction. Her family knew the whole truth about her time on the island, but she'd kept the details about Flynn's true identity from her friends. Everyone in town knew about the attack on the *Dreamer* and that she'd been a basket case ever since. Her unpredictable behavior had kept everyone around her cautious about referencing her time on the island in any way whatsoever. She addressed Zach. "I'm fine. What have you learned?"

"Flynn Brogan will keep the dog if you're not anxious to have him. Apparently Brogan insisted that you not be told that he was the interested party and that you should keep the Newfie if you want him. But the attorney said that in this case, friendship trumped their attorney-client relationship, and that he wanted you to know that Bismarck and Brogan have bonded. He said Brogan needs the dog."

"Why?"

"I don't know. That's all he said. I actually quizzed him about it, but he'd said all he intended to say, and he zipped his lip."

Gabi considered that. Flynn had taken two lives that day aboard the *Dreamer.* Maybe he suffered some of the same sort of blues as she did. Maybe Bismarck soothed his troubled soul. "Flynn Brogan saved my life. If he wants Bismarck, he should have him."

As one, those gathered in the medical clinic waiting room appeared to heave a sigh of relief.

Celeste rose from her seat and enveloped Gabi in a

hug, then linked her arm through Gabi's and told her, "I'm craving a soda. Walk with me to the vending machine?"

Since her mother looked like she was ready to pounce on her, Gabi quickly said, "Sure. Glad to."

As they turned a corner, Celeste observed, "You're feeling better, aren't you, dear?"

"I'm getting there," Gabi answered honestly. Celeste was so easy to talk to; she knew just what to say to soothe a person's troubles. Gabi had found that spending an hour with Celeste Blessing helped her psyche more than two hours with a shrink. "I think. The funk comes and goes in waves now rather than flooding me like it did for a while."

"Time does heal all wounds."

"Time and Eternity Springs," Gabi quipped.

"True." Celeste fed a dollar bill into the drink machine, selected a can of soda, then fished her change from the coin slot. "So, is your recovery respite coming to an end? Has the time come for you to resume your glassblowing lessons?"

"Yes, but not on Bella Vita Isle. My mentor is traveling a lot and can't teach me anymore, but he has recommended me to an artist in California and one in Minnesota. I'm hoping to hear from one of them about a possible apprenticeship soon. But if those don't work out, I'll apply to some of the university programs and go back to college."

"This fall?"

"No. The spring semester would be the earliest I could get in." Thinking about the delay helped her make a decision. She fed coins into the machine and bought a Three Musketeers bar. "That's not a bad thing, though," she added, trying to convince herself it was true. "I'll have two little Romanos to cuddle and love on. I just don't know what I'll do to support myself in the meantime. Before I discovered my passion for glass, I had an idea to start a concierge business to offer services to the vacation homes in the area. If I'll be in Eternity Springs for a year, I may give that a try."

"Actually . . ." Celeste pursed her lips, took a sip of her soda, and said, "I suspect you'll have plenty of paying work to do for the next few months."

Gabi gave her friend a wary look. "What do you know that I don't?"

"I have a friend who suffered a Lisfranc fracture in her foot, the kind of injury your mother sustained. It proved to be a severe injury that took many months to heal and required surgery. It's a good bet that your mother will require a manager to take care of Aspenglow Place while she recovers."

Suddenly the candy bar tasted sour. "Seriously?"

"I'm afraid so. I was with your mother when Rose showed her the X-rays and referred her to an orthopedist. Maggie was distracted and wanting to rush back to the waiting room as Rose was trying to explain the extent of her injury. I could see Rose's expression when she decided to wait to press the issue."

"Oh, poor Mom," Gabi said. "Of course I'll help her."

"I know you didn't like working at the B&B before."

"That was different. I was looking for a direction in life then, thinking Aspenglow might be it. It wasn't. Now I have direction, and honestly, as anxious as I am to continue learning, I'm really not in a rush. I can certainly wait until Mom is ready to go back to work."

"My friend couldn't manage stairs for almost four months."

"Oh, dear," Gabi murmured as the implications of the injury became clear. "She won't be able to get up to her bedroom."

"Not unless she gets Richard to carry her up every night," Celeste observed.

Gabi shook her head. Her mother wouldn't want to do that. She'd told Gabi just yesterday that she'd encouraged Richard to make that move he'd been contemplating, and he was leaving Eternity Springs at the end of the month. Apparently he'd floated the subject of marriage, and Maggie had refused him. After over three decades of marriage that had brought her a great deal of pain along with the happiness, she was gun-shy.

Gabi had learned about her father's infidelity only recently, when her aunt Bridget had accidentally included her on an email she'd sent to her sister Maggie. It had been a hard pill to swallow and hadn't helped her mood of late.

"We can switch places," she said, thinking the problem through. "I'll move into Mom's bedroom suite for the duration, and she can move into my rental house. She won't like it, but it makes more sense than anything else."

Celeste gave her a beatific smile. "I knew you'd be there for your mother. You're a good daughter, Gabi."

She shrugged. "I'm also still a little shaky. It won't hurt me one bit to hang around Eternity Springs a little longer."

They returned to the waiting room and joined in a game of cards that Zach was beginning to deal. Celeste had just pulled in yet another pot, this time worth $3.47, when Holly's footsteps came pounding down the hallway. Everyone went on notice. Gabi and Zach rose to their feet, and Maggie folded her hands and brought them up to her mouth.

Holly called. "Nana! Gabi! Lucca and Mama said for you two to come quick if you'd like to join us. The baby is about to be born!"

"We get to watch?" Maggie gasped.

"What a gift," Celeste observed.

Gabi grabbed the handles of her mother's wheelchair

and hurried up the hallway. They entered the birthing suite just in time to hear Hope's obstetrician say, "Give me a big push now, Hope. You've got it. Attagirl."

Hope let out a shout, the baby began to cry, and a thrill rushed through Gabi. With one more push, a little boy slid into the physician's waiting hands.

"A boy," Lucca said, his voice rough.

"A brother!" Holly exclaimed.

Maggie Romano gripped Gabi's hand and squeezed it hard as the doctor laid the baby on Hope's torso and handed Lucca the scissors to cut the cord. Hope spoke softly, her voice cracking with emotion. "A son. We have a son, Lucca."

A pair of joyful tears rolling down his cheeks, Lucca Romano said, "Welcome to our world, little man."

Hope gently cradled her son against her. "My newest miracle."

ELEVEN

Gabi loaded the last of the breakfast dishes into the dishwasher at Aspenglow Place, added detergent, and started it. She turned to her mother with a smile. "Well, that was a success, don't you think?"

"Absolutely. You've come a long way in the culinary department, sweetheart."

"One could almost say I'm a good cook."

"Whoa, now," Lucca said as he entered the bed-and-breakfast's kitchen through the mudroom at the back, his baby in his arms. "That's a pretty big leap, sis. Don't you think you should be happy with the fact that you're not sending Mom's guests to the hospital with food poisoning?"

"Oh, shut up and hand over my nephew." Gabi swooped little Marc out of his father's arms to begin her morning baby-holding time.

In the two months since the baby's birth, the extended Romano family had adopted a routine that suited them all. Early every morning, Zach picked up his mother at Gabi's house and brought her to Aspenglow in time to get breakfast started. Gabi had coffee ready, and she and Maggie discussed the day's tasks over a cup at the kitchen table. Then they got to work, and Maggie taught her attentive-for-the-first-time-ever daughter how to cook.

After breakfast, Lucca would stop by with the baby. Maggie sat in her wheelchair and Lucca deposited his son into Maggie's arms, and then he pushed the wheelchair like a stroller back to Gabi's house for a nice morning outing. Following her foot surgery, Maggie had advanced to crutches and a medical walking boot, but she still wasn't up to taking a stroll through town.

Maggie could have remained at Aspenglow Place for the day, of course, but mother and daughter had figured out early in the process that if Gabi was going to act as temporary manager, then everyone was better off allowing her to do it on her own, in her own way. That's why Gabi was alone in the house shortly before noon when she answered a knock at the front door and all but keeled over in shock. "Cicero?"

"Hello, Legs." He held a fair-skinned, redheaded toddler, and he shifted the girl from one arm to the other. "I'm not sure that it's safe for the hoodlums to come inside. Could you meet us at that park down the street so you and I can talk?"

Her gaze went past the glass artist to Aspenglow's front yard, where a boy of about seven chased another boy of about five around the oak tree. Another girl, a little older than the boys, leaned against an SUV. "Cicero," she repeated dumbly. "You're here. In Eternity Springs. With children. I didn't know you had children."

"God forbid," he said with a shudder. "They're nephews and nieces. I'm babysitting. The little monsters' mom needs some time to herself. She's living in Texas now, and the kids said they wanted to go fishing in the mountains, so I thought we'd pay you a visit. So, the park? Can you meet us?"

"Uh, yes. Of course. Let me put a load of clothes in the dryer, and I'll be right there."

"Excellent."

He turned around and saw that the boys had quit

playing chase and were now throwing rocks at something hidden in the branches of the tree. "Drop the rocks, you heathens."

The older boy dropped it, all right, with a full-armed throw straight into the tree. Seconds later a squirrel raced down the trunk and dashed across the yard, away from the boys and toward safety.

No wonder Cicero looked so harried, she thought.

She hurried through her task in the laundry room, then hung the BE BACK SOON sign on the front door and headed toward Davenport Park. Her thoughts were in a whirl. Why was Cicero here? She didn't buy this "visit" business one bit.

Surely he didn't intend to ask her to watch the children for him while he did something else, did he?

"Oh, holy cow," she muttered. What would she do then? She had no experience with children. As much as she loved little Marc and the other Eternity Springs kiddos, being around them scared her to death. Having responsibility for them? No way. She couldn't even take care of a dog safely! Gabi wasn't a babysitter.

Still, she had direction in her life because of him. She owed him. "Whatever he wants, I'll have to paste on a smile and agree," she told herself as she approached the entrance of the park.

She found Cicero sitting on a bench while the boys climbed all over the fort made of logs and the older girl sat off by herself reading a book. Wearing a pink dress adorned with watermelons, the little girl was picking yellow dandelions, and Gabi couldn't help but think it one of the sweetest pictures she'd seen in some time. Cicero watched the children, looking as intense as he had when he was creating a sculpture for a former president of the United States.

Gabi's heart went out to him. He didn't look comfortable with the children. She hoped their mother didn't need time to herself very often. Cicero wasn't suited for playing parent. And speaking of parents, where was their dad? She took a seat beside Cicero and said, "Fancy meeting you here, boss."

"Yeah." His mouth twisted in a rueful smile as he patted the seat beside him. "Who woulda thunk it?"

"So what's the story?"

He drew in a lungful of air, then exhaled harshly. "I have a proposition to make you."

A proposition? What sort of proposition? "Look, Cicero, just because I'm not officially your student anymore doesn't mean that I want—"

"Not that kind of a proposition," he interrupted. "I'm Flynn's friend, not an asshole. Well, not about friends and their women, anyway. My proposition has to do with work. Will you listen?"

"Yes." She'd hold her comment about his having referred to her as Flynn's woman for another time.

"I have news and an opportunity to present to you. First, you are going to be offered the apprenticeship in California."

Gabi's heart leapt. She'd heard nothing from either the artist in California or the one in Minnesota. She'd all but given up on those. Just last night she'd printed out a college application to begin filling out.

"However," Cicero continued, "I don't want you to accept it. I have something better. Gabriella, how would you feel about spending a year on the glass island?"

"The glass . . . whoa." She sat up. "You mean Murano? Italy? A year in Italy?"

"I have a friend, my own mentor, who's a master artist, and he's willing to offer you an apprenticeship as a favor to me. You'd start in the middle of September and stay through the summer."

The middle of September. Zach's baby was due any day now, so she wouldn't miss that blessed event. She had absolutely no reason to refuse and every reason to jump at the opportunity.

Excitement swelled within her as she said, "Oh, wow. Oh, yes. Absolutely. Of course I'll go."

Her pulse raced and her thoughts spun with dozens of questions. An apprenticeship in Murano was the holy grail. Finally, the most immediate question made it from her mouth. "Why would you do this for me?"

"I'm looking down the road and hedging my bets. I've decided to move my studio from Bella Vita to Galveston in order to be closer to my sister. She has cancer. She's a fighter and she'll beat this thing, but she needs help."

"Oh, Cicero. I'm so sorry."

He curtly nodded his thanks, then pressed on. "Working in South Texas doesn't solve all the problems. The heat has been brutal on the island this summer, and it's negatively affected our productivity. Galveston won't be any better, but a satellite studio in a place where the weather is cooler could be the answer. I think this Eternity Springs of yours might fill the bill. I like it here. It's not too far from Texas, so Jayne and the demons could come and visit. They'll be happy to get away to the mountains again this time next year."

"You're saying you're going to build a studio in Eternity Springs?"

"Yeah. And I'll need a gaffer. Mitch is willing to move with me to Texas, but he's a sand and surf man. He wants to spend his winters on Bella Vita. I figure after a year of intense study with Alessandro, you should be ready to work with me."

"As your gaffer?" she said, gasping.

"Yeah. I'll have the studio ready by the time you come home. Then we can tackle your retail tourist shop idea. That's gotta be your baby, Gabi. I'll handle commission and gallery work like always, but the everyday knick-knack stuff, forget it. In fact, if you want to have a partnership agreement drawn up to reflect that, it'd probably be a good thing. Mitch and I work on a handshake, but he doesn't have overhead selling out of the market. We'll need to dot our *i*'s and cross our *t*'s if we're going to have a storefront."

"Partnership? Me? With you?"

"Sure. That's what you wanted, isn't it? Wasn't your idea to sell touristy stuff in this little burg?"

"Yes, but . . ." Gabi's thoughts whirled. A storefront. A partnership. A gaffer for Cicero! "Cicero, I don't have the money for start-up costs right now. I've done a little research on SBA loans, but I'm not there yet. And a year in Italy . . . it won't be cheap."

"You'll earn a stipend in Italy that will cover your basics. I'll provide start-up funds for the retail shop. It will have to pay for itself eventually, but I'm willing to give you time to find your feet. So, are you in?"

"Yes! Absolutely, I'm in! Thank you, Cicero."

"Thank you, Legs. This summer all but did me in. I'm hoping that next summer Eternity Springs might just save my sanity. We got in late last night and rented one of those cottages at the healing center, one of the ones by the creek. Got up and went fishing this morning. Kids were thrilled to be back in the mountains. They like it here."

"It's a wonderful town."

"That Celeste friend of yours . . . she's just about awesome. I swear, the kids acted as if they'd found their long-lost grandmother."

"She's a special woman, and she does love children. You might want to warn them, though, not to mess with her Gold Wing. Celeste dotes on that motorcycle of hers."

"I'll do that," he replied, rising to see why the younger boy had started crying.

Gabi found watching her temperamental mentor deal

with youngsters more than a little weird, but her mind quickly returned to this surprise that had fallen in her lap today. Italy. Learning from a master. Excitement and exhilaration bubbled up inside her like champagne. This was what she'd wanted for so long. A purpose. A passion of her own. The chance to build something of her own here in Eternity Springs, where she'd live her life surrounded by loved ones.

But not a lover.

Immediately her thoughts went to Flynn. Part of her wanted desperately to ask Cicero about him. Another part of her shied away from letting his name escape her lips. Her emotions remained a tangle where that man was concerned. She was trying to put him behind her and move forward. She'd even had a dinner date with the hot new manager up at Storm Mountain Ranch. But the whole time they'd conversed over chicken marsala at the Yellow Kitchen, she had looked into his brown eyes and thought of blue ones.

When Cicero approached the bench, she couldn't stop herself. "How is Flynn?"

His step slowed and a strange look passed across his face. He repeated, "Flynn? What do you mean, how is he?"

"I don't think it's a difficult question. The last time I saw him he had just killed two men in order to save our lives, and he had paparazzi staking out his every move because the world likes to think he killed his wife."

"Do you?" Cicero interrupted, studying her closely.

"Think he killed her?" Gabi shook her head. "No, of course not."

"You're certain?" he pressed, a look in his eyes that she simply couldn't read.

"Yes," she snapped. "Aren't you?"

"Well, yes. I admit when I first met him and realized who he was I had my doubts, but then I went fishing with him. I was with him when he fought a thrashing, four-hundred-pound marlin into the boat. You don't do that kind of fishing with a man and not figure out his mettle."

Gabi nodded. "I won't say my instincts about men are always right—heaven knows I've been blindsided in the past—but you don't survive a pirate attack with someone without learning a thing or two about them, either. Flynn didn't kill Lisa Seagraves."

"No, he didn't." Cicero took a seat beside her and said, "He's left Bella Vita."

Left Bella Vita? But he loved the island. Loved the sea. "Is he on a vacation?"

"No. I mean, he left for good. He sold everything and moved."

"He moved!" Gabi repeated, her stomach sinking. "Where?"

Cicero shrugged and evaded a direct answer. "I don't think he's settled on a place just yet."

"Oh." The news made Flynn seem farther away than ever to Gabi. When she'd allowed herself to think about him, she'd taken some comfort in picturing him on the Tradewinds beach. And in the middle of more than one sleepless night, she'd toyed with the idea of returning there to see him. "So did the paparazzi become too much for him to handle there?"

"Actually, since that latest Hollywood murder trial started, the paps disappeared. Guess they all flocked to California. That was a good break for him."

"Cold, Cicero."

"But true. Media demands fresh meat."

Was that the case with men, too? Had Flynn found another woman? Gabi winced, ready to change the subject. "So, tell me what sort of place you're looking for to convert into your studio. Maybe I'll know a place or two to suggest."

"Actually, I think I may have found it already. If the inside is anything like I imagine it is, it could be the perfect space."

"Tell me about it."

"It's on Cottonwood and Second. An old, boarded-up church. When I mentioned I would be looking for studio space, your friend Celeste suggested I take a look at it."

Gabi knew the exact building he meant. "That's the old Episcopal church. They outgrew it and built a new place. It's been for sale forever."

"Is the inside like a normal sanctuary?"

She nodded. "High ceiling. Beautiful stained-glass windows. I would never have thought about converting a church."

"Me either, but your friend said she'd considered buying the building herself but didn't have a use for it. She said it has great energy, and she's convinced it will feed our artistic souls."

"Well, if Celeste said that, then you should listen to her. She's never wrong about stuff like that." Gabi thought about it further, her excitement returning. "The rectory is attached. It's an awesome space for the retail shop, and the tourist traffic goes right past it. Oh, boss, I agree with Celeste. It'll be perfect."

"Okay, then, tell me where to look for a summer home. I'm not ready to buy now, but I might as well look around while I'm in town."

Gabi considered the question, mentally reviewing available houses in town. "The good thing is that real estate in Eternity Springs works on a bit of a different schedule than the rest of the country. We have a fair amount of seasonal residents and they tend to put their places up for sale at the end of the season. You have more to choose from then than at other times of the year."

"Anything with a padded room? The heathens will be visiting."

"For you or for the children?"

They heard a whack, then a pair of cries. One of the boys had abruptly changed direction and they'd run into each other and conked their heads. "Me. Definitely me."

When he rose to check on the kids once again, Gabi followed him to help. They brushed the boys off, their uncle Hunter reassuring them that their heads were not in fact broken, and soon the boys were off and running again. Cicero stood watching, his hands on his hips, shaking his head in exasperation.

Then the little girl rose from the sandbox where she'd been playing and approached her uncle, silently slipping her hand into his. Gabi watched, bemused, as he smiled gently down at the little girl and ask, "Can I do something for you, Daisy May?"

She nodded.

"What is it?" The little girl crossed her legs. "Okay. Gotcha." Cicero glanced at Gabi and muttered, "Potty training."

The notion of Cicero having anything to do with potty training boggled Gabi's mind.

He looked around for the older girl and called, "Misty? Daisy needs to go."

Without looking up from her book, Misty said, "You promised me no more diapers all day if I babysat this morning so you could sleep later."

Cicero muttered a curse, then glanced at Gabi. "Restrooms?"

She pointed toward the cinder-block building. "Over there."

"Okay. Any chance there's a family restroom?"

"Afraid not. I'll take her."

"Thank you." He twisted his mouth in a rueful smile. "The complications of life that I've never before contemplated. Daisy, my friend Gabi is going to help you, okay?"

The girl got a bit of a panicked look on her face. "It's okay, sweet pea. I won't move from this spot."

"C'mon, Daisy. I see my friend Sarah walking this way pushing her baby in a stroller. After we potty, we should go say hi. She owns a bakery here in town and she almost always carries cookies to give away to the local kiddos. I'll be sure to tell her that you count as local because your uncle is going to build a studio here."

Daisy beamed up at her, and Cicero nodded his thanks. Gabi oversaw potty time, then introduced Misty, Daisy, and the boys—Keenan and Galen, Gabi learned—and Cicero to Sarah Murphy and her son, Michael. Through it all, little Daisy never said a word, though she did give Gabi a little finger wave goodbye when they left.

Sarah waited until they were out of earshot to say, "That's your glass artist? Wow, Gabi. And he's moving to Eternity Springs? It's like Nathaniel Bumppo, live and in person, walking our fine streets."

"Who?"

"Daniel Day Lewis. He played Natty Bumppo—Hawkeye—in *Last of the Mohicans*. I swear, looking at him makes me hear the swell of the soundtrack. He must be smitten with you to move—"

"Nope. Forget about it, Sarah. We've already come to that understanding. It's not going to happen. He's Flynn's friend and besides . . ." She paused dramatically, then finished, "I don't date business partners."

Sarah's brows winged up. "Dish, girlfriend."

Gabi relayed the proposal Cicero had made, and as she did so, she could barely keep from giggling. She wanted to sing and spin her way across Davenport Park, à la Maria von Trapp in the Alps above Strasbourg. She might have done it had she not cared about the state of innocent little eardrums.

"That's awesome, Gabi. I'm so happy for you." Sarah

threw her arms around Gabi and gave her a hug. "I know this is what you've wanted."

"It is. It really is." It was a new start, a new chapter in her life. Something to look forward to so she could stop looking backward at Bella Vita Isle. Backward at Flynn.

It was time. Now she knew that for certain. Any thoughts she'd entertained about returning to Bella Vita were done. Flynn had decamped for parts unknown. He was gone. That dream was dead. She had a new, exciting dream to live.

No pirates or paparazzi prey allowed.

TWELVE

Thunder Valley, Colorado

Snowflakes floated from the sky like angel feathers from heaven, blanketing the small clearing around the cabin nestled deep in the forest. Flynn stood in the doorway with Bismarck at his side, wincing at the bright white of the snow and contemplating a trip to the woodpile. "What do you think, boy? Do we have enough wood to last us until tomorrow?"

The decision, like all decisions, was difficult for Flynn to make. It was as if he lived at the bottom of the sea and every thought, every movement had to be pushed through a world of dark, heavy water that made him sluggish and weak.

Bismarck let out a yip, then made the decision for Flynn by starting outside. Bismarck thrived in the cold. Sometimes even when the December temperatures hovered in the teens Flynn had to coax him inside with treats. Taking his cue from the dog, Flynn grabbed his coat from the hook beside the door and slipped into it, then pulled the eye patch off his head and replaced it with the dark sunglasses he kept on the small, rustic table beside the door. He stepped out into the frigid mountain air, which served as much as anything to illustrate just how much his circumstances had changed since the holiday season last year.

Last year he'd hosted Matthew and Margaret, their three children, and their seven grandchildren at Tradewinds over the Christmas holiday through New Year's. They'd filled the house with joy and excitement, delicious scents, and delightful sounds. It had been the nicest Christmas Flynn had spent in a very long time.

Matthew had lobbied hard for Flynn to join them this year at their home in Miami, but Flynn couldn't do it. He couldn't endure being around that many people, and besides, he didn't want to scare the children with his Frankenstein scars.

He'd grown a beard since leaving the hospital. His skin was still so tender that he'd put off shaving at first, and then when he'd let Matthew and Cicero talk him into wintering in the Rockies, he'd figured it made sense to keep it. Now with his hair longer, too, he fit the mountain man image quite nicely.

Not that there was anyone around to see it.

He'd lived here on a twelve-acre section of valley carved away from Storm Mountain Ranch since the first of October. The land was fenced and posted, and except for the UPS driver, he remained blissfully alone. Well, for the most part. Celeste Blessing knocked on his door occasionally. Cicero had showed up twice, and after Matthew's fourth visit in as many weeks, Flynn had put his foot down. He wasn't a damned invalid. Not anymore, anyway. He could see again. He could walk again. His friends both had work and families that needed their attention, so he'd told them they weren't welcome again until after the New Year.

"You're becoming a hermit," Cicero had accused on his recent visit.

"Yes," Flynn had replied, pointing at his eye patch.

"I'm a hermit slash mountain man slash pirate, and I couldn't be happier."

"I can't believe you joke about pirates."

"Like they say, if you can't beat them, join them."

"They didn't beat you, Flynn. You're still standing."

"With a limp."

"Well, it's not a damned peg leg."

The way it ached some days, Flynn almost wished it were.

Then, because apparently torture was his new thing, Flynn had asked Cicero about Gabi.

His excuse was that he wanted to be sure that she was happily installed in Italy. The last thing he needed was to turn down an aisle at the Trading Post and bang his cart into hers. Not that he spent too much time in town. Online shopping was his friend.

Cicero had given him a long, skeptical look before updating Flynn on Gabi's activities in the most romantic city in the world. Knowing that she loved her new life both pleased Flynn and plagued him with what-ifs during the long, cold winter nights.

"Don't go there," Flynn warned himself aloud as he trekked through the snow toward the woodpile. He could deal with pirates, but that direction could lead to dragons.

Ahead of him, Bismarck was a flash of black on white as he played in the drifts. Watching him, Flynn felt his spirits lift a bit and a rare smile form on his lips. He wouldn't try to deny that this move had been a good thing for his dog. For Bismarck's sake, if not his own, the decision to come to Colorado for the winter had been sound. Bismarck was much, much happier in the cold than he'd been in the tropical heat of Bella Vita or even Miami.

He picked up the axe, placed a log on the tree stump that served as his chopping block, and began to work.

He could have used a chain saw, of course, but the physical exertion felt good. The physical therapist in the rehab hospital had worked Flynn's ass off in order to rebuild his muscles, which had atrophied after being bedridden for too damned long, so he wasn't a weakling anymore. He was glad that one part of his body worked. His mind was proving rusty.

He swung the axe, split the wood. Over and over. He paused a moment to wipe his sweaty brow, and he realized the snow had stopped falling. This was a pretty place. A peaceful place.

Peaceful . . . up to a point.

His gaze shifted toward his workshop, which so far was worthless. At least every other day he woke up with the full intention of going to work. He'd actually made it into the workshop on four different occasions. Each time, his mind remained in mothballs.

And that totally sucked. When it happened, Flynn felt as if he'd lost absolutely everything. As a result, he found it harder and harder to make the walk to the workshop. He was finding it harder and harder to get out of bed each day, too. If not for Bismarck, he might not do it.

"Can you be any more pitiful?" he muttered, his breath fogging on the cold air. He swung the axe a little harder next time. He continued swinging hard until he'd cut enough wood to outlast a three-week blizzard and had worn his arms, shoulders, and back completely out. He stood staring at the split logs splayed across the ground, debating whether he had the energy to gather any up and take them inside, when he heard the sound of an approaching vehicle.

Hmm. Didn't sound like the UPS truck. Cicero and Matthew knew better than to show up until after New Year's. Had Celeste Blessing decided to make a run at him again? She'd become quite the pest with her visits and invitations, though he had to admit he'd enjoyed that angel food cake she'd dropped off last week. She hadn't recognized him as either the man she'd visited on Bella Vita or the GQ killer, thank goodness, and that made him wish he'd grown a beard two years ago.

He figured she must be this friendly to every newcomer to the area. Maybe that was simply her nature. She'd certainly been kind to him when she'd shown up at Tradewinds. Nevertheless, he didn't want her hanging around Thunder Valley. He'd thought he'd put her off until after Christmas at least, when he'd agreed to attend her Christmas Eve open house. Flynn let out a long sigh, and his breath clouded on the cold mountain air. Had she figured out he didn't have any intention of showing up?

But the vehicle that drove out of the forest into his clearing didn't belong to Celeste. "This day just keeps getting better and better," he muttered as he leaned on his axe handle and watched the approach of the white SUV adorned with a light bar on the roof and a seal and the word SHERIFF on the doors.

Bismarck bounded to Flynn's side as a tall man wearing a cowboy hat, a blue coat identifying him as the sheriff, jeans, a gun belt, and boots exited the truck. He walked through the snow toward Flynn in a loose-limbed stride that Flynn recognized. Upon getting his first good glimpse of the sheriff's face, Flynn confirmed that he was about to meet Gabi's brother, Zach Turner. The family resemblance couldn't be denied.

Well, he'd figured this visit would happen sometime. In fact, he'd expected to see the sheriff during his first two weeks in Thunder Valley. "Hello there, neighbor," Zach called.

Neighbor, my ass, Flynn thought as Gabi's brother approached, his hand extended. Flynn ignored the offered handshake and rested his free hand on Bismarck's head. "Sheriff."

"Good-looking dog you have there."

"Yes, he is. This is Bismarck. But then, you know that, don't you, Sheriff Turner?"

Zach braced his hands on his hips and studied Flynn. "So, that's the way this is gonna be? Straight and to the point?"

"You tell me. You're the one who invited yourself onto my land."

"Okay. That approach works for me. What the hell are you doing in Eternity Springs, Brogan? Why the disguise?"

Flynn smirked. "I was invited, and my beard keeps my face warm. It's winter."

"Did my sister invite you?"

"No. Gabriella doesn't know I'm here. Your town ambassador invited me."

The sheriff folded his arms. "Celeste?"

"Yes."

"So why did you accept the invitation?" Blue eyes hauntingly similar to Gabi's glared accusingly from beneath the wide brim of his hat. "Are you thinking to insert yourself back in Gabi's life?"

"You can back down, Sheriff Guard Dog. I know she's in Italy. This valley is isolated. She doesn't need to know that I'm here. I very much don't want her to know that I'm here."

"She's coming back."

Flynn's spine stiffened in alarm. "I thought she wasn't returning until summer."

The sheriff shrugged. "Summer will be here before we know it."

"I'll leave by then." Or he'd tell everyone he was leaving, build a gate to keep the trespassers out, and simply drive a little farther to buy his groceries.

The sheriff looked at Flynn hard as if trying to see past the lenses of his sunglasses and straight into his soul. "Could we go inside, Brogan?"

Flynn was so tired he feared he might just fall down, but he didn't want Gabi's brother inside his home. "What, you couldn't find probable cause for a search warrant?"

Zach rolled his eyes in exasperation. "I don't want to search your house. I want to get out of the damned cold!"

Flynn let half a minute tick by while he made his decision. He could send Turner on his way; if he did that, he figured, the sheriff would probably go. He also figured Turner would likely be back. Wouldn't it be better to get it over with and put a stop to any further contact with the Romano family once and for all?

The devil on his shoulder whispered in his ear, *If that's what you really want, then why did you move to freaking Eternity Springs?*

Flynn wanted to bury that devil here and now, so he said, "All right. Come inside."

As he led Gabi's brother toward the log cabin, Flynn didn't try to hide his limp. Once inside, he kept his eyes closed as he removed his sunglasses and set them in their usual spot on the table. He found the eye patch in its spot and put it on, then turned to face the sheriff.

Zach Turner asked, "What are your intentions, Brogan?"

He couldn't help but snort. "Well, I intend to fry a hamburger for my supper. That's about as far ahead as I look."

"Toward my sister. Your intentions toward Gabriella. I know you had an affair. She . . . invested."

"That's over. We're over. You don't have to worry about that, Turner. It's fair to say that the one intention I still have in my life is to never see your sister again."

Except for in his memories. He still could see her there, where she was safe and happy and he was whole.

"Why should I believe you?" Zach asked. "Look at the evidence. You moved to her hometown."

Flynn knew the fastest way to cut through the bull. What was a little more embarrassment and humiliation after everything he'd been through? He didn't want to do it, but the quicker this was over, the better. He pulled off his coat, hung it on its peg, and didn't hesitate as he began to unbutton his flannel shirt.

With his back to the door, he flipped on the cabin's central light, gritted his teeth, and took off his shirt and undershirt.

Zach Turner's gasp was audible. "Holy shit, man. What happened . . ." The question died away as Flynn turned around and the sheriff got a look at his chest and then his face. "Oh, my God. What happened to you?"

"It doesn't matter. What you need to know is that I am no threat to Gabriella. I'm not the man I was last spring. I won't pursue her."

"I'm so sorry. I . . . wow. What you must have gone through."

"Pity rubs me the wrong way, Sheriff. The bottom line is that I survived."

Zach let that sink in a moment, then asked, "Did the attack on you have anything to do with what happened aboard your boat?"

Just get it over with, Brogan. He won't leave you alone until you do. "The father of one of the men I killed on the *Dreamer* that day exacted revenge. It left me beaten up, torn up, and a little bit crazy. I came to Eternity Springs because your sister and her friend Celeste said it has a healing energy, and frankly, the hospital had run out of tricks."

Zach's voice emerged low and solemn and serious. "Were you blinded?"

"Temporarily. I now have sight in both eyes, but I'm very sensitive to light." He motioned toward the eye patch. "This eye in particular."

As Flynn began pulling on his shirt, Zach's gaze lowered to Flynn's legs. "I noticed a limp."

"Pins, rods. Airport security is gonna be a bitch for me from here on out." Flynn wanted desperately to sit down, but his pride wouldn't let him. He did, however, grab the back of a chair for support.

"They used a knife?"

He nodded, not bothering to mention the burning sticks or the hammers.

"Gabi doesn't know?"

"No, she doesn't. And I'll ask you to keep it that way."

"Wait a minute. I don't lie—".

"I'm not asking for a lie. I'm asking for your silence, and you owe me. I saved your sister's life."

"She would want to know."

Testily Flynn responded, "Like the song says, you can't always get what you want."

Zach's mouth flattened in a grim line, but he showed no sign of retreat. "Mind if I sit down while we debate this?"

Frustrated by the man's tenacity, Flynn sighed and shrugged. "My log cabin is your log cabin."

The sheriff pulled a chair away from the kitchen table and straddled it. Zach observed, "It's true you saved her life, but one could argue that you put her into jeopardy to begin with by taking her on that godforsaken sailing trip."

"One could argue that. Look, Turner, I hate what happened to Gabi on the boat that day. It will haunt me until the day I die. However, it doesn't negate the fact that I killed two men before they managed to rape her. Give me your silence now, and that will be the last you hear from me."

Zach rubbed the back of his neck. "I don't know. . . ."

Flynn played his last card. Taking a seat at the table opposite Gabi's big brother, he spoke seriously and sincerely. "Knowing this happened to me would hurt Gabi. You know it would. Despite all my failings, she would be troubled by this news. She's too tenderhearted. You'll be doing her a kindness by sparing her the knowledge."

"I don't like secrets, Brogan. They're destructive."

"She would feel obligated. She'd want to try to fix it. To fix me. You know that's true. That's how Gabi is. But she's moved on with her life, Turner. She's pursuing her dream. Don't screw that up."

It was vital that Flynn win this argument. He couldn't see Gabi. He especially didn't want her to see him like this. It would destroy him. Never mind that she was still his first thought in the morning and the last each night before he slept. He was toxic, and he wouldn't hurt her further. "It's over for us both. Allow it to stay that way. Please."

Zach rose and walked to the window where outside, snow drifted from the sky once more. He stood unmoving for a long moment, then asked, "You'll leave before she comes home?"

"I will."

"Okay, then. It goes against my nature, but I won't tell Gabriella that you're here. I am going to tell my wife because I don't keep secrets from Savannah, but she'll keep it to herself. That woman could give the NSA lessons on keeping secrets." Zach lifted his hat off the rack where he'd left it upon entering the cabin, then once again, offered his hand for a handshake.

This time Flynn responded, his grip firm and sure.

"I won't bother you again, but if you ever need a sheriff or assistance of any kind, just holler. I left my card. It has my direct number. Use it if you need it."

"Thanks."

"Good luck, Brogan. I wish you well. I hope Eternity Springs does manage to work its magic on you."

Zach was halfway to his truck when Flynn called out. "Hey, Sheriff. Did you and your wife have that baby?"

Zach's huge smile warmed all of Thunder Valley. "We sure did. We had a healthy little girl."

"What's her name?"

"Grace. We named her Grace."

"Congratulations, Zach Turner. You are a lucky man."

After the sheriff's SUV had disappeared into the forest, Flynn contemplated leaving the wood where it lay and taking a nap. He was exhausted, physically and emotionally. He glanced at the clock. Only eleven. He should go out and gather enough wood for tonight at least, then eat a sandwich and take a nap. An afternoon nap was nothing to be ashamed of. A morning nap was different.

"All right, Bismarck. Time for another snow frolic."

Flynn ended up working for another hour, gathering wood for the wood box inside, then stacking the extra on the nearly depleted woodpile. With the task finally finished, he looked around for Bismarck. The dog loved to roam and explore, but he never went beyond the clearing into the trees. Sure enough, he was rooting at the base of a pine tree at the edge of the forest off to the west. Flynn let out a whistle, and the Newfie came bounding toward him.

Inside, he took a shower, then went to make a sandwich for lunch and frowned at the offerings in his refrigerator. He was down to the last of the deli meats and cheese. "Dammit, Biz, we'll have to make a supply run."

He glanced out the window, where the wind-driven snowfall brought blizzard conditions to mind. "We can put it off until tomorrow. The weather forecast calls for the snow to stop by midnight tonight. We will need to go in the morning, though, because tomorrow's Christmas Eve. I imagine all the stores will start locking up early."

He didn't mind the trips into Eternity Springs as a rule. Now, however, a trip to town meant braving the over-the-top Christmas decorations that hung everywhere a man turned. He simply wasn't in the mood.

After lunch, he lay down for the long-promised nap, but his mind wouldn't empty long enough to drift off. He replayed Zach Turner's visit a dozen times. Pictured Gabi in a glass studio in Venice two dozen times. Imagined himself, as the man he had been before the attack, with Gabi in a bedroom above a glass studio in Venice, and the thoughts went on long enough to make him need to take a naked dive into a snowbank.

The fantasies chased him out of bed, and self-disgust drove him to make another stab at accomplishing something, anything, in his workshop. Before he could change his mind, he pulled on his coat once more, snapped his fingers for Bismarck, and walked back out into the driving snow.

The workshop was a converted barn with tools of every kind imaginable, welding equipment, stacks of raw materials, and a computer powerful enough to impress even the geekiest of geeks. In addition to plenty of pacing room, it had a chalkboard, a whiteboard, his favorite office chair—a La-Z-Boy recliner—and a sound system recommended by Sam Wilcox himself. The workshop had been equipped with everything Flynn needed, wanted, or desired.

Except ideas with which to work.

He had realized that of all his losses, this was the most devastating. For almost all of his life, he'd had notions and thoughts and suppositions flittering through his mind like confetti. True, he hadn't always paid attention to them. He'd intentionally muted them when he was up to his ass growing the business side of Seagraves-Laraby. But they'd always been there. Even when Lisa had died. Even during the trial.

They'd gone silent that godawful night on the beach. It was like a black shroud surrounded him, and he and his ideas couldn't fight their way out. Yet.

He wasn't giving up. Flynn had to believe they wouldn't stay silent. His sight was coming back, wasn't it? The shadows faded a little more every week, he tolerated light better each week. Surely the ideas would return, too.

It was that tiny flicker of hope that had him holding the workshop door open for Bismarck before stepping inside. He hung his coat on a hook, turned up the heat, lit a fire in the hearth, then picked up a copy of *Popular Mechanics* and began to flip through it, seeking something, anything, that interested him.

Nada.

"Okay, try something else." He sat down at the computer, pulled up his StumbleUpon home page, and decided to try the word "valve." But as he set his fingers to the keyboard, his gaze fell upon the photograph of a basketball player. In an instant his mind engaged, though in a different direction from what he had sought. Not with a fantasy this time, but with a memory.

"I just love March Madness," Gabi said, watching him fill a large paper bucket with popcorn from the movie-theater-style popcorn machine he'd installed in the media room at Tradewinds. "Even when we're not involved as a family, it's still my favorite sporting event of the year."

Flynn chose two Kölsch beers from the mini-fridge and poured them into glasses. "What is your favorite part of the Dance?"

"All of it," she replied, her face glowing with excitement as she plopped down into one of the theater chairs, popcorn bowl in her lap, and accepted the beer with a smile. "'Madness' is the perfect word for it. It's the excitement and the energy of players and coaches and fans. What other sport gives you the opportunity to root hard for a team you couldn't find on a map to save your life, one you'd never heard of before Selection Sunday, knowing there's a chance they'll topple one of sport's giants? It's thirty-two games in two days! It's who gets to wear the slipper, who—"

"Slipper?" Flynn interrupted.

"Cinderella. Who will be that year's Cinderella team. And of course, it's bracketology."

"Brackets are my favorite part of March Madness," Flynn admitted.

Gabi sipped her beer and gave him a considering look. "How many bets do you have out? How many different brackets?"

He smothered a grin and attempted to dodge the question. "I'm not a gambler, Gabi."

"Everybody bets on March Madness. Even the knitting group in Eternity Springs has a March Madness pool going on."

"Well, there's our bet, of course, which has to be my favorite bracket bet ever. I do so look forward to watching you mow my lawn."

She laughed. "You're dreaming, big guy. You might as well stock up on soapsuds now. You'll be giving Bismarck his baths from now until the Fontanas come home. So, what other pools are you in? The one at the public market?"

"Yes."

"The one at the marina?"

"Yes."

"Any online?"

Four. One of which had a pretty hefty bet. *"Sure. Just for fun."*

"Hah. You're as much a part of the insanity as me."

He was insanely attracted to this bright, beautiful, bubbly personality who had swept into his world and chased the shadows away. The night's games began, and they settled down in front of the screen. She was delightful company for watching sports, knowledgeable and interested. He couldn't help but compare her to his wife. Lisa had liked to go to games with him when they were in college, but after they married, her interests changed. She preferred arts over sports. For a while he attended her gallery openings and she tailgated with him. He hadn't noticed when that stopped, or when they began living their lives so separately. Looking back now, he could pinpoint it to when she'd told him she'd changed her mind about wanting children.

Impulsively, he asked Gabi, *"Do you want kids?"*

"To do what? Pick brackets?"

Idiot, he chastised himself, and hastened to change the subject. *"Never mind. Say, I forgot the butter. Do you want melted butter on your popcorn?"*

"You have melted butter, too? Yes, please. How awesome is this? It's like a real theater—only with hoops!"

Bella Vita Isle didn't have a movie theater, so Flynn had created his own. *"I keep meaning to order in big boxes of Junior Mints. Maybe have a jar of dill pickles."*

"Oh, I always bought dill pickles at the movies. They were the cheapest thing at the concession stand, and my brothers hated them, so I didn't have to share. They were popcorn hogs. I never got as much as I wanted."

"In that case, consider the popcorn machine here yours to sample freely."

"You are a prince, Flynn Br . . . whoa. Did you see that three-pointer? Guy can't miss from downtown!"

Gabi grew focused on the game at that point. Flynn gently pried the popcorn bucket out of her grasp, added plenty of melted butter, then gave it back to her as she muttered, "Defense. Where's the defense?"

He watched her more than he watched the game, the way she shifted in her seat as the ball was passed on the court, the gestures she made with her hands. The expressive faces she made, the gasps and the groans. "For crying out loud, Longhorns. If you don't step it up, you're going to bust my bracket!"

She seduced him without trying and without awareness. When she tossed another few kernels of popcorn into her mouth, and her tongue darted out to lick the slick butter from her lips, he could stand it no more.

She squealed in surprise when Flynn scooped her up out of her chair and returned to his own seat with her in his lap, saying, "I know a little bit about those colleges in Texas. The University of Texas Longhorns, the TCU Horned Frogs, the Baylor Bears. One of my friends in grad school got his undergrad degree from Texas A&M. He told me the Aggies have a tradition that I thought was the best collegiate tradition I've ever heard of. He said when the Aggies score, the fans do, too. They get to kiss their dates." He glanced at the screen. "The 'Horns just put up a three."

He started to lower his mouth to hers, but Gabi put up a hand. "Wait, Flynn. That doesn't work. The Aggies and Longhorns are mortal enemies."

"What do we care? I'm a Georgia Bulldog and you're a Connecticut Husky. C'mere, Lassie." He took her mouth in a long, lingering, thorough kiss.

When they finally came up for air, Gabi said, "I love college sports."

A wet muzzle sniffing at his ankles jerked Flynn back to the here and now. As his hand went down to pet his dog, he could almost smell the popcorn drifting in the air of his workshop. He felt a sudden yearning to be with people. Not to speak to them or get involved in any way, but simply to be around someone other than himself. "Maybe we'll go on into town and hit the Trading Post this afternoon after all. What's a little snowstorm in the Rockies in December, anyway? We have snow tires. What could go wrong?"

Flynn knew the minute the words left his mouth that he'd made a mistake. Saying something like that invited trouble. But the fact that he had said them meant that he couldn't call off the trip now. That would push him totally over into the wuss department.

He might be scarred, half blind, broken, and blue, but he wasn't a wuss.

Twenty minutes later, with Bismarck beside him in the passenger seat of his pickup, happily gnawing one of the rawhide bones Flynn provided to keep him occupied in the truck, they left the property and turned toward town. The snowstorm had strengthened and, as was his luck, visibility had decreased. He called upon rusty skills learned while driving in Ann Arbor to navigate the twisting mountain road, but he managed it, and they arrived in Eternity Springs without mishap.

The streets were as busy as he'd seen them since he'd moved to Colorado. It was just two days before Christmas, and people were rushing to purchase last-minute gifts; probably some were just beginning their holiday shopping. The parking lot for the grocery store was packed, forcing him to park a block away. Glancing at his dog, he said, "This might take a little longer than I'd planned, boy, but I'll buy a steak with your name on it for being a patient dog."

Bismarck didn't bother to look up from his bone.

Flynn climbed out of his car and sauntered up Aspen

Street toward the store. As was his habit when passing the sheriff's office and Aspenglow Bed and Breakfast—places he associated with Gabi—he looked the other way. It was just easier.

That's why he didn't see the woman hurrying up the path to Aspenglow's front door pulling two large rolling suitcases.

THIRTEEN

Gabi's gaze snagged on the bearded man who loped along on the opposite side of the street. Something about him struck a chord with her. Was Bear, a former Eternity Springs resident and mountain-man taxidermist, paying another visit from South America with his wife? Maybe he was bringing stuffed parrots for the collection he'd donated to the school.

Then she dismissed him and turned her attention to the matter at hand—her surprise visit home for Christmas.

She was excited and wanted to giggle. Her mother was going to squeal like a teen girl at a boy band concert. She'd been so sad that Gabi wasn't coming home. She'd even offered to buy the plane ticket herself, but Gabi was too proud to accept that. Instead she'd shopped for deals and found flights with sometimes scary connections, but ones that didn't break her bank. She'd bid her hosts *buon natale* and begun the travel odyssey that ended—she lifted her hand and rang the bell, heard her mother's footsteps approach, heard the doorknob turn—now.

"Gabriella Brianna!"

But Maggie Romano didn't squeal like a teenager. She burst into tears. Loud, boisterous, distressing tears. "Mom! What's wrong?"

"You're here!"

"Yeah . . . ?" Gabi released the handles of her suit-cases.

"You said you weren't going to be here!" Maggie cried.

"I found a way to get here. Is there a problem, Mom?"

"Yes, there's a problem! I have two lovely new daughters-in-law and two glorious new grandbabies and a successful new business that I love and life is won-derful. I've been so blessed. But . . . but . . ."

Gabi took charge, abandoning her suitcases and step-ping inside, placing her hands firmly on her mother's shoulders and moving her toward the living room. "Calm down, Mama," she soothed, gently pushing Maggie's shoulders to guide her to sit on the sofa. "Tell me what's going on."

"It's Christmas!"

Oh, this was the annual Christmas meltdown. One year she'd cried over the fact that the grocery store had run out of yellow sprinkles for her sugar cookies. She'd had red and green, but what was Christmas without yel-low sugar cookie sprinkles?

"I know you think that this is my annual Christmas meltdown, but it's not."

"Okay."

"You kids just don't get it. You are all in that stage of life where your life expands to include new people, new loves. It's exciting and special. Yes, it poses challenges as far as holiday scheduling goes. You want to be in your own homes, beginning your own holiday traditions. As well you should. That's what life is all about."

Okay, she's obviously not talking about me right now. I'll be here on Christmas morning. Who won't be?

"But what you kids don't realize is that this is a time of loss for people my age, and we mourn it. I love my grandchildren, don't get me wrong, but I loved my babies, too. I loved Christmas morning and Santa Claus. I adored opening the windows of the Advent calendar with you all. I loved our family traditions to the very marrow of my bones."

"I know, Mom," Gabi said, sitting next to her.

"And I loved spending the holidays with my mother and my father. And with your father. Those days are over. Those people are gone."

Tears stung Gabi's eyes, and she reached over and hugged her mother. "I miss them, too."

"I know you do. All of you children do. But you miss them from your point of view. You don't miss them from mine. You don't know about working Christmas Eve with my mom in gift wrap at the local department store. You can't understand what it's like to remember coming home from midnight mass on Christmas Eve, then staying up all night to put scooters and bicycles together. They were wonderful times, and I miss them so much."

Gabi was at a loss about how to respond. "I'm sorry, Mom. I guess I've never thought about it in that way."

"Well, you should think about it. You should all think about it. Because it's time for me to make new traditions, Gabi. I'm not dead yet. Things have to change. You and your brothers will have to accept that. You won't like it, but it's a taste of what's to come. Life moves on whether we want it to move on or not."

"Okay," Gabi said. "That makes total sense, Mom. What do you want to change?"

Maggie filled her lungs with air, then exhaled in a rush. "This will be the last Christmas dinner I cook for the family. It's time. You can do it or one of your sisters-in-law can do it from now on. You can rotate. You can all go out to a restaurant if that's what everyone wants."

Restaurant? This is beyond meltdown! Whoa. Gabi sat back against the sofa. No more Mom's Christmas dinner? The whole idea made her want to cry. The fact that she wanted to cry made her feel like she was eight years old. "Mom, what is going on?"

"I'll continue to bring your grandmother's cake," Maggie continued, "although I should teach you how to make it so that you'll have it on the years I don't join you all for Christmas."

Now Gabi sat up straight. "What do you mean, the years you don't join us?"

"Next year I'm going away for the holidays. I'm not sure where I'll go or how I'll go or even who I'll go with, but I'm going to fill my holiday season with new and exciting things, and look forward instead of backward!"

Gabi blinked. It was if she'd been kicked in the gut. "Well. Welcome home, honey."

At that, her mother's eyes went wide and she clapped her hands over her mouth. "Oh, Gabi. I'm so sorry. That was just . . . oh, I'm a terrible mother." Maggie flung her arms around Gabi and hugged her tight. "I am truly so glad to see you. This is the best surprise. I was so dreading not having you with us tomorrow. Thanksgiving simply wasn't right without you. I couldn't have asked for a better gift for Christmas than to have you here with us."

Gabi patted her mother's back and wondered just what had been happening in Eternity Springs in her absence. Seriously, where were the boys when all this was going on? The Christmas meltdown had seemingly morphed into a midlife crisis, but why? *I go to Italy and my mother goes nuts.*

Maggie kissed Gabi's cheek and begged, "Forgive me for being such a dweeb."

"Dweeb, Mom?" Gabi tried to joke. "You're never a dweeb. Sometimes you're a dork. I could be persuaded to forgive you—for the price of a piece of Nana's Italian cream cake."

Maggie sniffed and wiped away the last of her tears.

"Blackmail on the day before Christmas Eve? Don't you worry that Santa won't come visit?"

"Naw." Gabi waited until her mother's gaze met her own to add, "I know that no matter what and no matter where, I can always count on Santa Claus."

Love shone in Maggie's eyes, and her tremulous smile reached into Gabi's heart. "Let's go into the kitchen and see what we might find on the cake stand."

As Gabi followed her mom into the kitchen, she reflected on the ever-changing landscape of their mother-daughter relationship. It had always been a good one. They had weathered Gabi's teens fairly easily, most likely because they'd been the only females in a household bursting at the seams with men, so they'd had little choice but to be allies. Her early twenties had been more difficult because they had to learn how to love each other as adults, but they'd managed. Now that thirty lurked just around the corner, Gabi found that her struggle was to view her mother as a still-young widow in her mid-fifties with a lot of life ahead of her.

But that meant letting go of the stay-at-home mom whose life revolved around her family.

Watching her mother slice two generous servings of Italian cream cake here on the eve of Christmas Eve, Gabi couldn't help but think of the Bible verse that in her mind was always recited to the music of the Byrds: *To every thing there is a season, and a time to every purpose under the heaven. A time to be born, and a time to die; a time to plant, and a time to pluck up that which is planted.*

Guess it's now reaping season for Romano holiday traditions, she thought as she took a bite of the famous Romano family Italian cream cake and failed to enjoy it quite as much as usual.

What a full year this past year had been. So much had happened in a relatively short time. Finding Holly, Lucca and Hope's wedding, two new Romano babies. Gabi's trip, her trials, her new direction.

And Flynn. Where was he this Christmas season? Was he happy? Did he have someone new to spend Christmas with? Did he ever think of her?

It served as the beginning of a bittersweet holiday for Gabi. Her brothers Max and Tony showed up just as she finished wrapping all her gifts and gave her that shocked-but-joyful welcome she'd flown across the Atlantic anticipating. When Zach and Savannah arrived with beautiful little Grace, she teared up and cried like her mother. Then Lucca and Hope arrived with Holly and six-month-old Marc, and soon the rooms of Aspenglow Place rang with laughter.

Even as Gabi participated in the festivities, a part of her remained separate and observant. The emotions rolling through her were different from what she'd experienced during the first holiday season following the death of her father. That had been grief. This was something different and difficult to define, a weird combination of joy and sadness, grief and gratitude, love and . . . more love.

For the first time, she got a glimpse of the holidays through her mother's eyes, and she got an inkling of the real reason behind so many of Maggie's Christmas meltdowns.

The next day, as had become their family tradition since Eternity Springs became the hub of the Romano family, they attended Celeste Blessing's Christmas Eve gathering at Angel's Rest. Her friends and neighbors were delighted to see her. No tears there, thank goodness. The little kids were so excited and just too darned cute dressed in their Christmas finery.

After filling a cup with spiced cider, Gabi wandered into the parlor—the "angel room," where the tree and holiday trimmings were done in shades of white and gold and every furnishing, accessory, and decoration tied into the theme of angels. There she found the Callahan twins wearing matching red velvet dresses and white tights and staring up in wonder at the angel figurine tree topper.

"She's the most beautiful angel I've ever seen," Cari Callahan observed.

"We better do what we can to keep Papa B. out of here," her sister, Meg, suggested. "You know how Papa B. is. He's liable to try to touch it, and he'd break it and Miss Celeste would be so sad."

Gabi followed the kindergartners' gazes to the topper. After four months in Italy, where her education had included personal guided tours of some of the great art collections Italy had to offer, Gabi looked at objects like the figurine atop the tree with a critical eye. As far as she was concerned, this fine porcelain, hand-painted angel wouldn't be out of place in the Uffizi. "She is gorgeous," Gabi observed, joining the twins' conversation. "There is joy in her face. She reminds me of Miss Celeste."

"My middle name is Joy," Meg said.

"I think she has faith in her face, too," Cari declared.

"You're just saying that because your middle name is Faith," Meg fired back. "What do you think, Miss Gabi?"

"I look at that angel, and I see joy and faith and hope and grace."

Cari clapped her hands. "Holly's mom and Sheriff Zach's baby girl!"

Gabi laughed, then turned when Celeste entered the room accompanied by a distinguished-looking elderly gentleman wearing a holiday red vest beneath a well-tailored gray suit. The girls gasped with alarm, then said, "Papa B., you can't touch the Christmas tree!"

"Why not? I want to see if an elf will fall out if I shake it."

"Papa B.!" the twins exclaimed, horror-struck.

Branch Callahan's hearty laughter and twinkling eyes made him look the part of Santa Claus on this Christmas Eve. "Unfortunately, we don't have time to test this tree. Your parents are looking for you, girls. We have to bust our britches to get to church in time to get a good seat in the back for the children's service."

"Good seats aren't in the back, Papa," Meg scolded as she took his left hand.

"That's right," Cari agreed, taking his right. "Daddy says the best seats are the ones behind the support column where the minister can't see you when you fall asleep."

"I knew I raised me a smart boy in my John Gabriel," Branch Callahan drawled, the Texas sound strong in his voice. He winked at Gabi and Celeste. "Thanks for another lovely Christmas Eve gathering, Celeste."

"I'm so glad you were able to join us," Celeste drawled right back, her voice full of Carolina.

Once the Callahans had departed, Celeste turned to Gabi. "It has been a lovely party, hasn't it? I do have one regret, however. My only regret is that our newest permanent resident didn't accept my invitation to join us."

"We have a new resident? Someone moved here this time of year?"

"Yes. Not long after you left for Italy. He keeps to himself, and while he isn't rude, he's not friendly by any stretch of the imagination. I've made overtures, but he politely rebuffs me. He seems very much alone. Very sad."

Gabi's brows arched. She seldom met anyone who managed to rebuff Celeste Blessing. "So who is he? Where's he from? Where is he living? What does he look like? I'm sure you've managed to ferret out some details, Celeste. You have such a way with people."

"He's very mysterious. He has a long beard and long hair, and he's worn sunglasses every time I've seen him. George, our new UPS driver, says he's seen him wearing an eye patch once. No one has managed to learn his name. All his purchases are made in cash, and the land sale and construction was made under a generic company name—Smith Industries. He bought the section of Storm Mountain Ranch that the Mitchells listed for sale, and paid a hefty bonus to get the cabin's bathroom updated and the barn remodeled fast. Brought in lots of tools, apparently."

"What has Zach found out about him?" Gabi knew her brother would have checked. The fellow sounded way too suspicious for the sheriff's peace of mind.

"He hasn't said. I'm sure there's no cause for concern or we would have heard. Like I said, I don't have the sense that he is trouble for us. I tend to think that we could be of help to him." Celeste shook her head and clucked her tongue. "Well, that's a concern for another day. It's Christmas Eve, and the time for good cheer. Now, your mother said you wanted to ask me something?"

"Not exactly. I want to give you a gift, and I'd like you to open it now, if you don't mind." She picked up a gift box wrapped in gold foil and handed it to Celeste, who smiled with delight as Gabi added, "I made it myself."

Celeste gasped with pleasure when she opened the box and spied the twenty-inch-tall figure with flowing golden robes and graceful white wings and crowned with a thin thread of a halo. "Oh, Gabriella. It's just fabulous. I absolutely love it."

"I started out with the intention of making an ornament for your tree, but as I gathered the glass, something came over me. I thought of you, and it was as if my own artistic spirit breathed to life inside me. It was the first time that had happened for me, Celeste, and it was such a high. I still have so much to learn and the piece has some flaws, but I want you to know that you inspired me, and this was my first work as a legitimate glass artist."

Celeste gave her a quick, hard hug. "I'm honored, Gabi. Truly honored. And I will treasure it forever."

Celeste removed the angel from its box and studied it, oohing and ahhing and beaming with delight. Gabi floated to Aspenglow on an artistic high that was reinforced after dinner when the family did their traditional gift exchange. Everyone was truly impressed by her talent and delighted with the gifts she'd made them. She joined them in church for the midnight mass as happy and fulfilled as she'd felt in a very long time.

Never mind that one just-in-case gift packed away in her luggage, a dreamweaver shaped like a sail in shades of Caribbean blue and sunshine yellow. She was determined not to think about that—think about him, wonder where he was or how he was doing—on this cold, dark winter's night.

So when the church doors flung open wide just as Father Hector Wilson wrapped up his homily and cold, bitter air swirled into the small church, she was caught unaware by the trouble that blew inside.

Flynn's Christmas Eve from hell began at seven o'clock that evening. After enjoying a long phone call during which he spoke with every member of the Wharton family, he'd poured himself an extra-tall scotch from a bottle already two-thirds gone and brooded while he sipped it.

And he stared at the phone. Memories of Christmases long ago played through his mind like a reel of film on the ancient 8 mm projector they'd had at home. Decorating sugar cookies with his mom, tramping through the mall with his father searching for the right gift for her, hot chocolate in the car as their little family drove around town looking at Christmas lights while listening to CDs of carols. Life had been good back then. Their little family of three had been bound by love.

Mom would hate what Dad and I have come to. She's probably up there in heaven scolding us right now.

Maybe that wasn't such a crazy idea. Maybe that was exactly what was happening. Why else would he be considering an action he'd never thought to take?

Flynn drummed his fingers on his thigh as he focused on the phone. He took another long sip of his scotch. He thought about the baseball glove Dad had given him for Christmas when he was eight years old.

"Screw it." He picked up his cell phone and dialed the number from memory. It rang four times before a stranger's voice, a young man's voice, answered, "Seagraves residence. Hello?"

Who's visiting Dad on Christmas Eve? Flynn wondered. "May I speak with the colonel, please?"

"I'm sorry. He and my mom are still at the airport. Nolan says they'll be pressing it to make it to church in time for the midnight service."

Flynn frowned, trying to figure out who this person might be. Buying himself a little more time, he asked, "He's flying tonight? On Christmas Eve?"

"Yes, I'm afraid so. Their plane had mechanical issues, so they were a day late leaving Paris."

Paris? At Christmastime? Dad wasn't a fan of Paris. "That's unfortunate."

"They didn't seem to mind extending their honeymoon by a day."

Honeymoon. Flynn's stomach dropped right through his cabin's wood floor. His father had remarried.

And he hadn't bothered to let Flynn in on the news.

The voice on the other end of the line asked, "Would you like to leave a message for him?"

"Tell him . . ." Flynn closed his eyes and had to clear his throat. "Never mind. No. No messa . . ." His voice trailed off as his mother's image flashed in his mind's eye. "Yes. I do have a message. Tell him Flynn called to wish him Merry Christmas, and that I added my congratulations on the marriage."

The man's voice raised an octave as he repeated, "Flynn? Flynn Sea—"

Click. Flynn disconnected the call and rose from his seat. Forgoing the glass, he grabbed the bottle of scotch by the neck and carried it toward the fireplace. How long he stood there, lost in thought and memories and resentment, he couldn't say, but it was long enough to get a good buzz. Eventually he dropped down into the easy chair and propped his legs on the ottoman, his feet toward the fire. It was hot, burning brightly. The room was toasty warm, so why the hell was he so cold inside?

He'd never felt quite this alone before.

He drained the last of the whiskey from the bottle and stared at the flickering flames, his mind going into dark, ugly places until he fell asleep, or maybe passed out.

The flames had died to glowing embers when he awoke to an aching head and the sound of Bismarck whining and scratching at the door. "What is it, boy?" he asked, his voice rough and still a little bit slurred.

Bismarck's whines didn't wane. Flynn attempted to recall the last time he'd let the dog out. Midafternoon? Hell, he couldn't remember. "All right, all right. Hold on a minute. I'm coming."

Flynn shuffled toward the door and opened it. Bismarck shot out like a bullet. "Wow. He must have really needed to go."

Except the dog didn't head toward his usual potty area. He barreled off through the snow toward the forest, a black shadow in the silvered moonlight. "Bismarck. Bismarck!" Flynn called. "Get back here, boy. Come!"

The dog showed no sign of having heard him.

Scowling, Flynn waited and watched. This wasn't like Bismarck at all. They'd worked hard on training when Flynn had been in the hospital. It had been part of Flynn's therapy. Bismarck always followed Flynn's commands.

"Something is wrong," he murmured, reaching for his coat. The dog's disappearance into the trees confirmed his suspicion. Bismarck never went into the forest.

Flynn grabbed a flashlight, his phone, and, after a moment's deliberation, a rifle, and took off after his dog, moving as quickly through the snow as a half-crippled man could. He slipped the rifle strap over his shoulders so that he wore the gun on his back as he jogged. He kept his flashlight aimed at the tracks—until an eerie howl sent shivers running up his spine. That wasn't a wolf, was it? Surely not. There weren't wolves in the southern Rockies . . . were there?

Whatever it was, Bismarck was headed for it.

Flynn ignored the pain in his hips and knees caused by his hurried steps. He was worried about his dog.

The animal howled again. Bismarck barked and barked and barked.

A child screamed.

"No," Flynn muttered. That couldn't be a child. It had to be a cat. Mountain cat cries sometimes sounded like a human's, didn't they?

"No! Stop. Go away!"

Oh, hell. Mountain cats didn't speak English.

Flynn gritted his teeth and picked up his speed, chasing after the fearful cries as fast as he could manage. Light from a nearly full moon spilled through the forest canopy helped to illuminate his path. His heart pounded, and his breaths came in harsh pants that left clouds of vapor in the air. "I'm coming!" he yelled, even though he doubted the kid could hear him over his own cries.

Then a truly bloodcurdling scream tore through the bitter cold night along with vicious barks and terrible growls and the sounds of battle engaged. *No. No. Please God, no. Don't let me be too late.*

He burst upon the scene within a minute's time. His mind took snapshots of the event. A girl, maybe eight or nine years old. Bismarck battling with another animal . . . dog, wolf, some combination of the two, he couldn't say. In seconds, Flynn assessed and analyzed, then acted.

Drawing his gun, he placed himself between the girl and the animals and waited for his shot. It was so dark. Both animals were dark. He couldn't risk a shot!

"Bismarck!" he shouted, making his voice loud and as commanding as it had ever been before. "Bismarck, heel!"

The dog reacted. He broke away from his foe just long enough, just far enough, for Flynn to make out the difference in the two animals. He pulled the trigger. The wolf went down. Flynn wanted to drop to his knees, too.

Instead, he turned to the screaming girl and rested his hand on her shoulder. "It's okay now, honey. You're gonna be okay. Give me a minute to make sure that the animal won't bother us any more. You shut your eyes. You don't need to look at this."

He hoped she listened to him, especially when he shone the flashlight on the prone figure and saw that he'd taken half its head off. Then, his heart in his throat, he shifted the light toward Bismarck. He lay at the base of a pine tree, blood staining the snow beneath him. *Please, God,* Flynn silently prayed.

The child was crying again, but he'd seen no sign of physical injury. Bismarck had defended her. What heart in his valiant friend. Tending to Bismarck had to come first.

Flynn knelt beside his dog. He was breathing, thank God, though in short, shallow pants. "It's okay, boy. We're gonna take care of you." He reached out and stroked his dog's head, taking a quick survey of visible wounds. Gashes everywhere. A tear along his neck that made it obvious the attacker had been going for Bismarck's throat. His right front leg lay bent in the wrong direction.

"It's okay, boy," Flynn repeated. "I'm going to take care of you."

He pulled his phone from his pocket and opened the mapping app, making note of the coordinates. Then, grateful he'd put the man into his phone contacts, he dialed Zach Turner directly. It rang three times before Zach said, "Hello?"

"It's Brogan. I have a situation. I need EMTs at these coordinates ASAP." He recited his location, then added, "I found a little girl alone in the woods. I don't know how long she's been out here."

Zach went directly into law enforcement mode, for which Flynn was infinitely grateful. "We're on our way."

"Good. I'll talk to her now and call you back when I have more details." He disconnected the call and turned to the little girl. "I called the sheriff and help is on the way. What's your name, honey?"

Her little voice trembled. "I'm not supposed to tell strangers."

"Fair enough," Flynn said, seeking to reassure her. "You can wait and tell the sheriff. I'll call you Sunshine, how about that? So, how did you come to be in the woods by yourself on Christmas Eve, Sunshine?"

"We're on our way to my brother's roommate's ranch for Christmas, and my daddy took a wrong turn and then when he tried to find the right way, he hit something big in the dark. I think it was a great big deer." Tears began pouring from the little girl's eyes, and the longer she told her story, the faster she talked until her sentences all ran together. "The car slid off the road and we fell. We hit a tree and the airbags went off, and I couldn't get Mommy and Daddy to wake up. They need help and I couldn't find their phones and I yelled and yelled but nobody heard me and I thought I saw a light and decided I had to go for help and then that big dog started following me through the forest and he growled at me and then the other dog came and started a fight and then you were here!"

"Okay. Okay. Do you know which way you came from?"

"No! I got lost when the dog started following me. He was very scary!"

"Yes, he was."

"He's dead, isn't he?"

"Yes."

"I'm glad. I'm glad he's dead. I love dogs, but he was not a nice one."

"No, he wasn't, Sunshine."

"Is the other dog your dog?"

"Yes."

"He saved me. Is he going to be okay?"

"I hope so. I really hope so." The sooner he got him to a vet the better.

"My name is Annabelle. Annabelle Spragins."

"I'm pleased to meet you, Annabelle. My name is Flynn. Is the ranch you are visiting called Storm Mountain Ranch?"

"Yes!" she said.

Flynn called Zach back and updated him. "The geometry of her story gives me a good idea of where you'll find the car. I should be able to pick up Annabelle's tracks and get there about the same time the ambulance arrives."

"Why don't you stay put? We'll find you."

Bismarck didn't have time for him to stay put. He'd

reach help fastest by meeting the EMTs. "We'll meet you there."

Zach must have heard the steel in Flynn's voice, because he warned, "Don't get lost, and I hope to hell that your cell phone has a good charge."

Flynn disconnected, slipped the phone into his pocket, then bent to pick up his dog. Quietly and soothingly, he apologized for causing him pain. "You are the best dog on the planet, Bismarck, and I'm going to do my level best to make sure that you come out of this as good as new."

He found Annabelle's tracks with relative ease and was able to follow them—and those of the predator—through the forest. He spied the car before the first responders did, and called Zach with the location. "We're two minutes from there," Zach told him.

Better that Zach got to the car first. "I think we'll slow down until . . . wait. I see movement. It's inside the car!"

"Help us!" a man's voice called out.

"Our daughter is missing," a woman cried.

"Mommy! Daddy!" Little Annabelle took off running.

The Spragins hadn't come through the accident without injury. Both parents had concussions. The mother's leg was broken. The father had a nasty cut on one arm and a serious puncture wound to one thigh. The EMTs had their hands full, and when one of Zach's deputies arrived, Flynn said, "I gotta get my dog to the vet. Can I take your truck?"

Zach handed over the keys with no hesitation. "Nic Callahan's house and clinic are on Pinion Street between Seventh and Eighth. She should be home. Her family went to the children's service earlier."

"Thanks, Sheriff."

"Good luck, man. I hope the dog is okay."

"Bismarck saved that little girl. You need to have someone follow our tracks. He'll find the animal that

Bismarck tangled with. I shot him. If I didn't know better, I'd swear he was a wolf."

Then Flynn gently placed his dog in the SUV's backseat and turned the truck toward town. Nothing mattered at this point but getting his dog to Nic Callahan.

He gripped the wheel with shaking hands and drove quickly but carefully. Behind him, Bismarck whined and whimpered and panted in pain.

"Hang on, boy. We'll have you to a doctor soon. You're a fighter. You just keep fighting." His voice broke on the last word, and he swallowed hard.

What a brave, valiant dog. Once again, Bismarck had saved someone from certain death. Once again, as a result, his own life hung in the balance.

He couldn't lose Bismarck. He'd already lost too much.

Flynn hadn't prayed that long night and day on the beach, but he prayed now. He asked for God's mercy. He begged for Bismarck's life. *Please, God. I can't lose him. I need him. Please.*

When the Newfie's pants and whines grew quiet, Flynn filled the terrible silence with his own desperate moan.

With the flashers blinking, he barreled into town, flew up Pinion to Seventh, and whirled into the drive beside the sign that said VETERINARY HOSPITAL. He drove the SUV right up to the vet office, then shut off the engine. "I'm going to get the doctor, Biz. I'll be right back."

Was that a whimper he heard? Hope filled his heart as urgency gave wings to his feet. He ran to the house next to the clinic and pounded on the door. "Dr. Callahan? I have an emergency. Nic Callahan?"

An older, white-haired gentleman dressed in a plaid bathrobe over blue flannel pajamas opened the door scowling. "It's after midnight, man. What are you—"

"My dog saved a little girl from being attacked by a wolf. The wolf got him. I need the doctor."

The old man's brow furrowed. "She's in church."

Frustrated, Flynn exclaimed, "Church! The sheriff said she already went!"

"She did, but the kids got sick, and they had to leave."

"Which church? Where is it?"

The man told him. Flynn ran to the truck, whipped back onto the street, and within minutes was yanking open the doors of Sacred Heart Church. "I'm sorry to interrupt," he declared in a loud tone. "It's an emergency. I need Dr. Nic Callahan."

Two women stood up. "I'm Dr. Callahan," the blonde said, alarm in her tone. "What's wrong?"

"Please, Dr. Callahan," Flynn said, his voice quaking. "You have to save Bismarck. You have to save my dog."

The blonde nodded even as the second woman gasped. Flynn finally looked at her.

Gabi.

FOURTEEN

Gabi thought she must be hallucinating. That man with the beard, the obvious limp, wearing an eye patch . . . an eye patch! . . . couldn't be Flynn. Never mind that he was the same height as Flynn and had the same voice as Flynn. That didn't mean he was Flynn. Didn't they say that everyone had a doppelgänger walking the earth somewhere?

She heard the echo of her father's voice repeating one of his favorite sayings: *Who the hell are "they"?*

Then she got a better look at the color of his eye and she gasped.

He looked straight at her, and she knew without a doubt.

This wild-looking stranger was Flynn Brogan.

She stood frozen in shock as he turned and hurried from the church. He held the door open for Nic and her husband, Gabe, who had followed her from the pew, and Gabi didn't breathe again until the door swung shut behind them.

Part of her wanted to rush right after them, but most of her was too shocked to move. "Gabi!" her mother said, tugging on her coat sleeve. "Sit down."

It was the easiest thing to do, so that's what she did. Father Hector resumed the mass, and Gabi participated by rote, her thoughts a million miles away. Or, actually, eighteen hundred miles away—the distance between Bella Vita Isle and Eternity Springs. *What is Flynn doing in Eternity Springs? What happened to him? Why the limp? Why the eye patch? Why the beard?*

He's here. Flynn is here!

His dog is hurt. Bismarck is hurt!

She leaned over and whispered to her mother. "I have to go."

"What?" Maggie whispered back, scowling. "What are you, five years old? We're almost to communion. Hold it."

"Not that kind of go. I have to leave, Mom."

Maggie looked at her daughter then, and her annoyed look switched to one of concern. "What's wrong, honey? You look ghastly. Are you ill?"

That's one way to put it. "I'm okay, Mom. I'll explain later."

She stood, and her mother lifted the kneeler to allow her to exit. "Where are you going?" Lucca asked as she moved past him.

"Bathroom," she replied, giving the expedient answer. Then, because the idea of telling a lie while in church made her wince, she ducked into the restroom on her way out and, because Gabi was Gabi, touched up her lipstick before leaving the church.

She was halfway to the parking lot before she remembered that she'd ridden to church with her brothers Tony and Max, so she didn't have a car. And of course Nic's vet clinic was at the far end of town from the church. It was a five-minute walk to pick up her own car, and by the time she let it warm up, it would be faster for her to just walk.

As she started up the street, she expected to have dozens of questions spinning through her mind, but instead her thoughts remained frozen and focused on the bottom-line issues. What had happened to Flynn? Why was he in Eternity Springs? And what had happened to Bismarck?

She was one block away from the Callahans' when she saw headlights come on and heard an engine start. She knew in her heart that it was Flynn and that he was leaving. That meant one of two things, she deduced, her heart twisting at both possibilities. Either Bismarck hadn't made it or Flynn was running away from her.

When the headlights turned in her direction, she didn't hesitate. Gabi stepped right out into the middle of the street. He might attempt to go around her, but she wouldn't make it easy for him.

The approaching headlights illuminated her, and Gabi lifted one arm to shield her eyes and held the other palm out, signaling stop. She held her breath, unable to guess what he would do. After all, never in a million years would she have thought that he'd walk into Sacred Heart during the Christmas midnight mass.

She could tell by the engine sound that he'd taken his foot off the gas, but the car—a truck, she realized—drew steadily closer. So, was this to be a game of chicken between her and a pickup? She anticipated the swerve that would take him around her.

Instead, the truck braked to a stop. She realized then that he was driving a sheriff's vehicle.

She took a deep breath, then approached the driver's-side door. He stood staring straight ahead, his jaw set, his hands clasping the steering wheel in a white-knuckled grip. He didn't lower the window. Frustrated, Gabi knocked on it and shot him a glare.

At least fifteen long seconds ticked by before the window slid down. Gabi asked, "Bismarck?"

"He's hurt. He needs surgery, but the doctor says he should make it."

"Thank God." She breathed a heavy sigh of relief. "I have a million questions."

Finally he turned his head, and even in the muted light of the street lamp, the glare he shot her was hot enough to melt the snowdrifts. "Well, I just have one. Why are you here? You're not supposed to be here. Cicero said you'd be gone a whole year."

Taken aback, she snapped, "Merry Christmas to you, too, Brogan."

"I didn't ask you to stop me," he said, his voice hard and angry. "I didn't want to talk to you. I left before my dog went into surgery in order to avoid you."

She caught her breath against the hurt his words caused, and it must have shown on her face, because he muttered a curse. "Look, it's been a helluva day. I don't have time for drama. I need to get this truck back to your brother so I can go home and get my own truck and get back here to wait for Dr. Callahan to finish with Bismarck."

"Just where is home?"

"All you need to know is that Bismarck will be okay and that I wasn't neglecting him. He acted heroically tonight, and a little girl is safe because of him. Now step away from the truck. I'm in a hurry."

"But Flynn, I think—" She stopped midsentence because she was talking to window glass and the truck was rolling away.

She stood in the middle of the street staring after him, her teeth chattering, her heart quaking, cold through to her soul. How long she remained in place, she couldn't say, but it wasn't until the church bells pealed that she stirred herself to move.

Flynn Brogan. Here. And hateful! But something was off. And the fact that he had Zach's truck . . . What in heaven's name was going on here? Why had nobody bothered to mention that Flynn Brogan was in Eternity Springs?

Gabi walked back to Aspenglow Place alternating between deep thought and moments when she couldn't think at all, only feel. The trip took a little over five minutes, and by the time she arrived, exhaustion pulled at her bones. She walked inside to find her brothers Max and Tony partaking in the traditional after-midnight-mass snack in the kitchen—pieces of Italian cream cake and glasses of milk. They looked up from their plates when Gabi entered the room. "Where did you go?" Max asked.

"That was Flynn Brogan."

The men shared a confused look, then Tony asked, "He called you?"

"No. The guy at the church. That was Flynn!"

"What guy do you . . . whoa, you mean the guy with the beard?"

"Yes!"

Max put down his fork. "That didn't look anything like the guy whose picture was splashed all over the tabloids. Why is he in Eternity Springs?"

"I don't know. He wouldn't tell me." Gabi absently cut a piece of cake for herself, then joined her brothers at the kitchen table. "Something's happened to him. Something bad."

"I think the guy is just bad news, Gabi," Tony suggested. "You should stay away from him."

She looked at Max to gauge his opinion. He shrugged. "What day do you go back? January second?"

"The first."

"I wouldn't let the fact that your ex is hanging around town spoil the little time you have at home."

Gabi didn't like hearing him referred to as her ex. Her jerk, okay, but not her ex. She nibbled at her lower lip and toyed with the cake on her plate. The boys didn't understand. It wasn't like she and Flynn had had a regular breakup. Their relationship had ended as a result of outside factors—namely, pirates!

Bet that would be a new one for a psychologist's couch.

"I need to know. Not knowing will drive me crazy for the next ten months. I mean, did he go off the deep end because he killed those two men? Has something else happened to him?"

Max polished off his glass of milk. "Ask Zach. He knows everything that goes on in this town."

"True." Gabi pursed her lips and considered it. "Why wasn't he in church, anyway?"

"Savannah said he got a call. A car went off the road up near Storm Mountain Ranch."

"On Christmas Eve? That's terrible." It also supplied a few pieces to the puzzle. Flynn and Bismarck must have been involved somehow. Flynn had borrowed the SUV to bring the injured dog into town. And Zach was probably still working the scene.

Gabi drummed her fingers on the table. He didn't want to see or talk to her—he'd said as much. Well, that was too damned bad. There was unfinished business between them. She'd been too wounded in the aftermath of the attack to tackle that business at the time, but she was stronger now. And Flynn . . .

Why had he come to Eternity Springs? And why had he come here looking like something that came down from the mountains twice a year?

"I want answers."

"There's a shocker," Max observed.

With half a piece of cake still on her plate, she abruptly rose and abandoned her dessert for her brothers to fight over. As she exited the kitchen, her mother descended the stairs wearing a festive red holiday robe and slippers. "There you are," Maggie said to Gabi. "Honey, good. You're home. Why did—"

"Not now, Mom," she said. "I'm on my way out."

"What? It's almost two a.m.!"

"Max and Tony will explain." She grabbed the coat she'd so recently taken off and headed out the door, pretending she didn't hear her mother's protests.

Again, she judged it easier and faster to walk rather than to take the time to warm up her car. Shoving her gloveless hands into her pockets, she hurried toward Cottonwood Street and the sheriff's office. The bitterly cold air stung her cheeks and made her eyes water. She tried to tell herself it was the air, anyway, and not her emotions. She wasn't sure just what she believed.

Flynn. He looked terrible. Broken. What had happened to his eye?

She spied lights on at the sheriff's office, but when she entered, she found the building empty. Little had changed in this building in the year since she'd left her job as deputy, so she felt right at home as she sat down in front of the radio and began monitoring the traffic.

She heard her brother say he was leaving the accident scene and heading back to town as soon as he dropped the dog owner back at his place in Thunder Valley. His deputy replied that he'd return to the office as soon as he finished taking statements. "No," Zach said. "Don't worry about it. You go on home, Bob, and get some sleep. I'll cover the rest of your shift. Merry Christmas."

"Thanks, boss."

The radio went quiet then, and Gabi considered what she'd learned. Flynn must be living in Thunder Valley. For how long? Had Zach known before tonight? If so, why hadn't he told her? She could understand him keeping the news to himself while she'd been in Italy, but they'd spent all afternoon and most of the evening together, and the blasted man hadn't said a word!

Thunder Valley . . . Celeste . . . the stranger . . . Gabi remembered what Celeste had said. Flynn Brogan had been living here for weeks at least. Zach had to have known about it. The longer she thought about it, the more she fumed. By the time her brother walked through the front door of the sheriff's office, she'd worked up a full head of steam. She sat with one hip on his desk, her arms folded.

Zach took one look at her and said, "Why am I not surprised to find you here?"

"What's the story, Zachary?"

Zach closed his eyes and shook his head. "I'm too tired for this."

"The sooner you talk to me, the sooner you'll get home to bed."

At that, her brother grimaced and rubbed the back of his neck. "I don't know all that much. He lives in a smallish cabin out in Thunder Valley. He bought the property not long after you left for Italy, but I only recently discovered who owns it. He intended to leave before you came home."

"You didn't tell me."

"No, I didn't tell you. He asked me not to, and he had good reasons."

Gabi tried to ignore the stab of hurt within her chest. Zach was her brother. "What are those reasons? Why did he come here?"

"He's . . . had a hard time." Zach frowned over his words. "I think he came here looking for some of that Eternity Springs angel dust."

"What happened to him? How was he injured?"

Now her brother folded his arms and gave her a steady look. "That's not my story to share. You'll have to get it from him."

"No way. You need to—"

"Enough, Gabriella. I'm not moving on this."

She knew the man well enough to recognize that when his voice took on a note of steel and his jaw went granite hard, she could push him no further.

"I'm having a hard time with this. You're more loyal to a stranger than you are to your own sister? How could you not tell me?"

"Because he asked, and because he killed two men in order to keep my sister safe, so yeah, I figured I owed him," Zach snapped back. He must have seen the flash of hurt on her face, because he immediately relented. "He told me he'd leave before you came home, Gabi. He said you two were over. When you showed up for Christmas I thought about telling you, but I didn't see any reason to stir things up. You were only going to be here for a week, and he rarely comes to town. I didn't think you'd run across each other. If not for that dog . . . who truly is some dog, by the way. He obviously has a heroic streak a mile wide."

"What happened tonight? How did Bismarck get hurt?"

He told her about the accident, and about the little girl getting lost in the woods. "It's going to start a brouhaha. That wasn't a feral dog. That was a wolf."

"We have wolves in this part of the state?"

"Apparently we do now. It's going to cause us some headaches. Brogan might want to make himself scarce after the holidays."

"He won't get into trouble for shooting a wolf that was about to attack a child!" Gabi exclaimed.

"No, but people will want to talk to him. I'll do what I can to protect his identity, but . . ." Zach shrugged. "The guy's a trouble magnet."

"That's a mean thing to say." Surprised by her immediate defense of a man who clearly didn't even want to talk to her, Gabi rubbed her hand across her eyes and murmured, "Oh, Zach. I don't know what to do."

Zach reached out and tugged her into his arms for a

hug. "Look, it's late. It's Christmas morning. Go home, Gabriella. You'll be better able to figure things out once you've had some sleep."

The man had a point. Gabi hugged him back. "Merry Christmas, Zach."

"Merry Christmas, Gabi. I'm glad you made it home for Christmas. Eternity Springs just isn't the same without you."

When she crawled into bed twenty minutes later, her heart was heavy and exhaustion clawed at her soul. But she couldn't fall asleep. She opened her eyes and stared toward her window and the faint shadow of the dreamweaver she'd hung upon her arrival. She'd made it on the sixth-month anniversary of the attack on the *Dreamer* after awakening from a nightmare-filled sleep. It was free-form, delicate and wispy, and a beautiful sunshine yellow and Caribbean blue. The blue of Flynn's eyes. She hadn't suffered a nightmare since hanging it above her bed.

She had, however, had an unusual number of sex dreams.

Now she stared up at the dreamweaver and thought of Flynn. Wondered about Flynn and his presence here in Eternity Springs. Questioned fate and destiny and God's purpose. "To every thing there is a season," she murmured.

What were the chances that this could be hers and Flynn's season?

Why would he be here, why would she be here, otherwise?

Mentally focusing on her dreamweaver, she drifted off to sleep. She awoke early on Christmas morning with a smile on her face . . . and a plan.

Back at the cabin and despite his exhaustion, Flynn seriously considered throwing a change of clothes into his duffel and taking off. If not for the fact that he had an injured dog at the vet's, he'd do it.

Gabriella Romano was back in town.

Maybe he should strip off all his clothes and walk naked in the snow until he freaking froze to death.

Instead, he climbed into his bed, where he tossed and turned and attempted to fall asleep, but just ended up thinking about Gabi Romano.

She'd looked amazing. Perfect. And while his eyesight wasn't at all perfect, he hadn't missed the confusion and hurt in her eyes . . .

He finally drifted off to sleep just as dawn broke on Christmas morning.

He awoke to the aroma of garlic sautéing in olive oil.

Whoa. Now that's a realistic dream. He must be craving Italian food. He'd have to make a trip to Ali Timberlake's Yellow Kitchen restaurant ASAP.

He pried his eyes open. Stared at the bedside clock. Eleven a.m. He blinked hard. Eleven a.m.!

The previous evening's events came rushing back to him. Bismarck. The wolf. The little girl. Bismarck.

Gabi.

"Oh, crap." He buried his head beneath his pillow. Damned if he didn't still smell garlic.

And hear singing.

Bad singing.

What the hell?

He tugged the pillow off his head. Opened his gritty eyes. Blinked. Still smelled garlic and olive oil. Still heard out-of-tune music—a seriously bad rendition of "I Saw Mommy Kissing Santa Claus."

He rolled up to a seated position. Gave his head a shake. Was this some sort of weird dream?

No, somebody was in his cabin. Not just somebody. He recognized that bad tune.

"What the hell?" he repeated, aloud this time. He threw off the covers and rolled to his feet, then, heedless of the chill, strode out of his bedroom into the cabin's main room.

Gabi Romano stood stirring a pot on his stove. She turned her head, offered him a brilliant smile, and said, "Merry Christmas, sleepyhead."

"I'm tripping, aren't I? I took a toke of some nasty weed or mislabeled pills, and I'm having a hallucination. Gabi Romano is not standing in my kitchen stirring a pot of . . . ?"

"Gravy, my father's Italian mother called it. It's red sauce. For the lasagna."

"Lasagna," he repeated dumbly.

"It's traditional Christmas Day fare in my family. We always have tenderloin roast on Christmas Eve, but Christmas Day is about cannoli for breakfast and lasagna for dinner. Of course, we usually have made it ahead of time, so the sauce has had time to mature, but like they say, needs must."

"You're making lasagna."

"Yes."

"What, your family sent you out here to poison me?"

She laughed. "I'd be insulted, but that wouldn't be fair of me, because you don't know what happened when I came home to Eternity Springs after Bella Vita. My mother taught me how to cook, Flynn. I listened this time. I'm pretty good, too."

"I'm dreaming, aren't I? But is this a nightmare or simply a dream?"

Again she laughed, and the sound drifted like church bells on the cold morning air. "Go put some pants on, Brogan. As much as I like looking at you in your boxers, I think we should probably talk before we pick up where we left off. Although you look like you can use some more sleep. Dinner won't be ready for a couple more hours, so feel free to catch some more sack time if you'd like. I'll be here when you wake up."

"No, you won't. I want you to leave."

"Sorry. I'm not going anywhere. Not until after dinner, anyway."

"You can't just barge in here and take over my kitchen."

"Sure I can. I've already done it. Unless you want to call the sheriff, maybe?"

That stopped him, as she surely knew it would. While he stood there scowling at her, she continued. "Give it up, Brogan. You are not going to win this one. This is Eternity Springs and it's Christmas Day and I'm going to cook you a delicious Christmas dinner."

A wave of frustration rolled through Flynn. He recognized that tone of voice. Short of bodily lifting her and tossing her and her pots and pans and red sauce out into the snow, he wasn't going to get rid of her. While the notion held a certain appeal, he hadn't sunk that low . . . had he?

Well, he didn't have to entertain an uninvited guest.

He turned on his heel and walked back into his bedroom, slamming the door shut behind him. He crawled back into bed, pulled his pillow over his head, and tried to will himself back to sleep. He was exhausted. He was frustrated. He was furious and angry and . . . alive. More alive than he'd been in months.

Hungrier than he'd been in months, too. He tried to tell himself the hollow sensation in the pit of his stomach resulted from the aroma of garlic and tomatoes, but as he drifted toward sleep, he acknowledged that Italian red sauce had little to do with it.

The Italian cook in his kitchen was stirring up more than Christmas dinner.

He slept hard and mercifully for a change, without dreaming. He awoke to the warmth of afternoon sunshine beaming through a window he ordinarily kept covered and the sensation of a soft, warm touch against his face. He opened his eyes, winced against the stab of sunlight, and quickly shut them again, muttering, "Dammit. The blinds."

"Oh," Gabi said, her voice sounding contrite as she moved quickly to close the blinds. "So you can see out of your injured eye? The light bothers you?"

Bothered him? Hell. Think a hot sword through his eyeball. He'd be damned if he'd say it and sound like a sissy, though. "I like it dark," he grumbled, his voice harsh.

Hers came back gentle as snowfall. "I wanted to look at you while you slept. I've missed you."

Missed him? Right. She hadn't tried to contact him, had she? Scowling, he reached for the bedside table and his eye patch, and once he had it in place, he gave her his fiercest glare. "You invaded my privacy."

"I should be ashamed," she said, her expression deadpan. "Your hair is darker than it was last spring—no more sun streaks. You're not nearly as tan. Guess wherever you went after leaving Bella Vita Isle, you didn't spend much time outdoors. But that beard . . . really, Flynn. I'm not on board with the beard."

"Were you always this chatty in the mornings?" he asked as he rose from the bed and stumbled toward the john.

"It's not morning. It's the middle of the afternoon and your Christmas dinner will be ready in just about twenty minutes. You have plenty of time to take a shower. If you want to shave, well, that's the beauty of lasagna. It keeps."

The woman invades my home, invades my sleep, and then nags me to bathe? And shave? He'd have liked to drop his pants in insult, except doing so would reveal scars he didn't want her to see. Besides, for all he knew, the Gabi Romano who'd pushed her way into his home today would take it as an invitation rather than as an insult.

He called Nic Callahan to check on Bismarck. Then, since he'd planned to bathe anyway and wasn't just reacting to her nag, he turned on the hot water for his shower. When he stood beneath the steaming stream lathering his hair and realized he was whistling, well, it was habit. That's all. He'd always whistled in the shower.

Well, he did up until last summer. If this was the first time he'd whistled in the shower since the attack, well, so what?

Lasagna wasn't to be turned down, after all. It was food, and he was hungry. *Yeah, right.*

Regardless, he wasn't going back down that road with her again. No way.

Despite his self-assurances, Flynn felt a bit defensive as he finished rinsing and switched off the shower and reached for a towel. Staring at his reflection in the mirror, he muttered, "Be damned if I shave."

Mollified, he dried off, dressed in jeans and a sweater, and went out to confront the pest . . . and maybe eat a little of that mouth-watering lasagna.

Gabi's fingers trembled as she dried the last of the pots she'd used and stacked it into her box to take back to Mom's. The changes she'd seen in Flynn had shaken her to her core.

There were crutches leaning against the wall in his bedroom. He hadn't used them last night when he burst into the church, but the bearded man she'd noticed upon her arrival in Eternity Springs, whom she now knew to be Flynn, had darn well limped. And his eyes . . . oh, his poor, beautiful eyes. He'd tried to hide his pain from her, but he couldn't.

Had he been in a car wreck? Had he been working on one of his inventions and been involved in an industrial explosion of some sort? Was that the reason for the beard? Was his face all scarred?

Looking deep into her heart, she asked herself if she cared. Did physical injuries affect her reaction to him? Was she that shallow?

No. Absolutely not. She hated his injuries because he was injured.

But dammit, she wanted to know how they had happened.

And I'm not leaving here until I get my answers.

Hearing him enter the room, she turned. *Why do I suddenly want to sing the theme song from* Beauty and the Beast? *That or* Duck Dynasty.

He looked as if he were walking to the guillotine rather than a delicious Italian meal. In his defense, he had reason to dread sitting down to a meal of her making, but then, this wasn't about the lasagna, was it?

"Why are you doing this, Gabriella?" he asked.

"I have questions. I want answers."

"Will you leave if I give them to you?"

She considered it. "I don't know. I guess it depends on your answers. I certainly won't go until after dinner, anyway. The lasagna is excellent. Would you like me to pour you a glass of wine? I brought a bottle of my grandfather's favorite Chianti."

His laugh had a bitter note. "Why the hell not?"

She lifted the bottle, then froze with the neck poised above his glass. "Wait a minute. Is there a reason you shouldn't drink alcohol? Drug interaction or something?"

A shadow passed over his face. "I haven't become an addict in the months we've been apart."

"That's not what I asked."

He scowled and tipped the bottle so that it poured. "I don't need a babysitter."

She wrinkled her nose. "That remains to be seen."

"Have you always been this big a pest?"

She shrugged. "I grew up with brothers. I learned to hold my own."

"I'll say," he grumbled, and lifted his glass. He took a fortifying sip, then asked, "How long do you plan to be in Eternity Springs?"

Gabi delayed her response by taking her own sip of wine. On her way out to Thunder Valley this morning, she'd realized that she might want to change her travel plans. However, she sensed now was not the time to fill him in on that. "My return ticket is for January first."

She watched him mentally count the days and frown. How flattering. She wanted to kick his shin. Instead, she took the salad bowl from his fridge and placed it in the middle of the table she'd set for two. Next she added a basket of warm garlic bread, and gestured for Flynn to take a seat.

He took his first bite rather cautiously, and wasn't able to hide his surprise. "This is delicious, Gabi."

"Thank you." He'd given her the same look she'd seen on the faces of her family members, so his reaction didn't surprise her. The way he proceeded to dig into it did. He acted almost ravenous, gratifyingly so. "When was the last time you had a decent meal?"

He paused then and looked surprised. "Eating hasn't been much of a priority for me."

That wasn't what she remembered from their time on Bella Vita. The man had loved his meals. "So much has changed, hasn't it, Flynn?"

He set down his fork. "Yes. You need to know that. Actually, that's all you really need to know."

"I disagree," she replied lightly, then extended the basket toward him. "More bread?"

He smirked but took a piece, and neither one of them spoke as they finished their meal. As Gabi set a piece of Italian cream cake in front of him, she said, "I called Nic

Callahan this morning. She said that Bismarck is doing well."

"I'm supposed to pick him up at six o'clock."

"My brother told me what happened. Bismarck is an amazing dog. He's a real hero. How did you find him, Flynn? Where did you find him?" She didn't miss the way his fist tightened around his fork.

"I looked until he turned up. He somehow made his way to a bird sanctuary. Lived off eggs."

"I'll bet he was excited to see you."

"He's a loyal friend."

"I can't believe he tangled with a wolf here in Thunder Valley. The ranchers in the area won't be pleased. Being Christmas, the news will spread a little slower, but once it does . . ." She shook her head. "The ranchers' association and government people will be bad enough. I don't even want to think about what it'll be like once the animal rights people get involved."

"This is private property," Flynn said.

"You don't really think that will make a difference, do you?"

He reached for the wine bottle and refilled his glass, then wordlessly asked if she wanted more. She held up her glass, he filled it, and they silently drank their Chianti and considered. "What a lousy piece of luck," he eventually muttered.

"Not for the little girl."

"No, not for the little girl." He sighed heavily, then said, "That's the best cake I've ever had."

"Full disclosure: my mother made the cake."

"Your mother is a nice lady."

"You met her? On Bella Vita Isle?"

"At the Trading Post. We both reached for the last package of Oreos at the same time."

Gabi clicked her tongue. "Those cookies are her secret vice."

"Not so secret. The store owner said he had a couple of packages set aside for her."

"Really now," Gabi replied, drawing it out. "Thanks for the ammunition. I'm sure I'll be able to use it sometime."

"You look like her."

Gabi couldn't help but laugh. "She's a pixie. I'm an Amazon."

"You're both beautiful women."

Gabi's heart went pitty-pat and yearning filled her. She wanted to know Flynn. She wanted to understand what happened with his wife and how he'd gotten injured and why he'd come to Eternity Springs. Where to start? How to get him talking about it?

Don't be a dweeb. Ask him. Pick one of the questions and roll it right on out.

"Why did you lie to me about your name?"

He frowned as if he'd gotten a taste of something sour. "I didn't lie. I changed my name legally."

"That's BS. I rattled off all sorts of personal things. You couldn't have mentioned that you had some baggage?"

He closed his eyes and pushed away from the table. "Give it up, Gabi. I appreciate the meal, but if you think that plying me with pasta will get me to spill the beans, then the butter has slipped off your noodles."

She couldn't hold back a laugh. "That's the worst collection of food metaphors I've ever heard."

He carried his plate over to the sink and rinsed it. "Go back to town. It's Christmas. You should be with your family."

"I know you didn't kill your wife, Flynn."

He fumbled the plate. It fell into the sink and split in two. He stood staring at the broken pieces, his heart racing. He didn't know how to react. He wanted to turn to her and sweep her up into his arms and thank her for believing in him, but at the same time, he wanted to deny that her words mattered.

"You're a good man," she continued. "A decent man. I hope that someday you'll be ready to tell me what happened, but in the meantime, I just want you to know that I believe in you."

These were words he'd longed to hear, so why did they hurt? Because except for Matthew, no one else had ever said them. Not his best friend. Certainly not his father. Blood streaked his left hand where he'd cut himself on the broken pottery. "Thanks for the supper, but I think you'd better leave now."

Knowing the value of strategic retreat, Gabi nodded. "All right. But this isn't over, Flynn."

"Yes, it is," he said, his gaze focused on the sink.

"I have questions."

"I can't answer them, Gabi. Have a good flight back to Venice."

She crossed the room to where she'd left her supply box and spied the small box wrapped in blue foil and tied with a silver bow tucked inside. With her hand on the knob, she paused. "You can play the Beast all you want, Flynn, but I'm not buying it. You're living in my hometown. Whether you did it consciously or not, you reached out to me. When you're ready to tell me why, I'll listen."

He didn't turn. He didn't respond. Gabi's heart melted a little as she watched him standing so stiff and tall and . . . broken. "Merry Christmas, Flynn."

She set the gift next to his sunglasses on the little table beside the door on her way out.

FIFTEEN

Gabi returned to Aspenglow Place to find her mother upstairs on the phone talking to one of her sisters and the Romano men gathered in the living room watching a particularly exciting NFL football game. Zach's baby, Grace Elizabeth, slept in a playpen in one corner of the room, while Lucca's son, Brian Marcello, snoozed in his infant carrier. She knew that Hope and Holly were visiting Holly's father at Angel's Rest, so she asked about the other missing family member. "Where's Savannah?"

Without looking away from the television, Zach responded, "I sent her home to cook and clean."

That nonsensical statement started a round of jeers from the other Romano siblings, Gabi included. Once Zach explained that his wife had gone home to take a nap, Gabi, a sports fanatic herself, joined her brothers to see if the Cowboys could pull it out against the Redskins.

After the game, and with her mother giddy over the opportunity to babysit, Gabi participated in a Romano family pickup football melee at Davenport Park. The Romano siblings gave no quarter to one another, nor, rightly so, any modifications due to Gabi's status as the only female in the game. As a result, she earned a strained hamstring while giving Max a bruised rib and Lucca a black eye. It was a grand afternoon, and just what she needed in the wake of her Christmas dinner with Flynn—a topic her family had studiously avoided, which told her it had been roundly discussed in her absence and that opinions about her actions differed. Such was the price one paid for being part of a large family in a small town.

She crawled into bed that night physically and mentally exhausted, so she didn't have too much time to dwell on the subject of Flynn Formerly-Seagraves Brogan but when she awoke the following morning, he was the first thought on her mind. Downstairs, she found her mother sitting at the table reading the *Eternity Times* and drinking coffee. "Good morning, baby. How are you this morning?"

"Confused. I need to spend some time doing some quality thinking, Mom."

"You should exercise. You always do your best thinking then. Your skis are at the front of the garage."

All of her stuff was in the garage, Gabi thought. She'd given up her rental house when she'd left for Bella Vita and, like so many children across America, stored all her belongings at her parent's house. "Do you know if my skates are easy to get to?"

Maggie grinned sheepishly. "Actually, they're upstairs in my room."

"What? Why?"

"I tried them on."

"Mom, you wear a size four and a half shoe!"

"I stuffed socks in the toes," Maggie said, defending herself. "About three pair in each skate." While Gabi gaped at her, she explained. "I wanted to see if I could stand in them. I was invited to go skating, and since it had been a million years since I'd gone, I was afraid I'd embarrass myself."

The casual note in her mother's voice told Gabi everything. Since Maggie's relationship with Richard Steele had ended amicably, this was a new development. "A date? You had a skating date? Spill, Mama."

Maggie waved the query away. "He was a visitor at the B&B. A nice man, but a temporary visitor. Nothing for you to be interested in. Go get your skates from my closet and hit Hummingbird Lake."

So Gabi did.

It was a beautiful, sunshine-filled morning with a few puffy white clouds high against the brilliant blue sky. A dozen or so other skaters had a similar idea, and the lower part of the lake closest to town was filled with children's laughter and parents' cautions and encouragements. Gabi warmed up around them, but when she wanted the speed that always helped to clear her mind, she made her way to the far end of the lake.

She skated long and hard, and while she didn't consciously think of Flynn, she thought about him the entire time.

At some point she became aware that a pair of skaters had joined her on this section of the ice, but only after she slowed her speed and began her cooldown did she look to see if she knew them. Ah, Sage Rafferty and her sister, Rose. They returned her wave and skated toward her.

"Gabi," Rose said when they were close enough to speak without shouting, "it's a good thing you aren't wearing a speed suit. All the dads on the ice would be craning their necks to watch you, and I'm sure it would lead to broken bones. I'd be forced to go into work on my day off."

Gabi turned the compliment right around. "Don't get too relaxed, Doc. According to my brother, Lenny Winston is liable to turn up with a case of 'flu' "—she made air quotes around the word—"by this afternoon."

Sage laughed. "Yes, our resident electrician has it bad for the lady doctor."

The three women skated slowly, side by side, as they continued their conversation. "Maybe you should go for it," Gabi said. "Lenny is pretty cute."

"He is," Sage agreed. "Unfortunately, he looks too much like the slug-eating rat bastard."

When Gabi's brows arched, Rose rolled her pretty forest-green eyes. "My ex."

"Ah, yes." Gabi knew Rose's story. She'd been with said slug-eating rat bastard for seven years. During that time, he'd kept putting off marriage or having children. When Rose was diagnosed with cancer and her treatment necessitated a hysterectomy, the bastard had dumped her, married, and fathered a child within a year. " 'Slug-eating rat bastard' is a generous term."

"Yes," Sage agreed. "I've cleaned it up because I'm a mother now. Poor Lenny does look like him. They both have those Nordic-athlete good looks. Rose needs someone tall, dark, and handsome. Like one of your brothers, maybe? Tony or Max? They're unattached, aren't they?"

"Stop it, Sage," Rose protested.

"Then there's our new mystery man. The beard is a bit off-putting, but that eye patch is strangely exciting."

"Enough, sister mine, or I'll share details about a certain prom night Colt would probably love to hear—not."

Sage's eyes widened, then she made a zipping motion over her lips.

Rose turned to Gabi and explained. "She never stops her matchmaking attempts. For someone who's single, there is nothing worse than a happily married woman. Make that women. Nic, Sarah, Ali, Savannah, and Hope all chime in whenever they get the chance."

"I feel your pain, sister," Gabi said.

"Although," Rose added, "Sage may be on to something where the mystery man is concerned. He is certainly intriguing. Did you hear about what happened Christmas Eve? How the mystery man and his dog saved Little Red Riding Hood from the big bad wolf?"

"This is the problem with small towns," Gabi observed. "Everybody knows parts of stories, but very few people know the whole story, and invariably it contains at most thirty percent of what actually happened."

"You're right," Sage said. "So, do you know the whole story?"

"I know a lot of it. I'm not comfortable sharing much of it unless the other parties involved give permission." Gabi ended that particular discussion by waving to another skater on the ice. Celeste Blessing altered her direction and skated toward them, a vision in gold and white with rosy cheeks and a winsome smile. A few feet away she cut her blades sharply, sending up a rain of ice shavings. "Isn't it a glorious morning! The perfect day for some outdoor exercise."

"We saw you riding your bicycle earlier," Rose said. "You are Eternity Springs's poster child for healthy living."

The women made small talk for a few minutes, and Gabi promised to meet them for coffee to catch up and tell them about her time in Italy before she returned to Europe. After the sisters skated away, Celeste observed, "Rose is such a strong, good-hearted woman. She's faced such obstacles in her life and persevered. She's like Hope in that way. I'd like to see her get a happily-ever-after like your sister-in-law."

"Yes," Gabi agreed, although distracted. She turned to Celeste and asked the question that had occurred to her the moment she saw Eternity Springs's matriarch skating toward her. "Celeste, did you know Flynn Brogan was in town?"

Celeste gave her an innocent look—and she did innocent looks better than anybody Gabi had ever met—but

Gabi wasn't buying it for a minute. "You did! What do you know about it? Did you have anything to do with bringing him here? Are you the reason he's here?"

"Don't be silly. He's here for you, of course."

Gabi's foot slipped and she almost took a spill on the ice. "Why do you say that?"

"Think about it, sweetheart. The man is wealthy. He could go anywhere in the world, but he comes to Eternity Springs? Why?"

"Because I told him how people come here to heal," she said. "You spoke to him after the attack. You're always telling people about the valley's healing energy. I'll bet you told him the same thing, didn't you?"

"Yes, but that only gave him the excuse to come to Eternity Springs. You're the reason behind the excuse. Surely you realize that, Gabriella."

Celeste had a canny way of getting to the crux of things. "He told you all this?"

"No. We haven't spoken more than a few sentences, and I didn't let on that I recognized him. I wanted to help him, so I went into welcome-wagon mode and tried to draw him out. But the man is stubborn. He's firm in his refusal of all of my invitations."

"Then why are you so certain that he came here for me?"

Celeste gave her a knowing look. "Aren't you?"

It was the ember of hope that existed in the deepest part of her heart.

"I don't know what to think, Celeste. There is so much about the man that I don't know."

"You have excellent instincts, Gabriella. What do they tell you?"

Without hesitation, she said, "He's a good man."

"I agree. He's a good man who has faced grave challenges but remains standing. Unfortunately, standing is not living. Flynn Brogan needs to learn how to live again."

She wanted to hope and believe and have faith, all of those things. But did she dare? "Do you think he's come here hoping I'd help him?"

"Do you?"

"I wasn't scheduled to return to Eternity Springs before the summer. He told Zach he'd leave before then."

"He might intend that. He might believe that's what he would do."

Gabi knew that Celeste was right. Flynn could have gone anywhere in the world. Yet he'd come here. Why? Because it was a connection to her. A connection to them. Even if he didn't want to admit it or couldn't admit it, he knew it, too. Deep down, he knew. She would just have to remind him. "But he's here. He came here."

"Yes, he came here."

"I'm here."

"You are," Celeste agreed, nodding. "But the man has walls as tall and thick as anybody I've run across in a very long time. I doubt you'll scale them in . . . how many more days before you return to Italy?"

"My ticket is for the first. If I go back, that is."

Celeste's smile was an intriguing combination of knowing and innocence. "Oh? Is that question on the table?"

"I think it might be, Celeste."

"You'd give up your dream of becoming a glass artist for a man with so many secrets?"

"No," Gabi fired back. "That wouldn't be healthy for either of us. But I've learned a lot not only about glass but about myself in the last six months. I allowed my feelings for a man to dictate the course of my career once before. I won't do that again. However, I've also learned the value of having balance in life. My teacher on Bella Vita, Cicero, was a tyrant in his studio. He's a temperamental artist in every sense of the expression.

Nothing and no one gets in the way of his work when he's in one of his storms of creativity. One of the masters I've studied with in Italy is the same way. But another one, Benedetto, has a different viewpoint. He told me he has years to become a better artist, but his children are only preschoolers for a very short time, and he has no intention of missing out on these years."

"He lives a balanced life."

"Yes. That's not something my father did. When my mother complained, he said he'd make his fortune when he was young and enjoy his grandchildren. Only he died before he ever saw those babies born. My father wasn't perfect, but I can take a lesson from that."

"You'll postpone your education?"

"Maybe," Gabi replied. *Probably.* "I fell in love with glass last summer, but I also fell in love with Flynn. I went from having no passions in my life to having two of them for a few short, wonderful weeks. As full and rewarding as these months in Italy have been, something has been missing."

"Someone has been missing."

"Yes." Saying it, Gabi realized it was true. "I love the glass studio. I love the heat and the sounds and the rhythm of the work. Someday I'd love to see a piece of mine on display at Vistas or in another gallery. But honestly, I think I might get a bigger kick selling them myself in a vendor tent at the Eternity Springs summer arts festival."

"Especially if Flynn is beside you making change?"

"Exactly." Her gaze drifted in the direction of Thunder Valley. "I don't ordinarily shy away from difficult tasks, but this one feels daunting. How do I breach his castle walls?"

Celeste patted her arm. "You'll think of something, dear. I have faith in you."

The affirmation from her intuitive friend gave Gabi

faith in herself, too. She skated back toward the crowded end of Hummingbird Lake with a determined smile on her face, her mind racing with possibilities.

Flynn awoke the day after Christmas in a weird frame of mind. Part of him wanted to follow through on the idea of packing a bag and beating a hasty retreat from Thunder Valley. Another part of him wanted to drive into town and ask Gabi to spend the day with him. Could he be any more confused?

Not that he needed to make any sort of decision, because he couldn't go to town even if he wanted to. Bismarck was on crate rest for three more days, and Flynn wasn't going anywhere without his dog.

Flynn hunkered down beside the Newfie, who lay curled up on the pillow inside his crate beside the hearth in Flynn's workshop. "How you feeling, boy?" he asked softly, stroking the dog's head. A glance at the clock showed it was too soon for another pain pill. "Want another treat?"

The dog's ears perked and his tail thumped the pillow twice.

"I thought so," Flynn said. He reached into the treat jar and drew out a biscuit. Watching Bismarck chomp it with relish warmed his heart, and a little more of his tension faded away. Despite the fact that Nic Callahan had assured him that the dog would recover, seeing it for himself helped tremendously.

Standing, he returned to his drafting board, where pencil lines marked the beginnings of a sketch on a page. Earlier that morning, while reviewing paperwork Matthew had sent him regarding one of the Barbecue-Meister patents, a glimmer of an idea had fluttered through his mind. Flynn's pulse had picked up, and he'd gathered up Bismarck and a few supplies and trekked through the snow to the workshop. He'd built a fire, saw Bismarck settled, and sat down to work.

A whole stack of crumpled pages lay discarded on the floor, but the one in front of him held promise. His blood was humming, and he whistled quietly beneath his breath. He sketched, erased, then sketched again. It felt good. Damned good. Creativity simmered inside him in a way it hadn't in months.

The sound of an engine proved to be an unwelcome interruption. Or at least that's what he told himself when he walked to the window. He pushed back the curtain, waiting expectantly for the approaching vehicle to move into view.

He expected his visitor to be Gabi. Never mind that he'd been less than welcoming the previous day. The Gabriella Romano he'd come to know on Bella Vita Isle wouldn't let that stand in her way.

Her arrival in Eternity Springs had caught him totally off guard, though upon reflection, he shouldn't have been surprised that she would want to spend the Christmas holiday with her family. The Romanos were tight. Now that he thought about it, his visitor probably would be not Gabi but one of her brothers. Or maybe all of the Romano men had come to roust the GQ Killer from the county.

Flynn scowled out at the bright white of the snow-covered valley floor. If the Romanos were here to get rid of him, they'd have to wait a couple of days until Bismarck was okay to travel. At that point, Flynn could beat a hasty retreat. He could hole up at one of the ski resorts until she jetted back to Italy. That was probably what he should do.

But he didn't think that was what he wanted to do. He wanted to tell the Romanos to buzz off.

Except for Gabi. He didn't want to tell her to buzz off.

He didn't want to see her, either. But he didn't want to not see her.

Dammit, at this rate he'd be a blithering idiot by New Year's.

The vehicle that came into view wasn't an SUV from the sheriff's department, or even the crossover that Maggie Romano drove around town, but a fire engine red snowmobile coming fast, driven by someone long and lean wearing a black jacket with red accent stripes and matching snow pants. Flynn's mouth twisted in a wry smile. He knew Gabi had come to call even before she brought the snowmobile to a stop, pulled off her solid black helmet, and gave her head a sexy shake. Her long auburn hair tumbled down her back and glistened like fire in the sunlight.

His mouth went dry, his prick went hard, and he cursed beneath his breath.

"If I had any sense at all, Bismarck, I'd barricade the door."

Instead he grabbed his jacket and his sunglasses, schooled his expression into a scowl, and went out to meet his visitor. "I thought you came back to the States to spend time with your family."

"I did. I have. But I talked to Cicero earlier and he gave me a message to pass along to you."

"What is it?"

"He wishes you'd pick up the phone when he calls. He wants to thank you for your generous donation to Dr. Trammell's pet charity. He said it greased the wheels, and Jayne was able to get an appointment. I gather the doctor is a cancer specialist?"

"Yes." One of renown, whose new-patient appointments were almost impossible to get. Flynn was glad he'd been able to help. Cicero had been a good friend to him. It felt good to do something in return.

"That was nice of you to do, Flynn."

"It was nothing," he replied, the tone of his voice putting a period on the topic.

Gabi tilted her head to one side, studied him, and took the hint. "Flynn, why don't you come with me and we can ride up to Teardrop Lake? I packed a lunch. It's a lovely day for a picnic; it's supposed to reach the forties this afternoon. We should take advantage of this unusually warm day."

The strength of his desire to go with her dismayed him. Lucky for him, he had a good reason to turn her down. "Teardrop Lake is over an hour away. I don't want to leave Bismarck for that long."

"How is he doing today?"

"So far so good."

"Can I see him?"

Flynn hesitated. Allowing her to see Bismarck meant letting her into his workshop. Allowing her into his workshop meant that curious Gabriella was bound to ask questions, and he didn't want to go there. But how could he say no? She loved Bismarck, too.

He needed to snarl at her and send her away. But he wanted so badly to be with her and bask in her warm glow. It wasn't fair to her. None of this was. But maybe he could just be with her for a little while . . .

"Tell you what. He's sleeping now, but soon it'll be time to change his bandages. I can use your help for that. Why don't you take me out on the snowmobile for half an hour, then we can come back here?"

Her smile sparkled like sunshine on the icicles hanging from the eaves of his cabin and warmed him. *I've been cold for so long.*

She drove the snowmobile like a maniac, scaring him, delighting him, coaxing rusty laughter from his throat. When she offered to switch places, he readily agreed, and didn't realize his mistake until she snuggled up against him, her arms reaching around his waist and holding him tight. It was heaven, and it was hell. Flynn turned the snowmobile toward home with a mixture of regret and relief.

He sent Gabi into the cabin to put water on to heat while he retrieved Bismarck from the workshop, thus avoiding any questions about his work. When he carried the dog inside after a short stop for Bismarck to do his business, she had both the teapot on the stove and a fire crackling in the hearth. Gabi sat cross-legged on the floor with Bismarck's Elizabethan-collar-shielded head propped in her lap, soothing and cooing to the dog as Flynn changed the bandages and applied salve to Bismarck's wounds. "The cone of shame," she murmured, clucking her tongue, referring to the protective collar. "Poor boy. How long will he have to wear this?"

"Until he heals to the point that he won't chew on his stitches. At least a week, I imagine."

"Well, this is Eternity Springs. I'll bet you heal in half the normal time, Bismarck. You're such a hero." She glanced up at Flynn. "Tell me how you managed to find him."

Flynn shoved to his feet and turned his back to her as he put the supplies away. "I think it's probably time for you to leave. I have to get back to work."

"Work? What sort of work are you doing these days, Flynn?"

He didn't want to admit to her that his creativity had dried up and he didn't do much of any work these days, so he offered a generic response. "Industrial design is my specialty."

"Are you working on a new product for the Barbecue-Meister, by any chance? Will you have something new for me to put under the Christmas tree for my siblings next year?"

"If you'll leave and allow me to work, I just might."

"Cool!" She walked toward the door, lifted her jacket

from the wall peg where she'd left it hanging, then sauntered over to him and pressed a friendly kiss against his cheek. "Speaking of Christmas gifts, I didn't accidentally leave that package wrapped in blue foil, you know. That's my Christmas gift to you. This is December twenty-seventh. It's okay for you to open it now."

He stood stiff as the pine trees in the forest beyond, his teeth clenched against the yearning welling up inside him. "Goodbye, Gabriella. Have a nice trip back to Italy."

A bleak light flashed across her blue eyes, and for just a moment her smile faltered. Then Gabi's natural determination reasserted itself, and she said casually, "My return ticket is for New Year's Day. You'll see me again, Flynn Brogan. Count on it."

Then, before he could dodge it, she kissed him once, hard and quick, on the mouth. "You really need to lose the beard, Brogan. I don't like it. It tickles."

"That's not happening," he replied. Watching her saunter out the door, her hips swinging with her sure stride, he muttered to himself and the dog, "I'm afraid it's the only armor I have against her."

Long after the sound of her snowmobile faded away, he stood without moving, thinking about her carefree kiss, wishing he had indulged the desire to pull her back for more, knowing he'd acted wisely by resisting the impulse. Once he finally shook himself out of his reverie, he decided to take Bismarck out for another business break, then sit and catch the college bowl game that was due to start in a half hour. The pre-game show should be on by now.

But once Bismarck was ready to return inside, Flynn led him back into the workshop rather than toward the cabin and the remote control. Gabi's mention of her brothers and their Barbecue-Meisters had prodded a thought from the back reaches of his brain. He sat down at his drawing board and began sketching out the idea.

He didn't get up and return to the cabin until the fourth quarter of the bowl game. The drawing he'd left on his board was the closest thing to a design he'd managed in . . . well, years.

His spirits high, he reached for his phone with the intention of dialing Aspenglow Place in order to share his news with Gabi. He stopped himself just in time. Opening that door would be foolish. Better she not have his phone number, nor he hers. It was better for them both for the cord to be cut once and for all when she returned to Italy.

He watched the end of the game and went to bed, content with his day. Unfortunately, his contentment didn't last past his second cup of coffee the following morning, when his cell phone rang. He didn't recognize the number, so he let it go to voicemail.

It rang again three minutes later.

Then three minutes after that.

And three minutes after that.

Flynn sighed. It had to be Gabi. He grabbed up the phone, connected the call, and demanded, "How did you get my unlisted number?"

"I used to be a cop. I'm an excellent investigator. Listen, Flynn, I'm going skiing with my brothers today, so I won't be by your place. I'd invite you to come along, but I doubt it would be good for your knees. So I've arranged an outing for us tomorrow. Do your injuries prevent you from riding a horse?"

It took a moment for his mind to catch up, taken aback a bit by the matter-of-fact way in which she mentioned his injuries. "What?"

"My niece Holly and one of her friends want to dogsit Bismarck for us tomorrow, so we'll be by around eleven o'clock. Unless the weather forecasters have it wrong, it'll be a great day to take a horseback ride up on

Storm Mountain Ranch. Barring a blizzard, I'll see you at eleven."

She disconnected the call before he managed to tell her not to bother to come. That, of course, would have been a waste of breath, because he knew that Gabi would do whatever she wanted to do. With each day that passed, he found it harder to summon the energy to attempt to stop her. With each day that passed, he came closer to admitting to himself that he didn't want to stop her. She was leaving in less than a week. What would it hurt to take this week and indulge in a little what-might-have-been?

So he went about his business that day and awoke the following morning a little earlier than usual, feeling a bit more positive than he'd felt in recent months. He did his usual morning physical therapy with more energy than usual, and when eleven o'clock rolled around and he spied the Range Rover coming up the drive, he realized he looked forward to the day more than any in recent memory.

Holly Montgomery and a cute little blond girl jumped from the car carrying bulging tote bags. "Hello, Mr. Brogan. This is my friend Marsha. How is Bismarck today? I know he has to stay in his crate and keep his cone on, and he might not feel very good. We brought books to read him. I know he can't understand the stories but my mama says he might like hearing my voice."

"I'm sure he will," Flynn said with a smile. "Come on inside and I'll introduce the three of you."

"Those girls couldn't be any happier," Gabi said a little while later as they left the cabin and climbed into her Range Rover for the drive up to the ranch. "Holly loves Hope's little Roxy and she wants another dog of her own so bad, but Hope and Lucca want to wait until the baby is a little older."

"That's understandable."

She chatted about her skiing adventures the previous day and kept up a steady patter of small talk between them. Flynn enjoyed that. They'd always been able to talk. Gabi Romano could make conversation out of anything. He'd missed that, having the connection with someone, the intimacy of just being with her and talking comfortably about nothing.

Flynn liked riding, and since his arrival in Eternity Springs he'd spent quite a bit of time on the trails of Storm Mountain Ranch. "Have you ever considered getting a horse of your own?" Gabi asked him when they paused at a particularly scenic overlook on the trail.

"I've thought about it. It depends on where I settle."

Like he'd ever really be able to settle. He'd probably be running from his past the rest of his life.

She went quiet for a time after that, though she seemed more pensive than melancholy. They rode in companionable silence until they reached the ranch building that served as the halfway point for the summer trail rides the ranch gave to tourists. Gabi opened the saddlebags on her horse, removed the sandwiches she'd packed, and passed one to him. "A scenic spot, space heaters, and bathrooms. It simply doesn't get better than this, does it?"

Looking at her, all rosy cheeks and sparkling eyes and happy smile, a forbidden thought fluttered through his mind: *It would be better with a bed.*

He quashed the thought.

"How about we take the shorter trail down to the meadow and let the horses run?" he suggested when they'd finished their lunch.

"Sounds heavenly."

Since he was more familiar with the trail than she, Flynn led the way down to the meadow. The ride took about half an hour, and three-quarters of the way into it, he realized that Gabi had fallen behind. Concerned, he turned his mount around and went looking for her.

He found her stopped in the middle of the trail gazing upward. Tears trickled down her face. "What's wrong, Gabi?"

"Look, Flynn." She pointed above her into the forest's winter barren canopy.

He stared up and frowned. He saw empty twigs and snowflakes caught on evergreen needles. Focusing closer, he caught sight of a spiderweb spun high above the trail, its gossamer threads damp and glistening in the sunlight. He looked for a bird or a squirrel or even a fox up a tree trying to identify the source of her tears. "What am I looking at?"

Her smile was bittersweet. "A dreamweaver."

It took him a minute to make the connection. "I thought those were glass seahorses and starfish that they make in Cicero's studio to sell to the tourists."

"Yes, but this is the real thing," she replied.

She pulled her cell phone from her pocket and took a picture of . . . whatever it was she saw. Flynn certainly didn't see it.

"This is so cool," she murmured. "Alessandro told me this would happen, that sometime I would see something that triggered an idea for a piece that would be a true work of art. This is it. This will be my first piece of art glass. I see it so clearly. It will represent my dreams woven into a symbol marking my way. You're a designer, an inventor. I'll bet you have these moments, too."

Once upon a time, yes. Uncomfortable with the thought, he deflected. "Was there a little something extra in your thermos at lunch?"

Now when she smiled at him, the bitterness was gone, and an emotion he recognized, yet denied, set her eyes aglow. "Not in my thermos, no." With a glance back up at the web, she murmured just above a whisper, "Something extra in my heart."

Flynn's mount shifted. Hell, maybe the mountain shifted, because he suddenly felt unsure and off balance. Gabi gave her mount a little kick, taking the lead position on the trail. "I truly do think this is the most beautiful place on earth. I hereby dub this path Dreamweaver Trail, and I am ready to move forward on it. Come along with me, Brogan. I promise you the ride of your life."

She headed down the trail and into the meadow, never once looking back, as far as he could tell. It was as if she just assumed he'd follow.

God help him, he wanted nothing more badly than that.

SIXTEEN

On December thirtieth, Gabi awoke tired, sore, and more than a little cranky. She considered herself to be in excellent shape, but these past few days had just about done her in. Skiing, skating, snowmobiling, horseback riding—and yesterday she'd talked Flynn into going ziplining. Her muscles were weary. Her bones ached. Nevertheless, she remained in a nearly constant state of sexual frustration.

The mountain man was proving hard to conquer.

He wasn't indifferent to her, Gabi was certain of that. He tried to hide it, and had they not previously been intimate, he might have pulled it off. Despite the fact that she was involved in something new for her—she playing the predator role, with Flynn her prey—her feminine instincts told her she'd made progress. She caught the furtive looks and sensed when the heat rose within him. At times the bulge in his jeans was unmistakable. He wanted her.

But the man was as stubborn as all of her brothers combined. While he'd quit attempting to send her away, he certainly hadn't welcomed her with open arms. In fact, he went out of his way to avoid touching her. However, when he was forced to touch her—helping her onto her horse and checking her saddle, for instance—his hand had lingered on her calf. And she hadn't missed how he'd buried his nose in her hair during their snow-mobile ride.

Which only made her go out of her way to touch him as often as possible.

"For all the good it does me," she grumbled into her pillow before rolling from the bed and heading for the shower. Though she had high hopes that with today's ef-forts, the status quo would change. Today she had some-thing more intimate than outdoor sports in mind as her strategic assault on Flynn Brogan's defenses continued.

As planned, she spent the morning at Angel's Rest with her mother and sisters-in-law on a Romano women spa outing while the men of the family handled the child care. The hot stone massage was just what her sore mus-cles had ordered, and the manicure, pedicure, and facial provided a welcome little jolt to her feminine confi-dence. Her mom, Savannah, and Hope had attempted to grill her about Flynn, but Gabi had deflected. It all was too fragile for her to discuss at this time.

She spent the afternoon playing auntie with the babies and Holly, then visiting with Sarah Murphy, Cat Daven-port, and Ali Timberlake at Sarah's house, providing the promised summary of her time in Italy. Her phone rang at 4:03, just as she'd finished telling her friends about her privately guided tour of the Sistine Chapel. Seeing the number, her heart began to sing. "Hello?"

"So what's the deal?" Flynn said, his voice gruff and demanding.

Her smile stretched wide, though she kept her voice innocent. "What deal?"

"Except for the day you went skiing and told me about it, you've been out here every day since Christ-mas. Today you just don't show up?"

Noticed, did you? "Did you miss me?"

"I started to worry about you," he snapped.

Satisfaction warmed her. Perhaps the mountain man was thawing a bit. "I told you what my plans were for today. Girl time."

"No, you didn't."

"Sure I did. In the note." *The note you obviously didn't read.*

"What note?"

"The one I left where I knew you'd find it—tucked beneath that package on the table beside your door." Silence answered her, underscoring the fact that the stubborn man continued to studiously ignore the Christmas gift she'd left for him. "Check it out, Flynn. I'll see you later."

She disconnected the call and did a fist pump in the air. Then she remembered she had witnesses. Sheepishly she glanced around, seeing the avid interest in the other women's faces. "Give it up, girlfriend," Sarah said. "What—or should I say who—has been keeping you so busy since Christmas that you couldn't fit us in until today?"

Gabi hesitated. These women were her dear friends, but they didn't know the whole story about her time on Bella Vita Isle, nor the infamous identity of the bearded man living outside of town. "I love local gossip as much as the next person, but if I promise to tell you all the entire story another time, will you give me a pass today?" Seeing the protest on Sarah's face, she quickly added, "This matters."

Her friends, being her friends, shared a look, then immediately nodded. Cat Davenport spoke for them all when she said lightly, "We'll hold you to it."

The gathering broke up, and Gabi had just exited Sarah's house when her phone rang again. She checked the number and drew in a breath. Flynn. Was he calling to tell her not to come? He'd sounded really annoyed. Had she overplayed her hand? Maybe leaving the note with her present had been a bad idea, but dang it, the fact that he'd continued to ignore her gift all week hurt her feelings.

"Hello, Flynn," she said, smiling and answering a wave from the local barber, who had exited the grocery store across the street.

"I have a problem with gifts," Flynn said bluntly. "It's nothing personal."

Gabi's step slowed. *He's sharing something with me.* "Oh?"

"That's how I found out my wife was having an affair. She bought a gift for me—a birthday gift. Her mistake was that she bought a gift for her lover at the same time. She mixed up the gifts. She tried to cover, claiming the store had mixed things up, but I knew better. She gave herself away."

Understanding washed over Gabi. She knew that feeling, the sickness in your stomach when you realized you'd been betrayed by someone you loved. "That's really lousy, Flynn." She felt awful for him, but at the same time, her heart was singing. He'd shared something important with her. Something deep and intensely personal. She was making progress!

"Yeah, it was. I've had a hard time with gifts ever since. It's stupid, I know, but that's why I haven't opened your gift."

"That's giving her power she doesn't deserve."

"I know that." He paused, then added sheepishly, "Now. I guess I didn't exactly realize it myself until now."

"So, I've helped you see the error of your ways," she said lightly. "Good. Once you know a problem exists, you can fix it."

"I don't—"

"Speaking of problems," she interrupted. "Now that you've read my note, I have one question. How are you fixed for popcorn?"

"I have popcorn," he replied, annoyance returning to his voice. "But about this movie night business. I haven't forgotten our discussions on the island. I know how much you love classic movies, but honestly, it's been a long day, and I'm beat. I'm warning you straight out that if you put on a Cary Grant DVD, I'm liable to fall asleep."

"I'll take my chances," she replied. "Now, I'm right across from the Trading Post and I can dash in and pick something up if you need anything. Razors, perhaps?"

At that, for the first time, she heard a smile in his voice. "Butter. Real butter. None of that fake stuff."

"For your beard?"

"See you at seven, Gabriella," he said, his voice soft and maybe, just maybe, welcoming.

Flynn disconnected the call, and Gabi crossed the street to the Trading Post grocery store, where she bought butter and stood for a long time in front of the shaving cream and disposable razors.

Two hours later, she was in front of her closet debating what to wear. She didn't have a lot to choose from. Most of her clothing remained in storage. She finally settled on one of her old favorites, jeans and a sapphire-colored cashmere sweater that clung to her cleavage and did nice things for her eyes.

Thinking about her eyes led her thoughts toward Flynn's. Talking about his wife had been a good sign, she thought. Maybe tonight he'd finally tell her what happened to cause the injury to his eyes.

At five minutes to seven she pulled onto the lane leading to his cabin. Light in the windows beckoned through the darkness of the winter night. He opened the door when she was still ten steps from the cabin. The aroma of freshly popped popcorn wafted from inside, but it was the sight of him that stoked her hunger. He wore jeans and a plaid flannel shirt. He'd lost at least twenty pounds since last spring, and he no longer had that sun-tanned, sun-bleached look, but neither detracted from his movie-star-handsome looks. If anything, the more defined angles and planes of his face served to emphasize his masculinity, and the eye patch made him rakish.

"Did you bring the butter?" he asked, by way of hello.

"I did." She set down her tote bag, then pulled off her gloves and hat. She shook out her hair, aware that he was watching her rather than digging in the bag for the butter. That gave her a little sensual charge that grew when he helped her off with her coat and his gaze lingered on her sweater.

Her voice was the slightest bit husky as she asked, "Want me to melt it?"

He briefly closed his visible eye. "I'll do it."

Hiding her grin, Gabi turned away to greet Bismarck, who was lying on his bed in front of the fire. "You've been sprung from your crate. Aren't you a good, strong boy?"

He thumped his tail but didn't lift his head from the pillow.

Gabi clicked her tongue and scratched his nose. "What's the matter, Bismarck?"

"I think he's depressed about having to wear the cone," Flynn said as the microwave hummed to life.

"Understandable." She gave the dog one last pat, then rose and wandered toward the kitchen, where Flynn had poured two glasses of red wine and filled a bowl with fluffy popcorn. She stole a handful of popcorn, then picked up a glass of wine and crossed the room to warm herself in front of the fire. "So what did you do today, Mr. Brogan?"

"I worked on the design for your brothers' Christmas present."

Delight filled her. "Really? How cool is that? Can I see?"

"No." He poured the butter over the popcorn, then carried the bowl and his wineglass to the coffee table. "What torture have you planned to subject me to tonight? Rock Hudson? Cary Grant? I don't suppose I dare hope for any John Wayne."

He's teasing, too. Smiling, Gabi handed him her tote bag. "I brought three to choose from. Any of them is fine with me. It's your call, Brogan."

He smirked as he reached into the bag. When he pulled out the movies and saw the selections, his brows arched in surprise and his voice rang with pleasure. "*The Godfather*? *The Hangover*? *Goldfinger*? I can't believe you brought these."

"I have four brothers. There are classics, and then there are classics."

His grin spread naturally, and he leaned down to kiss her. "Damn, woman, but I love you."

The minute the words emerged from his mouth, they both froze. His visible eye rounded as Gabi's heart beat triple time. His expression took on a deer-in-the-headlights look.

As the moment stretched, Gabi knew she needed to step carefully or risk giving back all her gains since the Christmas Day dinner. She should play it off as a semi-joke or something like that, so she said lightly, "Of course you do. I brought you a great soundtrack, infantile humor, and Miss Monneypenny and Pussy Galore."

He blinked. "Do you do that on purpose, Gabriella?"

"Sometimes, but not this time," she replied, wincing. She backed away from him and reached for her wine. "So, what are we watching?"

Blowing out a long breath, he said, "Best go with *The Godfather*."

"Excellent choice. Have I told you about the *Godfather* tour? I did it one weekend. It took us to a gorgeous little village called Savoca on the island of Sicily."

She rattled on about the island and the tour while he dimmed the lights in the cabin and got the movie started. When the Paramount Pictures logo flashed on his screen, she breathed a sigh of relief. She needed to think . . . and avoid thinking about that line in the movie about going to the mattresses.

Flynn's words played over and over in her head as she stared unseeing at the television screen. Gabi wasn't aware of downing her wine or accepting his silent offer of a refill. She didn't realize when she scooted closer to him or even notice when he put his arm around her and tucked her up against him.

He'd said the three little words. Not in a bold declaration like she'd love to hear, true, and he had been caught off guard by having said them himself. But the words were the words, and the man she'd seen in Sacred Heart Church less than a week ago wouldn't have said them in any way whatsoever. She had made progress. Big progress.

Did he know his thumb was stroking up and down her arm?

While Michael Corleone walked the hills of Sicily, in her mind's eye Gabi returned to Bella Vita Isle, where Flynn's thumb had stroked her arm . . . and the whorl of her ear, the back of her neck, the line of her collarbone. The valley between her breasts. Her nipples. With the gentlest of touches, teasing, taunting, until desire had swelled within her and she'd arched her back, aching, silently asking, begging, whimpering.

"Dammit, Gabi," Flynn muttered, his voice tight.

Had she spoken aloud? Had she wriggled? Perhaps. She felt swollen and needy. She wanted his bare skin against hers. She craved friction. She craved Flynn.

She turned her head to find him watching her, his eyes heavy-lidded and hot. "Dammit, Gabi," he repeated, and then he captured her mouth with his. He was hungry, seeking. His tongue slid between her lips with aching familiarity and his hands went into her hair, pulling her close.

His kiss was hard and hot and . . . not right. As a general rule, Gabi didn't have a problem with beards, and she thought the scruffy look was downright sexy. But Flynn's beard was distracting, not just because it scratched her and made her imagine beard burn in uncomfortable places, but because of what it represented.

Sadness. Separation. Secrets.

From out of nowhere, tears stung her eyes, and she tensed and stiffened as a whisper of uncertainty fluttered through her. Had things changed too much? Was this divide too much to breach?

Flynn either noticed or felt something uncomfortable himself, because he suddenly broke the kiss and pulled away. "Sorry," he said gruffly. "I didn't mean for that to happen."

No, he didn't. Just like he hadn't meant to say he loved her. He was fighting this battle with everything he had. Why? What did he know that she didn't? Was it something that truly could keep them apart? Was she tilting at windmills here?

Standing, he picked up the popcorn bowl and carried it to his little kitchen. Gabi decided then that the time had arrived to speak to at least one of the elephants milling about the herd in the room. "Why is that, Flynn? Why can't we—"

"Because I just can't," he snapped, and even in the shadowed cabin, she couldn't miss the way his body had stiffened. Then he softened his tone and added, "Because it's not fair to either one of us. It was a mistake to let this week happen. I see that now. I just . . ." He paused and cleared his throat. "I thought that since you're leaving New Year's Day, it wouldn't hurt anything to . . ."

"To what?"

He stood saying nothing, a shadowed figure in the darkly lit room. Suddenly she hated the darkness, hated the beard and the eye patch. All of it hid him from her. He hid behind them. "Talk to me, dammit. What do you want?"

Pain laced his voice. "To spend time together. To pretend that day aboard the *Dreamer* never happened. To have just a little bit of time together the way it was before."

"Before what? What happened to you, Flynn? Help me understand." She held her breath, praying that he would open up. For both their sakes, she had to crash through those walls. His heart was hers if she could just get to it.

But Flynn pulled back, reinforced those damned walls. "You should leave now, Gabriella. It's safer. The weather forecast calls for snow to begin before midnight."

Safer for whom? Freshly annoyed and tired of being shut out, she opened her mouth to tell him so, but Flynn continued to speak. "Since tomorrow is your last day home, you should spend it with your family. I'll tell you goodbye now."

"Talk to me, Flynn."

He lifted her coat from the hook where it hung and said, "Enjoy Italy, Gabi. I'm so glad that you are following your dreams."

If she followed a dream right now, she'd punch him in the mouth.

A dozen different sentiments bubbled on her tongue, but she swallowed them back. She needed to keep her focus on the end of the trail, to think through what he'd said and done tonight, and act deliberately. She settled for saying, "You are so stubborn. Maybe that's a good thing, because stubbornness helped you survive whatever trials you faced after I left Bella Vita Isle, but I have to tell you, it totally drives me crazy sometimes."

His only response was to hold her coat out for her to take.

In a flurry of feminine huffiness, Gabi grabbed the jacket and stormed from the cabin saying, "Good night, you mule-headed bearded goat of a mountain man." Then she leaned up and kissed him, fast and hard, catching him off guard. And then she left.

Gabi Romano liked having the last word.

She was halfway to town before she calmed down enough to think about what had transpired. Once she did, a faint smile played across her face. At least temper had burned away the sexual frustration she'd suffered. All in all, she counted it a successful evening.

And now she was done with movies, ziplines, and small talk. Tomorrow the heavy guns were coming out. Or, to be more precise, the heavy knife.

The man didn't have a clue what was headed his way.

A foot of new snow fell overnight, but New Year's Eve dawned sunny and clear. As Flynn escorted Bismarck outside, he decided he was glad the snow had filled in the tracks of Gabi's car. If only he could figure out how to create a snowstorm in his mind to wipe away his memories of the past week.

The hours of this day couldn't pass fast enough. He needed this year to be over in the worst way.

He'd been a fool to think no harm would come from spending the week with her. Hadn't she haunted his thoughts daily following her departure from Bella Vita? Hadn't her spirit lingered in every room at Tradewinds? The sound of her laughter . . . her voice . . . her moans . . .

It would be the same way here in Thunder Valley. "We may just have to find somewhere else to live, Bismarck," he said as his gaze fell on the Christmas gift he'd never found the nerve to open.

Damn, woman, but I love you. How easily those oh-so-difficult words had tripped off his tongue. Sure, it had been a casual remark and he'd passed it off as such, but the fact remained that Flynn didn't make casual remarks like that. Not using those three particular words, words he'd spoken only to three other women in his life—his mother, Margaret Wharton, and Lisa. His feelings for Gabi were nothing like those he'd felt for his mom or for Margaret, and as for Lisa . . . well, about all he could remember now was the heartache.

Flynn turned away from the Christmas gift, disgusted with himself. She'd called him a mule-headed bearded goat of a mountain man. She'd have been closer to the mark had she said he was a yellow-bellied, empty-headed idiot. Coming to Eternity Springs had been a stupid idea. He wasn't healing. He wasn't living. He was hiding. It was a humiliating fact for him to admit. And dammit, he was tired of hiding.

After spending an hour doing the daily workout his physical therapist had prescribed, he found that his bad mood persisted. He tried to drag himself out of the funk with work, but the creative energy he'd found during recent days had disappeared. Gabi filled his thoughts. Sexual frustration tied him in knots. The day didn't get any brighter, either, when he fielded a phone call from the local sheriff.

"Thought I'd give you a heads-up," Zach Turner said. "The holiday respite appears to be over. News about your wolf is out. I wouldn't be surprised if you have visitors in the next few days."

"Thanks for the advance word. This sounds like a good time to make myself scarce." Maybe from the entire state of Colorado. This might be just the impetus he needed to find a new place to live. Or hide. Or simply exist.

He no sooner hung up from talking with Turner than Bismarck let out an alerting bark. Someone was invading his valley. Gabi? It wouldn't surprise him. It wasn't like her to give up easily. She was liable to pay him a visit simply because he told her not to do it.

But when his visitor drove into view, he experienced a moment of panic. It wasn't the red crossover SUV Gabi had been driving on her holiday, but a van. A news van.

He muttered an expletive. Exactly when had the universe ruled that the only kind of luck he was allowed was bad luck?

He debated what to do. In the wake of the sheriff's phone call, he was almost certain that this had something to do with the wolf. Almost. Knowing his luck, this would be a reporter come to broadcast the fact that he'd found the GQ Killer.

"I damned sure don't look very GQ these days," he muttered, stroking his beard. He decided that the odds were in his favor. No one had a reason to connect Flynn Brogan, one-eyed mountain man, with Flynn Seagraves, murder defendant. All he had to do was brazen his way through. He donned his sunglasses and wide-brimmed mountain man hat and exited the cabin.

The van stopped and a reporter and cameraman climbed out. "Mr. Brogan? I'm Paul Simmons with Channel 8 out of Colorado Springs, and we're doing a follow-up on the Christmas Eve story. I'd like to ask you a few questions and roll some tape of the local hero. I think Bismarck is his name?"

It proved amazingly easy for him to give the interview, and Bismarck cooperated by offering up appropriate puppy-dog eyes and awkward plastic-collar, feel-sorry-for-me movements. At least this had been a local guy rather than network. The last thing this pretty valley needed was for a cloud of news locusts to descend. Nevertheless, by the time the van left his property, Flynn was strung as tight as that ribbon around the Christmas gift Gabi had left for him. Had he not needed to head into town for Bismarck's follow-up vet appointment, he would have made use of his gym equipment for a second round of daily PT. After all, hadn't the first done wonders for all his frustrations?

Yeah, for about ten minutes.

He was itchy when he loaded Bismarck into his truck and twitchy when he entered the city limits of Eternity Springs. He made sure to avoid Aspen Street, where Maggie Romano's bed-and-breakfast was, and he kept his gaze firmly on the center of the road as he drove to Nic Callahan's vet clinic. He didn't want to see Gabi again before she left town.

Because he wanted more than anything to see Gabi again before she left town.

Dammit, he wouldn't do it. It had taken every bit of strength he had to send her away last night. He didn't think he could do it again.

No, it had to be this way. He had to keep Gabi—and everyone—at arm's length, because as soon as he reached out, bad things happened. To him. To them.

It had happened too many times now. It was as if he were cursed. He couldn't believe anything else. Hell, it even affected poor Bismarck. If Flynn had let him go to some nice suburban family, he sure wouldn't have tangled with a wolf.

Or saved a little girl, the voice of reason in his head whispered.

Flynn didn't listen to that voice. He hadn't listened to it in months.

Nic was running a little late at the clinic, so they had to wait almost half an hour before she took Bismarck into the examining room. Within a few minutes, Flynn knew something was wrong. "What is it?"

"Honestly, I'm not sure. His incisions look fine, but he's running a fever." She asked him a barrage of questions, which he answered as thoroughly as possible, then said, "I want to do some blood work, Flynn, and keep him overnight for observation."

Flynn studied his dog and stroked his coal-black coat as he stared into his big brown eyes. Did they look feverish? Pained? He couldn't tell, but then, he wasn't a vet, was he? "Okay. All right. Whatever he needs."

"He just needs to heal," Nic said. "That takes time."

Tell me about it.

Flynn exhaled a heavy breath, his stomach tight with worry. "I can't lose him, too, Dr. Callahan." That was a lot to reveal to a woman he didn't really know, but she was part of Eternity Springs, this place where he'd come to lick his wounds.

Nic touched his arm, her voice reassuring as she said, "I'm not worried about losing him, and I'll admit I'm being overly cautious. Since you confided Bismarck's history to me, well, Gabi Romano is a dear friend of mine. All animals who come to me deserve the best of care, but Bismarck is special. I want him to return to the best of health as quickly as possible."

"So he's not dying."

"No. He's banged up and hurting, and he has a little postsurgical infection. Based on what you've told me about his behavior, I suspect some IV fluids and antibiotics will make him a new man by this time tomorrow. Plus, he's not unlike other dogs—as great as the cone collars are to help heal wounds quickly, they are hard on the canine psyche."

"He's depressed."

"And confused. And maybe a little scared. A lot has happened."

She could have been talking about him. Flynn almost checked his neck for a cone collar.

Nic finished by saying, "He just needs a little TLC from somebody who loves him. Then he'll be good as new."

"Oh. Okay. Good. That's really, really good." Flynn dragged his fingers through his hair. "I guess I won't worry, then."

"Don't worry. I'm just an overly cautious veterinarian."

"Okay, then." Flynn took a minute to scratch Bismarck behind the ears and rub his belly and assure him that he'd be back the following day with copious treats in his pockets. He left the vet clinic feeling a little lost.

He turned away from Aspen Street, intending to stay as far away as possible from Maggie Romano's bed-and-breakfast while he worked his way back home. But when he drove down Cottonwood Street, he spied the old Victorian mansion, Cavanaugh House, that was the heart of the Angel's Rest estate. Without giving it much thought, he turned onto the bridge that crossed Angel Creek and made his way up to the house. He'd rent one of the cottages that sat along the creek for the night. They were private. No wolf news seekers would find him there, and he'd be close to Bismarck. Plus, visions of Gabi Romano wouldn't haunt him from every corner of the room.

"Oh, dear," Celeste Blessing said as she flipped through her reservation book at the lobby desk. "Due to the holiday, I'm afraid the only accommodation I have available is the Honeymoon Cottage. It's our most luxurious, most expensive accommodation. Though I will say, the hot tub is very nice on a cold winter's night, and the bed is heavenly."

"That's fine. I'll take it."

He signed the credit card slip and she handed over the

key. He considered going straight to the cottage and taking a nap, but he knew he'd better make the run back to Thunder Valley, tend the furnace, and throw a change of clothes and his toothbrush into a duffel before returning. He should grab the thriller he'd been reading, too.

While he made the drive, his thoughts focused on Bismarck. He'd noticed a little seepage around one suture, but he hadn't thought it was anything serious. He knew that his own wounds had done plenty of oozing in the days and weeks after the attack. He'd survived just fine, hadn't he? Bismarck would, too.

With his attention back in Eternity Springs with Bismarck, he didn't pay much attention to the tracks leading up to his cabin. After all, the television van and his own truck had carved paths in the snow. He didn't notice the smoke rising from his chimney at all. So he wasn't at all prepared to walk into his cabin and find it already occupied.

Gabi.

Wearing . . . what in the world was she wearing?

It clung to her curves, a fire engine red . . . what was it? A dress? A shirt? It had half-sleeves, a plunging neckline, and a row of big black buttons that ran from her breasts down to the hem of the outfit, which just barely covered her ass. Black garters held up fishnet stockings. Her open-toed heels had to be at least three inches tall.

She held a pair of barber's scissors in her hands.

"What the hell?" he said, barely able to form the words since his mouth had gone Death Valley dry.

She reached up and pulled his sunglasses from his head. "Sit down, Scruffy. It's time we dealt with that beard."

The lights in the room were muted, and he saw then that she'd set up a barber shop of sorts in front of the fireplace by moving his leather recliner from its spot in front of the television. His nightstand and the small table from beside the door sat behind the chair to one side. On them sat a large bowl he didn't recognize, a towel steamer and tongs, a badger shaving brush, a scuttle, shaving soap, three dark-colored glass bottles—and a straight razor.

"What the hell?" he repeated. Just how angry had he made her yesterday? He had visions of Sweeney Todd.

She smiled at him, slow and steamy and full of confidence. "Don't worry. I learned by shaving my father, then I had a part-time job in college working in a barbershop."

"Did you wear an outfit like that?"

"Not exactly, no."

Guess the barbershop didn't want to be responsible for heart attacks.

She lifted the lid from the steamer and picked up the tongs beside it. "Sit down, Flynn."

"Gabi, seriously. What is this?"

"I'm going to shave your face."

"Why?"

"Because it's time you quit hiding behind that beard. It's time you quit hiding from me."

"Gabi—" he began, protest in his voice.

She interrupted, with a bit of an edge in hers. "It's New Year's Eve, Brogan. I'll be damned if I'm going to be such a wallflower that I spend tonight alone. I won't ask you to take me to the party at Angel's Rest, but I made dinner reservations at the Yellow Kitchen and you're going to take me. Even my mother has a date! One night, Brogan. Clean-shaven and wearing a jacket and tie. You can give me that much."

"I don't have a jacket and tie here."

"Be a problem solver."

"It isn't smart, Gabriella."

"Maybe not, but it's life. Life happens, Flynn, whether we live it or not. Tonight I want to live it. With you.

Now . . ." She pointed to the chair. "Sit down and let me get to work."

It was easier to sit than continue to argue, and besides, he didn't have the will to resist her. So he took a seat in his recliner and gave himself up to her tender mercies and ministrations.

She used the scissors on his beard first, cutting close to the skin, then she wrapped his face in a warm, damp, eucalyptus-scented towel. When her fingers began to massage his face, he almost groaned aloud.

She replaced the cooling towel twice and continued her massage, standing behind him, leaning over, her breasts occasionally brushing him. It was the most pleasurable torture he'd ever endured—and she was just getting started.

After the hot towels, she massaged oil directly into his skin. He closed his eyes and allowed himself to enjoy her touch. When she stepped away, he knew a keen sense of loss.

Then he heard the *click click click* of the shaving brush hitting the scuttle, and he opened his eyes to watch her work up a lather—in more ways than one. She was so damned beautiful, with her hair pinned up and a few stray curls escaping. And that damned outfit . . . a Halloween costume, he guessed. She was trying to seduce him. *And I just might let her.*

She brushed the warm lather onto his face in slow, sensual strokes while she softly hummed a tune he knew he'd heard before but couldn't place. Wood in the fireplace crackled and popped, and the scent of sandalwood from the oils and soaps she used on him blended with the oriental-spicy fragrance of her own perfume. It was as sensual a moment as he could recall, and Flynn abandoned any attempt to resist its allure.

Then he heard her pick up the razor and he opened

uncertain eyes. She gave a little laugh. "Trust me, Brogan."

He did. He closed his eyes and relaxed.

After allowing the lather to sit for a few minutes, she made the first pass with the razor with the grain, the fingers of her left hand gently pulling his skin taut when necessary, her breath warm on his face, her full, soft breasts teasing him deliciously.

She lathered him again, made a second pass with razor sideways to the grain, and then repeated the process for a third and final time. She told him she'd infused the next hot towel with lemon essential oil, and that the aftershave mask that came next would replenish the moisture in his skin.

"Now, a cold towel with lavender essential oil to soothe and relax," she said, her voice a throaty purr. She finished with a toner and a sandalwood-scented balm that she applied with her thumbs in slow, massaging strokes.

"So beautiful," she murmured, and her words brought him back to reality.

"Scarred."

"Yes." She took a step back, folded her arms, tilted her head, and studied him. "I suspect the ones inside are worse. I have to say, Brogan, the scar on your neck scares me to think about, but the one on your cheek . . . added to the eye patch . . ." She gave a sensuous shiver. "Call me unfeeling and shallow, but I find them totally sexy. A complete turn-on."

Then she did something no other barber had ever done to him before. She plopped herself down in his lap and tenderly kissed first the scar on his neck and then the one on his cheek. Reactively, his hands spanned her hips, and he felt her hands grab his shoulders. Hard. He remembered how she loved. Not a wilting violet. This woman gave as good as she got.

Then she kissed his mouth, absent the tenderness. This was total heat. She literally stole his breath away.

She threaded her fingers through his hair and held his head. Dammit, she held his heart, too.

She wiggled her butt and snuggled against his erection, and then used her tongue and teeth to drive him to the edge of madness.

And then, just as the thought of levering from the chair and carrying her to his bed began to sound like an excellent idea, she was gone.

Gabi stood two feet away, her chest heaving as she fastened the top two buttons he didn't remember undoing. Her lips were swollen, her hair tumbling from its pins. "Seven o'clock, Brogan. Pick me up at Aspenglow Place."

He shuddered out a breath and surrendered. "Okay."

SEVENTEEN

After Gabi left, Flynn spent a full five minutes sitting in his chair. Maybe this wasn't really happening. Maybe he'd fallen asleep in his chair in front of the TV and this was all a dream. Except his eyes were open, and his face felt like a baby's butt.

"Okay, then," he said, speaking out loud—to himself, since Bismarck wasn't around. "You're in this. One night. It's only one night."

Was it a mistake? Was it destiny?

Was it just lust?

Whatever it was, he should make it a damned good one.

From that moment on, he was a man with a mission. First off, he placed a call to Matthew. After a few minutes of small talk and catching up about the Wharton family holiday, he got down to business. "Matthew, are my extra clothes stored here or in that rental unit in town? I need a suit."

"They're in your workshop. There are a couple of wardrobe boxes in the far north corner behind the lathe."

"Shoes, too?"

"Yes, and shirts and ties and a dress coat, of course."

Of course. Flynn grinned. Matthew Wharton was a

true friend. Flynn had been a lucky man all those years ago when the hungry attorney charged into his office and convinced him that Seagraves-Laraby needed his services.

"So, are you going out tonight?" Matthew continued.

Flynn hesitated. He couldn't say anything to his friend about Gabi or he'd never hear the end of it. "Some TV people showed up today to ask about the wolf. Local media, thank goodness. For now, anyway. I want to be ready in case it all goes to hell."

"Oh." Matthew's voice sank with disappointment. "Well, if it gets to be more than you want to handle, I'm a plane ride away."

"Thanks, Matt. Give Margaret a kiss for me, and tell her I said happy New Year to you both."

"And to you too, Flynn. To you too."

Flynn stood staring at his phone for a moment. It occurred to him that Matt had been more of a father to him over the past three years than had Nolan Seagraves. A weird combination of sadness and satisfaction washed through him. Why had he never realized that before this moment?

Maybe he had to truly let go of his hopes where his father was concerned if he wanted to see Matthew for what he truly was.

He made up his mind that his New Year's resolution would be to make sure that Matthew and Margaret knew how much they meant to him. In the meantime, he had a date to plan. Since there would only be this one night, he might as well do it right.

He checked the time, made a plan, then retrieved his clothes from the wardrobe box in the workshop. How had he missed noticing this box?

Because you've hardly noticed anything since the attack, that's why.

"Well, maybe that's changing," he muttered as he

headed back into town. Or maybe he'd return to his numbed and clueless state after Gabi left again. Time would tell, and in the meantime, he wouldn't worry about it.

Upon arriving in town, he checked into his cottage at Angel's Rest, tried on his suit, and was relieved that it didn't look any worse than it did, considering he was twenty pounds lighter than the last time he'd worn it. Next he visited the Trading Post, then the liquor store, and the florist. Finally he made a vital stop at the drugstore. He had just enough time to shower and dress before making the short trip to Aspenglow Place.

At a stop sign, he glanced in the rearview mirror and saw his scars. Not Frankenstein, he could now admit. The surgeon had done a good job and the scars on his face weren't all that noticeable, the worst one being the gash the bullet had carved aboard the *Dreamer*. Gabi had seen them, of course, when she shaved him. He wondered how she'd react to the rest of them. Would she be repulsed? For the first time in longer than he could remember, the thought of getting naked in front of a woman gave him pause. Maybe he should have gone through those additional surgeries after all.

He took his foot off the brake but hesitated a moment before pushing on the gas pedal. *Are you sure you're ready for this? After protecting yourself for so long, are you going to be able to set it aside? And why are you doing it? For Gabi? For yourself?*

Yes, to all of the above.

There was a greeting card quote he'd seen floating around the Internet that said, "Life shouldn't be counted in the number of breaths you take, but by the moments that take your breath away."

For Flynn, this was one of those moments.

He continued to the B&B, parked along the curb, and

walked up the front step. Approaching the front door, he recognized that he'd most likely regret this in the morning, but for now, for tonight, Flynn Brogan was going to live. Breathlessly.

While Gabi readied for her date, she wondered if she was wasting time and energy. Would the man actually show?

Sure, he'd agreed in the heat of the moment, emphasis on the word "heat," but what had happened after she left? Her phone had rung three times that afternoon, and each time she'd expected to find Flynn on the other end of the call. Maybe she'd made a mistake by not taking the barber session to the conclusion toward which it had been headed, but dang it, she had some pride, too. She'd done all the pursuing over the past week, and frankly, that was new for her. In the past, men pursued her. This shoe-on-the-other-foot thing had just about reached its limits.

At five-thirty when she went upstairs to begin the process of getting ready, she'd almost broken down and called him. That would have been a strategic mistake, however, so she managed to keep her fingers off the keypad. If the man stood her up, he stood her up. Her dreamweaver trail would have led straight off the cliff. If that happened, she wondered if she'd have the gumption to drag herself up and put the pieces back together to keep trying.

Telling herself to think positively, she nevertheless prepared for her date as if going to war. If he did show up, she'd darn sure be ready to join the battle.

After going for the bombshell look that afternoon, she chose a classic little black dress for her look on New Year's Eve, pairing her old standby with new heels she'd purchased in Milan and the glass necklace and earrings her teacher had given her for Christmas before she left

Italy. She kept her makeup understated and wore her hair up in a smooth chignon.

Her mother had already left, so she was alone in the house as seven approached. She descended the stairs and debated opening a bottle of wine. If he didn't show up, she'd probably drink the whole thing herself, and could there be anything more pitiful?

Then, three minutes before the hour, the doorbell rang. Gabi sucked in a deep breath, checked her lipstick in a mirror, and answered the door.

Her heart almost stopped. He looked so hot, and while "GQ" fluttered through her thoughts, she refused to go there. It wasn't fair to him. "Hello."

"Hello. You look gorgeous, Gabriella."

"As do you, Mr. Brogan."

So began a most magical night. Eight o'clock dinner reservations allowed them time to have that glass of wine before heading to the Yellow Kitchen. Then their meal was a leisurely experience of casual conversation, soft lighting, romantic piano music, and delicious food and wine. They danced on the small wood parquet dance floor, and it was heaven being in his arms. They stretched the meal out until almost nine-thirty, and when they left the restaurant, he held her hand.

"A TV crew visited my cabin this morning to do one of those feel-good interviews about Bismarck saving the girl from the wolf," he told her. Gabi's step slowed, but he didn't give her a chance to speak before his hand tightened around hers and he continued. "Because I thought it best to get away from there for a few days, I rented a cottage—the last available—at Angel's Rest when I brought Bismarck into the vet. I'd like to take you there now. It's new, private, and very nice. But if you have your heart set on attending someone's party, then—"

"No!" she quickly said. "That sounds fine. It sounds great."

"Good." He opened the passenger side door of his truck for her, then leaned in to kiss her quickly before easing it shut.

Gabi dropped her head back against the headrest and shivered in anticipation. She hadn't been misreading the signals he'd transmitted over dinner! She hadn't thought she was wrong about that, but with Flynn Brogan—this version of Flynn Brogan, anyway—a girl was never sure. And when he led her into the honeymoon cottage at Angel's Rest, not a single iota of doubt remained. He'd set the scene for seduction—in a honeymoon suite, no less.

As Flynn helped her with her coat, her gaze noted the champagne bucket, two flutes, and chocolate-covered strawberries sitting on a table to one side of the fireplace, where kindling sat stacked and waiting for a match. The floor cushions in front of the hearth were right off the pages of *Arabian Nights* and through a half-opened doorway she spied a bed as big as Hummingbird Lake. "I knew that Celeste had plans to build a few more cottages, but she's outdone herself with this."

"Wait until you see the private courtyard. It has a hot tub and plunge pool and enough heaters to keep a person warm even on a night as cold as this one."

"Really?" Her eyes widened with interest. "Show me."

"Anything you'd like, my lady," he replied, his gaze warm, his voice deep and smooth. "The courtyard is this way."

He led her into the bedroom where, yes, the bed was oversized, and toward a pair of French doors. He flipped a set of switches on the wall; outside, lights flooded on and tall patio heaters flared to life. The infinity-edged hot tub was huge and inviting, with clouds of steam rising into the night air and little waterfalls spilling from it into the plunge pool some five feet below. "Oh, wow,"

Gabi breathed. "This is fabulous. It makes me want to . . ." Her voice trailed off.

"Strip off your clothes and slip into the water?"

She hadn't realized he'd moved so close, but now he was there beside her, his hand lifting to trail down the side of her face, from forehead to temple to her cheek. He cupped her jaw and lifted her face. "Happy New Year, Gabriella."

"Happy New Year, Flynn."

His smile was tender. Expectant. "You're so beautiful." Taking her hands in his, he lifted them to his lips and trailed kisses along the tops of her fingers. Without words, he pulled her fingers to his face. Responding to his lead, she gently caressed his scars, and he leaned into her touch with a strangled moan.

He needed this, she realized. The touch, the acceptance. She saw that more than ever in this moment.

Then he kissed her. And kissed her. And kissed her.

Taking her in his arms, he slowly danced backward to the bed as zippers and buttons were undone quickly. Soon they were entwined upon the soft bedding and Flynn came down over her, kissing her neck, trailing a path down to her breasts. Impatiently her hands threaded in his hair and her hips rose. She remembered how he felt. She remembered how she felt. How they felt together. Tears stung her eyes.

Gabi felt like she'd finally come home.

He made love to her in the big wide bed and again beside the fire. They ate strawberries and drank champagne from flutes, then he spilled the frothy liquid onto her naked skin and used his tongue to taste and tempt and tease and drive her insane. His mouth was warm and wet on her belly, and the erotic shock of what followed left Gabi boneless and sated.

A little before midnight, he opened another bottle of champagne while she grabbed two of the fluffy white robes from the closet. With the lights dimmed, they slipped naked into the steaming water of the hot tub and gazed up at the star-filled sky, and when Flynn entered her just as the sounds of cheers and bells and horns began to sound and fireworks exploded over Humming-bird Lake signaling the new year, she lost the ability to think at all.

Later, when they lay entwined upon the bed drifting toward sleep, she thought about the stars and how her brother Lucca often said that he'd fallen in love with his Hope beneath the star-filled night sky over Eternity Springs. With Flynn lying naked and warm against her, sated and pleasantly exhausted, she knew a joy that she hadn't experienced in months.

This was right. She and Flynn were right. This was a new year, a new beginning. Happiness welled up inside her, and Gabi smiled into the dark.

She shifted position, spooning against a now obviously sleeping Flynn, wiggling her butt to get even closer. She'd be sore in the morning. Wonderfully, deliciously sore. *Gabi old girl, the shave strategy worked like a charm.* She drifted off to sleep with a smile on her face.

She dreamed that she was floating on her back in a warm, gently rocking moonlit sea.

Above her, the heavens shine with millions of stars. She smiles at the beauty of the sight and hope fills her heart.

But I'm not in Eternity Springs. Where am I?

Her legs sink and begin to tread water. She turns around, searching . . . there a boat. The name Dreamer *is painted blue against a white hull.*

A man appears on deck. Flynn. "Hey, beautiful. Conch salad ready in five."

"Conch salad makes you horny," Gabi calls back, laughing.

But then her laughter turns to a scream as figures rise up behind him. Flynn is falling into the sea, past the hull of the Dreamer, *which has turned from blue to red.*

Gabi awoke, her heart pounding, her throat tight with fear. Where was she? What . . . oh. The events of the night flooded back. She was in bed with Flynn. In the Honeymoon Cottage. In Eternity Springs.

Not aboard the *Dreamer* in the Caribbean Sea.

Relieved, she blew out a breath. Well, now. That had been icky. She hadn't had a pirate dream in a couple of months. She had thought—hoped, prayed—they were behind her.

The stargazing and the sex must have triggered it, she decided. After all, the last time she'd indulged in either one, she'd been in the Caribbean. Rolling over to face Flynn, she studied him. There was just enough ambient light to illuminate his features, relaxed in sleep. Did he have nightmares about that day?

For the first time in months, she deliberately allowed her thoughts to return to their doomed sail aboard the *Dreamer*. How exciting it had been. She'd felt as if she'd been living a movie. A romantic fantasy.

A joy that need not have ended. Three evil men had changed the course of her and Flynn's lives—Bismarck's, too—and they'd paid for it with their lives. Had they had wives and children? Families who mourned them? Had the monetary gains from a life of piracy been worth the risk and, in the end, the ultimate price?

She wished that she and Flynn had plotted a different course that fateful morning. How would their lives be different today had they not run afoul of those criminals? She wouldn't have another soul on her conscience, that was for sure. Flynn wouldn't have two on his.

He'd been through so much. She recalled the moment earlier tonight when she got her first glimpse of his naked torso. It had taken real effort not to gasp, and now, thinking back on it, shielded by the darkness and his slumber, she allowed her tears to silently fall. Reaching out, she gently trailed her fingers over ridges of scar tissue that hadn't existed last spring.

Many, many ridges. Not just on his chest, but everywhere: his back, his buttocks, his thighs, his calves. No accident had done this. Someone had hurt him badly—on purpose. With a knife and something else. Some of these scars were burns. Who had done this? Why? Did it have something to do with his murdered wife? Anger ripped through her, raw and hot.

The need to know what had happened to him washed over her like a tidal wave. She knew something of his life before Bella Vita Isle, so much having been written about him after his wife's murder. But after Bella Vita? She'd found next to nothing in her online searches. Certainly not a speck of information about his being . . . what? Attacked? Beaten? Tortured? She was tempted to wake him up and demand explanations before he could think and throw up another layer of bricks. Or would that destroy all the progress she'd made thus far?

Oh, Flynn. What did they do to you?

The trauma he'd suffered had changed him.

Instinctively, she dipped her head and gently kissed the ridge that bisected his chest from his collarbone to below his hip, taking her time, working her way down every inch of the scar, wishing she could somehow touch the wounds deep inside him with her kiss. From that scar, she moved to another and then another and then another.

"Gabi . . . ," he whispered, his voice gritty with sleep.

Just at what point he awoke, she couldn't pinpoint, but when she kissed her way down his hip to find his fist clenched tightly at his side, she knew that he was conscious of her ministrations. At the discovery, she hesitated. Maybe she was pushing too hard.

"Touch me," he said, the words a plea. "Just touch me . . . I need to feel your hands on me."

"Will I hurt you?" she asked softly.

"Maybe. Probably. But the memory will be worth it."

"Oh, Flynn." So Gabi didn't stop. She kissed her way down one leg and up the other, kissed his knuckles, his arm, his shoulder, then up to his face. The wetness she found there could possibly have been her own tears, but she didn't really believe that. His breathing was labored. Measured. He was fighting a battle from within. A last-ditch effort. She swallowed a lump of emotion in her throat, then softly, sweetly, kissed first one closed eye and then the other. He was still so beautiful.

"Flynn . . . ," she breathed, then she kissed him again. "I love you." And again. "I love you." *Let down those walls, my love.*

The third time she kissed his mouth, he came to life. He kissed her back, hungry and passionate and bordering on angry. With few preliminaries, he rolled her over and entered her. With every stroke, she sensed his burning anguish. He'd always been a powerful lover, but this was different. With every pound of his hips against hers, she knew he was exorcising the demons that haunted him. It was pure need. Gabi simply held on and let him take her, and when he threw back his head and let out the wounded-animal cry of her name, it was like something escaping him.

He collapsed on top of her, and for a long moment his harsh breathing was the only sound in the room. Then he muttered an epithet and rolled off of her. "Gabi . . . hell, I'm sorry. I was . . . I didn't . . . You didn't . . . I'm sorry. I'm so sorry. Did I hurt you? My God, I don't—"

She placed her hand on his arm. "Shhh . . . I'm okay, Flynn. You didn't hurt me."

"I just . . ."

"I know." She kissed him, a lingering, soft kiss. Savoring the moment, she closed her eyes. His lips were pliant and sweet. "It's okay. I'm okay."

And before long, he was making love to her again. Gabi welcomed him into her body, her heart, her soul.

EIGHTEEN

Flynn awoke with the first rays of dawn, way too early considering that he'd gotten such little sleep the night before. The memory of Gabi's cries, her voice, and her body spooned against his drifted through his mind, and without opening his eyes, he smiled lazily. A man could get used to that. To her.

No sooner had the thought formed than a heavy weight settled on his chest. He wouldn't have the chance to get used to it. Gabi was leaving today, which was a good thing. Better to rip that bandage off fast. He'd learned that lesson well enough over the past few years.

Hell, the only reason he let her see him was because she was leaving, so he wouldn't have to deal with any aftermath. Like questions. Like having her kiss his scars and cry over him.

He knew what she'd want next. She would want to *talk*. She'd want details about his injuries, about Lisa's death. She'd want to slice him open and root around in his weaknesses and insecurities. Well, he had no interest in that.

I'm glad she's leaving, he told himself.

Liar.

Okay, he wasn't glad, but it was better for her this way. Having her around this past week had been a nice diversion, but that was the thing about reality—it's real. His reality was that he had no business infecting Gabi's bright life with his darkness.

He wondered what time her plane left. Probably not too early or she would have mentioned the need to be up and out. He'd indulge himself and hold her for a few more minutes, then he'd go take a shower. Maybe she'd take the hint and leave and avoid a messy goodbye.

Goodbye. That's what it would be. What it would have to be. He'd need to find a new place to settle before she returned for good, but that had been his plan all along. He shouldn't freak out about it.

She felt like heaven in his arms, all soft and warm and sweet. He missed sharing a bed with someone. The right someone. *Oh, well—like they say, life sucks and then you die.*

Then, tired of his own pity party, Flynn eased away from Gabi and strode into the bathroom. He turned the water to just short of scalding and stepped beneath the spray. He showered for a long time, allowing the steamy heat to soak into his cold bones. Finally he reached for the faucet handle and had the water halfway shut off when he heard a noise behind him. He looked over his shoulder. *Okay, then. Guess a messy goodbye won't be the end of the world.*

A naked Gabriella Romano stepped into the shower, and within seconds it wasn't the hot water generating the heat.

Forty-five minutes later, after shower sex and one more round in the bed, he lay working up the energy to move when he sensed her gaze upon him. Sure enough, he opened his eyes to see her watching him. "Tell me what happened to you."

A memory flashed. The tip of Vicente Villarreal's knife playing with Flynn's balls. He shuddered and rolled from the bed. "Do you want some breakfast? There's a basket with breakfast cookies, and there are bacon and eggs in the fridge. I'm happy to cook."

"Flynn—"

"I'm starving, myself." He found his jeans and a Georgia Tech sweatshirt and pulled them on, then went to the cottage's small kitchen, where he pulled a pound of bacon and a carton of eggs from the fridge. Moments later, Gabi joined him wearing one of the plush spa robes from the closet.

She drew a deep breath, then said, "I'm hungry, too, Flynn, but I'd like some answers with my eggs."

"Is scrambled okay?"

"Eggs or answers?"

He set his mouth. "What time is your flight? I assume someone is driving you to Gunnison to make your connection to Denver?"

"Distraction won't work with me, Flynn Brogan. Not this morning. This is too important."

"No, it's not. This is you being curious."

"It's not curiosity. I see your scars. I feel them. I need to know, to understand you."

"Let it go, Gabi," he snapped. When a mulish look came over her expression, he pressed on, speaking more forcefully, but choosing his words with less care. "Just because we had New Year's sex doesn't give you a key to my private business."

"New Year's sex? That's what you think it was?"

He wouldn't look at her. "Wasn't it?"

She folded her arms. "Now, that's just mean."

He ripped open the package of bacon and shrugged. He was feeling pretty mean. She was treading into some dangerous territory, and he wasn't going along for the ride.

"Who hurt you, Flynn?" she repeated. "Tell me!"

Silently he snorted. Had he wanted to answer—which he damned well didn't—where to start? Lisa? Her sister?

His best friend? His father? *You're edging into that pity-party place again, Brogan.* "How many slices of bacon would you like?"

Her toes began to tap. "I think you and I are having our first fight."

"I'm having four. I'll make you two."

He set six pieces of bacon into the heated skillet, and as they began to sizzle, Gabi Romano did, too. "I swear, sometimes I think you could give my brothers lessons on how to be stubborn, and believe you me, that's saying a lot. Okay, here's the deal. I'm going to fall back to the technicality that you said it to me first, which you did, even though I know you didn't mean to say it. That sits better on my pride, and besides, I don't think people say such a thing even in an offhanded way if they don't mean it."

What in the world was she talking about?

"Flynn, I love you. I told you that last night, but you might think it was just sex talk. Well, it wasn't. I love you, and I know in my heart that you love me, too."

Oh, crap. "Don't do this, Gabi. Please. We've had a nice week, a fun New Year's Eve, but that's all it was. It's all it can be. It's best for both of us that way."

"Why? Explain it to me."

"No." He couldn't go there. He never would. His time on the beach had been ugly and he refused to think about it, much less talk about it. "There's no need for it. Last night was our goodbye."

Damned if she didn't smile at him and shake her head as if he were a mistaken child. "You have stubborn down to an art form, but you are not a good liar. How anyone who knew you could think you lied about the circumstances surrounding your wife's death is beyond me. Tend your bacon, Flynn."

He frowned down at the frying pan, then used a fork to flip the pig. How had he totally lost control of the conversation? Hell, of the entire past week! Anger began to churn in his gut, and he snapped, "I'm not your lap dog."

That wiped the smile off her face. "Do you always lash out when you feel threatened?"

"Are you always such a—" He bit off the word before it left his mouth. She didn't deserve that. From the very beginning, Gabi had called 'em as she saw 'em. She didn't lie. She didn't prevaricate. If she said she believed he loved her, then his actions had given her reason to believe so. If she said she loved him, well, then she loved him. *Oh, Gabi. I'm so sorry.*

She was dead wrong if she thought he couldn't lie through his teeth when necessary, but he'd try starting with the truth. He set down the fork. "Look, Gabi. You are a lovely, wonderful woman, and I've enjoyed spending time with you. If I were looking for love from any woman, I'd hope I'd be smart enough to look in your direction. But I'm not in the market. I wasn't last spring, and I'm certainly not now."

As he picked up another egg to add to his bowl, he saw no sign that his words were getting through to her. Talk about stubborn.

"Besides," he continued, "it's a moot point. You're returning to Italy today, and I have no intention of attempting to carry on a long-distance relationship. I won't say I regret last night, because I don't. I do regret if last night gave you the wrong impression about my . . . um . . . feelings."

"I'm not."

He waited a beat. "Under the wrong impression?"

"Returning to Italy."

Involuntarily, Flynn's fist tightened around the egg until it broke in his hand. He barely even noticed. "What do you mean, you're not returning to Italy?"

"Did you ever open the Christmas gift I gave you?"

"What does that have to do with you needing to catch your flight?"

"You haven't opened it." She sighed with disappointment. "It's a dreamweaver. It's the color of your eyes and sunshine, and it's shaped like a sail. It took me seven tries to get the color and shape just right. Open it, Flynn. Hang it. It will bring sunshine into your life and chase away the shadows of bad memories. I gave it to you because I think you need it, and . . . really, Flynn. Wash the egg off your hand. You're making a mess."

"Quit telling me what the hell to do!" He picked up another egg and squeezed it until it broke, then he flung the slimy mess away. It hit the refrigerator door and dribbled onto the floor.

Shocked by his outburst, Gabi took a step backward.

"You are the pushiest woman I've ever met!" he continued, the fear inside him putting an ugly note into his voice. "You show up uninvited at my house every day for a week, then you top your seduction off with that little shaving trick. Despite everything, I'm still a man, Gabriella. It worked. We had sex. This is the morning after, and it's time for one of us to leave. I suggest that it be you. Keep going all the way to Italy."

The rosy color drained from her cheeks, leaving her complexion ashen. Upon seeing her reaction, Flynn's stomach rolled with shame and guilt. That only made him angrier. "I don't need your dreamweaver sunshine in my life. I like living in the shadows. It works for me. I want to be alone. I like being alone. I want you to leave me the hell alone!"

"Stop it!" she burst out. "You're just trying to drive me away because I'm asking questions and pulling down your walls."

"I'm trying to drive you away because it's over. I hate to be cruel about this, but you don't really leave me many options. I'm a wealthy man, Gabriella. I'm a wealthy, infamous man. I can pretty much have whomever I want, when I want, and that suits me just fine. I'm sorry if that doesn't fit with the little fantasy you've been building in your head, but that's the way it is."

"I'm not leaving until we settle this."

"Settle? What do we have to settle? As far as I'm concerned, we're done."

Outwardly calm but inwardly quaking, he knew he'd better put an end to this fast, before he lost it. Rinsing his hands, he casually added, "Of course, I'd be happy to upgrade your plane ticket to first class, Gabi. Last night was very nice."

That did it. Finally. Her eyes flashed and went round. "So what is that? Payment for services rendered?"

He shrugged. Hiding the trembling in his hand, he turned the bacon. Outwardly calm, inwardly dying. There was no turning back at this point.

"Okay, so that's it." She spoke in a deadly quiet tone he'd never heard before, a voice filled with resignation, one that said he wasn't worth the fight. Her beautiful blue eyes remained clear and free of tears. "Fine. You win. I'm gone."

Thank God.

"And to think that I was ready to throw away the opportunity of a lifetime for you, and you won't even let me into your world just a little bit. You want to live behind walls, fine. That's your choice."

You're right. It is. It's my only choice.

"That doesn't work for me. I thought maybe you might be ready to break through that, and I would have helped you. Guess that was my mistake or my temporary insanity."

He met her gaze without flinching or giving his inner turmoil away. "Must have been."

Her eyes shot fire, but her tone dripped honey as she added, "Oh, and about the upgrade, Flynn? Let me assure you, money doesn't buy class. Nor does it buy sense or integrity. And I won't settle for less."

She stalked off to the bedroom, leaving him with runny eggs on his hands and on his face, slamming the bedroom door behind her. Five minutes later she was back.

Flynn glanced up from dumping his scrambled eggs onto a plate. Gabi glared at him, full of fire and fury, and he thought he'd never seen a more gorgeous, glorious woman in his life.

"You sure had me fooled, Flynn Brogan. That day on the *Dreamer* when you saved us, I thought you were the bravest man alive. I never guessed you were such a coward."

With that, head held high, Gabriella Romano didn't spare him another look as she sailed out the front door of the honeymoon cottage at Angel's Rest.

And out of his life.

NINETEEN

In the wake of Gabi's departure, Flynn decided that he'd rather face television cameras than the memories inside the honeymoon cottage. He picked up Bismarck—now free from the prison of his cone collar—along with a bottle of new antibiotics from the vet and returned to his cabin. His nice, dark, lonely cabin.

"Welcome home," he muttered.

He tried to tell himself he was glad for the solitude, but he'd never been very good at lying.

He helped Bismarck down from the truck cab, and they entered the house. It felt cold and empty, and so Flynn went directly to the hearth where he built a fire. Soon flames flickered and sap in the wood spat and crackled, and warmth filled the room. But Flynn couldn't get warm as the cold reality of regret and loss settled into his bones.

He'd lost a lot in his life. His wife, his reputation, his best friend, his father . . . but this? This was like someone had cut out his heart and stomped on it right in front of him.

Despite the fact that it wasn't even noon, he cracked the seal on a bottle of scotch and settled down to get sloshed. Hey, it was a holiday, after all.

He sat with his legs outstretched and crossed at the

ankles, his glass propped on his belly as he stared into the fire. *Flynn, I love you. Tell me what happened. . . .*

His hand gripped his glass hard as the sounds reverberated in his memory.

"We're gonna skin you alive, gringo. After we cut your dick off and shove it down your throat." Maniacal laughter rises on the night air like smoke from the fire burning on the beach.

Firelight glints off the curved blade of a fillet knife. Pain explodes as the knife slices into tendons.

Tell me what happened, she'd said. *Tell me. Tell me. Tell me.*

"Rather somebody shoot me and put me out of my misery." He took another long sip of his scotch. Why the hell had he ever thought it was a good idea to move to Eternity Springs?

Because the idea of the place had called to him, appealed to something inside him that he seldom acknowledged or recognized. They said that Eternity Springs was where broken hearts came to heal. Well, broken hearts were one thing, broken souls something else. He'd hoped for too damned much.

Flynn sipped his whiskey and brooded. How long he sat there, he couldn't say, but as the minutes passed, anger and despair grew inside him. He rose and began to pace the room, driven by an emotion . . . a need . . . that he couldn't define. He wanted to lash out. He wanted to fight. He wanted to beat somebody up.

That somebody being himself.

He couldn't erase the memory of Gabi's eyes, her devastation at his words. He'd driven her away just as he'd intended. Just as he'd wanted to do.

Liar.

He downed his drink, poured another. His hand tightened around the crystal glass, and he was seconds from drawing back his arm and letting it fly when a knock sounded on the door.

He halted mid-pace, his head whipping around, an animal on alert. If this was another reporter or a PETA person, he swore he'd go protective-Bismarck on him.

Unless . . . could this be Gabi? Could her valiant heart have driven her to make one more effort at convincing him to stop being an ass?

If this was Gabi at his door, what would he do?

Maybe he could just tell her that he was too broken. After all, shattered glass couldn't be repaired. That's what he was. Shattered. And she needed to start over with another piece, a whole piece.

Bismarck rose and padded to the door, wagging his tail. Okay, then. His visitor must be Gabi. *Well, here we go again.* Flynn set down his drink, dragged a hand across his bristled chin, and opened the door. His heart sank. Not Gabi. "Celeste."

"Hello, Flynn. May I come in?"

She stepped forward before he could deny her. Instinctively, he stepped back and allowed her inside.

Celeste's bright smile seemed to light up the dim room. "You were in such a hurry to check out this morning that you left your credit card at Angel's Rest."

She set it down on the table, right beside Gabi's Christmas gift, and Flynn frowned. "Oh. You didn't need to go to the trouble to bring it by."

She smiled brightly. "It's no trouble. Besides, I wanted to get your feedback about our accommodations. Was the honeymoon cottage all that you had hoped?"

All that he had hoped? Flynn did something then that he couldn't explain. Maybe it was the lack of sleep, the excess of emotion and liquor, or possibly the fact that Celeste reminded him a little of his mom, but he opened his mouth and confessed, "Gabi loves me."

"Of course she does."

"I don't know why. I certainly don't deserve it." Especially not after today.

Celeste laughed and patted his arm. "Don't act so surprised. You knew she loves you. That's why you moved to Eternity Springs. Because you love her, too, and you wanted to give your love a chance."

He dragged his fingers through his hair. "I don't mean to be rude, ma'am, but that's crazy."

"Are you trying to claim that you aren't in love with Gabi Romano?"

Flynn remained silent.

"I thought not."

Now he began to pace. "It's not that simple. Loving her is the easy part. But I'm a walking disaster, Celeste. I think I'm just meant to be alone."

"Balderdash. Don't be ridiculous. None of us are meant to be alone, dear boy."

Balderdash? His lips twisted, but he didn't argue with her. One simply couldn't argue with Celeste Blessing.

Bismarck rubbed up against her leg, demanding attention, and Celeste knelt on one knee to pet him and scratch behind his ears. "I've heard you've been feeling bad, you poor thing," she said. "I'm so sorry about that. You've certainly faced more than your share of challenges in your young life, haven't you?"

Watching her pet and comfort his dog, Flynn had the weird sensation that she was petting and comforting him.

"You might not recognize it," Celeste continued, "but your trials have made you stronger. You are not a walking disaster, and you will triumph over your demons. Nothing defeats a valiant heart."

Valiant. Definitely not an everyday word, but there it was again. It certainly fit Bismarck, and Gabi, too.

Celeste looked up at him, her gaze serious and unwavering. "You have a valiant heart, too, Flynn Brogan."

He closed his eyes as a curious sense of yearning filled him. Kind, positive words. They were worth more than diamonds.

She rose and took his hand, giving it a squeeze as she continued. "But your heart is also tender. You are an inventor, a dreamer. Dreamers by nature have tender hearts, but at this point in your life, your valiance must overcome. Look inside for it, Flynn. It is still there. Your dreams have been dashed, but they haven't been destroyed. Don't abandon them. Fight for them."

In a low tone, he voiced his greatest fear. "I'm afraid I'll destroy her. I won't mean to do it, just like I didn't mean to destroy my wife, but that was the end result. I couldn't live with doing it to Gabi, too."

"How did you destroy your wife, Flynn?"

"I didn't kill her," he asserted quickly. "That's not what I mean. I failed her. I failed her when she needed me most."

"How would you fail Gabi?"

"I don't know. That's the problem. I didn't know I was failing Lisa at the time. I acted with the best of intentions, and it led to disastrous consequences. I didn't murder Lisa. I was rightly acquitted by that jury. But . . ."

"But?"

From the depths of his soul came the fear, the fact, that he'd never admitted, not even to himself. "My father was right. The bottom line is that I should have prevented what happened. I'm responsible for her death."

"He said that to you?"

Flynn nodded and explained. "A high IQ doesn't make a man smart, Celeste. Lisa paid the price for my poor judgment, and now the thought of failing Gabi . . ." He closed his eyes and shook his head. "It would have been better if I'd died on the beach that night."

Celeste's voice held an unusual edge. "Dear boy, I hope that sometime I get the opportunity to meet your father and tell him exactly what I think of his opinions. Bad parenting carves scars on the soul that take a long time to heal. Talk about something destructive . . ." She clicked her tongue in exasperation. "Think with that high-powered brain of yours rather than your emotions. We are talking about Gabriella Romano. I repeat, Gabriella Romano! Betrayal by her slug of an ex and her weak best friend didn't destroy her. Taking the life of a deranged killer in her sister-in-law-to-be's bedroom didn't do it. A pirate attack on the high seas didn't bring her down for long, for heaven's sake. Give the girl more credit! She is a warrior woman, and she is fearless when it comes to her heart. She's given that treasure to you."

"I didn't ask for it," he protested.

"Nevertheless, it's yours. So what's the worst thing you can do to this most precious gift?"

"Break it. Considering my history, I probably will break it."

Celeste sighed and shook her head. "There you go using emotion instead of logic again. Such a lack of faith in yourself, Flynn. You'll need to work on that, but it's a discussion for another day. Back to Gabi. So, say you break her heart. Then what?"

"What do you mean?"

"What happens when you've broken our Gabi's heart? Will she be destroyed?"

He snorted. "She'll probably come after me and kick my ass."

"Exactly. You know her well. And knowing her well, you must see that while you could hurt her, you will never destroy our Gabriella. Don't look at her through the prism of your past, Flynn. Her strength is proven, and she has chosen you to be her partner. So you see, the question at hand is not whether you have the power to destroy her, but whether you have the strength to stand beside her."

Flynn went still and his pulse rate increased as her words echoed through his mind.

Celeste reached up and patted his cheek in a way that was reminiscent of his mother. "Don't be afraid to leave the shadows. Take off your eye patch, leave your sunglasses behind. Don't delay. The time is now. The cure for what ails you is here." She placed her hand over his heart. "Where valiance dwells."

She gave Bismarck one more scratch behind the ears, then departed.

Flynn stood in the middle of his lonely cabin trying to find his balance after the earthquake Celeste Blessing had just unleashed upon his world. For all of the repercussions rolling through his head, one truth became clear. Of the many fears he had to conquer, one stood out from the rest. One imminent consequence he couldn't survive.

He'd damned well better find his courage and do something about it. Fast.

Gabi refused to cry over a man. It was one of her most closely held principles. So the tear tracks on her cheeks and the redness in her eyes had nothing to do with Flynn-the-Idiot Brogan.

In the bedroom Gabi was using at Aspenglow Place, Maggie Romano eyed the suitcase on the bed and the storm of clothes spread across the floor and every piece of furniture. She picked up a shirt that Gabi hadn't worn in at least three years, shook her head, and sighed. "Do you want some help, honey?"

"Yes. Give the boys baseball bats and tell them to go pound some sense into that . . . that . . . *scimunito*!"

"What did you just call him?"

"*Scimunito*. It means 'idiot.'"

"Oh, I need to learn that." Maggie lifted a skirt off the floor. "You know, dear, now that you've dragged all these things out of storage, it would be a good time to sort through them and make a bag for Goodwill."

"You're right. I'm not in the mood to watch football with the boys downstairs, and I'm not doing anything else, so I might as well." Gabi eyed the skirt in her mother's hands. It had been one of Frank Sobilek's favorites. "We can start the Goodwill bag with that skirt, Mom."

Maggie folded the skirt and set it on a corner of the bed. "You know, dear, it's not too late to change your mind. Zach could use his lights and siren and get you to the airport in time to make your plane."

Gabi shook her head. "No. I've made my choice, and I don't back down from a fight. I'm going to take today and lick my wounds, but then tomorrow I'm diving back in."

"That's my girl." Repeating a longtime habit, Maggie crooked her finger. Gabi smiled and bent down so that her diminutive mother could kiss her forehead. "I'll go downstairs and get a couple of trash bags for the donation pile."

"Thanks, Mom." Mother and daughter shared a smile. Both knew that Gabi's gratitude had to do with lots more than the fetching of a trash bag.

Maggie had been in the kitchen making coffee when Gabi blew in from her overnight with Flynn and rushed upstairs without so much as a good morning. Maggie immediately went into mother hen mode. She'd waited out her daughter's angry tantrum and storm of tears, then she'd convinced Gabi to take both a bath and a nap.

She'd awakened more clearheaded, but still sad and frustrated. Flynn had hurt her. After such a wonderful, glorious night—the best night of her life—he had to go and be such an ass. That crack about upgrading her ticket . . . he'd pay for that.

She wondered if he really thought his little performance this morning in the kitchen had driven her away.

That, after his performance in the bed, the shower, the hot tub, and in front of the fireplace? Did he think she couldn't recognize when she was having sex and when she was being made love to?

"Fool-brained, hardheaded, obstinate numbskull," she muttered. She needed to remember that the scars the man had inside were obviously worse than those he had outside, but sometimes when he opened his mouth—or, for that matter, failed to open his mouth—that was simply hard to do.

She picked up the little black dress she'd worn the previous night. No way was she getting rid of it. She thought she just might wear it every time she wanted to remind Flynn of his stupidity. She had just hung the dress in the closet when her mother reappeared in the doorway. "Gabi, quick. You have to see this. And be quiet!"

Curious, she followed her mother down the hallway toward the staircase landing. Maggie brought her index finger to her lips and mouthed, "Listen."

Gabi heard Lucca say, "You have some testicular fortitude to show up here."

"Balls the size of church bells," Tony agreed.

"Just answer my question, please," the familiar deep voice rumbled.

Flynn! Gabi's chin dropped in shock, as she gave her mother a flabbergasted look. Maggie pointed to the end of the wall, where, if she was careful, Gabi could peek around the corner without being seen.

On silent feet, she approached her spot and peered carefully around and down. Flynn stood encircled by the Romano men—Zach, Lucca, Tony, and Max.

Max asked, "So what's in it for us if we tell you our sister's travel plans?"

Zach folded his arms and drawled. "He's gonna tell us it'll result in harmony, peace, love, and unicorn farts for all eternity."

Unicorn farts? Gabi swallowed a laugh.

"I'm going to tell you that I need a chance to speak with her before she boards her plane."

"You made her cry, asshole," Lucca said. "You don't deserve a chance with her."

"I know that better than any of you. Now that we all agree that I'm an asshole, will you please answer my question?"

Tony pressed him. "Why should we? Give us one good reason."

"I love her. I need to tell her that, and I need to answer questions she has about some very personal issues."

"What? You have an STD?"

Gabi could almost hear the grinding of Flynn's teeth. "Questions about my wife's death and how I came by my scars."

Gabi brought her hand to her mouth, gasping. Without making a conscious decision, she walked forward, and the movement at the top of the stairs caught Flynn's notice. Seeing her, he appeared to release a long sigh of relief. "Hello, Gabriella," he said. "I'm so glad you're still here. Could we talk?"

Her pulse pounded so hard she suspected he could see it from downstairs. "All right."

Zach stepped in front of Flynn. "Are you sure, Gabi? We'll be happy to throw him out on his ass if you'd like."

"Yeah," Lucca, Tony, and Max chimed in.

"You can certainly try," Flynn observed.

A warm rush of love swept over Gabi at her brothers' posturing. Standing there in a little circle were the five men she loved most in the whole world. "I'm so lucky," she murmured.

Flynn pinned her with a fierce stare. "Want to grab your boots and coat? I'd like to walk and talk if that's okay with you."

"All right. I'll be down in a few minutes." She started back to her bedroom, then paused and turned around. To her brothers, she said, "Don't hurt him. That's my prerogative."

Zach's petulant voice followed her down the hallway. "You spoil all our fun."

Because Gabi was Gabi, she took time to change her clothes and fix her makeup. It wasn't until she outlined her lips that she realized something had been different with Flynn. It was the middle of the afternoon on a bright, cloudless day. He hadn't been wearing his sunglasses or his eye patch.

Why not? What had changed?

Dozens of questions rolled around her brain as she descended the stairs. Lucca, Max, and Tony had returned to the football game. She didn't see Flynn, but Zach stood in the entry hall waiting for her. "You okay, Gabriella?"

"I am."

"If you have any doubt whatsoever, you say the word and I'll take care of Flynn Brogan."

She wrapped her arms around his waist and gave him a quick, fierce hug. "I love you, Zach."

"I love you, too, little sister. You just say the word and I'll . . ."

"I know." She kissed his cheek. "Is Flynn outside?"

"In his truck. Said he wanted to get the heater running in the cab so you wouldn't be cold. Fact is, he wanted to be away from us."

"Can you blame him?"

Her brother shrugged. "Don't let him off the hook too easily, warrior woman. Savannah and I had to fight our way to the finish, and that made our marriage stronger in the end."

"Thanks for the advice. Now, go back to the football game, Sheriff."

Opening Aspenglow Place's front door, she stepped out into the cold mountain air and spied Flynn leaning against the passenger side door of his truck, waiting for her. She approached him saying, "I thought you wanted to walk?"

"I do. In the valley, if that's okay with you. I think it'll be easier for me to talk there."

"Okay."

He opened the door and Gabi climbed inside. They didn't exchange so much as a single word during the twenty-minute drive to his house. But when he pulled up in front of the cabin, shifted into park, and killed the engine, he said, "Which do you want to hear about first? My wife or my scars?"

"I'll listen to whatever you have to say."

"Okay, then." He opened his door. "Let me check on Bismarck. Do you need gloves? A hat?"

"They're in my coat pocket."

Gabi followed Flynn inside his cabin and watched, smiling faintly, as he opened Bismarck's crate and talked to him, scratching him behind the ears. It was only when he rose to take a biscuit from the treat jar that she noticed the window. More precisely, what was hanging in the window.

A dreamweaver shaped like a sail in shades of yellow and Caribbean blue.

Her heart lifted. He'd not only opened her Christmas gift, he'd hung it up. Her spirits high, she turned to him with a brilliant smile . . . but the expression on his face killed it instantly. He looked as if he were headed out to face a firing squad, not take a stroll through the pine-scented forest on a sunny winter afternoon.

Gabi let him lead the way, and he traced the path they'd ridden after the wolf attack, the one she'd designated to be her personal dreamweaver trail. Only after they'd left the clearing and entered the forest did he begin to talk.

"Before I say anything else, I'm sorry about what I said in the cottage. You didn't deserve that. I won't make excuses for myself because there aren't any beyond the fact that I'm a horse's ass."

"Apology accepted," she said quietly.

They walked another five silent minutes before he finally began. "Gabi, have you ever considered what the Callahans, the Murphys, the Raffertys, and everybody else would think about having the GQ Killer living among them?"

She wasn't surprised by the question, but she was frustrated. Flatly, she said, "You didn't kill your wife, Flynn."

"No, I didn't. I want you to know how much it means to me that you know it, too. My father holds me responsible, and my best friend believes I did it."

"The same best friend who slept with your wife?" she pointed out. "Your father . . . well, that's just stupid. He must be one of those fathers who never get to know their children."

"My father knew me. I thought he did, anyway. I thought we were close."

"I thought that about my father, too. Come to find out, he'd been keeping a string of mistresses all my life. Looks like we were both wrong. So, why are your father and your friend so clueless? It was a circumstantial case. Why did they buy the prosecution's version of events?"

"So you are familiar with that?"

Her lips curled. "You mean the 'You were enraged because your wife betrayed you with your best friend, so you drugged her and stuffed her in the freezer in your basement' theory? Yeah. Sheer brilliance, that."

Playing devil's advocate, he pointed out, "The syringe containing the sedative had my fingerprints on it."

She wrinkled her nose and dismissed his point with a wave. "Obviously planted evidence."

Flynn shook his head, an enigmatic smile on his face. "Your faith takes my breath away, Gabi."

"The prosecution's stupidity does that to me. You're an engineer. You invented the Barbecue-Meister and all sorts of other things. And you'd be so stupid as to leave damning evidence like the syringe behind? Really?"

"It was misdirection on my part," he said, repeating the theory.

Gabi gave an unladylike snort. "Ridiculous. So, tell me the behind-the-scenes stuff. How soon did you know they were coming after you?"

"Almost from the beginning." He told her about the investigation and how the detectives had quickly focused on him. "I had no idea that she'd been telling people she was afraid of me. That little tidbit hit from out of the blue."

"Why did she do it?" When he hesitated, she prodded, "You have to have a theory. What do you think happened, Flynn?"

He kicked at a pinecone lying in the snow. "I have a theory, but I couldn't even convince my own criminal attorneys that it had merit."

"Tell me about it."

"I think Lisa set the whole thing up in order to frame me, not for murder, but for attempted murder. Lisa wasn't trying to die. She was trying to get attention from me and Will, but, more important, from the criminal justice system. Unfortunately for everybody, her designated rescuer let her down."

"I don't understand. Who was supposed to rescue her?"

He gave Gabi a sidelong glance. "Her sister, Wendy."

"Her sister," Gabi repeated, halting in her tracks, unable to hide her incredulous reaction. "Her sister the movie star?"

"I know. Impossible to believe." Flynn shrugged. "I think she counted on Wendy to raise the alarm, and for whatever reason, Wendy didn't do it."

Gabi's brow furrowed. "But why would Lisa go to such lengths to get attention?"

"I can't prove it, because she was never professionally diagnosed, but I am certain that Lisa had Munchausen syndrome. Do you know what that is?"

"People who hurt themselves to get attention?"

"Yes. She was never officially diagnosed because she wouldn't cooperate, and she didn't fit the Munchausen pattern of repeated hospital visits or too many laboratory tests, but I am certain of it. She exhibited signs of it the entire time that I knew her, though I only recognized it in hindsight.

"She was originally a medical student in college, but she missed so many classes due to illness that she eventually changed her major. I just thought she was a sickly person. Then I came home early from work one day about a year before she died, and I saw her cut herself with a kitchen knife. On purpose."

"Oh, Flynn. That must have been horrible."

He shoved his hands in his coat pockets and nodded. "She tried to tell me I was mistaken, but I'd seen it. That's when I first suspected something was wrong, and I did some research and read about Munchausen's. I tried to convince her to get help. I begged her to see a doctor. When I tried to force the issue, she grew irate. Things got really ugly between us, and that's when I let her down. I quit trying to get her to get help. That failure of mine will haunt me until the day I die." Gabi touched his arm in support.

"I think that's when she turned her attention to Will as a way to get back at me. It's also when the Munchausen's took a turn toward a new audience—the criminal justice system."

"She wanted attention from cops?"

Flynn nodded. "After she died, I recalled reading about a category of Munchausen patients who present themselves to law enforcement authorities as victims of crime. They'll report being victims of everything from petty complaints to serious crimes—rape, assault, kidnapping, and even murder. They'll present self-inflicted injuries to back up their claims. I think that's what happened. Her plot was supposed to punish me, because she hated me by then, and garner the attention she craved from medical and law enforcement personnel, and her famous sister, too."

Mentally donning her former-cop hat, Gabi said, "Walk me through what happened that day. How do you figure she did it?"

He pinned her with a look. "You're giving this consideration."

"Of course. Why wouldn't I?"

"My attorneys thought I was the crazy one. I had suspicions with nothing to back them up."

"Lawyers." She sniffed with disdain. "They won your case, so I guess we shouldn't complain too much, but you weren't vindicated. That's been a hard thing for you to live with. Now, tell me about that day."

Flynn grabbed her hand and brought it to his mouth for a kiss. "Okay. Lisa lured me to the house with a promise to return a personal treasure of mine, the wool afghan my mother had crocheted that I'd inadvertently left behind when I moved out. That put me at the house at the right time."

"Opportunity," Gabi said, her gaze following a squirrel that bounded through the trees above.

"Yeah. I think she injected herself with a sedative that she somehow got her hands on, possibly during one of her visits to see her sister, from one of those Hollywood quacks who masquerade as doctors."

"The syringe had your fingerprint, not hers."

"Yes, which provides means. Since her affair with my best friend provided motive, she tied it up in a nice little bow. But I think she had a second syringe. I think she flushed it before the drug took hold."

"Sneaky."

"Typical. The syringe with my print on it had to have been something she saved from before we separated. I found them in the house more than once. Lisa loved her meds. I believe she left the syringe with my fingerprint on it for the cops to find, then crawled into that freezer in the basement confident that her sister would raise the alarm. Only, Wendy didn't do it, and Lisa froze to death."

"I can buy Lisa's part. Explain to me about Wendy."

Flynn grimaced, and it was obvious he didn't want to answer her. Gabi's antennae perked up. He wasn't comfortable talking about the movie star. She had the sudden suspicion that she knew why.

He took aim at another pinecone and kicked it away. "We know from phone records that Lisa called Wendy that morning, but we only have Wendy's version of what was said. She claimed it was just a casual conversation between sisters. I think it could have been more. It fits their pattern. Growing up, Lisa was always needy, and Wendy always came to her rescue. I think it's entirely possible that Lisa gave her sister a crazy story and Wendy ignored it—to tragic consequences."

"Why would she lie about it? Why the histrionics in the courtroom?"

"Her career. She wouldn't want to risk damage to her career. Frankly, she got some good mileage out of being the victim's sister. Lots of publicity."

"That's just sick."

"It's show business."

Disgust rolled through Gabi. "Is that what the switching allegiance and the courtroom outburst were all about? A publicity stunt?"

"That was probably part of it. Mainly, though, she wanted to get back at me." Flynn rubbed the back of his neck and confessed. "She made a pass at me. Told me she was in love with me, that she'd always been in love with me."

Bingo. "You shot her down?"

He nodded. "And nobody rejects Wendy Stafford."

"Aha," Gabi said. "So now we have motive on Wendy's part. That's why she turned on you halfway through the trial, I'll bet. She thought with her sister gone, she'd have a chance with you. But you didn't cooperate."

"Nope."

"So she goes from supportive family member to grieving loudmouth." Gabi huffed, then shook her head. "I never have thought much of actors. So, did you ever confront her with your theory?"

He nodded. "She acted shocked. Denied everything. But she is an actor, Gabi. A talented one. I think she's been acting all of her life, in fact. I don't know what happened to those girls in the house they grew up in, but I suspect it wasn't good."

"There has to be a way to prove your theory," Gabi said, anger spurring her to follow his lead and kick a pinecone. "You need to be exonerated. She needs to pay for what she's done to you. Who were your investigators? I'm sure your legal team hired the best, but I'd like to take a look at their files. Have Zach take a look, too. Sometimes fresh eyes can see new things. Did you investigate their childhood? If we could establish a pattern of Munchausen going back that—"

"Gabi," he interrupted, reaching for her arm and pulling her to a stop. "No. I've been down that road, believe me. It leads nowhere."

"But—"

"No, honey." He put a finger against her lips. "Look, I'll ask Matthew to send you all the files and you can go through them to your heart's content. But I can't let you assume that this is a problem that can be solved with extra effort—even totally dedicated extra effort. Because here's the deal. Even if Wendy Stafford went on national TV and admitted to my suspicions, some people would still believe that I'm guilty."

"But—"

"You know it's true. People like to believe the worst. I defended myself in the courtroom, but I can't do a damned thing about the court of public opinion. And you absolutely can't make decisions about the future based on a hope like that."

She went still. "What are you talking about? Any decision you make about the future is always based on hope."

Grimly he said, "That's my point. In our case, they damned well need to be based on reality. I need to tell you about reality, Gabi. I need to tell you about the night I found Bismarck."

TWENTY

Flynn dropped his head back and turned his face toward the sky as he recalled that long night and endless day. It would be so easy to get tugged into the vortex of agonizing memories, but he fought the urge, and began. "After the attack on the *Dreamer,* I felt . . . impotent. I couldn't turn back the clock. I couldn't cleanse your soul of the burden of having taken another life or erase the two deaths I had on my conscience."

Gabi's expression reflected second thoughts. "Flynn, I don't need to know. You don't need—"

"No," he interrupted, putting up his hand. "Let me finish this. Just . . . don't say anything. Let me tell you so that I never have to talk about it again."

She swallowed hard, then nodded.

"What I could do," he continued, "the only thing I could do, was look for Bismarck. I believed there was a really good chance that Bismarck had survived. I wanted to find him. For his owners. For you. For myself. Finding him became my obsession. I started searching, and I went public with his story and the search. I asked for help finding him."

Flynn risked a look at Gabi. She had her hands shoved into her pockets, and she walked as if braced against a fearsome wind instead of the slight breeze whispering through the forest. They walked another twenty-five yards before he spoke again. He told her about his arrival at the bird sanctuary, about anchoring in a cove and hearing Bismarck's barks. He explained how he swam to shore, then was hit on the head.

"I woke up spread-eagled on the sand. The father of one of the pirates had already found Bismarck. Like everyone else in the Caribbean, he knew I was looking for him. I worked in a grid, so it was easy for him to pinpoint where I'd be within a day or two. He set me up."

"Villarreal?" she asked. "Wasn't that his name?"

Flynn nodded. "He was looking for vengeance, with a couple of sadistic minions to help. He told me up front that I wouldn't leave the beach alive, but I wouldn't die nearly as soon as I wished. He was right."

Obviously shaken, Gabi reached out to Flynn, but he shook her off. He could accept no comfort at this point, not now that he'd steeled himself for the telling of his tale. "They tortured me."

Gabi's eyes closed. She shuddered.

"I don't know if I can say much beyond that. . . ."

She waved her hand, wordlessly telling him that she understood, that she would not push him for details. Instead, she asked, "How did you survive?"

Relaxing a bit, Flynn lifted his mouth in a terrible, crooked smile. "A combination of canine defense and the devil getting his due. I wasn't lucid throughout, but I do remember Bismarck barking. I thought they must have him chained or tied up. Then quite a few hours into it, right about the time I think they were about ready to get serious with the fillet knife, Bismarck went Cujo."

"He attacked?"

"Oh, yeah. The sounds he made changed. No more barks. He started howling—a horrible, haunting noise—and suddenly it was headed right at us. He'd gotten loose.

I couldn't really see him, but the expressions on the others' faces told me he must have looked pretty damned frightening. He scared the old man to death—literally. Guy had a heart attack and fell down dead before Bismarck put a mark on him."

"That was too easy for him," Gabi said, a bit of a bloodthirsty note to her voice.

Flynn smirked and continued, "After that, Villarreal's minions dropped their knives and ran off screaming. They stole my boat and left me on the beach. At that point, I wanted to die in peace, but Bismarck wouldn't let me. He kept licking me and nudging me and whining into my ears."

"God bless him. Who found you?"

"My lawyer. I missed a phone appointment with him. He got concerned, instigated a search. They located the Formula pretty fast, and convinced the minion to talk." Now the faintest of real smiles touched his lips. "Margaret, Matthew's wife, likes to say that Bismarck and my bulldog lawyer saved my life."

"Thank God for them both."

Flynn nodded. "Yeah, though I didn't think so at the time. It would have been much easier to die. And a lot less painful. But in the end, I lived. That's the story. I spent some time in a hospital, more time in a rehab place, and then I moved here."

Now he stopped and turned to her, caught both of her hands in his. Fiercely, he insisted, "Bismarck and Matthew saved me, but so did you, Gabi. You gave me Eternity Springs. This place called to me. I really believe it helped me to heal. The locale, the people . . . this truly is a special place. And even though you were in Italy, you were here. You were here."

Gabi closed her eyes, but failed to hold back tears. Despite her obvious emotion, her voice came out strong and sure. "We are both lucky to have found Eternity Springs."

"I would like to make this my permanent home. I don't know if it's possible, but I would like to at least make a run at it."

"Why wouldn't that be possible?"

Tentatively he suggested, "It may prove to be too much. Face it, Gabi. I'm still the GQ Killer."

Her brow dipped in confusion over shimmering blue eyes. "I don't understand. Do you think the neighbors will complain?"

"Yes! Real life isn't an hour-long TV drama, or in this case, a detective show. It doesn't get all wrapped up in a nice little bow at the end. Real life is messy. In real life, the good guys don't always win and villains don't always pay. I've accepted the fact that my father and best friend and most anyone who's read the front of a tabloid newspaper while standing in line at the grocery believe that I'm evil incarnate. It's annoying, but I can live with that."

He tugged on her arms, unfolding them, then took her hands and kissed her knuckles. "But then there's you. That's a lot to ask of a woman. I'm a lot to ask of a woman. I'm not a good bet, Gabriella. I'm still the GQ Killer, and I'm still the broken son of a bitch who spent too many hours at the hands of sadists. I can live with it. What I don't know is if I can ask you to live with it, too."

Gabi went as still as the snowy forest, and he reached up to cup her cold, rosy cheek. "I love you, Gabriella Brianna Romano. I love your passion and your strength. I love your warrior woman attitude and your girly-girl style. You have the biggest, most valiant heart of anyone I've ever met and you have given that heart to me. It is the most wondrous gift, and at the same time, a most terrible burden. I can't bear the thought that someday, I could be responsible for it being broken."

"Why do you think you'll break my heart?"

"I'm the GQ Killer, Gabi. You are the precious, beloved daughter, sister, friend, and neighbor of the people of Eternity Springs. You are the brightest light in this town, and while I don't know how I could live without you, I'm afraid that I'm going to bring you into the shadows with me."

Blinking back tears, Gabi pushed against his chest. "You drive me crazy. Help me out here, Brogan. I love you. You love me. I get that. What I'm not so clear about is what happens next. You're going to let our friends and neighbors decide our future?"

"That's not what I'm saying. But in a way . . . yes. I think I have to come clean with more than just my beard around town, and you can see how the repercussions affect you. You need to think long and hard about being with me. Knowing how strong you are . . . I'm hopeful. I admit that. But it's going to tear me up inside when my black reputation rubs off on you. I'm afraid I'll be the weak one in the relationship and we won't be able to survive it over the long term."

"Oh, for crying out loud. What you're saying is that we have to make sure that the GQ Killer doesn't strike again, right? And just what will the murder weapon be? Rapier tongues? Cold shoulders?"

"Wait until you live it. It's nothing to joke about."

"*Scimunito!*" she exclaimed. "I have one problem with this whole scenario, Brogan. You did a halfway decent job just now. This is a very romantic spot—a quiet forest, the scent of pine perfuming the air, the chirp of winter birds providing background music. Your words, your sentiments, fill my heart to overflowing. But the ending still needs a little work."

"I don't understand."

"For a brainiac, you can be so clueless. Let me spell it out to you. When a girl receives a declaration of love like the one you just gave me, it's usually accompanied by a kiss. Not just hand kisses, either, though I will say I like that particular habit of yours. I mean the kind of kiss that—"

She didn't get the rest of the words out because he moved like lightning and swept her into his arms, capturing her mouth with his in a long, thorough kiss that was as romantic as he could make it.

When they finally came up for air, he held her in a fierce embrace and quietly declared, "I love you, and I want a life with you more than anything. I will do the very best I can to make it work. However, I won't stand by and see you hurt because of me. I will walk away before I let that happen. You must understand that."

"Oh, Flynn. So many people have let you down, haven't they?" She tenderly brushed his hair away from his eyes and said, "I do hear you, and I understand why you feel the way you do. However, I'm going to bet on our friends and family and on this town. You just watch, Flynn Brogan. Something tells me that your official welcome to Eternity Springs is going to be more than you ever dreamed. Hope and dreams, my love. That's what we do here in Eternity Springs."

They had begun walking again after the kiss, and their path through the forest had circled back around to the snowy meadow where his cabin sat. He was struck by the beauty of the scene, the log cabin surrounded by snowy mountains. It wasn't a big house. It wasn't fancy. But it suited.

"You left the lights on in the cabin," she observed.

"Yeah." A slow smile spread across his face. "I did."

"Let's go inside and light a fire, shall we?" Without

waiting for his response, Gabi strode off toward the house.

Flynn followed her in from the cold, into the light.

On the evening of New Year's Day, Savannah and Zach Romano had invited friends and family to their home for what Savannah deemed the Great New Year's Calorie Cleanup. Everyone was encouraged to bring whatever holiday treats still lurked in their cookie tins, refrigerators, and pantries that they wished to have out of their house prior to the official start of their New Year's diets. Gabi suggested she and Flynn attend.

"It's not just a girls' night. The guys will be there, too, to scarf food and watch football. I think it will be a great place for you to roll out your news."

Flynn lifted his head from the bed, where they'd spent the balance of the afternoon. "Seriously? You want to jump right into this tonight?"

Gabi slapped his bare ass and climbed from the bed, heading for the shower. "No time like the present, Brogan. They'll all wonder why I changed my travel plans, so this will be a great way to roll the whole thing out among friends."

"Friends will be the worst," he protested, his formerly excellent mood evaporating.

Paused in the bathroom doorway, Gabi challenged him with a look. "You've seen *Charlie Brown's Christmas,* haven't you? Remember the character Pig Pen? He had a dust cloud around his feet all the time. Well, you're like Pig Pen, only instead of a dust cloud, you have a rain cloud above your head. Let the sun shine, Brogan. Eternity Springs is a sunny place."

An hour later, as he carried a tin of peanut brittle and chocolate fudge up the walk to her brother's home, he halfway expected his own personal thunder and lightning to break out at any moment.

Savannah opened the door and did a double take, seeing him sans beard for the first time. "Doesn't he clean up pretty?" Gabi asked.

"Very nice," Savannah said. She accepted the tins he offered, then went up on her tiptoes to kiss him on the cheek. "Welcome, Flynn. I'm so glad you chose to join us. I'm really looking forward to getting to know you better."

"Thanks." He gave her a sheepish smile and added, "Though I think your husband would like to kill me."

"Well, sure. You're sleeping with his little sister. That's what brothers do."

"She has four of them," he said glumly.

Savannah laughed and threaded her arm through his. "Lucky for you that Gabi is such a good friend. The women in her life outnumber the men. Come on in. I'll protect you."

Gabi trailed behind them as Savannah led them into a large open kitchen and family room where a crowd of people already congregated. Some of them he'd exchanged casual conversation with in the past. Others he recognized from town. He'd never been formally introduced to any of them. As they began greeting Gabi with exclamations of surprise, she gave him a warning look that told him his anonymity was reaching its end.

"No, I didn't miss my plane, I had a change of plans." She smiled brilliantly at Flynn, then continued, "Friends, I want to introduce you to the very special man in my life, Flynn Brogan. Flynn is the man who saved my life in the Caribbean last spring. Flynn, I'd like you to meet Cam and Sarah Murphy, Sage and Colt Rafferty, Rose Anderson, you know Nic Callahan, and this is her husband, Gabe."

Flynn shook hands and said hellos, thankful that his palm wasn't sweaty. Another group of laughing people came in, and Gabi continued her introductions. He shook hands with Mac Timberlake and his wife, Ali, and Jack and Cat Davenport. Once that was out of the way, Gabi added, "Flynn has been living incognito out in Thunder Valley. You might not recognize him without his beard and sunglasses."

"You're our mountain man?" Rose asked, her deep green eyes sparkling with interest.

"I'm afraid so," he replied.

Everyone welcomed him with such honest, open friendliness that he felt like a total fraud. The longer it went on, the worse he felt, so when tiny, dark-haired Sarah Murphy nudged redheaded Sage Anderson with her elbow, grinned wickedly, and said, "Gabi's been holding out on us," he'd had enough.

"For good reason," he declared. His voice grim, his chin and his defenses rising, he added, "You should know something about me before you welcome me so warmly. Just about a year ago, I changed my name. I was born Flynn Seagraves."

Gabi linked her arm through his. "The tabloids dubbed him the GQ Killer when he went on trial for murdering his wife."

The room grew quiet. A couple of the people shot quick looks toward Zach, who stood in the kitchen calmly tossing back kernels of caramel corn.

Then Mac Timberlake said, "You were acquitted, I believe."

"Yes."

Gabi said, "Mac used to be a federal judge."

Lovely. Just effing wonderful.

Then a curious thing happened. Sarah Murphy walked over and gave him a hard hug. "Thank you for saving our Gabi. We love her so much, and the thought of losing her is too much to bear."

Then Cam Murphy held out a plate. "Want some Fritos and bean dip, Brogan? We have a pool going on the game. Five dollars a square. How many do you want?"

A little bewildered, he popped a chip into his mouth, then dug in his pocket for his wallet. After he handed over a twenty for four squares, Cat Davenport handed him a red plastic cup filled with champagne and said, "I think it's time for a toast. Jack, Gabe, see that everybody has something to drink, would you please?"

Once that was done, Nic Callahan did the honors. Giving him a warm smile, she lifted her glass. "Welcome to Eternity Springs, Flynn Brogan. You're gonna love it here, I promise."

Overwhelmed by the unexpected show of acceptance, he stammered out a thank-you, then sent Gabi a pleading look to bail him out. Her eyes gleamed with amusement as she lifted her voice and announced. "Hold on a minute, everybody. There's one more thing about Flynn that you need to know. Guys, you'll especially want to hear this."

She waited until the room once again was quiet, then waited another dramatic moment. Zach said, "Hurry up. It's almost time for kickoff."

"Ladies and gentlemen, it is my pleasure to present to you the inventor of . . . the Barbecue-Meister."

Every male chin in the room dropped, then they all started talking at once.

Flynn Brogan sat down to watch football with a whole roomful of new best friends and the woman who loved him at his side—stealing Fritos dipped in bean dip off his plate.

EPILOGUE

Gabi sank her feet into the blissfully warm water of the pedicure bowl, wiggled her toes, and shook her head at Flynn. "No, not that one."

He glanced at the bottle of nail polish in his hand. "You said red. This one is red."

"It's not the right red."

"Oh, for crying out loud," he grumbled.

She knew better than to smile at his petulant expression. Patiently, she explained, "I have to look my best for this."

"Why? We're going to see Cicero, not the Queen of England."

"I'm a puddle of nerves about this visit to Galveston. Looking my best will help my self-confidence."

Now he looked positively disgruntled. "You shouldn't be nervous. What's the worst he can do?"

"Seriously?" Gabi shot him a chastising look. "The man is a fire-breathing dragon in the studio, and he's not going to be very happy once he discovers that I didn't return to Italy. It's very possible that he'll turn his fire on me when he sees me. If I'm going up in flames, then I want to look good doing it."

He folded his arms, tilted his head, and studied her. "You really are nervous, aren't you?"

"Yes!"

"Now, Gabi." Compassion replaced the ire in his eyes. He crossed to the polish rack, removed every shade of red, then carried the bottles back for her to make her choice. "No need for nerves. You are hands down the most confident, courageous woman I know."

He said it with such sincerity that she knew he believed it. His conviction gave her faith in herself. She chose the color titled Tango For Two, and said, "Thank you, Flynn. For the polish, and for so much more."

They smiled into each other's eyes and a huge wave of love welled up within Gabi. This man was everything she'd ever wanted. Abruptly, she said, "I've changed my mind. There's a blue over there on the polish rack. Second row, third bottle from the left. Would you bring that one to me?"

"Blue nail polish? Really?"

"Really. It's called Caribbean Me Away." She'd keep to herself the fact that she'd associated it with him from the first time she'd seen it, and that she'd never wanted to wear it until now. No matter how wonderful Flynn was, she'd yet to meet a man who understood about a girl and her nail polish.

As he handed the bottle to her, the nail tech entered the room carrying a stack of fluffy white towels, fresh from the warmer. The receptionist followed at her heels. "Flynn, so sorry we kept you waiting. Marcel is ready for you now."

Gabi spied his wince only because she watched him closely. "He's an excellent stylist, Flynn."

"Stylist." He sniffed. "I've always gone to barbers."

"Then you should have gotten a haircut before Fred closed the barbershop for his two-week Christmas holiday in Florida."

Flynn sighed, then followed the receptionist. A moment later, he was back. He leaned down, kissed her

quickly, then murmured into her ear. "By the way ...
about that dragon? I'm the only man allowed to set you
on fire."

Gabi's laughter followed him into the salon.

The nail tech sighed and said, "You are so lucky, Gabi."

"Don't I know it!"

As the tech went to work on her pedicure, Gabi relaxed
against the massage rollers and enjoyed the pampering.
She exchanged small talk with the tech and caught up on
the latest small-town gossip making its way through the
salon. But when sunshine broke through the clouds and
sent a ray of sunshine beaming through the windowpane,
she was distracted by the prism of color it cast against the
white curtain. In her mind's eye, Gabi saw a rainbow in
glass. In a dreamweaver.

Her thoughts flashed back to the day she met Mitch.
*Where are you from, beautiful lady? Is it winter where
you live? You must buy a dreamweaver and take our
warm sunshine home with you so that on dark, dreary
days you can look at it and see your dreams.*

She'd done exactly that, hadn't she? On that sun-
washed, Caribbean spring afternoon, she'd gazed into
glass and discovered a dream. Over time, like a gather of
molten glass on a rotating punty, that dream had grown
and changed shape. Now she was about to stick it into
the two-thousand-degree oven that was Hunter Cicero's
artistic temperament in order to reshape it once again.
Maybe that was one of the biggest lessons she'd learned
in the past year. Dreams were meant to be fluid.

"What are you looking at, beautiful?"

She glanced up to see Flynn standing beside her once
more, his hair neat and trim and the same length as the
day she first met him. *Dreams are fluid, and the people
in my life are solid.*

She spoke past a little lump in her throat to say, "Celeste needs a suncatcher for the window of her spa."

"Then you should make her one."

The smile bloomed from deep in her heart, where aspirations began. "Yes, I think I will."

"Good. So are you ready?"

"As soon as my polish is dry."

He glanced down at her feet and slowly shook his head. "Those are the bluest toenails I've ever seen, Gabriella."

"Caribbean Me Away, Flynn Brogan," she responded, giving them a saucy wiggle.

A short time later, all pampered and polished and prepared, Gabi Romano opened the door and stepped into the crisp mountain air, ready to reach for her dreams, her soul mate at her side.

Read on for a preview of Emily March's next novel
in her Eternity Springs series:

Teardrop Lane

January
Galveston, Texas

The throbbing beat of U2 blasted from speakers
mounted from the metal rafters of the old warehouse as
Cicero extended the long metal blowpipe into the crucible and gathered glass. Heat from the furnace burning at
two thousand degrees hit like a fist, but he didn't notice.
The image of the sculpture drawn in pencil on the top
sheet of his sketchpad filled his mind.

Wondering why Gabi Romano had shown up with his
friend and her lover, Flynn Brogan, in tow when she was
supposed to be in Italy serving as an apprentice to the master glass artist Alessandro Bovér, could wait. The image
burning in his brain took precedence over everything.

As he closed his lips around the end of the pipe and
blew life into his work with a first puff of air, Gabi stepped
into the role of gaffer. Wordlessly, he accepted her assistance and blocked out everything but the work, losing
himself in the seductive and compelling fog of creativity.
For a stretch of unmarked time, the two worked in a silent and practiced ballet of molding the glass, applying
heat, shaping and blending, and blowing.

Hunter Cicero played with fire for a living and he was
very, very good at it.

The graceful figure in his mind gradually took shape in the glass. At some point in the process, his own apprentice, Mitch Frazier, sauntered through the door, then stopped in surprise upon seeing Flynn leaning against the wall, casually observing, while Cicero sat at his workbench and Gabi extended the blowpipe into the furnace to reheat the glass. Mitch seamlessly joined the creative effort.

The trio spent another forty minutes at work before Cicero decided the piece had taken final form. With a well-placed tap of a pair of metal jacks, he separated his sculpture from the punty and it fell into Gabi's gloved hands. Cicero set the punty aside while she placed the work into the annealing oven to slowly cool to room temperature. He grabbed a bottle of water from the fridge and drained it in one long draw.

He switched off the music, then spoke to Mitch first. "You were late."

"Sorry, boss." Mitch pulled the rubber band from his long Rastafarian braids and allowed them to swing freely down past his shoulder blades. "I stayed out late last night and overslept."

"Use your alarm next time. Better yet, save the late nights for weekends. I don't want you here when you're tired. You'll be careless and have an accident and your mother will kill me."

The woman would do it, too. Cicero had barely made it off Bella Vita Isle alive after he'd convinced his apprentice to accompany him to Galveston and help establish a handblown-glass studio that catered to the tourist trade.

Cicero finally turned his gaze on Gabi, who stood twirling a long dark curl around her finger. She offered him a tentative smile, and he narrowed his eyes and scowled at her. The woman was smart to be nervous; seeing her here did not make him happy. "Did you get lost on your way back to Italy?"

Gabi visibly braced herself. "No, Cicero. I'm not sure I'm going back."

Her statement came as no real surprise. Cicero wasn't stupid. Obviously, she and Flynn had reconciled, and she'd decided to cut her apprenticeship short—by nine months. Was she about to bail on the Eternity Springs project, too?

Maybe, he thought, his stomach sinking. If she was together with Flynn, why wouldn't she? The man had more money than Midas. Mindful of his own not insubstantial investment in the small Colorado mountain town and the stack of bills piling up on his desk, Cicero felt his temper rise. "What's wrong with you? Working in Alessandro's studio is the opportunity of a lifetime, one that countless other artists would kill for. What about all that talk you spouted about your dream and your passion? You're going to throw it all away?"

"I don't intend to throw anything away," she replied, her chin coming up. "I said I wasn't sure that I was returning to Italy. Cicero, last summer you came to me with a business proposal. Now I'm coming to you to propose a modification to that plan. Will you sit down and discuss it with me?"

Annoyed at the flash of relief over her assurance, he allowed his frown to deepen and shot a glance toward Flynn. "Are you part of her scheme?"

Flynn lifted his hands, palms out. "I'm an interested bystander, here to support you both."

Honesty glimmered in his friend's eyes, so Cicero hooked his thumb toward the small room off the studio, where an old, gray metal desk and two ratty chairs sat piled high with paper. To Mitch, he said, "I need you to shift the Valentine's Day goblets for Beachcomber's Gifts to the top of your work list."

"Really?" Surprise glinted in the young man's brown eyes. "I delivered a dozen of them last week."

"Yeah, well, yesterday a seven-year-old went on a rampage in the shop."

"Oh, mon!" Mitch exclaimed, the Caribbean strong in his voice. "Kids are such a . . ." His words trailed off when he noted the pain in Cicero's expression. "Wait. Was it . . . ?"

"Keenan." His seven-year-old menace of a nephew.

Mitch winced. "I'll get right on 'em, boss. No worries."

"No worries," Cicero repeated in a mutter as he followed Gabi and Flynn into his office. He cleared a stack of manila folders off a chair so Gabi could sit, then opened the small refrigerator and pulled out bottles of water. He tossed one to Flynn, another to Gabi, and took one for himself before clearing off the chair behind the desk and taking a seat. He twisted the lid off his water bottle, drained half of it in one drink, then said, "Bottom line it, Romano. What do you want?"

"First I'd like to explain why I want what I want. You see—"

Cicero interrupted. "It's the middle of a work day and I have an appointment at two. I don't have time for explanations. Cut to the chase, Gabriella."

"Okay. Well."

She wiped her palms on her jeans, and despite himself, Cicero was tempted to smile. Ordinarily, Gabriella Romano was one of the most self-assured women he'd ever met. The only other time he'd seen her this nervous was when she'd been working up the nerve to ask him to teach her to blow glass. "Spit it out."

She nodded, then spoke in a rush. "Instead of returning to Italy to finish out my apprenticeship, I want to divide my time between Texas and Colorado, working with you and Mitch here in Galveston and getting the retail shop in Eternity Springs ready to open for the upcoming tourist season."

Cicero took another long sip from his water bottle while he considered her idea. He'd called in a favor to get her the spot in Alessandro's studio in the first place, so he didn't like to see her bail. "What does Alessandro say about that?"

"He's fine with it. He thinks you can teach me everything I'll need to know because . . ." She paused, grimaced, and muttered, "This is more humiliating to repeat to you than I had anticipated. Alessandro tells me I'll never be an artist, so I can learn everything I need to know from you."

Ouch. "I can't decide if that's more an insult to me or to you."

"Me, definitely. He thinks you're the second coming of Chihuly, while I'm competent and enthusiastic, a hard worker, entertaining company, and lovely to look at, but I don't have fire for the fire."

"Huh." Cicero sat back in his chair and studied her. "Do you agree with his assessment?"

"Absolutely not!" Gabi made no attempt to hide her annoyance. "I have plenty of fire. But I also have family. I missed them. I was homesick. Last year was . . . difficult."

Difficult was an understatement, Cicero knew. In May, she had been aboard Flynn's sailing yacht in the Caribbean when it was set upon by pirates. She had taken one man's life that day; Flynn had killed two. The fallout from the event had wounded Gabi's heart and all but destroyed Flynn, but they had fought their way back to health and now, apparently, to one another.

Flynn rested a supportive hand on Gabi's shoulder, and she reached up to hold it. "I value the months I spent in Italy so very much. The experience was fabulous and I learned a tremendous amount. But now I need to be in

Eternity Springs. It's where my heart is whole and where my fire is free to burn.

"Alessandro is a fine teacher, Cicero, but so are you. It's possible that he's right and I'll never produce gallery-quality work. But maybe he's wrong. Maybe if I'm home and happy and surrounded by loved ones, I'll be able to create something spectacular. Eternity Springs is a special place. Just ask Sage Rafferty. She'll be the first to say that living in Eternity Springs inspires her work."

Sage Rafferty had made a name for herself in the art world for her boldly colored, whimsical paintings. She owned Vistas art gallery in Eternity Springs and had contracted with Cicero to represent the work he produced locally. Sage did speak enthusiastically about her home-town, and he knew better than to dismiss the power of inner peace for an artist. Wasn't the lack of it showing in his work lately?

And yet, he missed so much studio time these days. It wouldn't be right not to warn her. "My hours here aren't regular. It'll take you eight years to learn from me what Alessandro would teach you in eight months."

"I can't believe I'm saying this, but you underestimate yourself, Cicero."

No, underestimating himself had never been an issue of his. "Ha-ha, Romano."

"You also have more patience with your apprentices, and that makes it easier to learn."

Cicero scoffed. "I'm not patient at all."

"I didn't say you had an abundance of patience. I said you had more than Alessandro." She leaned forward in her chair, her blue eyes gleaming earnestly. "I know this plan slows down my progress, but it also allows me to be around to watch my niece and nephew grow. I didn't realize how much that mattered to me until I left home. They changed so fast that first year. I don't want to miss it."

"So you're giving up your opportunity for kids? Somebody else's kids, at that?"

"This from the man who traded the aquamarine of the Caribbean for Gulf of Mexico gray in order to be nearer to his sister and her children?"

Cicero's gaze shifted to the stack of invoices on his desk. Houston Oncology. MD Anderson Cancer Center. Physician's Services. "The two situations are completely different."

Gabi's eyes softened with sympathy. "How is Jayne doing?"

"Good," he replied, trying to believe it. "She's good." Then, to ward off any further questions about his sister, he added, "You can watch kids grow on the Internet. You don't have to be in the same town."

"But I want to be in the same town. I recognize that it's a trade-off. Life is a series of trade-offs. I can be passionate about glass and passionate about people, too. I'm searching for the right balance between the two. I know you understand that. You would never have left Bella Vita otherwise."

No, balance had nothing to do with his return to the U.S., though he did understand the concept.

"I can be of help to you here in Texas, Cicero. My training in Italy was intense. I'm good enough for tourist work. You can shift things like Valentine's Day goblets to me and free up Mitch to help you with your work."

Cicero sat back in his chair. "You have it all figured out, don't you?"

"I've put a lot of thought into it, and—oh!" She snapped her fingers. "I forgot to mention the remodel schedule. This time of year, construction hands are thrilled to have indoor work, so it won't be any trouble at all to speed things up." Having made her argument, Gabi sat back and waited silently, if not quite patiently.

He picked up a pen and drummed the tip against the desktop, thinking. Again he surveyed the clutter on his desktop and mentally shifted his money around. Getting the Eternity Springs shop up and running early could be a godsend to his cash flow. He'd already sunk a pretty penny into purchasing the old church property and starting the remodel. Materials were paid for. He still had some credit left. Maybe once they finished up the loft apartment he'd intended for himself, he could rent it out. Maybe . . .

Maybe he could think of something more selfish for himself to do, but he'd have to try damned hard.

Murano. Venice. Italy. The three years he'd spent there had molded him into the artist he was today and showed in every piece he produced. She simply didn't know yet how important this time was to her art.

"Gabi, I don't agree with Alessandro. I've seen pictures of the work you've been producing, and I believe you do have the talent to be an exceptional glass artist. I would be doing you a disservice if I agreed to this. Alessandro is—"

"Not as good as you," she interrupted. "He might have more experience and a flashier reputation and a studio in the most famous glass city in the world, but Alessandro isn't as good as you are, and he will never inspire me the way you do."

The vehemence in her tone along with the declaration itself took him aback. What had Alessandro been thinking to say the woman lacked fire? Flynn Brogan is a lucky man. Then, just to goad her, he arched a brow toward Flynn. "You let your woman say such things to another man?"

"*Let* me!" Gabi exclaimed.

Flynn laughed. "Gabriella Romano is very much her own woman, as you well know. It's one of the reasons why we both love her."

"True enough." He gave her a wolfish once-over and added, "I should never have yielded the field to you, Brogan."

Flynn's expression oozed self-satisfaction. "Doesn't matter. You never stood a chance with her."

"Confident of yourself, aren't you?"

"Excuse me. I'm sitting right here!"

Both men ignored that.

Cicero recognized the instant when Flynn's gaze went from amused to serious. He propped a hip on the corner of Cicero's desk, and his voice resonated with sincerity as he said, "I'm confident in her. As you should be. Our Gabi is loyal and honest and insightful. She has excellent instincts. She is passionate about her work and passionate about her world. Listen to her. Believe in her."

Cicero absently fanned the corner of the stack of invoices on his desk, and in an uncommon moment of openness replied, "I'm afraid I've lost the ability to believe in much of anything."

Gabi reached out and covered his hand with hers. "In that case, you need to get to Colorado as quickly as possible. I know it sounds corny, but you can believe in the magic of Eternity Springs."

"It changed my life," Flynn agreed. "It can change yours, too."

"I don't need magic. I need a miracle."

Gabi's smile went as bright as the furnace. "Hey, we do miracles, too. Just ask my sister-in-law, Hope."

Before Cicero could respond to that, a colorful whirlwind of noise and motion burst through the studio front door.

"Uncle Skunk!" Seven-year-old Keenan exclaimed. "Where are you, Uncle Skunk?"

"Hey, Uncle Hunk," called nine-year-old Misty. "Wait until you hear what happened at school!"

Jayne Prochaska carried two-year-old Daisy in her arms and offered him an apologetic smile. "Junior? I'm so sorry, but Amy isn't answering her phone and I need to run into Houston. Could you watch the kids for a little bit?"

"Unc Nooner!" Four-year-old Galen exclaimed. "Do you have any candy?"

"Uncle Nooner?" Flynn repeated, his brows arched and his lips twitching. "Man, am I going to have fun with that."

Cicero opened his mouth, then shut it. What could he possibly say? He closed his eyes briefly, shook his head, then grasped the lifeline Gabi had offered. "I'll agree to your proposal on one condition."

Warily, she asked, "What's that?"

"Babysitting."

"How much babysitting?"

"I won't abuse you. Much."

Gabi made a theatrical grimace, though he could tell her heart was singing. "All right, we have a deal . . . Uncle Hunk."

February
Eternity Springs, Colorado

Rose Anderson removed her stethoscope from her ears and patted the silver-haired gentleman on his knee. "You heart sounds just fine, Mr. Henderson."

"It's not my heart that's paining me," he grumbled. "I told you I broke my ankle!"

"I think it's sprained, but the EMT will be here to transport you to the clinic any moment now for an X-ray. Dr. Coulson will fix you right up."

"Dr. Coulson! What about you? You're my doctor."

Inwardly, Rose sighed. "I'm not on call tonight."

"Then why are you wearing your white coat?"

Rose searched for patience. She wasn't going to discuss details about her upcoming laundry day with Gilbert Henderson. "Dr. Coulson will take excellent care of you. There's no need for concern."

The septuagenarian scowled. "He's not as pretty to look at as you. His bosom doesn't brush up against me when he examines me."

"For this we can all be grateful," Rose dryly replied.

"You're a prize to look at, Doctor Rose. The Irish is stamped across you. I've always taken a shine to redheaded, green-eyed girls. Bet you burn in the summertime if you're not careful. How come you're not married?"

The question could have made Rose angry, but she'd grown accustomed to its being asked. She didn't hear it as often since moving to Eternity Springs—one of the pluses to small-town living. People ferreted out what they wanted to know about you pretty quickly, and word got around even faster. Her friends, acquaintances, and patients knew her story by now.

Unfortunately, Mr. Henderson had a bit of dementia going on.

Ignoring the query, she said, "I know the ankle is tender now, but unless Dr. Coulson finds something on the X-ray, I predict that you'll be back to dancing in a couple of weeks."

Her patient crooked his finger for her to bend closer, then he all but bellowed into her ear. "What about s-e-x? It is Valentine's Day, after all."

Yes, my personal Halloween. Rose patted his knee and told herself that she didn't care that this senior citizen had a more active love life than she did. "Talk to Dr. Coulson about that."

Thankfully, the EMTs showed up and helped Gilbert

Henderson from the Angel's Rest activities center. As Rose tucked her stethoscope back into her bag, Celeste glided up and asked, "Gilbert is okay?"

"Gilbert is the Energizer bunny of Eternity Springs's seventies set, and he'll be just fine if he stays off that ankle for a few days."

"Good. I'd hate for anything to cast a damper on our first official Angel's Rest Valentine's Day Dance. It's been wonderful so far. And just look at our honorary king and queen. Have you ever seen a more romantic pair?"

Rose followed the path of Celeste's gaze to where Flynn Brogan and Gabi Romano swayed to Elvis singing "Can't Help Falling in Love," wrapped in each other's arms, lost in each other's gaze. "They are . . . sweet."

Sickeningly so.

Celeste continued, "We've had some fabulously romantic marriage proposals here in Eternity Springs already, but I will say I'm partial to how Flynn proposed. The way he reengineered that yacht into an ice boat so he could take her sailing on Hummingbird Lake in order to pop the question shows not only a brilliant mind for design but also a truly romantic nature."

Rose's disdain melted a bit. She didn't give a whit for romance, but a brilliant mind had always turned her on. Of course, that was what had led her into trouble more than once, wasn't it? "They make a nice couple. Has Gabi said when the wedding will be?"

"I think they're still negotiating. Gabi wants to plan a wedding—she does love that sort of thing. He would like to elope."

"I'm sure they'll work it out," Rose said, zipping up her physician's bag. She lived in the garret apartment of Cavanaugh House, the Victorian mansion at the heart of the Angel's Rest grounds. She wanted to get home to a hot bath, a glass of Cabernet, and the postapocalyptic novel she was reading. Exactly why she particularly enjoyed that genre of book, she couldn't say, but she read every one that came out. Maybe because she identified with the premise. Wasn't the life she was presently living postapocalyptic in its own way?

"I'll be at home if you have any other accidents, Celeste," Rose told her, thinking she might snag a brownie off the refreshment table on her way out. "Just give me a call."

"Oh, Rose," Celeste protested. "Won't you stay and enjoy the dance with us? Not everyone here has a date, you know. We particularly designated it as a singles-welcome event."

Rose's gaze found the newly engaged couple once again, and then trailed over to where her sister danced with her husband, their expressions unfortunately sappy for a couple who should have moved beyond that dreamy-eyed stage by now. "Thanks, but I need to— Oh, no."

She switched back into doctor mode the instant she spied the boy covered in blood dash into the room. She took half a step forward, then stopped and reassessed. Not blood. Food coloring? Or paint? Probably paint.

The kid was maybe seven or eight years old, and he wore red-stained jeans, a red-stained Oregon Ducks jersey, and a panicked expression. The reason for the panic became immediately obvious.

A man burst through the door in hot pursuit. His hair was dark as midnight and flowed nearly to his shoulders, framing a face that belonged on an Old Master's painting depicting a fallen angel. Eyes the color of chocolate gleamed above sharp cheekbones and a blade of a nose. His lips drew back over straight white teeth in a tight, predatory smile. "Get back here, you little hoodlum!" he hissed, his path taking him toward Rose. "I swear, I'm going to string you up by your shoelaces and make you listen to show tunes for two hours straight!"

The boy stopped in the middle of the hall, glanced wildly around for an escape, then darted straight for Rose. He hit her legs with enough force that she swayed and took an inadvertent step backward as he cried out, "Save me!"

Rose met the stranger's grim gaze and asked, "What's wrong with show tunes?"

headline
ETERNAL

FIND YOUR HEART'S DESIRE...

VISIT OUR WEBSITE: www.headlineeternal.com
FIND US ON FACEBOOK: facebook.com/eternalromance
FOLLOW US ON TWITTER: @eternal_books
EMAIL US: eternalromance@headline.co.uk